S0-BCQ-922

CROOKED TREE

CROOKED TREE

by
Robert C. Wilson

University of Michigan Press
Ann Arbor
&
The Petoskey Publishing Company
Traverse City

Copyright © 2005, 1980 by Crooked Tree Industries, Inc.
All rights reserved

Published in the United States of America by
The University of Michigan Press
&
The Petoskey Publishing Company
Manufactured in the United States of America
2007   2006   2005   5   4   3   2   1
ISBN 0-472-11531-6
Library of Congress Cataloging-in-Publication Data on File

No part of this publication may be reproduced, stored in a retrieval system,
or transmitted in any form or by any means, electronic, mechanical,
or otherwise, without written permission of the publishers.

For
Mom and Pop

Acknowledgments

A number of people provided me with valuable assistance and I wish to thank them: David Bain, William T. Baker, Dr. William Benninghoff, Hon. Patricia J. Boyle, Dr. John Cosgriff, Jack Dangar, Albert Elias, Walter Gibbs, Dave Higbee, Jay Kaufman, Rich Krisciunas, Mike Lang, Mike Marion, Brian Marzec, Dr. Philip Myers, Brad Schram, Peter Skolnik, John Thompson, Mike Wholihan, John and Katie Wilson, Jean Wilson, and James Axel Wilson. I apologize for any names I have neglected to mention; my appreciation for their efforts is no less sincere.

All references to Ottawa legends and beliefs were based on my independent research and of course any inaccuracies are to be blamed solely on me. However, three people with special knowledge of the Ottawa provided needed verification on many points: Veronica Medicine, Curator of the Chief Blackbird Ottawa Indian Museum, Harbor Springs, Michigan; Ray Kiogima, who provided the Ottawa translations; and Mary Belle Shurtleff.

I am especially indebted to the following people for their special contributions: Jeanne Corombos, Terry Boyle, Brian Cleary, my agent Diane Cleaver, Joe Coccia, Audrey Graham, my editor Phyllis Grann, Andrew Wilson, and Mike and Sheila Wilson. Their encouragement and help was essential and is gratefully appreciated.

This edition is the direct result of the continuing interest and encouragement of people like Mary Erwin at the University of Michigan Press and Bill Dana of the Great Lakes Booksellers Association, as well as the many bookstore owners and readers who have graciously expressed many kind comments regarding my work. In particular, I'm appreciative of the efforts and support of Brian Lewis in making this edition possible.

I
Mush Qua Tahs

1

The isolated dirt road cut a narrow swath through the forest. Its rutted trail had yet to feel the midmorning July sun. The ground was still cool.

Moist sand scattered in tiny clumps with each shuffling step. Laboriously the man trudged along the trail, his fleshy fingers gripping the stained leather handle of his briefcase. To his untrained ears it was quiet. As he moved down the sandy road the lightest of breezes carried his scent before him.

A few hundred yards ahead, two black bears rose abruptly on their hind legs, one standing slightly taller than the other. Their heads turned slowly from side to side, their twitching nostrils tasting the air currents. The odor was unmistakable. And it was growing stronger.

The female brought its paws gently to the ground. Then its mate did the same. The scent kindled danger in their memory, a danger they had bolted away from many times before. But something told them this time it was different. The bears remained where they were.

The man's feet grew moist, sliding in his loose-fitting shoes. Gritty dirt ground between his toes. The route had never seemed this long before, but never before had he been forced to walk it.

County Road 621 between Mackinaw City and Wabanakisi, like many in the ring-finger area of Michigan's mitten, followed the course of an old Indian path. And the Indians had not plotted their trails with the modern highway in mind. The path and later the road tortuously skirted a dense wilderness roughly paralleling the bulging northwest coast of the lower peninsula.

Crooked Tree State Forest was an irregular-shaped green blotch on the official state map, sprawling over 175,000 acres. For the most part it was a vast unsettled expanse of pines and oaks, rivers and lakes, crosshatched by forgotten lumber trails kept barely passable by jeeps and snowmobiles. Most people avoided the dirt-road shortcuts, but James Davis drove his Buick as if it had four-wheel drive.

When he had decided to squeeze in an early appearance on behalf of a client in Mackinac County Circuit Court, he knew he would not be on time for the McCutcheon trial in Wabanakisi. His certain tardiness was excusable, he felt, because a large fee made it so. He had not counted on his adversary in Mackinaw taking that matter as lightly as he took McCutcheon's case.

Already late, he raced from the parking lot, his tires spitting gravel in a dusty plume. Fifteen miles south of Mackinaw, County Road 621 veered west for several miles before looping back toward Wabanakisi. Instead of following 621 to the right, Davis angled into a dirt cutoff. Before, it had always saved him valuable minutes on the forty-mile drive.

The car bounded and jerked over the uneven surface, Davis alternately accelerating and braking. Deep in the engine, the pistons grated in hot cylinders. A red light flashed unnoticed above the speedometer as a growing clang hovered in the car's wake. An unlubricated bearing glowed with heat, the piston rods absorbing the stress. But the strain increased.

Davis stomped hard on the gas pedal as the Buick swooped into a sandy depression. With a grinding pop a rod snapped. Released with explosive fury, the piston broke from the crankshaft and sprang against the hood. The metallic crash echoed noisily off the trunks of countless trees as it rippled through Davis' tensed skin.

The crippled car veered to the side of the road. "Son of a bitch!" Davis spat, slapping the dashboard. He glanced quickly in the rearview mirror for another vehicle. Seeing no trailing clouds of dust, he wrenched himself from behind the wheel and got out of the car. His watch told him he was already an hour late for the nine-o'clock trial. He knew there was no cell reception here, but tried his phone anyway. Nothing. He snatched his briefcase from the seat and began walking along the dirt road. It would meet 621 shortly, he thought. There, he would flag a car.

Though the woods was now more than just a blur, Davis was still blind to the individual details of the dark tree trunks and leafy underbrush on both sides of the road. His vision was fixed straight ahead in a glowering tunnel. To him, the woods was the woods. It all looked the same.

As still as the silty surface of the black puddles under the cedars, the bears separated the smell of danger from the hundreds of competing scents and tracked its approach. Their bulky, shaggy bodies poised in rigid attention.

Plodding vigorously ahead, Davis tugged at the knot of his tie. Glinting drops of sweat collected between stretched tendons in his neck. Deaf to the subtle noises generated on either side, hearing only the heavy rush of his own breath, Davis pulled off his sport coat and hooked it over his shoulder on a bent finger. His shirt clung to his back in one large wet square.

He stopped and gazed along the dirt road. The highway was not in sight.

The alien scent halted its drift. The bears' instincts urged them to run, to retreat deep into the woods. But something equally primal and more imperative froze them where they were.

Davis looked at the leafy crowns above him. Dominant oak leaves jittered nervously in a growing breeze. His skin chilled. An involuntary tremor ignited deep inside. He shook his head, his heavy cheeks quivering, as if to shake the creeping discomfort.

It was the trial. It *must* be the trial, he told himself. The twinging uneasiness, the gripping tension, was the same as he had felt when he awoke. It was the normal pretrial apprehension, he insisted.

Davis reached an unfeeling foot forward. Then the other. His knees creaked as he struggled for control. Warmth began to return to his skin. But still the feeling persisted.

The bears moved carefully through the dense cedars, their heavy paws falling softly on the moss-covered ground. The narrow clearing was near. The bears approached cautiously.

Air rasped through Davis' dry throat. Saliva thickened inside his lips. He glanced anxiously into the woods. Child's fears, he told himself, trying to reason with unsettled nerves. Ahead the road began to dip. The ground to the left of the road remained high. To the right, it sloped down from the dirt track, the oaks giving way to the olive green of conical-shaped cedars.

The alien scent filled the bears' nostrils. As its source walked toward them, the fear of danger grew as well. The female angled away from its mate, directly into the wind. In the low twisting branches under the impenetrable canopy of cedars, they were all but invisible from the clearing.

The deep silence of the thick lowlands pealed mutely in his ears. Passing through a visible swarm of gnats, Davis felt the sharp bite of a deerfly on the back of his neck. He swatted at it with his coat-burdened hand, but the fly evaded the awkward attack and buzzed mockingly around his head. Davis broke into a trot for a few steps. His chest swelled.

The bears padded toward the clearing. They were out of sight of each other, yet they sensed their positions. Ahead, through the trees, their weak eyes could distinguish a shape moving in the ribbon of sunlight.

The pulsing silence was interrupted. Davis became aware of a heavy thumping to his right. He paused, peering into the dead branches. He saw nothing. Yet the rhythmic pounding continued. A branch broke, its distinct snap crackling through his head. Davis turned and moved hurriedly, his feet scuffing the sandy roadbed.

The bears sensed the intruder had increased its speed. It was now between them. In the clearing, but between them. Abandoning caution, they loped without disguise.

The sounds were real. Heavy footsteps were unmistakable. Davis lurched forward, his stumpy legs pounding the loose soil. What was it? his mind screamed. Blood surged through his temples. His heart crashed wildly in his chest. The realization erupted in his mind: He was being stalked!

The soft ground ended abruptly. It rose to the treeless passage. The male bear's curving claws dug into the steep embankment. It moved effortlessly up the slope.

Davis glanced to the side. His eyes were blurred with stinging sweat. The shadowless forest flashed white in his mind. A dark shape entered the blur. He tried to focus. It was moving. His eyes cleared. Yet his mind could not comprehend.

The bear stepped deliberately down the middle of the clearing, head lowered, jaws slack. A gravelly rasp churned in its throat. A gummy string of saliva oozed between its daggerlike teeth and slimed toward the ground.

Davis stood motionless, his eyes fixed on the approaching shape. It's impossible. Bears are shy, afraid of man.

Fear no longer weighted the male's thoughts. Although the scent of danger was almost overpowering, its instincts had been stilled. Frenzied anticipation surged through its blood.

Davis pivoted slowly. No sudden moves. The car. Back to the car. The bear was protecting its territory. It would not pursue. As he turned, he kept his eyes on the beast and began to inch away, looking over his shoulder. The bear's pace was unaltered. He reluctantly pulled his gaze away. Northward. Back to the car.

"Nooo!" Davis' quiet gasps exploded in terrified emotion. Another black shape. Another bear!

Panic seized his thoughts. He spun around. It was still there. They were closing in. His jacket slipped from his fingers and dropped to the ground. He stepped awkwardly toward the edge of the trail. An embankment sloped steeply downward. A trembling foot slid a long first step. Another. Davis hurtled down the ridge. His knees stiffened and locked at the bottom, and he plummeted to the ground.

It was escaping! The creature had bolted away. The bears' restrained muscles exploded with pounding fury. With a thrusting burst they lunged after their prey.

Davis struggled to his feet. He felt the earth trembling from the approaching beasts. He stumbled toward the thickness, soft ground pulling at his shoes. His briefcase lay open at the base of the ridge, papers spilling from inside.

Excited grunts escaped with each breath. The intruder was running directly into their realm. Their territory!

Jagged twigs scratched his face. Davis waved his arms wildly as he struggled through the twisting branches. He sank deeper into the cedar swamp.

The bears rushed stiff-legged down the slope. The upright figure was disappearing into the trees. But there was nowhere for it to hide.

Black muck seemed to grasp his feet. Davis lunged forward. Gnarled roots slippery with moss upset his balance. The pounding was just behind!

The bears splintered through the cedars in a relentless charge, dashing unimpeded by the brittle branches. Only yards ahead, a struggling form jerked erratically.

No escape! his mind shouted. Upward. Climb! Davis lunged for a low-hanging branch. It snapped in his hands. Again he leaped. The second branch held. He strained with aching muscles to pull himself up. Slowly his body squirmed off the ground. His lungs seared in writhing pain.

Seeing their prey dangling unprotected, the bears lunged.

A roar crashed in Davis' head. It boomed under the suffocating blanket of cedars.

He tried to raise his feet, but they were snagged. Stabbing pain shot up his left leg. Immense pressure seemed to be collapsing his bones. Davis screamed.

The she-bear jerked its powerful neck. Davis thudded to the ground, ripped from the branch. The bear released its grip on his foot with a guttural growl. Davis tried to twist away, but a lightning forepaw hammered his side. The snapping of his ribs crackled in his ears.

Davis spun to his back. Dual jaws of ivory daggers drooled in snarling fury. Reflex action brought his arms up to shield his body, but the quick thrusting heads of the bears reacted even faster.

Dulling pain surged inward from the wounds, numbing his chest as it spread. Creeping upward, the dullness stilled the mad cries gurgling deep in the man's throat. Then with a merciful thrust of steellike claws the dullness smothered his thoughts. In a moment, all that disturbed the quiet of Crooked Tree was the snuffling grunts of feasting carnivores.

Through the dense cedars, the warming sun touched the roadbed, and the drying sand began to crumble grain by grain into vanishing footprints.

2

Axel Michelson walked toward his office. He was prepared for trial, but no manner of preparation ever seemed to stifle that special excitement, an excitement bred of nervous anticipation and long hard work. The apprehension of a jury trial was always the same. The judge, court stenographer, and bailiff were comfortable people. They always acted predictably. But a jury introduced new variables into the game.

A cup of black coffee steamed on Grace's desk when Axel strode into the reception area. "You've had two calls already this morning," she greeted.

"I can guess one," said Axel, catching his breath. "Mrs. James called to tell me what that rotten, no-good soon-to-be-ex-husband of hers did last night."

"You're right there."

"And the second was a distraught seamstress who wants to sue Oligopoly Sewing Machine Company because one of their not-so-fine products ran amok and sewed her fingers together."

"Wishful thinking. Don't you know you have to be a big shot to get the fat contingency cases?" Grace teased.

"But I am a big shot. Didn't you see my name in the *Bay City Times* in the state-forest article? That's hot stuff. The environment's big news."

"Yes, and I noticed they spelled your name wrong again." Grace laughed, hoping to ease Axel's pretrial tension.

Grace knew well the jittery feeling preceding a new jury case. She had been a legal secretary for ten years before Axel even took the bar exam, and could read attorneys as well as any judge. It was this same sense of character that had led her to choose Axel as her new employer two years ago when Samuel Hetcham died.

Her first contact with Axel Michelson was two summers before that as a client during her divorce. Mr. Hetcham had referred her to the newest attorney in Wabanakisi, an ex-associate from a Detroit corporate law firm who was hungry for work. While he competently guided her through the maze of legal procedures, it was not his legal skills but his humanness that impressed Grace most. She had not thought it possible for anyone to deal on a rational level with her separated husband the way Michelson had, all the while minimizing the bitterness and shielding her two daughters from it.

Grace reached for a folded copy of the Detroit Free Press and handed it to Axel. "I think this editorial will make you feel better."

"Oh?" Michelson's eyebrows raised, the McCutcheon trial suddenly forgotten. He took the paper and walked through the open doorway into his office. Settling into his swivel chair, he leaned back and leafed through the second section, looking for the editorial page.

Suddenly he sat up straight and folded the paper flat on the desk. His eyes raced through the column in the upper-left corner headlined "Crooked Tree Faces the Ax." It was what he had been hoping for since he first filed suit on behalf of the Ottawa tribe. One of the state's big daily newspapers had finally taken a stand against further real estate development in the Crooked Tree State Forest. What a newspaper says is not supposed to have any effect on what a court does, but Michelson knew that Federal District Judge Frank Moss would have read the editorial. And he was delighted.

But that hearing wasn't until next week. The Arnold McCutcheon personal-injury suit was set to begin shortly, and Axel knew he could not afford the luxury of lax concentration. Not with insurance defense specialist James Davis as his adversary.

Eleven months ago, during a heavy August rain, as Arnold was hurrying down the wooden stairway of the Wabanakisi Mercantile, one step cracked. His leg plunged through the rotten wood, impaling itself on a corroded spike that had probably fifty years of infection on it. Considering the doctor's bill, surgery, and his pain and suffering, Arnold figured he needed more than two thousand dollars. And more than likely a jury would agree, his lawyer had decided.

Axel snapped the clasps on his briefcase. As he stood, his image reflected a half-dozen times in the glass-covered bookshelves behind his desk. The bookshelves, like the building itself, held their age gracefully.

When built in 1903, the Salling, Hanson Building was headquarters of one of the most successful lumber companies in the middle of what was once the world's purest stand of white pine. Lumber from the Salling, Hanson & Company could be found across the country in many fine structures built toward the end of the nineteenth century. For his own building, it was said old man Hanson personally chose the trees to be felled and saw to it that the finished timber had no knots to blemish the walls. It did not matter that paint would cover any marks—Mr. Hanson simply loved perfection as much as he loved wood.

Rasmus Hanson was not born to lumbering. But like many Danes who immigrated to the United States in the 1860's, he was drawn by Michigan's "green fever" to the frigid northern lumber camps.

Within a few short decades, the seemingly unending landscape of white and red pines in northern Michigan was barren. The "green gold" that started the rush had yielded unparalleled riches, ten times the wealth realized from the California gold strikes. When it all ended, Danes like Rasmus Hanson retired on their earnings, while others, like Oscar Michelson, left the long shanties of the winter camps and tried farming the sandy soil. The unprotected windswept countryside raged with fire, scorching the nutrients from the already anemic dirt. Many farmers wandered south to the big cities, where timber money was financing an industrial explosion. Years later, some of their ancestors returned to the north. The picturesque beauty of the second-growth forests and the crystal-clear lakes lured many of them to Wabanakisi County. Axel Michelson had a better reason for moving. He was married to a descendant of Chief Shoppenaw, onetime tribal head of the Ottawas of Crooked Tree.

Though no longer the sole humans in the area, the Ottawas still accounted for 40 percent of the county population, with half of these living within the boundaries of a small reservation several miles north of town. No one knew the exact site, but somewhere within the reservation once stood perhaps the largest Indian village in northern Michigan. It had been settled by the Ottawas in 1742, one hundred years after their tribe was uprooted by war and driven westward by the Iroquois Confederation of Five Nations.

A mammoth white pine, its top hooked by the westerly winds, marked the new home of the Ottawas. The tree served as a beacon for Indian canoeists traversing the choppy lake waters in their fragile birch-bark craft. The Ottawas called the area wau-go-naw-ki-sa, "the land of the crooked tree." Like the Anglicized Ottawa name for the area, the crooked tree survived, miraculously preserved from the crosscut saws of the lumberjacks.

It was a few minutes after nine, but Axel did not hurry down the side staircase of the Salling, Hanson Building. It was only a short walk to the courthouse. His office was at the north end of a two-block-long business district that comprised all of downtown Wabanakisi. The shops and offices that fronted on the east side of Main Street stood on the edge of an incline that slanted down to Lake Muhquh Sebing. Some of the stores had basement-level entrances from the grassy corridor that separated them from the lake.

Stretching out to the west behind Main Street for about a half-mile was the old residential part of Wabanakisi. Beyond the last row of wooden frame houses was a green belt of trees and heavy undergrowth. This narrow, wild strip of land sat atop a modest sand dune that sloped down to the wide expanse of Lake Michigan.

Lake Michigan and Muhquh Sebing were connected by a narrow canal that cut through Main Street at the north end of the business district. Main Street spanned the canal by means of a drawbridge, which had to be raised for the mast of any sailboat in the twenty-two-foot class or larger. At this time of the year, with the cottages along Lake Muhquh Sebing filled with their Detroit or Chicago owners, the little drawbridge seemed to be up as much as it was down.

As he walked southward toward the City-County Building, Axel glanced to his left between the stores. The sun reflected off the rippling lake in silvery patches with each flickering undulation of the waves. Lake Muhquh Sebing was no more than three miles in breadth at its widest, but its slender length reached almost twenty miles. "Muhquh" and "sebing" were the Ottawa words for "bear" and "lake," so named by the Indians for the once abundant black bear that had reigned over the area before the coming of the white man. Besides bringing the muhquh to near extinction in the area, the early white settlers added the redundant "lake" to Muhquh Sebing.

Michelson ran quickly up the few steps to the Wabanakisi City-County Building, a building which could not have been uglier if it had been planned that way. It was a squat, fortlike structure with a huge aluminum-sided monstrosity of a turret that served as its centerpiece. What made it all the worse was the memory of the stately old courthouse that once stood on the same ground.

The heavy oak door of the courtroom swung noiselessly inward. "The heat was so intense," Axel heard Harry Forstyk, the clerk, saying, "that the sand along the beach melted into glass."

"Is that right?" Mrs. McCutcheon gasped incredulously.

"No, it's not," Axel interrupted as he walked toward plaintiff's table. "It was ice from the fire hose."

"And how would you know?" Harry challenged. "You weren't there."

"No, but Charley Moozganse was, and his version is a little different from yours."

"Moozganse! That moose's asshole was so drunk that night the alcohol in his kidneys would have ignited like gasoline if he had been anywhere near. Did he tell you how I saved the town by stopping the spread of the fire?"

"I didn't realize the town was in much danger. From the way I understand it, the old Muhquh Sebing Hotel was down by the lake fifty yards from the nearest building."

"They call me Fireplug, don't they?"

"Yes, that's true," Axel admitted. He did not choose to add that Harry earned himself the nickname by telling the story so often. "Now, what about Davis? Has he checked in yet?"

21

"Do penguins wear ice skates? He's only twenty minutes late now. I'd give him another half-hour."

The extra time could be valuable, Axel thought—a chance to calm his client, as well as himself. As he huddled with the McCutcheons at the Formica-topped table, Harry ambled slowly toward a door marked "Jury" at the rear of the courtroom.

Standing in the narrow hallway between her kennel and the animal hospital, Janis Michelson stared through the window. While her eyes followed the antics of three boys playing with the dogs in the penned area behind the building, her thoughts were on Axel, on the trial he was beginning. She felt tense, preoccupied, sharing the same pretrial apprehension she knew he was feeling. The worst was always the beginning, she thought. By lunchtime, she knew, she would feel better.

The front door banged loudly, drowning the jangle of the bell above the entrance. Walking into the front room, at first Janis thought no one was there. But then she noticed the light brown pony tail of Grace's daughter, her head barely reaching the top of the counter.

"Marcy! What do you have there?"

"My snake is sick, Mrs. Michelson. I took her next door, but Dr. Routier told me to bring her to you."

"He did, did he?" Janis said as she stooped beside the little girl. "I guess I'd better take a look."

Marcy handed her a clear glass jar with a coiled garter snake at the bottom. "You'll be able to make her better, won't you?"

"I'll do my best." Janis unscrewed the tin top, perforated by random spike holes, and lifted the snake from the jar. "What's her name?"

"Gertrude."

Janis held the snake before her dark eyes and petted its striped head with one finger. Its eighteen-inch body drooped just slightly longer than Janis' thick black hair. "Gertrude looks fine to me. Why do you think she's sick?"

"Because she won't do anything. She just lies in her jar and doesn't move."

"Oh, I don't think you have anything to worry about, Marcy. Gertrude's not sick. She's just acting like all snakes would if they were in a jar."

"But she hasn't eaten a thing since I found her. That's three days. She'll starve."

"What have you been feeding her?"

"Cheerios."

Janis grinned. "I'm afraid snakes don't like Cheerios."

"But with sugar?"

"No, not even with sugar." Janis held the snake above the open jar and lowered it tail-first. "My grandfather used to tell me a wild animal is an animal only because it is free. When it is caged, it loses so much, it becomes not an animal, but an object, no different from the twigs and dead grass you placed at the bottom of this jar."

"Do you think that's what happened to Gertrude?"

"I think so."

"Maybe I should let her loose, then."

"That would probably be best, Marcy. And I'm sure Gertrude would feel much more like a snake again."

Marcy leaned forward and hugged Janis tightly. "Dr. Routier was right. He knew you would know what to do."

Judge Wilfred T. Jensen slapped his pen to the pad of paper with a decisive snap. The clock had just hummed electrically on the hour. Ten o'clock. Leaving the sentence unfinished, he rolled his chair away from the desk and sprang out of the soft leather without a hint of his seventy-six years.

He stepped through his chamber's door into the courtroom, his black robe, open down the front, sailing behind him. "Young Mr. Michelson," he declared.

Axel looked up from plaintiffs table. "Good morning, Judge."

"It is a good morning, and I hate to be wasting it here with all those perch and bass out there just waiting to be caught. What's the delay?"

Axel glanced quickly at his watch. "We're still waiting for Davis." His tone was apologetic, though there was no need for his apology.

"And not even a call, Judge," Harry Forstyk added. "Those jurors are getting mighty restless with so many of them cooped up in there."

"I don't blame them, but I guess there's not much we can do about it right now." Jensen's hands gestured helplessly under the loose-fitting sleeves of the robe. "Axel. I saw the piece in the *Free Press* this morning. What's the latest on Crooked Tree?"

"Judge Moss in Bay City granted our request for a temporary restraining order. There'll be a hearing on the preliminary injunction next week."

"You know, whoever in Lansing granted those licenses to develop housing in a state forest should have his head examined." Jensen leaned against the siding of his bench. "I wish you luck. I've been hunting there since I was a boy, and I'd sure hate to see the forest harmed."

"Most of us feel the same way, Judge," Arnold McCutcheon noted. "But the county has been changing. With so many new people here, people from the city, priorities have changed. It's already affected the wilderness. There are fewer deer, bear, everything."

"I don't know about there being fewer bear," Harry said. "I've heard a lot of campers say they've been seeing them at night. The bears may have been almost wiped out fifty years ago, but they came back. Maybe because of that hunting ban in the seventies."

"Or maybe they're just smarter now," Jensen offered.

"Could be. In any event, it should be a good hunt this November."

Axel shook his head. "Hunting deer, I can understand. Venison can make a fine dinner. But why bear? Who ever eats bear meat?"

Harry guffawed. "I eat it, that's who."

"I'm not surprised, with that thick hide of yours. And it sure wouldn't be the first time you were in a class by yourself."

"Even if I didn't eat their meat, I would still hunt them for the thrill of it. Just because they're shyer than a kid with braces on his teeth and run at the first whiff of a man doesn't mean they can't kill you with one swipe of their paw."

"That may be so, Harry," said Axel. "But you know as well as I do at least half the black bear around here are shot while they are sound asleep in their dens. I don't think shooting a hibernating animal taxes the courage of any hunter."

"I agree, Axel. I agree. And you'll never find Harry Forstyk tracking a bear to its winter den."

Judge Jensen interrupted. "That's heartening to hear, Harry. Now, how about tracking down Davis and hauling his tail in here."

"I'll try, Judge, but I never was much good at trapping that kind of game."

The black-and-white patrol car cruised northward along the winding asphalt road. Deputy Sheriff Brockington held an easy grip on the steering wheel with his right hand, his left elbow protruding from the open window. His muscles felt the dull relaxation that comes from being awake all night.

Brockington had the two-a.m. shift and should have been off duty a half-hour ago. He would have been if he hadn't told Jerry Shank he would fill in for him for a few hours. It was the dentist, this time. At least once a week it always seemed to be something. But Brockington didn't care, as long as his afternoons were free. His afternoons were for his sons. He didn't enjoy working from two until ten every morning, but it was the only way he could guarantee being with his kids during the summer.

The oldest two boys were now on the same team, and the Little League playoffs were to begin that afternoon. On the mound and at shortstop, they were the stars of the team. Brockington smiled as he thought about next year, when the youngest would be able to follow in the footsteps of his two older brothers. And he just might be the best of the bunch.

As usual, County Road 621 was almost barren of traffic. But Brockington was in no hurry. All he had to do in Mackinaw was deliver a single subpoena, and then he would be free to head home.

3

"Okay, Harry. Fine. Tell the judge I'll have somebody check the road. Matter of fact, I've got a car up that way right now."

"Thanks, Sheriff. If he shows up here, I'll call back."

Luke Snyder replaced the phone and swiveled to face the desktop radio. Depressing the transmitting bar on the microphone stand, he called for the patrol car.

"Brockington here," came the tinny reply.

"Dave, something just came up. Where are you now."

"I just dropped the papers off with the sheriff up here and was on my way out of town."

"Good. I've got a missing-person report I'd like you to check on. An attorney. He supposedly left Mackinaw about nine-thirty and was heading for Circuit Court here. He hasn't arrived yet, and I want you to be on the lookout for his car on the way back. Do you mind?"

Brockington glanced at the digital clock on the dash. Eleven-thirty-two. Two hours until game time.

"Dave? Listen, I know you've worked all night. If you'd rather not, I'll send somebody else out."

"No, Sheriff. No problem. I can handle it. I'll check the side of the road and stop at Hingman's Bar. Maybe they saw him."

"And the cabins along the way, too. He may have stopped at one of them."

"All right. What kind of car?" Brockington fished a spiral notebook from his pocket.

"Blue Buick Le Sabre," Snyder reported, reading from a pad

of paper. "License TKB 123. Name is Davis. James Davis."

Brockington clipped the microphone to the dash and eased back into the seat. It was only the first game, he considered. As long as they didn't lose, there would be more. And with his kids playing, they couldn't lose.

Michelson walked through Grace's empty office, his heels clicking on the hardwood floor. A young man in his early twenties sat hunched over a stack of books at a table opposite Michelson's desk. His shoulder-length black hair hung straight across the sides of his face. He scribbled a hurried note on a yellow pad before looking up. "Hi, Ax. How's the trial going?"

"It's not, Larry. Davis didn't show," Axel said.

"He didn't show! That sounds even too much for him."

"He'll have an excuse this time, I'm sure. They think his car broke down somewhere between here and Mackinaw. The sheriff's looking for him now." "Just what we don't need. Another delay."

"Maybe it will work out all right. If adjourned until after next week, we can concentrate on the injunction."

"Good. I could use a little help with this research."

Michelson laughed. "I told you clerking for me this summer wasn't going to be cake. And besides, second-year law students are supposed to love research."

"Yeah, but don't forget I'm only part-time."

"I'm just trying to help in your legal education," Axel shrugged. "Let me try to get hold of my wife, and then we'll talk over what you've got so far."

Michelson twisted the phone so it faced him as he stood in front of his desk. Leslie Routier at the kennel answered. "No, Mr. Michelson," she said. "She went home early today. She was sick. Didn't you know?"

"No, I guess I didn't. I've been busy..." Axel's words trailed into thought. She hadn't *appeared* sick. "Thanks, Leslie, I'll call her at home." He dialed again and waited. Six, seven rings. No answer. Axel pulled the receiver from his ear. He could hear someone coming up the stairs.

Ted Hiller smoothed his lower lip across a mustache of perspiration as he pushed through the door. Michelson greeted him with a handshake. "Good to see you, Ted."

"Thanks, Axel. Just thought I'd stop by to say hello," Hiller said, his heavy jowls vibrating as he spoke.

"A busy plumber can't be stopping by just for a social call," Axel prodded.

"No, I guess not," Hiller drawled. "You being the center of attention around here lately, I thought I'd come see how it's affected you." The two men stood even at about six feet, but Hiller's eyes stared down at Axel's chest. His short-cropped black hair would be as straight as Larry's if he let it grow, but its length was just another way he kept his distance from his heritage. Like most Ottawas, Ted had prospered right along with the growth of northern Michigan. But many, particularly those who lived on the reservation, had yet to bridge the economic gap to comfortable middle-class living.

Michelson leaned back on Grace's desk and folded his arms. "It hasn't affected me a bit. Has it you?"

Hiller looked sharply into his face. "The injunction could hurt this town real bad. That new development would hold a lot of homes and bring in a lot of people." Hiller paused, waiting for Michelson to reply. But Axel remained impassive, preferring to let Hiller struggle with the difficult words. "You know, it's not easy for the merchants to make ends meet every year, especially when most of the people leave when it starts to get cold. And the merchants, I can tell you, are very anxious for those new homes to be built."

"I suspect, Ted," Axel began with cautious respect for his friend, "that there are a good deal more people around here who are not merchants than who are, and I also suspect . . . no, I can say with a fair degree of certainty that most of them would just as soon not see more people move up here."

"That may be true, Axel, but you know as well as I that it's the businessman who controls the money around here. And that's a very important fact of life for young attorneys who may later wish to run for state senator or judge." He was much more blunt than Michelson had expected, and he did not know how to take it.

Seeing his hesitation, Ted continued. "Listen, I could care less whether that area is developed or not. I know, I've got the contract to do the plumbing on those new houses, but hell, I've got too much work as it is. I'm just telling you for your own good that you're not the most popular man around here, since getting that injunction."

"First of all, it wasn't an injunction. It was a temporary restraining order, which means it lasts only ten days unless I get an extension or convince the judge to grant a preliminary injunction. And secondly, I'm afraid I have no choice but to pursue the matter as strenuously as the legal system permits. You see, my clients, the Ottawa tribe, have a vested interest in keeping Crooked Tree State Forest unspoiled. When they deeded all the land around here to the U.S. government, including where this town sits, in exchange for that tiny reservation, the government agreed to keep the land near the reservation free from settlements. In effect, by treaty, they were given the right in perpetuity to hunt in that land and to insist that it remain untouched."

"I know that, Axel. I'm an Ottawa myself. And there is nothing I am more proud of than my heritage. But the development might help my people on the reservation even more than the merchants. And I can guarantee you that not one Indian up there survives solely by hunting in those woods."

"I fail to see," Axel said, "how putting in a lot of fancy houses with 'Keep Out' signs all around will help the Indian at all. And there's also the simple matter of wanting to save the trees. Crooked Tree is one of the few really wild areas left in this state, certainly in the lower peninsula, and neither I nor almost anyone else I talk to wants to see it destroyed."

"Neither do we," Hiller said with near-exasperation. "It's not as if they're going to bulldoze the whole goddamned woods. Hell, the state forest covers a hundred *thousand* acres, or is it two hundred thousand? All the real-estate people want is a mere eighty-five."

"I'm sorry, Ted, but I don't subscribe to the 'You'll-never-miss-it' theory. We've surrendered too much as it is. Each new encroachment not only reduces the wilderness by just that much, but also opens the rest to more extensive contact with man. And you know what a poor track record we have for keeping wild areas wild, once they're within beer-can range."

"Come on, Axel," Hiller snorted, "be reasonable. The wilderness is going to remain wild. No one's going to be able to get into the deep woods."

"Oh, but they will. There'll be that many more trail bikes and snowmobiles racing through formerly inaccessible areas of the woods, scaring the shit out of the deer, bear, whatever. And what does that do? It forces them to retreat even farther into the woods, shrinking their food area even more. So some animals starve, and sooner or later we discover one species no longer lives there anymore."

Hiller managed a grin. "As far as I'm concerned, the only good b'ar is a dead b'ar."

Larry laughed from the doorway. "You may think a bear's best place is in the home . . . in front of your fireplace, but you seem to be forgetting our people believed the black bear was our cousin."

"Yeah, I forgot about that. About the same time I forgot about the manitous that control the world and the stars being soul villages in the sky."

"You should be glad you're talking to Larry and not his grandfather," Axel said.

Hiller shrugged, an easiness to his movement for the first time since he walked in. "Charley Wolf's beliefs died out for the same reason you're going to lose that lawsuit: Progress. As they say, it's inevitable."

"You know something, Ted? I'm afraid you just might end up being right. But if you are, it's going to be over my strongest legal challenge."

Hiller edged toward the door. "I can see I wasted my time trying to talk some sense into you."

"Not at all. I was glad you found time to get your nose out of plugged-up toilets long enough to stop by for a visit. Call me anytime when you want to talk about saving the state forest land."

"Oh, you can count on that, Axel. The Chamber of Commerce is going to try to intervene on behalf of Sunrise Land and Home Company.

"Good. It'll make us seem more the underdog."

Turning to leave, he said, "Say hello to Janis for me."

As Hiller's footsteps retreated down the stairs, Axel turned to face Larry. His concern was un-camouflaged. The prospect of a second adversary, an adversary with supposed community support, would make their burden much heavier.

Deputy Sheriff Brockington nodded to the woman in the door as he slipped the gearshift into reverse. The high-powered Dodge patrol car rumbled as it moved slowly over the dirt driveway.

No one had stopped at her house that morning, Mrs. Weaver had said, but Brockington was not thinking of Davis as he backed onto County Road 621. He was thinking of the woman's youthful face and how it appeared paled by lonely hours in the woods. She had wanted him to stay. Her eyes practically beseeched him.

The road snaked away from the isolated house, graying asphalt cracked like a dry riverbed. Brockington drove slowly, his trained eyes alert for fresh oil spots on the highway or upturned gravel on the shoulder. Davis hadn't been seen at Carriway's cabin, nor had he stopped for help at Hingman's Bar. Brockington knew there were no other buildings visible from the road between Mrs. Weaver's and Wabanakisi that could have attracted a disabled motorist. Why wouldn't he have called on his cell? He must have made it at least into town, he thought. Yet, if he had, he certainly would have appeared at court. Even Davis would not stand up a waiting courtroom.

A few miles down the road, on the outer bank of a southward bend, a dirt trail broke the forest barrier. Brockington slowed his vehicle and peered down the narrow clearing. There was nothing. Just like at the northern end of the dirt track.

Brockington eased his car onto the shoulder and came to a halt. His hands twisted forward and back over the plastic steering wheel as he stared straight ahead along the empty 621 toward Wabanakisi. Only fifteen more miles. He glanced at the glowing numbers of the dashboard clock. Twelve-twenty. He could be home in time for a quick lunch before the game.

Brockington angled back onto the pavement, but instead of accelerating toward town, he swung the patrol car in a wide loop and eased through a deep pothole bordering 621 in front of the dirt road. The track alternately widened and narrowed as it wound into the woods. Occasionally, tufts of wild grass sprouted from a hump between the tire ruts in a rugged show of resilience to the four-wheel-drives that regularly rumbled over the trail.

To either side, the dominant white oak formed a swaying

buffer from the breeze. To Brockington it suddenly seemed easy to comprehend how the intermingled crowns could absorb a man without so much as a snapped twig.

The road began to slope gently downward, and to his left the ground fell away even more. As the land changed, the foliage changed with it. In a matter of a few dozen yards the white cedar grew exclusively, forming an almost impenetrable barrier of twisting trunks and bramblelike branches.

Brockington nosed his car along, glancing into the deep cedar thicket. In springtime, much of the dark moss-covered floor would be submerged in a few inches of cold, black stagnant water. In July, moss formed a molded blanket over the protruding roots of the cedars.

The trail gradually rose, the cedars giving way once again to the oaks. Sticky perspiration began to stain Brockington's shirt in the unventilated car. He rolled his window down halfway. Shade enveloped the road, the afternoon sun blocked by trees on a hill to his left.

At the top of the hill a black shape jerked itself into a state of alert. The bear had heard a noise uncommon to the forest. Its poor eyesight could not focus on the black-and-white automobile a few hundred feet through the trees. But the bear knew it was there, and it sniffed the air vigorously for a clue as to the nature of the beast.

Rounding the hill, Brockington raised his hand to protect his squinting eyes from the bright sunlight. It was a moment before he noticed the blue Buick Le Sabre. Brockington brought his car to a halt in the middle of the dirt track, almost corner-to-corner with the Buick. He pulled a spiral notebook from his shirt pocket and compared the license plate with his scribbled notes. The number of the Buick matched the missing Davis car.

Brockington felt a grim satisfaction as he got out of his car. He approached the Buick, eyes intent on diagnosing the trouble. He leaned on the driver's door and peered into the empty car. The keys dangled from the ignition. Brockington slipped behind the wheel and turned the key to accessory. He watched as the red bar of the fuel gauge rose steadily. When it passed half full, Brockington switched it off and pulled the keys from the steering column. After slipping them in his pocket, he glanced over his shoulder in the back, then rubbed his hand across the fabric of the front seat and bent down for a close look at the floor. Nothing unusual. No sign of trouble. He flicked the hood release.

The deputy pulled himself to his feet and slammed the door. Circling the car, he observed no trace of Davis. Any tracks, he noticed, would be indistinguishable in the thick sand. At the front of the Buick, Brockington slipped his fingers in the vertical opening between the hood and the grille. The latch would not budge. Dropping to one knee, he bent his head low to the ground and attempted to look up into the engine. Unable to see, he returned to the patrol car, unbuckling his holster as he walked. Laying his gun on the front seat, Brockington reached for a flashlight attached under the dash.

The bear had crossed the narrow clearing and was shuffling slowly toward the noise. The light breeze carried an unmistakable scent to its nose as it headed directly into the wind. Tall three-lobed ferns fell soundlessly in its wake, leaving a lacy trail of twisted green tendrils.

Brockington lay on his back and pulled himself under the front of Davis' car. With his flashlight he could see where the hood latch was slightly bent. He reached for his handcuffs in his rear pocket and used them to pry the metal back into shape. The deputy sheriff inched his way from under the car, rolled to his stomach, and pushed himself up. He reached his hand into the slot, and this time the latch gave way. Raising the hood, Brockington bent over the crippled engine. He felt a sense of relief when he saw the blown piston rod.

Brockington turned and cupped his hands around his mouth, shouting, "Davis!" His voice was strong. His uneasiness had departed. Brockington shouted again, louder. After another silent moment, Brockington started to walk down the road, pausing to lean through his car window to place the flashlight on the seat next to his gun.

The bear became motionless as its senses tracked the movement of its prey. Its eyes almost glowed as if it was night under the dense cover of the brambles. Matted fur stained brown protruded from its snout and chest like a necklace of thorns. The bear's steady concentration was on the approaching scent. It was alone this time. Its mate was asleep in their den of fallen cedars.

Brockington ambled from side to side of the road, looking

carefully at the embankments for any trace of Davis. With a hot July sun beating down on the woods, the forest floor became a veritable oven under the canopy of leaves. Brockington cupped his hands and shouted, "Davis!" several more times, only to hear his own echo in return.

From the underbrush twenty-five feet from the clearing, the bear could see the upright animal. The noises did not bother it. It had heard them before. And like before, it would be easy. It would be over swiftly. The bear's steeled claws clenched the dirt.

The bushes to the left of Brockington moved. He took two quick steps toward the noise. He could see nothing, but something was there. The leaves rustled sharply as a hidden creature tried to free itself. Brockington reached to unsnap his holster. It wasn't there!

A dark shape burst from under the bramble ferns. Brockington jerked his forearms to his face as he stumbled backward. The creature was in the open. Brockington heard a deafening whoosh as he caught a glimpse of a brown-and-white fan-shaped feathered tail rising in the air. The grouse flushed from its nest, beat the still air violently as it fled the intruder.

Startled, the bear broke its concentration. It tried to assimilate the foreign noise, and it stumbled backward in confusion. Then it turned and sped deep into the woods.

Brockington stared frozen in place as the grouse disappeared over the trees. It was a moment before he could manage a nervous smile. Back at the car, he opened the door and slid onto the vinyl seat. Unclipping the hand-held microphone, he signaled Wabanakisi. "This is Brockington, just off 621 about fifteen miles north of town. I found Davis' car, but there's no trace of him."

"Can his car be driven?" asked the voice through the speaker.

"No, it looks like he blew a piston. I suggest you send a wrecker up here to haul it out."

"Okay. Give us your exact location." Brockington did. "Any idea where he went?" the voice continued.

"He must have walked south from here down to 621. Maybe there he got a ride."

"Probably. See any trace of him?"

"Nope. I came in from the south on the trail and didn't see a thing."

"All right, Dave. Why don't you drive back to 621 and wait for the wrecker. I'll dispatch one right now."

Brockington agreed and signed off. Driving back to the highway, he tried unsuccessfully to shrug off his disappointment. He would miss the entire playoff game for sure.

4

Janis Michelson crushed the small clump of dirt with her fingers and shook the loose soil to the ground. She tossed the weed onto a pile of recently uprooted green plants. Pausing to wipe her brow with the back of her dirty hand, she surveyed the small patch of growing vegetables. The corn stood about two feet high in three rows lining the north edge of the garden. Among other vegetables identified by seed packages attached to sticks poking out of the ground were radishes, onions, lettuce, zucchini, and tomatoes.

Staring at the maturing plants, Janis thought of her first attempt at growing food, a five-foot-square corner of her mother's garden when she was nine years old. Janis pictured her working in that first garden, wearing her carefully hand-sewn deerskin clothes, her hair in long tight braids. Her mother had worn her traditional Ottawa dress only rarely, but that was how Janis always remembered her.

Her mother used to call her Mtigwah Jeegwung. There was no comparable word in English. Literally, it translated as "new fern," but beyond its descriptive function it was a word of beauty, of innocence, of emotion. The Ottawas had many words for the ferns that blanketed their forested world, each one defining a particular shape, a special quality, an age. Mtigwah Jeegwung meant more than just a new fern. The word encompassed the fragile elasticity of the early shoot, the pale, almost whitish green of the velvet stalk, the gentle curve of the unfolding tendril, the tiny, papery fronds beginning to peel away from the bud.

As she rested on her knees, Janis pictured herself kneeling beside her mother in that first garden, listening as she said, "My little Mtigwah Jeegwung, your grandfathers have lived on this land for longer than man can remember. They were part of it. And so am I. And so are you." Janis listened as her mother retold the proud stories of their chiefs, the powerful stories of their manitous, the funny stories of the people.

Her mother died after Janis' fourth garden, and every summer since then Janis had tilled a small plot of land. Working on the soil was how she remembered her mother, her past. Janis wondered what it would be like to have her own mtigwah jeegwung work beside her and listen to her family's stories. But she was so busy with the kennel, and with Axel working as well, there was no time.

This summer was the first year Janis had planted this particular soil, having moved into their newly built house the fall before. The house stood on ten acres of land Janis had inherited from her father. The land had been in the family since 1894 as part of a compromise over early white encroachment into Crooked Tree. The original treaty provided for exclusive Indian use of the state forest, but under the pressure of a growing white population the treaty was "amended," permitting the settlers and lumberjacks to hunt and fish in Crooked Tree, while a strip of land was carved from the edge of the state forest and parceled out among the male Indians. Most of the land had long since reverted to the state, as the framers of the agreement knew it would, for unpaid taxes. But Janis' family had maintained good title, and now she and her husband were the only human inhabitants for miles, practically surrounded by the state forest.

Janis rose and brushed the moist soil from her knees. She felt much better now. The nervousness of the morning was gone. The edginess was calmed. She had known all she needed was some time alone in her garden. And it had worked.

Axel's car idled patiently in the middle of Main Street as the drawbridge reached its full height. Two small craft were coming back into the protection of the inland lake after a day's sail. Standing erect, the roadway looked like a fragile screen door, the metal grating seemingly too weak to support the weight of traffic.

After the bridge lowered, Michelson followed the traffic north through town. He felt tired, as though he had been in trial all day. It must be the uncertainty, he thought. He knew exactly which dirt road Davis' car had been found on. It was only a few miles north of his home.

Most of the cars had turned off 621 when Michelson saw the flashing orange light of an emergency vehicle approaching. It was a tow truck with a blue Buick hoisted behind. He recognized Davis' car, and after he passed, he watched it grow smaller in his rearview mirror.

After a few minutes the Crooked Tree came into view. A tiny silhouette in the distance, it stood on a sand dune overlooking Lake Michigan. Like the Ottawas returning in their canoes, when Michelson saw the Crooked Tree he knew he was almost home.

Axel eased off the accelerator as he steered onto the narrow tree-lined driveway and drove the few hundred yards to his house. Their ten acres stretched from County Road 621 to the edge of the Crooked Tree State Forest. The house was close to the east edge of their property line, sitting by itself among the flora of the forest. There were no neighbors other than the animals of the woods, and except for the occasional raccoon that rummaged through their garbage, their neighbors did not disturb them.

Michelson parked on the concrete apron in front of the two-car garage. During winter, both cars would be under the protection of the roof, but during summer, wheelbarrows, rakes, or bicycles seemed to take up the extra space. Axel followed the jagged line of stepping-stones to a paved sidewalk that led to the front door. He climbed the four stairs up the low ridge of ground that stretched in either direction deep into the woods, forming a kind of earthen terrace to their house. It always amazed Axel how the ground could have been so easily carved by the glaciers and how long lasting were their landforms.

Janis was asleep on the couch when Axel entered the front door. He walked softly by her to the bedroom, loosening the knot of his tie. There was something special about his wife when she was asleep. With eyelids gently closed and lips barely touching, her face reflected a pureness of beauty unblemished by taut muscles or conscious thoughts. As Axel stared at her from the bedroom door, he felt a tender love that nipped softly at the tips of his unsteady nerves. He finished changing his clothes and came to her side. He knelt on one knee and leaned forward to wake her with a kiss.

At his touch, her eyes jerked open. Her body tensed as her lungs rapidly sucked in air through clenched teeth. She gripped the couch and pushed herself deeply into the cushions, her face frozen in fear.

Axel jerked his head away, as startled by her reaction as she by his waking her. "Honey, honey, it's me!" he said breathlessly.

The hissing of air through her lips ceased. Her body remained taut, but her face relaxed slightly. While she did not speak, her eyes questioned.

"It's me, honey, only me," Axel repeated. He neared her slowly, putting his hands on her shoulders. At his touch, her muscles slackened. He felt her begin to tremble. He eased his arms around her back and held her close. "I'm sorry, Janis, I'm really sorry. I should have known better than to sneak up on you like that." He felt her head nod slightly on his shoulder.

Janis pulled herself away, bringing her face a few inches from his. There was a trace of a tear in the corner of her eye. They stared at each other for a long moment before her lips curved slightly upward in a cautious smile. Finally she exhaled heavily, saying, "You almost scared me to death."

"Scared you to death," he exclaimed. "What about me? My heart practically stopped when you jumped."

"Well, if it had, you would have deserved it." She pouted. They laughed easily now, kidding each other. Axel brought his legs up to the couch and stretched out beside her.

Janis kissed him gently and said, "I'm sorry I reacted so dramatically. It must have something to do with not feeling so well today."

"Leslie told me you left work early this morning. How do you feel now?"

"I feel all right. Just a little tired." She paused thoughtfully.

"Actually, that's all I was this morning, just a little tired. At the kennel I couldn't seem to get rolling, so I just came home."

"Well, that's great," Axel said. "I wish I could lie around in bed all day when I felt a 'little tired.'"

"No, I guess it was more than that. I felt weak. Sick, maybe. I was in bed until going into the garden this afternoon." She lowered her eyes from the ceiling and said with mock seriousness, "What do you mean you wish you could lie around in bed when you're a little tired? If I let you, that's what you'd do all weekend. Isn't that right, Fred?" She used his middle name as a reminder of when he used that name exclusively. When different-sounding names were no longer embarrassing and he grew proud of his Danish heritage, Axel released his first name from hiding behind an initial in his signature.

"No, that's *not* right, Axelqua." He added the root of the word "squaw" to his name, at one time a proper way to address an Ottawa wife.

Ignoring his taunt, Janis rested her head on his shoulder and asked, "How did the trial go today?"

"It didn't. The other attorney never showed up. They found his deserted car on a dirt road a few miles north of here, but not him." Axel felt her shiver involuntarily.

"Did they find his body yet?"

"Body!" he exclaimed. "Come now, let's not bury him prematurely."

"I'm sorry, honey. I thought that's what you meant." Janis began to finger the buttons on his shirt.

"You may yet prove to be right. Actually, if I'm honest with myself, I fear the worst too."

Axel felt her hand glide down to his thighs, stroking them gently. Her lips grazed his neck as she undid his belt. When she slipped her hand into his pants, Axel knew they would have a late dinner.

The sun sets late in July. With daylight saving time, the fiery globe does not dip below the Lake Michigan horizon until after nine. It was dusk before the dishes were rinsed and stacked in the dishwasher. Janis and Axel dragged their tired bodies into the bedroom and prepared to retire.

The one-story house was in the shape of a stubby L, with the top of the L, the garage, pointing to the south. The driveway approached from the west, rising slightly over the low earthen ridge. In addition to the front entrance into the living room, there was an inside door through the garage. This door led into a small laundry room with a lavatory. The kitchen and dining area stretched along the back of the house from the garage to a sunken family room. Two bedrooms were at the north end of the house, and the stubby foot of the L, aiming westward toward the heart of the state forest, was divided between a den and part of the master bedroom. Behind the dining table, between the kitchen and the family room, was a double-width sliding glass door that overlooked the garden and the woods.

Janis was already in bed when Axel came in from the bathroom. He sat on the edge of the bed and reached to the Bose radio, adjusting the alarm time-set. As he stared at the dim glow of the clock face, a barely perceptible grinding diverted his attention. "Jan, do you hear something in the kitchen?" he whispered.

She rolled over groggily and perched herself on one elbow. After a silent moment she said, "No, I don't hear anything."

Axel stood and walked to the door. He listened intently. It was still there. But faint. Janis looked at Axel with wide eyes. She had heard it too. "Something's out there," Axel declared. "Sounds like clawing."

"Maybe a squirrel on the roof," Janis offered.

"Maybe," he said. Axel reached for his flashlight on the dresser. As he moved through the common passageway between the bedrooms, living room, and family room, he flicked on the beam.

He walked softly to the top of the two steps separating the family room from the dining area. The cone of light searched the sliding glass door. It was closed tightly; the wooden stop bar lay in the runner. Axel panned slowly over the kitchen with the flashlight. There was a sharp clinking of glass, like two dishes bumped together in the cupboard above the sink. Axel dashed over and flung the cupboard open. The noise ceased. The beam flickered off the gleaming surface of a hanging coffeecup as it slowly rocked on its hook. Cautiously he reached toward a stack of plates.

"Don't!" It was Janis.

Axel twisted quickly. It was a mistake.

"Look out!"

He felt it on his hand before he could move. Furry, with needlelike claws. He could feel no pain, yet blood erupted from the fleshy heel of his palm as the creature slashed its head from side to side.

"Ah-ah-ah," his voice hyphenated frantically as he spun around and around on the linoleum. "God damn, god damn, let go!" The writhing head moved forward, toward the veins in his wrist. "No!" The flashlight banged to the floor. Axel gripped the wriggling body with his freed right hand and wrenched it from his wrist. Janis came running from behind as he flung it to the counter.

"Get it," he screamed. "Don't let it get away." Axel fell back against the wall, pressing his bleeding hand into his stomach. The small striped animal was momentarily dazed. It recovered quickly and sat up on its haunches. Janis wrenched a frying pan from a hook on the wall. "It's a chipmunk," she shouted incredulously.

"Kill it," Axel wheezed. "Rabies."

The chipmunk did not move, its eyes glinting in the darkness. Janis hovered before the counter, pan upraised. She did not move.

"Janis, it may have rabies. Kill it!" he pleaded.

Janis remained immobile. The chipmunk's reflective eyes were fixed on hers. Axel forced himself from the wall, grimacing with pain. He seized the frying pan from her hand and stumbled toward the counter. The chipmunk broke its pose and tried to dart away, but Axel caught the hind end with a shattering blow. As it squirmed on the counter top, Axel brought the pan down once more. The small bones cracked, and it ceased moving.

He staggered back as Janis collapsed to the floor. Axel ripped a towel from a rack by the refrigerator and bound his hand tightly. He soaked a sponge in cold water at the sink and turned to his wife. She lay unconscious in the middle of the floor. Her face was drawn and her lips parted. Axel bent down to her and squeezed cold water onto her forehead.

Janis rolled her head away from the sponge, sighing.

"Come on, honey, get up," he said. "You have to drive."

She blinked and struggled to rouse herself.

"Oh, God, Axel. Look at your hand!" Blood had soaked through the towel and was dripping to the linoleum floor.

"I know. You have to take me in to the hospital. Let's hurry."

"But let me look at it first. We have to stop that bleeding."

"No, let it bleed. Let's just go."

Janis hurried into the bedroom for some clothes, while Axel opened the cabinet under the sink and pulled out a paper bag. He held its open end by the counter's edge and scraped the dead chipmunk in with the frying pan. Janis brought a pair of pants and a sweatshirt out for him and then rushed out to the car. Axel dressed with difficulty, favoring his injured left hand. With one sleeve dangling from the sweatshirt, he hurried out to join Janis. When he slammed the car door shut, she backed off the concrete apron and gunned the car down the gravel driveway to 621 and the hospital.

5

"I've been practicing medicine in the north woods for twenty-nine years, and this is the first time I've treated a chipmunk bite. Porcupine quills, bee stings, horse kicks, and even a pig bite one time. But chipmunk bites? Never."

Axel did not know if Dr. Lewis was expressing surprise or disbelief. He asked, "Did the lab results from last night reveal anything I should be worried about?"

"No, Axel, the critter was not rabid." Dr. Lewis shifted uncomfortably on the stool, crossing his legs. He leaned toward the padded table, resting his elbow across his thigh, and said, "Tell me again how the thing bit you."

"It didn't just *bite* me Doctor, it *attacked* me." Axel noticed Lewis' eyes narrow, regarding him closely. "It leaped out of the cupboard and tore into my hand. It didn't just nip at me and try to get away, it acted savagely."

"I don't doubt it struggled violently. When an animal is endangered, it tries to protect itself. If it must fight to survive, it fights the only way it knows—with all its strength. It sounds like you had the animal cornered, it was scared, and it tried to defend itself."

"But *speed* is its defense, not its teeth." Axel was frustrated. He had been through this with the intern twelve hours earlier when he'd had his hand treated at the hospital. "It could have jumped on the counter and run off. You know how fast chipmunks are."

"But that's the point, Axel. You stood between it and the

counter. It had to attack you so it could get away."

"It was not trying to get away, though. It was trying to attack me. I could swear it was struggling to get at the veins in my wrist."

Dr. Lewis rubbed his chin and stared at the wall above Axel's head. "I'm not convinced, Axel. I still think it was just trying to get away."

Axel sighed. "Doctor," he said slowly, measuring his words, "after it was on the counter, it just stood there. It did not move. It did not try to escape. Only when I swung the pan did it try to get away."

Dr. Lewis nodded his head gently, but his expression was non-committal. "Well, if it did act as crazy as that, you're lucky it didn't have rabies." The doctor motioned for his arm. "Let me take a look at it today."

As the doctor examined his hand, Axel winced with pain. The belligerence he felt a moment before dissolved. He had spent the last ten minutes trying to convince a rational person that a chipmunk had tried to kill him. And for what? What would it prove if it had? That the chipmunk was crazy? Axel realized that he had made too much out of the incident, that Dr. Lewis was right.

Charles T. Lewis was usually right. Besides being the most respected medical man in the area, he was generally sought out for his opinions on various community issues. When it looked like the proposed sewer system around Lake Muhquh Sebing was going to be scrapped a few years ago because of prohibitive costs, Dr. Lewis told a city meeting that the sewer was needed to protect the lake from pollution. The sewer was installed and the lake was saved from the pressures put on it by the growing population.

"It will stay swollen for a few more days," Lewis said, "and will become even more black and blue by tomorrow. Don't worry about that, but if it gets red and infected, give me a call. I'm glad to see no tendons were severed."

"Thank you, Doctor." Michelson shifted uneasily, adding, "I'm sorry I carried on so about the chipmunk. I feel kind of silly now."

"Oh, so what. It was quite an experience, I imagine." Lewis pulled a small pad of paper from his shirt pocket. "It may hurt

for a while, so I'll give you a prescription for some pain pills."
Dr. Lewis handed him the slip of paper and rose from the stool.
The two men walked from the small examination room into the
doctor's office. Axel noticed a shoe box on a corner of Lewis'
desk where he kept magic tricks to amuse the children. Axel
remembered when he brought Grace's daughter to see Dr. Lewis
and to calm the girl down Lewis took a light bulb from his box,
screwed it into his mouth, pushed his nose, and it lit up. "I
would like to see your hand sometime next week," Lewis said,
"so why don't you make an appointment on your way out."

After conferring briefly with Emma Whitesun, Axel left the
clinic and stepped into Main Street, squinting in the bright sun.

After Janis dropped her husband off at the doctor's, she
crossed the drawbridge and hurried through town. She was
going to be a little late for work, but Dr. Routier would not
mind, and Leslie would have the kennel open by now. Dr.
Routier's veterinary hospital was southwest of Wabanakisi,
near the Lake Michigan shoreline. His hospital occupied half of
a narrow one-story brick building. Routier owned the building
and rented the other half to Janis, who operated a dog kennel.

In lieu of rent, Janis kept the vet's business records and did his
billing for him. It was a fine arrangement for Janis. And the fact
that Dr. Routier's eighteen-year-old daughter, Leslie, worked for
her at the kennel and lived nearby with her parents and was
able to watch things at night made it all the better.

Janis pulled her car to a stop beside the eight-foot Cyclone
fencing that formed the exercise area for her kennel. As she hurried toward the building, sand stung her face from the
windswept beach one hundred yards behind the hospital. She
tugged the door shut behind her, glancing at the clock on the
wall. It was ten a.m. Not bad, she thought, for spending half
the night at the hospital. She deposited her purse behind the
counter and walked through the corridor that connected the
kennel to Dr. Routier's offices.

"Hi, Mike," she said to a young man wearing a white jacket.
"Are things busy in here today?"

Mike Routier smiled as he turned to face Janis. "It's quiet so
far. You feeling any better?"

"No worse. Last night Axel was bitten by a chipmunk, of all

things, and I had to take him in to Emergency."

"A chipmunk!" Mike laughed. "What was Axel doing, stealing his acorns?"

Janis smiled, and was thankful it was not she who had to live down a chipmunk attack. Looking over his shoulder, she asked, "Is your father around?"

"Yes, but he's in the middle of a spaying right now," he said, nodding toward one of the back rooms. In another few years Mike hoped to join his father as a veterinarian himself. He was still a year from applying to vet school in Lansing, and in the meantime he spent summers at home assisting at the animal hospital.

"Okay. If he's looking for me, I'll be next door catching up on some paperwork."

"Paperwork!" he said. "Haven't you seen Leslie yet?"

"No, why?"

"I'm afraid you have more than paperwork. You'd better find her right away."

Janis hurried back through the hallway past her office and into the dog pens. Leslie was on her knees, massaging the throat of a sullen German shepherd. Janis smiled a quick greeting, then asked, "What's the problem? Mike said something's up."

"This morning when I opened, I found Mrs. Tarrie's poodle gagging. I thought he was choking to death, so I quickly got my dad. He checked him over and said it was tracheobronchitis."

"Oh no," Janis groaned. Her chest sank dejectedly as she considered what "kennel cough" could do to her business. Glancing down the row of cages, she asked, "Which other dogs besides the poodle have started coughing?"

"This one," Leslie said, patting the German shepherd. "And I've found what looks like phlegm on the floors in most stalls. I think only three dogs of the eleven aren't sick yet. I've got the three separated, so hopefully they may be okay."

"Is that why the Doberman and the collie are in the pen outside?"

"Yes, and that small scruffy dog seemed all right too. I took him over to our house, and Mom's keeping an eye on him."

"Good thinking, Leslie. I should get the big dogs out of here too." Janis reached down to scratch the shepherd behind the ears. "What did your dad say to do about the sick ones?"

"He gave me some white pills and antibiotics. Here," she said, pulling a folded piece of paper from her shirt pocket. "He wrote down how many to give each dog, depending on their size."

"Thanks," Janis said, scanning the scribbled instructions. "I'm going to look at the dogs in back." She refolded the slip of paper and handed it back to Leslie.

Both dogs broke for the heavy metal door as Janis pushed it open. They swaggered up to her, vying for attention. She bent to one knee and brought both heads to face her. "You two are going to stay at my house tonight," she said as she scratched them vigorously on their sides. The Doberman leaned forward suddenly and licked her right across the lips. "Blah!" she exclaimed as she rubbed her mouth on the back of her hand.

Her knees cracked as she rose from the ground. She opened the door just enough for her body to slink inside while keeping the anxious dogs out. Leslie had just placed a capsule on the back of the shepherd's tongue and was holding his mouth shut until he swallowed it.

"I think I should get those two dogs out of here as soon as possible," Janis said. "If you don't mind, I'd appreciate it if you could take them out to my place and drop them off."

"I'd be glad to. Do you want me to leave right now?"

"Yes. Here are the keys to my car." Janis slipped her keys to the kennel off the ring before handing it to Leslie. "Maybe you can just leave the dogs in the garage and shut the door so they won't run off."

"Okay, will do." Leslie gestured toward the row of cages. "I've given the first dosage to the dogs in these three, so you'd better do the rest."

"All right. By the way, you remember how to get to my place, don't you?"

"Sure," Leslie said as she took the two cloth leashes from a hook on the wall. "I'll see you later."

"'Bye," Janis said. She picked up a small clear plastic container of pills and examined them closely. She held them tightly as she led the German shepherd back to his pen. From there she could see Leslie in the back gathering the two dogs and putting them on leashes.

Leslie unlocked the gate and walked the dogs to Janis' station wagon. They hopped in the backseat, their eyes following Leslie as she circled to the driver's side door. After adjusting the seat, Leslie pulled the car out of the parking lot and drove toward town.

After she crossed the drawbridge and accelerated on the open road, the warm air circulated gustily from her open window. The Doberman pushed his head over her left shoulder, nosing his face into the wind. Leslie glanced into the back seat at the collie, who sat panting. County Road 621 played hide-and-seek with Lake Michigan, alternately plowing through thick stands of trees and open expanses that provided a clear view of the lake. The froth of the waves snaked a fragmented white line in an unending assault on the beach. A solitary triangular sail cut a seemingly effortless course far from land. Great sloping mounds of sand, dotted with glacial debris and patches of dry grass, plunged into the emerald waters, resisting for the moment the relentless pounding of the waves. Soon the angled trunk of the massive Crooked Tree appeared on the horizon, and Leslie began looking for the gravel cutoff to the right. Seeing it, she slowed to turn. An impatient van passed her in the left lane, bringing excited barks from the dogs in the backseat. As she pulled into the narrow aperture through the trees, the car was enveloped by silence.

Leslie drove up close to the garage before the disk brakes ground to a gritty halt. She jumped out and whisked the back door open, ready to grab the leashes as the dogs leaped out. Instead, the animals remained motionless, cowering. Leslie would have laughed if they had not looked so afraid.

She reached in and picked up the leashes, giving them a gentle tug. "Come on, you two, let's go. You both were practically jumping out the window on the way out here." Leslie paused, waiting for them to move. They did not, so she pulled strenuously on the leashes. They resisted for a moment, then climbed reluctantly out of the car. Leslie led them to the middle of the garage and unclipped them. She bent down and petted each softly on the head. "There, there," she cooed, everything's all right. You'll only be closed in here for a few hours. Don't be afraid." Her soothing voice seemed to lessen their involuntary trembles.

As she closed the garage door, Leslie could hear one of the dogs whimper sorrowfully. Unnerved by the low moan, she turned to walk to the car. A sudden gust of wind broke the eerie stillness, slamming the back door shut. Leslie brought her hand to her collar and hurried to the car. Backing away from the garage, she left fresh tire tracks of sand on the pavement. She could not explain why, but she felt a sense of relief when she turned the station wagon onto 621.

A small brown sack with a Wabanakisi Pharmacy label stapled to the top rested unopened on the corner of Axel's desk. As he studied a sheaf of estate papers, there were two quick raps on his ajar door, and Grace stepped in. "Luke Snyder is in the office," she said. "Can he see you?"

"Sure, ask him to come in." Grace swung the door wide and beckoned for the sheriff to enter.

"Good morning, Luke." Axel shook his hand and motioned toward a chair. "I hope you've come with good news about Davis."

"I'm afraid I haven't, Axel. But then again, I don't have bad news either. I just wanted to stop by to tell you how the situation stands right now, seeing as how it was your case and all."

"I appreciate that."

The sheriff continued, "We've searched 621 and all the side roads from here to Mackinaw, and there's no trace of him anywhere. Gas stations and houses along the way reported that no stranded motorists stopped in yesterday, and he hasn't turned up at home. We had his picture on the news last night, and so far no one's called." Snyder paused, letting the extent of his efforts sink in.

"So what do you think, Luke? Where did he go?"

"I guess he was either picked up and robbed, or he's out in the woods someplace. The state police are sending up a crew from Petoskey to help me on the case and they hope to get some tracking dogs up here tomorrow, so if his body is in the woods, we'll find it."

Michelson nodded, and stood to escort the sheriff to the door.

"Hey, what happened to your hand?" Snyder inquired, eyeing the bandages for the first time.

"Oh, just an accident at home," Axel said vaguely. He felt a flash of embarrassment at the thought of what Luke could do with the knowledge of his disablement at the hands of a chipmunk.

Janis shook her hands, splattering water on the wall above the sink. She took the towel from Leslie and rubbed her hands dry. They were completing the final cleanup after a long day of scrubbing and disinfecting.

"I'll give them another round of their medicine before I go to bed tonight," Leslie said.

"That would be great, Leslie. I appreciate it. I'll be in early tomorrow, so get a good sleep and come in whenever you want."

Leslie said good night and walked through the corridor to her father's office and out his back door. She strolled lazily across the sandy ground toward the lake and her family's house, propped on wooden stilts near the beach.

Janis collected a couple cans of dog food and dropped them in a half-empty bag of cereal mix. She looked around the kennel, trying to remember what she had forgotten. Her memory jogged, she reached for the phone and dialed Axel, telling him she would be in front of the Salling, Hanson Building in a few minutes.

When she drove down Main Street, Axel was standing on the curb, briefcase in hand. "Hi, honey," he said as he climbed in the front seat.

Janis leaned over as far as her seat belt would allow and kissed him on the cheek. "How is your hand today?" she asked.

"Fine. The Darvon was a lifesaver."

"Did you get the pills from Dr. Lewis?" Janis turned her head to check for traffic and pulled the car away from the curb.

"Yes, he looked at it and said it would get worse before it gets better and gave me a prescription to keep me from howling."

"But did he say you would be okay?" she pressed.

"Oh, sure," he said. "Oh, I forgot to mention, the chipmunk did not have rabies."

"That's good news. I may need a healthy attorney soon."

"You? You going to file for divorce?"

Janis shot a quick smile to Axel. "Can dog-kennel operators be sued for malpractice?"

"Not exactly, but sure, they can be sued for negligence." He turned to face her, his curiosity pricked. "Why? What did you malpractice today?"

"Most of my charges came down with bronchitis."

"Bronchitis?"

"Tracheobronchitis, in the throat. It's highly contagious among dogs." She told him briefly about the disease and how it can run rampant through a kennel.

"You said 'most of your charges.' What did you do with the healthy ones?"

Janis chuckled and glanced at Axel. "You'll meet two in a few minutes."

The trees blurred by the side windows as the little car sped along the highway. Patches of shade mottled the cracked asphalt surface as oak leaves danced in the wind, tethered to waving branches by rubbery twigs. Tomorrow, the Friday stream of weekend travelers would wend its way into northern Michigan's back roads, but at the moment the Michelsons were alone on 621.

The paved corridor of 621 disappeared behind them as the gravel road leading to their house curved gently through the woods. "My cousin Greg called again today. He's been trying to enlist me in preparations for the summer Ottawa festival, and I just about decided to help him out, before today," Janis said. "I hate to do it, but I'll have to put him off for a few more days, or at least until things are straightened out at the kennel. If by chance he calls tonight, could you tell him I'm sick and in bed? Okay?"

"Oh, don't be silly. Just tell him what's happened and you can't spare any time right now. Then, if he—"

"Damn," Janis interrupted. "Don't tell me the dogs got out." She stopped in front of the sliding garage door, raised about three feet from the ground.

"Maybe Leslie tied them up in there, or in back," Axel offered.

"No, I told her to close them in the garage, and she said she did when she got back. I just hope they have stayed close by and not run off chasing squirrels into the woods."

They got out of the car, and Axel raised the garage door to its full height. Finding nothing unusual, Axel circled around behind the house, where his wife stood, hands on hips, eyeing the still woods, her piercing whistle quickly swallowed by the density of the trees.

"Why don't you go inside and call Leslie to make sure the

dogs were in the garage when she left," Axel said. "I'll look around back here."

"Okay," she said as she turned toward the house.

"By the way, what kind of dogs are these?" Axel asked.

"A collie and a Doberman pinscher. I think the collie's named Satch and the Dobe Diablo."

"Oh, that's just great," Axel said. "I'm going to be wandering in the woods looking for a Doberman named Diablo. I hope I don't find him."

Janis laughed. "He wouldn't harm a flea. He's just a friendly house dog."

Axel had been joking, but he looked at Janis and said more seriously, "They may be sick. You don't suppose that would cause them to attack?"

Janis said reassuringly, "Not a chance. If anything, tracheobronchitis makes them tired and lethargic, just like you would feel if you had the flu."

Axel nodded and walked past the garden to the edge of the woods. It was difficult to discern where the Michelson backyard ended and the forest began. Except for the land on which the house stood, and the garden, they had made slight change in the landscape. Axel had cleared the area immediately around the house of ferns and small bushes, but he disdained plowing up the ground and planting grass. They had built there to be close to nature and did not want to surround themselves with an artificial landscape.

Axel shouted the dogs' names as he moved slowly into the woods. Perhaps because he was looking for movement and listening for the dogs to come crashing through the woods, it seemed quieter than usual.

Waist-high ferns toppled effortlessly with each step, leaving a broken tear in the forest's second canopy. Fallen trees and scattered branches, some suited in moss, littered the ground, forming obstacles for Axel to step over. He stopped to cup his hands around his mouth. "Satch! Come here, boy! Diablo!" Axel surveyed the forest floor with his eyes, straining to hear approaching steps in the woods.

Protruding from behind the trunk of a tree Axel saw a yellowish shape. He moved quickly closer, eyes unflinching from the scene. As he neared, he could see the distinctive long straight hair of a collie. "Come here, Satch!" he called. The dog did not move. Axel halted. It lay against the tree, its back bent awkwardly around the trunk of the Norway pine. The dog's tan-and-white fur was stained with dried blood. Axel fought a sense of revulsion and bent down close to the animal. Heavily matted fur below its neck showed where its killer had attacked. It must have been the Doberman.

Axel carefully looked about for any trace of the other dog. Feeling safe for the moment, he plucked several ferns from the soft forest floor. He bunched their stalks together and lodged them in the Y of a low-hanging branch to mark the spot.

Avoiding looking again at the collie, Axel started to walk quietly back toward the house, his eyes darting from side to side. His bandaged left hand pounded with pain as perspiration collected on his lip. Trying to step gingerly around brittle twigs and dead leaves made the short walk back seem interminable.

Axel froze, his eyes riveted straight ahead. Low to the ground, directly in his path, lay the Doberman. The dog did not lunge, but remained motionless. Its head rested on its paws, unblinking eyes fixed on Axel and teeth frozen in a silent snarl. He fought the urge to run, knowing he could never outrace the dog. The fear he felt the night before resurfaced, magnified.

Michelson inched slowly to his right, leaning down to pick up a dead branch. With measured steps he began to move in an arc around the dog, keeping it in his steady gaze.

After circling twenty feet from where he first saw the prone animal, Axel paused and studied it carefully. It must have seen him, yet it had not budged. He took a cautious few steps toward the Doberman. The short black hair behind its ears seemed unnaturally rippled. Moving closer, Axel saw why it bared its teeth but did not growl. The skin had been torn from the side of its head.

Axel walked up to the dog and nudged it with his stick. It rolled on its side. Without the long hair of a collie to hide its wounds, Axel could see clearly the ripped neck of the dog. He glanced back to where the ferns hung from the Norway pine, fully fifty feet away. Feeling sick to his stomach, Axel dropped the branch and walked toward the house. Without answers for himself, he did not know how he would explain this to Janis.

6

Wrapping flies was delicate work. The polypropylene had to be wound tightly around the thin metal hook, securing the feather in a flushed position. Patient, nimble fingers were required. It did not matter that the fly did not look like a fly. It only mattered what the fish would think.

Karl Waldemeir pulled the line tight and snipped the end off with a short scissors. He held the hook by the end and rotated it in front of his eyes. The feathers jutted out like extended wings, while a piece of rabbit fur teasingly clothed the bare metal. Karl placed the hook in a clear plastic box divided into compartments, snapped the lid shut, and put it in a larger box with the rest of his fishing tackle.

He carried the fishing box up the basement steps to the kitchen, and surveyed the rest of his gear. A small satchel of clothes rested atop a rolled sleeping bag, a collapsible cot, and a canvas tent. Karl reached in one of two cardboard boxes and rummaged through the cooking utensils, towels, and silverware. Feeling his small stove on the bottom, he retracted his hand and looked into the other box. Satisfied that he had sufficient canned goods and other food, Karl flicked the light switch and walked into the living room.

Settling into a lounge chair, Karl reached for a book. Peering over his shoulder was the one-eyed gaze of a soaring goose, profiled in oils on an eleven-by-fourteen-inch canvas. It was one of a series of wildlife pictures Karl had painted and hung throughout his house. Next to the goose was a duck, flying in the same direction. On the opposite wall, a black bear looked down from the heights of a mature beech tree. The birds had been painted mostly from memory, but the bear was copied from a postcard. Despite the many times Karl had camped up north, he had rarely seen black bears in the wild.

Waldemeir was content, quietly looking forward to the weekend. His gear was all packed and ready to load in his four-wheel-drive Blazer. Tomorrow he planned to leave work early, come by his house, and pick up his things. He would be on the road by two and at Crooked Tree State Forest by early evening.

It was a cloudless night at Crooked Tree. Without their insulating layer, the radiated heat from the earth escaped into the upper atmosphere and it became quite cool. Staring through a break in the trees at the stars, Axel stood by his garage, numbed not by the temperature but by the senseless killings of the dogs. They could not have killed each other, he reasoned. They were too far apart. But then who? The question had troubled him for several hours, and each time, his analysis resulted in the same answer: Someone upset at his participation in the Crooked Tree injunction.

He lowered his eyes and walked into the garage, pulling the door down from the inside. Satisfied it was locked, he turned his attention to the large brown plastic garbage bags. There were no tears, and the paper-coated wire was securely twisted around the bags, as tight as it was earlier when he and Janis had placed the dogs in them.

At first Janis had not believed Axel when he told her about the dogs. She had insisted on seeing them for herself. Even as she looked down on their lifeless bodies, she still would not believe. Standing next to the ferns jammed in the branch of the Norway pine, she had cried softly. "Axel ... ?" The words would not form in her mouth.

"I don't know, Jan. I just don't know."

"They wouldn't have done it to themselves, would they have?"

"No, they're much too far apart for one to have crawled injured like that."

"Leslie said the door was shut tightly. Who would have wanted to break in here? Who could have done such a thing?"

Axel was silent. He thought about Hiller's visit the day before. He thought about the varied interests that stood to gain a lot of money by the proposed real-estate development in the state forest. He felt disgust, to be sure; but at the same time, he sensed a feeling of guilt. If true, it was his actions that had brought this on his wife.

"Jan, it's possible that our opposition in the injunction is more desperate than I thought."

"What do you mean?" she demanded. "That the dogs were killed in revenge just because of your involvement in that case?"

"Not so much revenge as warning."

Janis' lips slowly parted as she considered the implications. "It just doesn't make sense," she said at last.

"Of course it doesn't. Hacking open the throats of dogs doesn't make sense either. But it happened. And they sure didn't open that garage door themselves."

"I don't know, Axel. It sounds so crazy." "It's just a possibility, Janis. That's all I'm saying."

"You've been in big cases before and nothing's happened. What makes this so different?"

"Yesterday Ted Hiller tried to put the friendly pressure on me to bow out. He even went so far as to suggest my law career could be in jeopardy."

"Ted? Ted Hiller?" Her tone was incredulous. "You think he had something to do with this?"

"No, not with the dogs. But if he was so moved to try to influence me in the lawsuit, there could be others with bigger stakes invested who might try stronger means of persuasion."

Janis was resolute. "I've known Ted all my life, and I'm sure he wouldn't have anything to do with this."

"I'm not arguing with you. I could be totally wrong about the whole matter. But I think the safest thing to do would be to report it to the sheriff."

Almost reluctantly Janis left the dogs in the woods and followed Axel back to the house. Standing in the kitchen by the sliding glass door, Axel dialed the sheriff in Wabanakisi. An unfamiliar voice answered. "Trooper Adams speaking."

"I'm sorry," Axel said, "I was trying to get the county sheriffs department."

"This is it, sir," the crisp voice said. "A few state police officers and myself are operating out of here for the time being."

Axel remembered what Snyder had told him about the state police coming up from Petoskey to work on the Davis disappearance. "Well, is Deputy Sheriff Perlstrom there, please?"

"Yes, sir. One moment, please."

Axel heard the receiver being placed on the table. He knew Luke was off duty normally after five and that Perlstrom handled the office evenings. Olaf Perlstrom was in his late fifties, and as far as he was concerned had retired from active status. He had been sheriff in Wabanakisi County for years until Luke Snyder outpolled him narrowly in an election eight years ago. After that, he took a job as deputy under Snyder and worked what was usually an easy night at the City-County Building, playing cards with whoever would stop by, and answering the telephone. Even though now a deputy, his former position made him act like a senior adviser.

"Hello, Perlstrom here."

"Hello, Olaf. This is Axel Michelson calling."

"What can I do for you?"

"We've had some trouble out here," Axel began grimly. "Somebody broke into our garage and killed two dogs Janis had home from her kennel."

"Oh, that's terrible," he said. "Damn kids are getting worse all the time."

"I don't think it was kids, Olaf."

"Yeah? Well, then, what happened?"

"Most of Janis' dogs at the kennel got sick today, and she brought two home and left them in the garage. When we got back this evening, the door was raised slightly and the dogs gone. I found them in the woods out back. Their throats were torn open."

"Jeez, that's terrible," Perlstrom repeated. "What makes you think somebody broke in and did it to them? I mean, did you see anybody, find any footprints?"

"No, but somebody had to open the garage door. And the only motive I can think of would be someone threatening me because of the Crooked Tree injunction suit I initiated."

"Oh, I don't know. The dogs were sick, right?" Axel said they could have been. "A couple of sick dogs, closed up in a strange place, they could have struggled with the door and raised it enough to get out. It wasn't locked, was it?"

"No."

"There you have it," Perlstrom concluded. "I had a dog once that could push up my garage door with his nose anytime he wanted out. And that's probably what your dogs did. Nosed their way out, and once out, being sick and all, they tore each other up. Dogs always go for the neck, you know."

"That's impossible," Axel said. "They were at least fifty feet apart, and nothing could have moved that far with its neck torn open."

"You would be surprised. I bet one dragged itself off before it died."

"Oh, come on. They were both dead long before whoever it was that killed them was through with them."

"So you think it's more likely that somebody killed those dogs as a threat to you?" Olaf said curtly.

"Not more likely. Just a possibility."

"You said they were out in the woods?"

"Yes, behind the house."

"Well, then, answer me this. If it was supposed to be a warning to you, why didn't they leave the dogs in the garage, where you would be sure to find them?" Perlstrom paused dramatically.

"Who knows why they dragged them out there. They had to be nuts to begin with, don't you think? I don't see the least bit of logic in anything about the whole business."

"I'm sorry, but I think you're just getting carried away. Listen, if I was going to deliver a message, I wouldn't tie it around a pebble and toss it in your backyard and hope you would stumble over it. I would wrap it around a rock and throw it through your front window. And how high was the garage door? You said it wasn't open all the way?"

"About three feet."

"If a man did it, don't you think he would have raised it higher so he could walk in without stooping?"

"Maybe they ran out when he opened it," Michelson snapped. "Who cares about the door or where they were. The fact remains there's a possibility someone broke into my house and killed two dogs as a threat to me. And there's a chance that they may be back, maybe when my wife is all alone. Now, I think that's sufficient cause for you to come out here and get the dogs and at least investigate the situation."

Olaf spoke testily. "Listen, you're exaggerating, and I've got more important things to do than worry about a couple of damn dogs. Davis is still missing, and until we find him, our office is too busy for dog runs."

Exposed to Perlstrom's famous temper for the first time, Axel understood how he built up enough enemies to eventually defeat himself at an otherwise very reelectable position. He cut the conversation off as civilly as he could and hung up the receiver.

Janis came over to Axel and took him in her arms, hugging him tightly, her head sideways against his shoulder. "Perlstrom's a bum, everybody knows that," she said. "We shouldn't have bothered calling him."

"You're right, but he did raise an interesting point."

Janis released her tight grip and pushed her head back, eyeing him curiously. "What's that?"

"Why were the dogs out in the woods? We may never have found them out there, or at least perhaps not for a long time. What kind of warning is that?"

"Who knows, but what's important now is what to do. We can't just let the dogs lie out there. Maybe Dr. Routier could determine how they were killed."

"Okay, why don't you give him a call," Axel said. "Meantime, I want to take a look at something."

Axel walked through the kitchen to the side door and into the garage. The two-car-wide garage door was parallel to the ground above his head. It was a series of metal panels, each about six inches wide, that bent as the door was raised along slotted runners. Axel reached for the cord hanging from the end of the door and pulled it partway down.

He followed the inside bottom edge of the aluminum door from one side to the other. He found no scratches or other evidence of the dogs' trying to get out, but just to the left of center, the door was dented inward. Axel bent under the door and stepped outside. The dent was about five inches across and bowed perhaps as much as an inch inward. Four parallel scratches in the paint rose from the bottom up.

Axel heard Janis come into the garage from the house, and he raised the garage door above his head. She walked toward him, saying, "Dr. Routier said to put the dogs in plastic bags and bring them in to him tomorrow. He said it may be possible to figure out what killed them."

"Come here, Jan, look at this." Axel gestured with his bandaged left hand. "It's dented from the outside. See? Somebody jammed something in and raised the door. This proves somebody was here and that the dogs didn't let themselves out."

"Why would they do that if the door was unlocked?"

"Maybe it jammed."

Janis ran her fingers over the dent. "Do you think they will be back?"

Axel reflected for a moment before answering. "I don't know. They might." He did not look at Janis. Instead he turned away, looking down the driveway and into the woods. He believed deeply in saving the forest from the exploitation the development threatened. And he had taken an oath not to reject the cause of a client because of personal considerations. But he also took an oath to preserve and protect his wife.

"Don't," she said.

"Don't what?"

"Don't quit the case. And don't worry about me. I'm not afraid. And besides, someone who would do something like this to a dog wouldn't have the courage to do anything to a person."

She had known what he was thinking before he opened his mouth. He felt warm and very close to her. "I won't quit the case." Axel grasped her tightly to his chest. "And thanks."

The rectangular nylon tent fly covered most of the living-room floor. It was narrow at the back, and flared to an extra width of fifteen inches at the front. Marsha Gutkowski was on her knees, applying a stick of wax to the seam that ran the length of the fly.

Normally she would not have to reseal the seams, but the tent had seen much use. Since her third year at Western Michigan University Marsha had spent much of her free time camping. She and her roommate, Kate, had decided that year there was no better way to spend a vacation. The two girls resembled each other in description but were different in appearance. Both were about five feet seven inches, of medium build, with long brown hair. But Marsha had sharp features, piercing eyes and a mouth that when closed could barely be discerned from a distance, while Kate had plump cheeks, round eyes, and a perpetual broad smile. After college the two had found teaching jobs at a Catholic high school in Kalamazoo and continued to room together.

In the living room Kate examined a stack of foil-wrapped pouches, grouping them according to a seven-day menu she and Marsha had prepared. The freeze-dried food in the pouches was not the most appetizing nourishment to live on for a week, but its light weight would make any portages with the canoe that much easier. The women were in no rush to leave early in the morning, but they wanted to have everything packed and ready to go by the time they went to bed. The summer-school session had ended that week, and they were taking a short canoe trip through the Crooked Tree State Forest. They had arranged to rent a canoe at Pike Village, south of Mackinaw City, and were going to float along the Big Two Hearted River, which started in Michigan's inland hills and wound through the Crooked Tree wilderness to Lake Michigan.

Three days of easy paddling were probably all they needed to reach Lake Michigan. They hoped, however, to set up a stationary camp somewhere along the river. But there was no schedule. Planning was loose. And extra food gave them a leeway of four days, if the trip lasted that long.

7

The Friday-morning sun illuminated the Michelsons' bedroom, waking Janis before the alarm. Axel stirred slowly, reaching his arm from under the covers to the clock, his fingers
searching for the button on the top. When the whine stopped,
he lay back, staring at the ceiling, and did not get up until he
heard the shower running. As he walked toward the bathroom,
his left hand began to throb. He took one of the pain pills that
Dr. Lewis had given him. After carefully unwrapping the stained
gauze strips, he examined the cuts. They were swollen, pink
where the skin was stitched, with yellowish-brown bruises circling most of the hand. He applied hydrogen peroxide with a
cotton ball to his wounds and dabbed the white foaming pus
with a Kleenex.

He dressed without showering, remembering the intern's
instructions to keep the hand dry. Janis was still in the shower
as he walked through the house to the garage. Grimly eyeing the
garbage bags, he opened the tailgate of Janis' station wagon,
hoisted the dogs one at a time onto it, and slid them into the
car.

Axel wondered what he would do if Routier's examination
bore out his early suspicions. If someone had killed the dogs,
they would certainly be back, perhaps with greater evil in mind.
It would be insane to stay in the house and wait for them, but
the injunction proceedings could drag out for years. He did not
want to be driven from his house, and he knew Janis felt even
stronger than he about that. It was her family's property, and

the forest was her ancestors' land. Axel loved the woods for its own sake, but to Janis it was part of her. It was part of her history, her heritage. To leave the land, Axel knew, would lead to his wife's divorce from part of herself. But to stay could be worse.

Janis watched as the swirling soapy water at her feet turned clear. She thought of herself a dozen years before, as a zoology major at the University of Michigan, staring down at a half-dissected cat on a table. She thought of a stillborn fawn she helped deliver when she worked for a summer at a small zoo in Traverse City. When she closed her eyes, the cat, the fawn, disappeared from her thoughts, and she pictured herself the night before staring down at the dogs in the woods. Something had tried to take shape in her mind at the time, but the image would not form. Now she tried to remember, tried to focus on that fleeting thought. But in the shower, her mind was even further removed from the image. Shrugging, she turned off the water. It couldn't have been important.

Kate and Marsha had finished a hearty breakfast of eggs and sausage and were getting ready to leave. They brought their camping equipment and supplies down to the car and stacked it carefully on the ground. With a car like Marsha's Volkswagen, packing it was an art.

As Marsha backed the car out of its parking space and steered toward the road, Kate fumbled through the glove compartment searching for the Michigan highway map. They knew which roads to take, but Kate just liked to see it graphically. She traced the M- 131 route northward, along the western part of the state. The heavy red line ended about thirty miles north of Grand Rapids, and 131 changed from expressway to a normal access road for the greater part of the trip. The drive would be longer on the two-lane highway than if it were all expressway, but they did not mind.

Marsha glanced at her watch as they left the Kalamazoo City limits. It was ten a.m. They would be at Crooked Tree by midafternoon.

Dr. Routier bent low over the collie, examining it carefully. Janis sat on a stool in the small wood-paneled room, eyeing

Routier expectantly. The dog was stiff, and rotated easily on the shiny metal tabletop.

"The way this flesh is torn, I would have to say it does look like some kind of animal bite. The Doberman could have done it, but not in the shape he was in." The vet stood straight but kept his eyes on the dog. He pondered the alternative explanations, but nothing seemed to satisfy his professional mind. "I suppose," he said at length, "this could have been done by some kind of pick or other hacking tool. But that seems unlikely as well."

"Why is that?" Janis asked.

"Because if a man was swinging down at a dog, he wouldn't catch him under the neck. At least, not the first blow. And there are no other marks on the dog."

"The garage door was dented at the bottom, and there were four parallel scratches in the metal. Whatever tool they used there could have been used on the dogs, don't you think?"

"Possibly. Maybe a hoeing rake with curved tongs, swung upward from the ground. That could explain how they got it in the neck."

It seemed logical and Janis nodded, adding, "But I just can't understand why, if it was supposed to be a warning to Axel, as he thinks, the dogs were out in the woods where we might never have found them."

"Maybe they hadn't intended on leaving them out there. Maybe after they caught and killed them in the woods they were going to drag them back to your house." He looked at her with quiet eyes and said softly, "Then maybe you and Axel drove up the driveway."

Janis tightened as an involuntary chill swept through her. Her face tense, she shuddered. "You mean they were there, watching us?"

"Janis," he said reassuringly, "that's just a possibility."

Not feeling reassured, she stood and approached the examination table, looking at the torn neck of the collie. Her eyes narrowed suddenly and she bent her head close to the dog. She raised her fingers before her steady gaze and seized a solitary black hair from the collie's fur. She held it before the veterinarian, pinching it between her fingers.

"About three inches," he said. "Too long for the Dobe's." He bent over the dog and searched its fur carefully. He reached his hand to the neck and grasped another black hair. "It could be hair from another dog in the kennel, or even one of your hairs."

"Or maybe the killer's."

Routier looked at her. "Yes, that could be." He turned and opened a drawer in a cabinet along the wall. He pulled out a small white envelope, used for holding pills, and carefully dropped the hair in. He held it for Janis as she slipped the other back hair in. Turning to the Doberman, lying on a second table, he said, "If we're lucky, he'll have some too."

It had more. "Get me another envelope, Janis." He pulled several black hairs from between its teeth and placed them in the second envelope. After labeling and sealing both packages, he said, "Okay, Janis. I think we have our first real clue. I'll send these to Lansing for analysis, and they should be able to determine what sort of beast they're from."

A dark blue van with the state crest of Michigan emblazoned on the door drove into the parking lot behind the Wabanakisi City-County Building shortly after noon. It had made the trip from Lansing in about four hours. The state police sergeant got out of the passenger seat and walked toward the rear entrance, while the driver remained where he was. As the sergeant entered the building, he could hear the muffled barks of the dogs in the van.

Luke Snyder greeted him and introduced him to the deputies and other state police officers. Sergeant Rademacher shook hands all around before sitting at a long table. He was one of the few officers assigned to the canine unit.

"As I understand it," the sergeant began, "the man's car was found on a back road, deserted, and there's been no sign of him since."

"Right," Snyder replied. He went on to briefly outline the search effort thus far.

"Well, it sounds like we should begin with the dogs near where his car was found," Rademacher observed. "If he was kidnapped or wandered along the highway looking for help, we would have heard from somebody by now. My guess is he's out in those woods not too far from where his car was. The problem is, it's real easy for the dogs to lose a trail in these woods. It's wet and swampy in places, and there's a lot of wildlife out there to cross them up. I say this with every confidence in the dogs, but I just want you gentlemen to know the difficulties we face."

Rademacher looked at the faces around the table. Some nodded, some stared impassively, and some looked away. Captain William Selzer from the Petoskey State Police Post spoke first. "Thank you, Sergeant. We understand the situation. Now I suggest we drive to the scene and begin the search."

"Oh, hell." Deputy Sheriff Shank could not contain himself any longer. "'The scene' has been searched and researched many times over. I've covered every inch of ground out there, and I can tell you: Davis is not in those woods."

Snyder interrupted Shank by standing. "Listen, Jerry. Until we do find him, we're not eliminating anything. And I don't care how many times it's been gone over." He knew Shank resented state police intrusion into county business. He did too, but in this case it was necessary. "I suggest we get started," he said.

The state officers in their blue uniforms and the county in their green rose and walked wordlessly through the corridor and into the parking lot. Before they entered their cars, Snyder gave general directions to the state police. Snyder's car left first, driving over an em-bankment and into the street, followed by a blue state-police car, the van, and finally a second county car. Crossing the drawbridge, rubber tires whistling on the steel grating, the caravan accelerated, leaving behind the first weekend arrivals.

The Blazer backed up the driveway, stopping with its tailgate next to the side door. Karl had worked through lunch so he could justify leaving early. His boss would not have hesitated letting him leave early, but Karl's sense of fairness did not permit it.

Much as he hated to spare the time, Karl stopped in the kitchen to fix a quick bite. He was too hungry not to. He slapped together a bologna sandwich and swallowed it practically whole between gulps of milk. Leaving the glass and mustard-stained knife in the sink, he hurried into his bedroom and slipped on an old pair of khaki trousers and a flannel shirt.

Surveying his camping gear, Karl began a familiar routine. He started with the cardboard boxes of food and cooking utensils.

He finished with his tackle box and fishing rod, folded in three sections and packed in a four-foot plastic tube. With the Blazer loaded, Karl slammed the tailgate shut, locked it, and then locked the side door of his house. Climbing in behind the wheel, he pulled the sun visor down and reached for a small dog-eared spiral notebook. He turned to a page toward the end of the book and wrote down the mileage at the bottom of a row of figures. He glanced at his watch and noted the time as well. He hoped to be setting up camp in Crooked Tree by eight o'clock, five and a half hours away.

The caravan of police vehicles stood in a line along the dirt road. The sun flickered through the nearly unbroken canopy of trees, casting an occasional spear of light off a windshield into the woods.

The uniformed officers stood in an uneven circle around Sergeant Rademacher. "Since the terrain seems varied and even swampy in parts, sections of his trail may be stronger than the others. Because of this, it will be best if we split up, giving each dog a chance at finding the scent."

Rademacher paused, looking northward along the dirt road. "How far did you say it was until the dirt road meets the highway?" he asked.

A deputy replied, "I'd say we're a little south of the halfway point of the 621 loop."

"So it's conceivable that Davis may have thought he was closer to where he came from and headed back that way," Rademacher surmised.

"That could be, but it's unlikely," Sheriff Snyder said. "I'm sure he knew this trail well, and he was hurrying to get to court. I don't think he would have started walking the other way."

"I see." Rademacher nodded. "But since we've got enough dogs, we'll search both directions anyway." Three German shepherds tugged impatiently at their leashes, pulling Rademacher forward a step. The driver of the van was only slightly better in control of another three dogs. Directing his partner to turn over two of the leashes to two of the officers, Rademacher did the same. Motioning along the sides of the road, he outlined the search pattern. "I'll walk along the road southward, and you two," he said, gesturing to a deputy and a state police officer, "walk parallel to the road, about fifty feet deep into the woods. That way, if my dog misses the trail, one of you should cross it somewhere. Dick," he said, turning to the driver of the van, "you do the same that way, all the way to the road." He looked around, waiting for questions. No one spoke, so he said, "Let's get started. Sheriff, do you have the clothes?"

"Sure, let me get them out of my car." Snyder retrieved a small bundle of clothes and a pair of shoes from the backseat. Sergeant Rademacher held the bundle before the dogs, letting each memorize Davis' scent. With the dogs anxious to move, the officers broke into three groups, two heading off with the dogs and one remaining with the cars.

Sergeant Rademacher proceeded southward along the dirt road, allowing his dog to roam from side to side. To his left, Trooper Adams guided his dog into the woods. Angling away from the trail road to the right was Deputy Sheriff Shank.

Shank stepped through the log- and leaf-littered forest floor over ground he had covered several times the day before. It all looked the same to him, and trampled ferns testified to the thoroughness of his search. As he paused, the German shepherd he held on a leash turned its head as if to ask: What's the delay? Its pointy ears perked. Shank sighed and started to trudge up a slight hill. At the summit of the hill Shank stopped again. He carefully looked down the hillside he had just walked up, scanning the ground for any signs of a body. He had stood at almost the same spot the day before, peering over the same area and seeing the same things: Trees, ferns, and grass.

He looked toward the road where Rademacher was walking slowly from side to side. The sergeant's dog had not picked up a scent either, Shank saw, and probably would not.

No, he thought. Davis was not in these woods. If he was, he would have been found. He had been picked up and taken someplace else by somebody along the road. The dogs and the search were a waste of time. Of this, Shank was sure. But he was a deputy, not the sheriff.

Looking down the slope he was about to descend, Shank could see his path led directly toward a line of conical-shaped cedars. He nudged the dog, and they began to walk down the hill, the dog alternately sniffing the ground and raising its head to look around. Shank took long strides, letting gravity pull him along. As he moved faster down the hill, the dog picked up speed, staying always a fully extended leash in front. Shank tried to slow down, but the dog was in control. The deputy's foot slipped on a fallen moss-covered tree trunk, and he tumbled to the ground. The dog's neck jerked back as Shank's weight brought it to a quick halt. "Goddammit!" he shouted as he struggled to his feet. He grabbed the dog by the collar, spun it around to face him, and gave it three sharp slaps across the head. The dog recoiled, cowering on the ground. "Can't you walk without pulling on that damn leash?" he shouted. "You're supposed to be trained. What the hell's wrong with you?" The dog remained on the ground, its head resting on its paws. "Now, get up," Shank snarled as he grabbed the dog by the scruff of the neck, "and let's go."

The dog moved more slowly now, occasionally darting a glance up the slackened leash. The ground, ribboned with twisting roots, evened out below the level of the road. Shank paused to wipe his sleeve across his forehead and decide which way to walk through the cedar swamp.

Branches grew low on the cedars, and when they were eventually starved by the sun-blocking upper branches, they lost their leaves and died. But they remained fastened to the tree, creating a skeleton of projecting twigs that interfered with Shank's progress. The dog, as unbothered by the roots as by the branches over his head, had increased the tension on the leash once again, straining as if trying to pull away from the deputy.

Some distance in front of Shank and the German shepherd, heavy footprints circled a rotting corpse. The prints of the bears were large and broad, with the unmistakable impression of all five toes. The black bear is plantigrade, like man, with the heel and ball of the foot touching the ground. By contrast, the whitetail deer, built for speed, would stand on the tips of its toenails. Looking closely at the tracks around the corpse, it could be imagined that the soft black dirt held the imprint of a naked human foot.

Shank noticed the gouged trunk of a cedar to his left. Bark littered the ground next to the tree, while some hung in flaky strips. The trunk was lined with deep vertical scratches gouged at varying heights and depths. Shank had tracked bear often enough during hunting season to realize what the scratches meant. The cedar was a "bear tree," scratched by any number of bears that had passed by it over the years. No other tree near it would be gouged in like fashion. By clawing the bark and sometimes rubbing their backs on the fresh gouges, the bears marked their territory-like the urinary post of wolves. Sniffing the tree later, another bear could tell how recently the first one had passed, and its sex.

The dog's nostrils worked vigorously as it nosed its way around the base of the tree. Shank had to loop the tree himself to untangle the leash. The dog was reluctant to leave the cedar, but yielded to the strong pull from Shank. He would have to remember this spot, he thought, come November and hunting season.

Not far past the "bear tree," the dog abandoned its random sniffing and tugged hard on the leash. The sudden pull jerked Shank forward.

His foot plunged into black muck covered by a shallow puddle. Pale green slime floated on the stagnant, water. He yanked his foot from the muck and kicked the dog in the flanks, black ooze splattering in its fur. The deputy swore and dragged the dog several paces ahead to a dry spot of ground, where he grasped a dead limb and scraped his shoe, as the dog cowered beside him on its belly.

With most of the muck cleaned from his shoe, Shank pointed the branch at the dog and growled, "That's the last time you're going to do something like that. You hear?" He paused, breathing heavily, eyes fixed on the dog. "Now, let's get the hell out of this damn swamp." He pulled the dog up and tramped toward 621. As they moved out of the cedar thicket, the lifeless eyes of James Davis stared at their retreat, a battered briefcase and a wrinkled sport coat lying by his side.

The ground gradually rose until the oak was once again dominant. Shank moved quickly through the woods, the dog obediently at his side. It did not sniff the ground or wave its head back and forth any longer. It just pranced close to the deputy, fearful of doing anything to renew his wrath. Within a few minutes Shank could see County Road 621. When he stepped out of the woods onto the shoulder of the highway, he saw Rademacher and Trooper Adams waiting for him at the entrance of the dirt road. He approached them triumphantly.

"Nothing, eh?" Shank said.

"No, not yet," Sergeant Rademacher responded. "I thought he might be on a trail a couple times, but if he was, he lost it back in the low area. What about you? Did you find anything at all?"

"No, not a trace of anything. And I say the more time we waste out here the more time we give to whoever got him to get somebody else."

Rademacher did not respond. With a disgusted glance toward Adams he turned and began walking back toward the cars.

8

The hill sloped gently from its modest height southward to the river. The trees were larger than in many other parts of Crooked Tree, but they were not quite as dense. The early evening sun cast shadows across the hillside like mammoth horizontal steps.

At the foot of a towering white pine, a mass of bramble fern quivered. A furry black head pushed its way through the woody stems and small green leaves and protruded into the open. With the pine protecting his back, the black bear had a clear view of the approach to his den before him, and he surveyed the hillside carefully. He saw no danger, yet he trusted his eyesight not nearly as much as his sense of smell. The bear perceived scents when molecules in the air made contact with receptor molecules in his nasal epithelium, a thin membrane stretched accordion-like over scrolls of tiny bones in the nose. While all mammals perceive scents the same way, their capacity to smell varies greatly. The epithelium of a human, if unraveled, would cover about two hundred and fifty square millimeters—the size of two thumbnails. In the bear, the epithelium would spread over half of his body surface.

Assured by his nose, the bear ventured from his shallow hole under the thick brambles and stood on his hind legs, stretching his muscles. After a good yawn, he plopped on his haunches and scratched his stomach with daggerlike claws. When satisfied, he folded his arms across his chest and let himself roll over backwards onto the barren twigs of a fallen sapling. A contented moan came from deep in his throat as he rubbed his back on the sharp branches of the dead tree.

The bear rolled to his side and pulled himself up on all fours. Tufts of black hair were left dangling on the branches of the tree as the bear ambled down toward the river. A month after he emerged from hibernation, his winter coat started to deteriorate. The shedding process brought interminable itching, and the bear got great pleasure out of using whatever he could find for a backscratcher.

On the wet ground near the water, the bear strolled lazily. His head swung slowly back and forth as his eyes took in everything immediately in his path. The bear paused, studying a rock partly buried in dirt. He circled the rock, nose close to the dirt line. He touched it with his paw and followed the lower edge of the rock around, with his claws digging slightly into the dirt. The bear twitched his arm suddenly, and the rock flipped in the air like a biscuit in a pan. A colony of silver beetles scampered every which way in the glare of the light. The bear's head lurched downward, its tongue lapping at the scurrying bugs. In just a few seconds the beetles were gone and the bear raised its head from the tasty snack.

He ambled away from the river toward a clearing in the woods, a favorite blueberry patch of his. Although he was classified in the order Carnivora, he was truly omnivorous. His teeth resembled man's, and despite his bulk, he was adept enough to pick individual berries with his front incisors from between the tiny leaves on the twisting blueberry bushes.

Coming into the clearing, the bear noticed movement in the center of the berry patch. The wind brought the scent of bear to his nostrils. Already downwind, he approached slowly. Two cubs, born the winter before while their mother slept in her den, frolicked playfully together. They nipped and scratched and wrestled puppylike with each other.

The bear surveyed the surrounding area for their mother. Seeing nothing, he continued his approach. Food was plentiful for the bear during the summer, and he did not need the nourishment a cub would bring. But this was too easy to pass up. Surely the bear would not bother hunting for game, nor would it extend itself in any chase. But an untended cub was like picking blueberries off the bush.

The bear had advanced within twenty feet before the cubs

stopped their playing. They stood quickly erect, their ears perked. The young bears remained unmoving for a moment before one cub broke the pose and turned its bewildered head in search of its mother. She was not to be seen. The other broke for the trees in a flash, realizing that was where its only safety lay. The first cub started a dash in the opposite direction, the adult in pursuit. It was not a fair race. The cub tumbled to the ground far from the tree line. The adult stood in front of it, ready for the pounce, but as it raised its paw for a slashing blow, the air was pierced by the mother's call. Her shriek pounded terror into the head of the bear, freezing his paw in midswing. He turned to face the mother, charging from the woods at thirty miles per hour. She pummeled into him in an instant, sending both bears sprawling to the ground. Rising quickly and standing erect, they faced each other with arms outstretched.

The mother barked a command at the cub and it was gone. The male feinted a jab with his paw, but the mother stood her ground, returning a growl that would echo through the trees for miles. She leaped at the bear and pulled him tightly to her body, lashing at his neck with her teeth. The male pushed away and dropped to all fours. He slapped the ground between them with his heavy paws. She bared her teeth, and her menacing growl bounced off the trees once again.

The male backed up a step. The mother moved quickly forward and slashed at him with her forepaw. He dodged and retreated farther. She dropped to all fours and charged, stopping an arm's length away. He moved back quickly, then turned and darted for the trees as the cubs had done a moment before. The mother pursued to the edge of the clearing, where she watched as the intruder loped into the forest.

He slowed his gait and stopped after a few seconds, turning to glare at the mother. Then he raised himself to standing position and stretched his arms out to their full length. He snarled a warning as bloodcurdling as the mother's had been. She remained motionless, staring. His strength demonstrated, the bear dropped to the ground once again and turned to trot away, feeling not in the least defeated.

The bear preferred solitude, and continued to move away from the mother and her cubs. He was unharmed from the skirmish and only slightly disappointed over the loss of a meal. Food was plentiful in the woods, and there were much easier meals to be had.

Kate and Marsha stared silently into the burning embers of the fire. A five-inch-wide furrow in the dirt led to the log they sat upon. They were tired, but for some reason they felt they could not retire until nightfall. So they sat by the fire with half-closed eyes, waiting for the day to end.

They had arrived in Pike Village in midafternoon and had had no trouble finding the canoe livery. Large signs announced its approach for miles. Marsha had parked her car by a large sign with "Minnehaha's Fun Canoes" lettered across the bottom. The top of the sign was cut irregularly, profiling a smiling Indian maiden merrily paddling from the middle of a canoe. The livery itself was little more than a wooden shack with a lean-to projecting from one of the sides. The screen door squeaked on rusted hinges as the girls entered.

"Excuse me," Marsha said to an upraised newspaper. "Are you the owner here?"

The newspaper folded and fell to the man's lap. He said nothing, but regarded the girls slowly from head to toe. He pulled a wooden blue-tipped match from his teeth and held it poised in his fingers, pointing at the girls. "Yeah, that's me," he said at length.

Marsha continued, "I called the other day and reserved a canoe. My name's Marsha Gutkowski."

He made no effort to move, other than stroking the stubble on his cheeks. "You're the one that don't know how long you're gonna be gone?"

"Yes, maybe a few days, maybe the whole week. We don't know."

"You're going to leave your car here and have me pick y'up?"

"That's right."

"Then how the hell am I supposta know when to come get you and my canoe if you don't know when you're gonna stop?"

"I thought we settled that on the phone," Marsha said. "You said to call you from one of the landings."

"Maybe I said that, and maybe I didn't. Anyways, I've been thinking. I just might be busy when you call." He put the match back in his mouth and resumed chewing.

"We'll be in no hurry. We can wait."

"What about my canoe? They ain't cheap, you know."

"Listen, our car's going to be right out there," she said, pointing to the bright yellow-and-orange sign. "And besides, I'm sure you do this all the time. It's your business, isn't it?"

The owner raised his feet to a table and pushed his chair back so it balanced on two legs. "Sure, it is. But normal times, girls ain't my usual customers. Maybe for a day, but not overnight. I didn't know you was two girls."

"And what the hell difference does that make?" Kate exploded.

He smirked and rubbed a dirty hand over his soiled T-shirt. "If you don't know, sister, you better go ask your momma."

"Oh, go fuck yourself and fuck your canoes," Marsha blurted. The man's mouth dropped, and the match fell to his stomach. The front legs of the chair crashed heavily to the floor. He started to say something, but Marsha and Kate were out the door before he made a sound.

Shuffling into the parking lot after them, the man shouted, "Hey, bitch. Go on that river. Maybe some rattlesnake poison will clean that filthy mouth of yours."

In gear, Marsha accelerated, her spinning wheels raising a cloud of dirt and dust. The man turned his head and coughed as the car sped away.

"Now what the hell do we do?" Marsha sighed.

"Who cares, it was worth it," Kate said. "Did you see the look on his face?"

"Yeah." Marsha grinned. "It was worth it."

"Anyway, I'm sure there are other places around here to get a canoe."

There were other canoe liveries, and with the help of a gas-station attendant they found one a mile or two down the river from Pike Village and that much closer to Crooked Tree.

After agreeing on terms and arranging the pickup, the girls loaded the canoe and set off. The current was a brisk three miles per hour at this point, but it would decrease as the river neared Lake Michigan. The Big Two Hearted River twisted on a jagged course for over a hundred miles, but the aerial distance from source to mouth was no more than thirty. Paralleling its course, sometimes no more than a few miles apart, was the

Little Two Hearted River. It eventually joined the main branch in the middle of the state forest.

Because of the swift current, Marsha and Kate did not have to extend themselves with their paddles to make good time. But they wanted to get away from the town and the cottages that lined the riverbank in spots. Once inside the wilderness of the state forest they would slacken their pace and look for a campsite.

They had canoed for almost an hour without seeing a house before a dark-brown-stained wooden sign appeared on the banks of the river. "Entering CROOKED TREE STATE FOREST" was carved in bold letters. Below, in less striking print, was "Fire danger: High Today." The "High" was painted on a removable wood plaque that swung free on a hook.

They had quickly agreed on a place to camp and were now just waiting for the campfire to die. In the unfamiliar quiet of the woods, it was somehow comforting to contrast the density of the city this morning with the isolation of their little camp by the river. It was relaxing for Kate to think that they might not see a single person for the next few days.

Karl felt as if a layer of cellophane snugly encased his eyeballs. He squeezed his eyelids tightly shut and massaged them briefly with his index and middle fingers and thumb. Resting his right hand on the middle bar of the steering wheel, he opened his driver's-side window. The cool evening air rushed into the car, alerting his senses. Waldemeir was not ready to fall asleep at the wheel; he just wanted to enjoy the last few miles into Wabanakisi.

In town he made one quick stop to pick up a cup of coffee at the Creamery. He balanced the Styrofoam cup between his legs until he had crossed the drawbridge. Accelerating on the open road leading north from Wabanakisi, he pried the plastic lid from the container and sipped the hot liquid.

Nearing his turn, he finished the last few gulps. He bit the empty cup, letting it dangle from his lips. He enjoyed sinking his teeth into the soft Styrofoam and would discard the cup only after leaving a trail of tooth marks around the rim.

The Blazer slowed and edged off 621 to a dirt road. It was one of many old logging trails that ribboned the northern woods. One of the main problems of the shanty boys, or lumberjacks, was getting the heavy timber from the cut site to the logging camp. They proceeded in the most direct fashion possible, winding their sleds piled high with logs around and through the noncommercial trees to the mill. The heavy load cut deeply rutted trails through the woods. Some eventually became the path for highways; others fell into disuse and became overgrown; and the rest, through occasional use, remained two-rutted trails.

Karl's memory was unerring as he made the proper cutoffs and followed the right branches of the Y's. He had long ago settled on this remote site as his favorite camping spot, and as he drove over the remote smoky roads, dust nipping at the rear of his car, he felt as if he was driving to his own summer home. When the ruts themselves started to boast grass, Karl knew he was almost there.

He slowed to a crawl and peered through shadowy trees. Spotting the flaky bark on the trunks of three huge red pines, Karl pulled his car off the track and nosed it into the woods. Blocked by the thickening forest after a few yards, he halted the slow advance of the wheels and turned the ignition off.

It was still light, but the sun would be setting within a half-hour, and darkness would not be far behind. Karl decided to bring to the campsite only what he would need that night and come back for the rest in the morning. He slid the canvas tent along the smooth floor and hoisted it to his shoulder. With his other hand he grabbed a sleeping bag and began toward the triangle of red pines.

The campsite perched on high ground maybe twenty feet above the water. The swift-flowing stream was bulged by the flow of the Little Two Hearted River. The confluence of the Big and Little Two Hearted where their twin courses blended into one, was upstream from Karl about a mile. The early Indians had noticed the similarities in the streams and had called them Nizhode Sibi, Twin Rivers. The same word, accented on the last syllable, Nizhode, meant "two-hearted." Unfortunately for historical accuracy, the French missionaries mistakenly gave it the latter translation.

With the tent facing the river and away from the predominant winds, Karl hiked the one hundred or so yards back to the car. Conditioned by the city, he took pains in locking the doors before returning to the camp for the night. Passing the three red pines, he noticed that the flaky bark of one of the trees was more ragged than it should be. He stopped to inspect it. The bark was scraped clean in parts, and the entire trunk was circled with long deep scratches. The sight perplexed him, and he stood for some time with two cardboard boxes stacked in his arms, staring at the tree. Raccoons or squirrels digging for insects? Karl had never tracked bear before.

9

The list of names filled the sheet of paper on Janis' desk. With the muffled sound of dogs barking behind a closed door, Janis stared blankly at her writing. No sense calling the owners of the dogs again. They had all been notified. Or had they? Suddenly Janis could not remember if she had called.

"Excuse me," a voice boomed.

"Oh, I'm sorry," Janis said. "I didn't notice you come in."

"You should wake up, dear. I've been standing right here." The woman had the unmistakable deep dried tan of year-round sun: Florida in winter, and north when it became too hot. "My husband and I are going on a sail, and Reginald cannot be left alone."

"Reginald?"

"Yes. This is Reginald." The woman placed a miniature poodle on the counter, its curly white hair an almost identical match with that of its owner. "I don't like the idea, but I'm going to have to leave him here. It's dreadful how he takes to water."

"I hate to tell you this, but I have no room for Reginald."

"But that's impossible," she gasped. "He gets seasick."

"I'm sorry."

"It's such a glorious Saturday. You wouldn't want us to waste it, would you?"

"Can't you just leave him home and have a neighbor let him out?"

"That's out of the question. Whom could I trust?" The

woman's voice iced. "I was told this was a trustworthy establishment."

"I assure you it is. But, well, some of my dogs are sick, and I can't take any more in."

"Oh, I see. Very well, then." The woman scooped up her dog and strutted toward the door. As she left, Reginald yapped once over her shoulder.

Janis sighed as the door clicked shut. On its window, black letters, in reverse from her angle, read: "Saturday Hours Noon-5." With the woman's car leaving the empty parking lot, Janis reached for the telephone.

"Mrs. Routier? This is Janis at the kennel. Is Leslie there? . . . Oh. I just wanted to tell her I'm going to be leaving now. It's three o'clock and the dogs are all fed and there's no reason for me to stick around. . . . No, I'm leaving the swinging doors open, so she doesn't have to stop by tonight. . . . But she'll be able to stop by tomorrow as usual? . . . Good. If anything comes up, I'll be at the school in Ottawa Village tonight and at home all day Sunday. . . . Thanks, Mrs. Routier. Good-bye."

Janis' hand lingered on the receiver as she stared at a stack of mail next to the phone. The unopened envelopes were addressed either to her or to Dr. Routier. Underneath, an accounts book lay opened. As if her hand was amidst poison ivy, she carefully retracted it.

Pausing only to lock the door, Janis hurried out of the building. She eased her foot from the gas pedal only when the town was behind her. She really didn't have to hurry. The meeting on the injunction in the village wasn't until eight. Breathing deeply, she rubbed the palm of her hand upward across her forehead. If only the feeling, the tension, would leave, she thought. If only she knew what it was.

Axel heard the car pull up in front. He laid his pen on the pad of paper and left his file on the table as he walked to the side door.

"Hi, honey," he said as he kissed Janis on the cheek. "You're home early."

Walking past him toward the family room, Janis said, "There was nothing more to do. I couldn't have taken any more dogs."

"But I thought you had a lot of paperwork to do."

"I did it." The lie blurted out without thinking. She opened her mouth to correct herself, but said nothing. It was not important.

"Great. Larry called and invited us over for dinner before the meeting."

"Tonight?"

"Yes. I tried to call, but you must have just left."

"And did you say we would come?" Janis demanded, her voice slicing the air.

"Well, yes." He hesitated. "There's nothing wrong in eating over there, is there? You like Larry, don't you?"

"Larry's fine. And so is dinner over there." The crispness was suddenly gone from her voice. "I'm sorry I barked, Axel. I guess I'm just tired."

"Maybe you should skip the meeting."

"No, I'll go. I want to go." After a convincing smile, Janis disappeared into the bedroom. She really did want to go. She had been planning on it. Yet something made her feel she should stay.

Enveloped in her thoughts, Janis did not speak to Axel again until their car passed the dirt-road cutoff on County Road 621. "That's where they found Davis' car," she said.

Axel did not know if it was a question or an observation, but seized the opportunity to break the silence. "Yes, about halfway through. Which way do you suppose he would have walked if he came out here?"

"Oh, I don't know. Toward town, I suppose." Her voice was flat, uninterested. Axel decided not to push it. She would come out of it on her own.

Midway through the westerly loop of 621, after the road began to curve slightly to the east, Axel slowed and turned down a weathered strip of asphalt. The heavy woods diminished into scattered farms. Stalks of corn stood high, a month from harvest. Cherry trees dotted the rolling country in modest orchards, but corn was still the dominant crop, as it had been two hundred years ago when the Ottawa settled in the area.

Only a dozen houses or so were clustered in the village, with most of the Indians on the reservation scattered on small farms. The village itself could provide the bare necessities for them, but any major shopping had to be done in town. One gas station identified by a thin metal Mobil flying-horse sign was next to a general store. Beyond that, the only other commercial building was a bar owned by Henry Longfellow. Over the years Henry had turned his bar into a museum of carved driftwood and tables fashioned from stumps.

The Michelsons drove by the school to the foot of the inland side of the dune. From the other side it rose from the shore of Lake Michigan to a modest height of two hundred feet. It was a fairly stable dune, covered for the most part with wispy blades of grass and dominated at the otherwise sparse summit by the Crooked Tree, its hooked tip pointing toward Ottawa Village, one hundred feet below the crest of the dune.

Larry Wolf lived where the sandy hill began its gradual rise. The one-story house had been built in the 1940's by his grandfather and father, using reclaimed lumber from the railroad station in Wabanakisi that was torn down to make room for a larger stone structure. The elder Mr. Wolf had worked in the old station since he was a young man, cooking meals for the engineers and for railroad hands and keeping the place clean. Lumber was scarce during the war years, and even if it was not, Larry's grandfather would not have been able to afford it. So when the plans were made for the new station, Charley Wolf volunteered to tear down the old one in exchange for the salvageable wood. He and his son worked a long summer pulling the building apart plank by plank and nail by nail. The wood was loaded on an old pickup truck and hauled to the reservation, where the two of them erected their house, using the best of the lumber and the old nails hammered straight.

Axel parked the car and walked up the front sidewalk with his wife. Above the dunes and still a ways from shore, Axel noticed the dark line of a cloud front approaching the land. He hoped it would bring rain. The dry forests needed it.

The house was clean and in good repair, but the white paint, dulled by the summer sun and tortured by the winter winds, hung in tattered shreds from under the eaves and by the gable. At one time Larry's grandfather would have been on the ladder scraping and painting at the first sign of peeling, but age showed on him and he was unable to work as he once had. And Larry had been trying to find the time to do the work the past two summers.

Above the wooden steps leading to the porch was an ornately carved plank, stained brown and deeply inscribed with "Wabanakisi." It had once hung above the door to the old railroad station, and since it did not match the motif of the new stone structure, no one minded when Mr. Wolf carted it off with the rest of the lumber. It had been the work of an unnamed Ottawa craftsman in the early years of the twentieth century. To the left of the letters was a likeness of the Crooked Tree, looking much the same as it did today. To the right was carved a silhouette of the cousin of the Ottawas, the black bear. Janis paused on the steps and stared up at the sign.

"Beautiful work, isn't it?" Axel said.

"Yes, it is," Janis responded. She lowered her eyes to the floor and negotiated the last step.

The screen door swung open, and Larry held it with his arm. "Hi, Axel, Janis," he said. "Come on in."

Janis smiled and said hello. They stepped by him and walked into the living room, settling onto an old couch. There was a loud flush of a toilet, and Larry's grandfather appeared shortly after. "Don't get up, don't get up," he said as he hopped across the floor, hurrying to Axel before he could rise. "I know how hard it is to pull out of those cushions. It's like you're sitting in an inner tube."

He bent over, with his hands searching behind him for a wicker rocking chair. "How are you, Janis?" he asked as he eased himself down.

"I'm fine," Janis said. "You look in good health. Are you still keeping in shape?"

"Yep. I walk up to Crooked Tree every morning. It's good for my heart, you know." He cracked a smile and raised a bony finger. "I used to walk up there for fun, to see the sun rise over the forest. It's a beautiful thing to see that orange light waking up the trees. But I haven't been up early enough to see the sunrise in years." He laughed. "I do it now because the doctor told me to exercise."

"He may have said to exercise, but I don't think he had in mind a hike up that hill every day. I like the view from up there too, Mishoo, but I prefer the sun setting over the water. It's more my time of day."

"Well, if you could get yourself out of bed early, you would see what I mean." Charley Wolf turned to Axel. "What's all this talk Larry's been filling me with all day, something about trees suing the real-estate people in court?"

Axel leaned forward, resting his bandaged hand on his knee. "In order to sue somebody in court, whether for an injunction, as in our case, or for anything, you have to show that you have some recognizable interest at law in what you're suing for. In other words, it's to make sure you aren't bargaining away somebody else's rights. Now in this case, the land is owned by the state. The state made the leases, and the state does not want to break the leases. In order for the Ottawas to get an injunction prohibiting the real-estate development, they have to show that while not owning the land, they have a recognizable interest in it. In our suit, we are basing our standing on the old treaty and the interest in hunting it supposedly gave the Indians. Now Larry says, why should we have to establish this kind of property interest in an environmental suit where much of the ecological abuse is wreaked on the abuser's own land. There are some regulations that help, but it's not enough. If no one can show an interest in the land, then the abuser can do what he wants. In this case, the abuser is the state. Larry's argument is that the environment is what is being irreparably damaged, and it should have the right to come into court on its own behalf."

"You mean just as any person could?" Janis asked with disbelief.

"Sure," Larry said. "All sorts of fictional persons are allowed to sue on their own—corporations, municipalities, trusts, and even ships at sea eventually were granted standing by the courts."

The idea did not strike Charley Wolf the least bit odd. While they debated, a steady frown became fixed on his face as the furrows in his weathered skin seemed to deepen. "Our grandfathers had a respect for nature," he interrupted at last, pronouncing each word as if it were the year's first ear of corn balanced in his hands, his voice cupping and protecting each one. "They knew how much greater the forces of nature were than themselves. They saw into the souls of the animals, and they found themselves. They knew the bear as a cousin and paid him the respect saved for elders, knowing that he may very well hold the soul of their grandfather. They did not hunt for fun, but for food and clothing and housing and tools. And when they killed, they did not cast aside the victuals and cart off a trophy. They offered his spirit appeasement and asked forgiveness for having had to kill him." His words carried a certain disbelief and a sadness, both moods lying over a quiet outrage like a blanket smothering a fire.

Charley Wolf was an old man, and he looked like an old man. His face was creased with wrinkles, and white hair, long lacking in natural oils, hung dryly to the bottoms of his ears. "Our grandfathers," he continued, raising a bony finger in the air, "learned to respect the land and the forests. They learned early the strength of the manitous. An Indian hunter once allowed himself to grow too proud. He forgot he was subject to the powers of nature and acted as though the animals and lakes and trees were there to serve his glory. For his arrows he insisted on the heart of the cedar. An entire tree would be felled and left to rot, except for a sliver from its core, which the hunter fashioned into a single arrow. One day the hunter sighted a Mitche Muhquh, a bear as great as he had ever seen. He approached with great stealth and shot an arrow as true as his skill allowed. The Mitche Muhquh stood on his hind legs and bellowed a roar that shook the leaves off the trees and sent ripples across the water. The arrow stopped in midflight, reversed its direction"— he raised a rigid arm and clenched his five fingers in a point— "and drove into the hunter's heart." He slammed his fingers to the center of his chest. "The hunter fell on his back, and the arrow grew into a white birch. As the hunter once stole the hearts of trees, the Indians for all time would steal his skin for their canoes and wigwams."

The room was silent for a moment. Axel glanced out of the corner of his eye at Janis. She sat studying her lap, as if she were in a doctor's office crowded with strangers. "Mr. Wolf," Axel said, "if you could speak as eloquently to the court this Wednesday, we would have no trouble winning our case."

Larry stood up and started walking to the kitchen. "It's getting late," he said. "If we don't eat, we'll miss the meeting."

Axel could not decipher Larry's mood, but Janis' was no secret. She shot an irritated glance at him as they rose to go to the dinner table. As she followed Axel out of the room, Charley Wolf remained seated for a few moments, and with one eyebrow raised higher than the other, his gaze bore into her back.

Larry brought a pot of chicken from the oven and set it by Janis at the table. She served herself and passed it along. Larry made a second trip to the kitchen and came back with a white crock, holding it by the edge with a towel in one hand and a hot pad in the other.

Steam billowed into the air as Larry lifted the glass cover from the crock. "Mindahmin," he announced. "I ground the corn myself." Looking at Axel, he said, "This was once the main dish for the Ottawas."

"Yes, I know. I've had it at some of the festivals."

"But that wasn't prepared the old way, ground by hand and seasoned with herbs collected from the woods," Charley Wolf said. "More than likely it was made with a blender and using spices from a can." Axel glanced at Janis. She did not seem amused. "People have forgotten the old ways," Charley Wolf said sadly.

"Oh, come on, Mishoo. What difference does it make how it was made?" Larry said. "The important thing is the corn porridge. It's a symbol, or a reminder, of our heritage, and that's all."

"But that's not all. Preparation of food was a religious event. The manitous watched, and a continuing food supply depended on them being satisfied."

"I didn't think you still believed all that stuff about spirits, all those old legends," Larry said.

"Maybe I do, and maybe I don't. All I know is that those beliefs helped our people to survive for hundreds of years. And they did quite well until . . . ." Charley Wolf trailed off, Axel thought in deference to himself. "Can you imagine," he continued, "our grandfathers killing their cousin the muhquh without asking his forgiveness, and then not having tobacco with him after the hunt? Maybe that was primitive, maybe foolish. But at the least it taught us to respect the animals, to respect nature and the food it provided for us. People forgot the old ways, and now they shoot the muhquh in its den and call it sport. Then the greatest indignity. They don't protect the bones from the dogs, muhquh's most hated rival. The dogs tear its flesh and scatter its bones, leaving its spirit to wander about the countryside looking for the rest of itself." He spoke slowly, his words torn from deep in his throat. "Our people will someday regret the passing of the old ways. They will be sorry."

The old schoolhouse was crowded. Forty metal folding chairs stood close together, each one of them occupied. A few people were leaning against the side wall or sitting on the window ledges. The Ottawa Council, the elected body of the Crooked Tree–area Indians, was seated in the front row. Axel Michelson stood behind a desk cluttered with his papers, facing the assemblage.

"The first thing we had to do was stop the bulldozers. This had to be done right away, and as I explained to the council, we had to petition the court for what is called a temporary restraining order. We won, and the TRO went into effect for ten days.

"Now we have to convince the court to grant a preliminary injunction until a full hearing can be held on the question. A preliminary injunction is similar to a TRO in that its main function is to maintain the same situation until a full hearing can be held, which at the earliest is months away."

Axel picked up a yellow pad from the desk in front of him. "Now, at the preliminary-injunction hearing we have to show that unless it is granted, our interests will be irreparably injured. That won't be hard. If the injunction is not granted, the land will be cleared and the damage will have already been done by the time of the full hearing. But the judge will have to balance our interests against the hardship the injunction will impose on Sunrise Land and Home. Their hardship includes not only the business delay but also the laying off of employees and the loss of income to the community, and you can be sure this is what they will be stressing to the judge. In essence, the judge is going to ask himself who would suffer more if the preliminary decision goes against them and they ultimately win."

Axel finished his prepared remarks and suggested a short break before answering questions.

He stepped down and started to walk over to the side of the room where Janis, Larry, and Charley Wolf were seated. Janis got up quickly to meet Axel, leaving Larry and his grandfather behind. She put her hands on Axel's shoulders and brought his ear down to her mouth. "I've got to get out of here," she whispered huskily. "That man is driving me crazy."

"What do you mean?" Axel said, pulling his head back to look her in the face.

"I mean just what I said," she snapped. "Through your whole talk I don't think he took his eyes off me once. I could feel him peering at me the whole time."

"Oh, you're imagining that," he consoled. "I looked in your direction, and Mr. Wolf was looking my way each time."

"And then, when it started raining on the roof, he leaned over and began whispering about Nanabojo and Peepuckewis."

"That harmless old story?"

"Listen, I'm going home, and that's all there is to it. Now why don't you give me the keys and you can catch a ride with someone else."

"Okay, okay," Axel said with a trace of irritation. "But let me talk to Larry. Maybe he can give you a ride."

Axel left his wife and strolled over to Larry and his grandfather. "I've got a favor to ask, Larry. Janis is restless sitting here, and I wonder if you could take her home for me?"

"Now?"

"Yes, I would appreciate it."

"Sure, I would be glad to."

Axel turned to look for Janis behind him, but she was not there. "She's over by the door already," Charley Wolf observed.

Walking toward the door, Axel whispered to Larry, "With the at-tack on the dogs the other day, I wouldn't feel comfortable with her going home alone."

"I understand. Maybe I could take my car and wait until you get home."

"That's a good idea. This shouldn't be much longer than another hour or so."

"Are you going to be my chauffeur?" Janis asked as they approached.

"Yeah. All set?"

"Yes," she said. She kissed Axel on the cheek. "I'm sorry, honey. See you later."

As they left, Axel turned and walked to a back corner of the room where a coffeepot rested on a folding table. He fished in his pocket for a small vial and popped the plastic lid off. He tapped a pain pill out in his hand and swallowed it with a gulp of the coffee. It was the fourth Darvon he had taken that day.

There were more questions than Axel had anticipated, and when the meeting finally ended, he realized that it was eleven o'clock. He was startled to see Larry sitting next to his grandfather.

"What are you doing here?" Axel asked. "Is Janis with you?"

"No, she stayed back at your house. She wouldn't let me stay with her."

"What do you mean, she wouldn't let you stay?"

"She just wouldn't let me come in," he repeated. "She was very adamant about it."

"That's terrible. You knew about the break-in. Whoever it was may come back. I don't see how you could have left her there alone."

"Axel. She all but threw me out. She absolutely insisted that I not stay."

Michelson was silent for a moment. Calmed, he said, "I'm sorry, Larry. I shouldn't have jumped on your back. How was she feeling?"

"She seemed tense, like she was all evening. Other than that, she was okay." Axel stroked his chin contemplatively. "Do you think anything is wrong with her?" Larry asked.

"No. No, I don't think so. She's just been under a lot of strain lately, with the dogs and all. I shouldn't have made her come tonight." Michelson finished packing his attaché case and began walking to the door.

"Want me to follow you home, Axel?" Larry offered.

"Thanks anyway, but I'm sure everything will be all right." Axel walked toward his car. He was not at all sure that everything would be all right.

10

The yellow squares quilting the log erupted in an occasional flame. The cracked surface of the log folded outward as the wood burned. Karl Waldemeir sat on a folding canvas stool staring at the burning embers. He was tired after a long day fishing, but he was relaxed. Outside of a couple canoes that passed his campsite during the after-noon and the roar of an off-road motorcycle racing through the woods, there was no sign of other people. That was the way Karl wanted it, and that was the way it usually was when he came to the Big Two Hearted River.

It was close to sunset, and the sky looked like it was going to rain. He had not been out to his car since morning, when he brought in the rest of his gear. Before turning in for the night, he wanted to make sure the Blazer had not been tampered with by man or beast.

Walking through the woods, he paused at the red pine with the ragged bark. The deep gouges could not have been caused by raccoons or squirrels, he thought. It was a much more pow-erful stroke that caused the damage. Bear? It could be. He knew black bear lived in Crooked Tree, but in all his years of coming to the Big Two Hearted River he had yet to see one. Still, if they were around, they could be a pest if food was left tantalizingly unprotected. He decided he would take extra precautions to see that nothing a bear might like to eat was in easy reach. He moved away from the tree and into the deepening shadows of the woods.

The bear stood above a small mound of sand, carried grain by grain above the thin surface layer of black soil by a colony of ants. It studied the mound for a moment before reaching its paw down. The bear knocked the top off the anthill and placed its paw on the ground by the scattered sand. Ants swarmed from beneath the surface, some to ward off enemies of the colony, others to repair the damage. The bear watched placidly as its paw was attacked by the ants, swarming over and into its thick black fur. When practically covered with in-sects, the bear sat back on its haunches and patiently picked at its fur until almost all the ants were eaten. Then the bear lowered its paw to the anthill and captured a second feast of the insects.

Satisfied with the high-protein appetizer, it ambled away from the depleted ant colony, guided by an instinctive urge to eat. When the snows fell in November and the bear settled in its winter den, it would need four inches of fat and three inches of fur to keep it warm for the winter. If it was a true hibernating animal, its respiration and circulation would slow and its body temperature would decrease to about the same as the surrounding air. But the bear was not a hibernator. It merely lapsed into a deep sleep and stayed in its den all winter in order to survive a period of food scarcity.

The bear stopped its nightly foraging to scratch its back. It squatted on its rear and stretched up against a tree. As it rubbed the rough bark, it moaned a contented sigh. Leaving tufts of black hair clinging to the tree, the bear fell forward and continued its hunt. Most of its meals were vegetarian. It would eat almost anything, but plucking berries from a bush or grazing on grass was much easier than chasing rabbits or negotiating around a porcupine's tail. The bear did, however, enjoy an occasional meal of a small animal, and this was the time of day most forest creatures preferred to come into the open in search of food.

Marsha and Kate could no longer hear the rushing of the Big Two Hearted River. The sound of the water splashing on the rocks receded into the distance as they walked farther into the woods, hoping to catch sight of some animals coming out for their evening feed.

They had not covered much distance on their first full day on the river. They floated with the current for the most part, paddling only to keep the canoe on course, and at four o'clock had set up camp on high ground close to the river. It was a good place to stop and had served as the overnight campsite of many other canoeists. Now, walking through the woods, Kate whispered, "What kind of animals are we looking for?"

"Anything, actually. Almost all the animals come out about dusk to feed. If we can come across a clearing where the sun was able to get to the ground and a lot of grass and ground plants grow, we'll see something for sure."

The women moved deliberately, trying to avoid twigs and dead leaves. They did not want to announce their approach. Rather than clearing, the woods became denser. The trees were predominantly hardwood, with a scattering of hemlock. The hemlock grew well under the thick canopy of the hardwoods, it being one of the few coniferous trees that could. It might take one hundred years for the short needles of the hemlock to reach the sun, but when they did, the tree could survive for another five hundred.

Kate grabbed Marsha's arm suddenly. There was a shuffle of leaves somewhere to their left.

"Let's spread out and start heading over there," Kate whispered.

"Okay. I'll go up a little, and you head that way," Marsha said, pointing in the direction of the sound.

There was something moving slowly through the woods. They couldn't see it yet, but they could tell it had an uneven, almost clumsy gait. They were close to it now, and for the first time it heard them. It stopped long enough to determine from which direction the intruders were approaching. Marsha saw the ferns tumbling and yelled to Kate, "There it is!"

It was moving as fast as it could away from them, but the women quickly caught up. Kate was the first to see the rounded mound of quills, and ran in front to head it off. The porcupine stopped, panting heavily. Marsha came up from behind. "He's scared," she observed.

"That's okay, Porky, we won't hurt you," Kate said. "We just wanted to see you."

The porcupine turned its body back and forth, keeping both women in view. "Don't get too close to its tail," Marsha warned as Kate moved closer.

"I won't. I just want a good look at those quills." Kate crouched down a few feet from the porcupine. "Look at those things. That's amazing. No one in their wildest imagination could have invented such a crazy-looking creature."

"Yeah, I know. I wonder how it evolved," Marsha said as she took a step closer. The porcupine suddenly tensed its quills and lunged away from Marsha toward Kate. It moved much quicker than Kate thought it could. She fell backward as it swung its tail. She pushed with her feet and hands and moved awkwardly on all fours, her back to the ground. The porcupine did not pursue, but tried to get away as well.

"Did he get you?" Marsha asked as she hurried to Kate.

Kate sat on the ground, breathing hard. "No," she wheezed. "But almost."

Marsha looked over toward the porcupine. It was a few feet off the ground and inching slowly up the trunk of a tree. Marsha started to laugh. She could not resist it. The color returned to Kate's cheeks, and she smiled nervously. "Fine outdoorsmen we are," Marsha said. "Scared half to death by a fat old porky-pine."

Kate started to laugh too. "Well, we deserved it," she said. "We probably scared him half to death first." She raised her hand to Marsha. "Here, help me up."

Marsha pulled her up and said, "We'd better head back. It'll be dark pretty quick, and the last thing I want is to be lost out here all night."

"Yeah. Who knows what other evil creatures lurk out here."

Marsha chuckled, and the two women started to walk toward the river. The porcupine watched them retreat from a safe distance overhead. They were long out of sight and smell before it started to climb down again.

"You know, I worry sometimes about myself," Kate said as they neared their campsite. "I suppose I like to think I could handle a crisis situation. That I could react fast. But the only way to really know if you can handle it is to get yourself into a tight situation and see what happens."

"So what are you getting at? You want to put a little thrill in your life?"

"No. But I was thinking. A porcupine shakes his tail at me,

and I just about go to pieces. I was just wondering what would have happened if it was something to be really scared of. I mean, I don't think I could have handled it."

"Don't be so hard on yourself. If it was something to be really scared of, you wouldn't have been crouching down looking it over. You would have been more careful and aware of the dangers."

"Yeah. Maybe so," Kate replied, her voice drifting into thought.

The bear stood in the middle of the clearing, chewing grass. Not too far away, a family of deer grazed nervously along the edge of the woods, keeping a wary eye on the bear's movements. The bear ignored the deer. It could probably catch the fawn if it tried, but that would require too much energy, energy better saved for adding insulation to its frame.

The bear's teeth were adept at grinding, at chewing the grass. Like pigs and men, it had the mouth of an omnivore, with molars along the side and in the back, rather than the carnassial teeth of a strict flesh eater; but the bear's canine teeth were formidable weapons, and powered by strong jaws, could tear the bark off a tree.

The bear was not a quiet eater. The gnashing of its teeth could be heard by even human ears at some distance. Bending its head to the ground to uproot another mouthful of grass, the bear stopped in midchew. It raised its head with a jerk and pointed its snout in the air. The deer scattered in an instant. Standing on its hind legs, the bear sniffed the air, its eyes no wider than a slit. Its head seemed to sway in the breeze, lazily searching, waiting for something to come to it. The bear tensed and dropped to all fours. The earth pounded as it began to trot purposefully into the woods. It headed toward the Big Two Hearted River.

Karl doused the fire with a large pot of water. He decided not to bother walking down to the river for more; the rain when it came would do the rest. He kicked some sand on the embers to keep live ashes from blowing away. Too much sand would form a layer of insulation, protecting it from the rain, and the fire could smolder for days.

Karl brought his cooking utensils inside the tent and laid them down near his fishing gear. He unzipped the sleeping bag and eyed the lining carefully for spiders or anything else that might have found its way inside during the day. As much as he enjoyed the outdoors, he never could get rid of his phobia of bugs. Satisfied the bag was ready, he stepped outside for one last chore.

It was dark now, but the bear did not slow its pace. What little light there was a membrane at the end of the eye mirrored back onto the retina, in effect, permitting the eye to see objects twice. This efficient use of limited light made its night vision about as good as its vision during the day. It also meant that its eyes turned into miniature reflecting disks. The brighter the source of concentrated light, the brighter its eyes would glow.

Kate and Marsha flipped the canoe upside down and placed most of their gear under it. There was not much room in the tent except for them. It was comfortable for two, but quickly became cramped and uncomfortable with the addition of any bulky object. Satisfied every-thing would stay dry under the canoe if it rained, they set about ensuring they would stay just as dry.

Marsha went to the front of the tent while Kate checked the back. Tightening the guy lines, they stretched the fly tautly over the tent. With each end slightly higher than the middle, the tent could with-stand stronger winds. Satisfied with the three inches separating the two sheets of nylon, Marsha unzipped the screen door and they climbed in for the night.

The bear moved easily, quickly, its heavy paws thumping an even rhythm on the forest floor. It weighed four hundred pounds and was covered with a thick layer of fat and shaggy fur, but it stalked through the woods like a deer. Its head was held above its shoulders, leveling the hump on its neck. Its stride was deliberate, relentless.

Karl sorted the food in the cardboard box. He was not worried about an animal getting into the cans, but one could be attracted to the box of potato flakes, bread, or cheese. He made sure they were wrapped tight before folding the flaps of the cardboard box closed. He slipped the box into a plastic garbage bag to protect it from the rain and then unraveled a length of rope and tied it around the box. He looked overhead for a suitable branch. Stepping a few more feet away from the tent, he bunched the other end of the rope and tossed it into the tree. The rope cleared a branch without snagging and fell to the ground. Karl hoisted the box about seven feet from the ground and secured the end of the rope around the trunk of the tree. He tugged once to make sure it was tight. With the box gently swaying out of the reach of animals, Karl entered his tent for what he hoped would be the last time that night.

The bear stopped suddenly and reared up on its hind legs. Something unexpected had been detected. Slowly, out of the darkness a black shape emerged. The bear watched warily as a second bear approached. It felt like bolting away through the woods. But it did not. Instead, it dropped to all fours and let the other bear approach, its eyes glinting in the darkness. The bears stared cautiously at each other, almost muzzle to muzzle. The intruder backed off slowly and began to move in the direction the first bear had been trotting. Without a second thought the bear began to follow the intruder.

"I'm going outside," Kate announced.
"What on earth for? It's going to start raining any minute."
"Don't worry, Mother, I'm a big girl."
Marsha sighed and rolled over. Kate unzipped the screen door and crawled out. She stood with hands on hips and surveyed the woods. It was quiet, but there was something hidden out there and Kate could feel it. It was a force that simmered under the calm of the night. It concealed itself under the chirping of the crickets and the gathering clouds. But it was there, waiting to erupt. Kate could feel it herself, a tingling of her skin and a quickening of her heart. The forest was ready to awaken under the storm, and Kate wanted to see the violence unleashed.

The contained fury of the bears leaked into the night air with each winded grunt. The air rushed from their lungs at an even tempo, punctuating the resonant thuds of their paws crashing to the ground. They marched steadily in single file, an easy lope belying a quiet tension. They were hunters, and they sensed the anticipation of a kill.

Karl lay on his cot in his sleeping bag, staring at the ceiling of his tent. Even though his eyes were wide open, he could not have seen his hand in front of his face. He could hear the trees swaying and their leaves rustling in the wind. He knew it would not be long before he would hear rain tapping on the canvas.

The bears slowed their pace to a walk. They stopped long enough to raise their noses high and sniff the air. After a moment they began to spread apart, moving away from each other and from the course they had been on. They moved purposefully, without hesitation. They knew their prey was close.

A white birch dying as the river stole the soil from its roots protruded from the embankment parallel to the ground. Kate sat on the trunk of the tree and stared at the dark reflecting band of water beneath her. It was as black as the shadows in the woods, but a glossy black like wet paint.

Something crashed behind her in the woods. She stood abruptly and spun around. Nothing. She noticed the wind was bending the trees.

The bear could hear the familiar sound of water rushing. It shook its head violently and circled in place. It looked up at the canopy of rustling leaves. A storm was coming. The bear looked in the direction of its partner and paced back and forth. It could not see the other bear, but it knew where it was.

Kate could feel the breeze filtering through the trees. It enveloped her, pulling her from the birch tree. She walked past the small green tent and into the woods. She felt sublimely at ease. No people. No buildings. Just the ferns brushing at her legs and the twigs scratching each other. She was alone, and she couldn't be happier.

The bear clawed at the ground. It lowered its head below its shoulders, waving it slowly from side to side. It was the strongest creature in the woods. It had no natural enemies. Slowly it started moving forward. One hundred feet away, another bear was doing the same.

"Kate?" Marsha called. There was no response, so she called a little louder, "Kate, are you there?" Marsha felt an involuntary chill. She pulled herself reluctantly out of her sleeping bag and unzipped the tent door.

The air hissed between the teeth of the bear. Its head was steady as its powerful legs alternated with deliberate caution. It was no longer guided by smell alone. The bear's gaze was fixed on an unnatural shape, out of place in the woods. It saw its prey.

Karl could not seem to close his eyes. Perhaps it was the wind, he thought. He had not expected it this hard. Maybe it would bring down a dead branch on his car. Dammit! a voice pounded in his brain. Fall asleep! He was unsettled. He would never fall asleep that way. He tried to calm down. He closed his eyes. His nerves forced them open.

The bears could see their target. They kept well hidden from it, glancing at each other, as if waiting for the other to act.

Fresh leaves brushed by Kate's face. The trees took the brunt of the wind, but enough filtered through to ruffle her hair. She didn't care if she got wet. She didn't care if she was caught in the storm. The fury of an enraged wilderness captivated her as she walked deeper into the black.

"Kate?" Marsha called. She saw no one by the river, but she heard something in the woods behind the tent. She stepped quickly in that direction. Twigs cracked. She saw a shape in the shadows.

Their heavy black fur blended with the darkness. Only gleaming eyes could betray their presence. But they were hunters. They knew how to surprise prey.

Karl unzipped his sleeping bag down the side and slipped a leg out. He was sweating. He had to cool off. He felt he should move his car from under the trees into the clearing of the road. But he did not get up. For some reason, he could not move.

Kate broke from her trance. There was something in the woods. Marsha swallowed hard. It was too dark to see a thing. Karl wiped a sweaty hand across a sweaty brow. The bear stood abruptly on its hind legs and roared, its head waving to the blackened skies. "Kate!" Marsha screamed into the wind. Karl sat straight up in his cot.

Stealth abandoned, the bear charged forward, slashing through the fabric with its claws. Its partner dropped to all fours and followed. The tent split wide open. Karl stared in disbelief. A silhouette of a bear hovered over him. His hands were frozen in fear to the wood frame.

Steellike claws slashed the other side of the canvas. The tent toppled. Karl fell off his cot to the ground, screaming. The bears tore the collapsed tent open, oblivious to all but their squirming prey hidden inside the canvas.

Karl felt a dull pain across his lower back. He tried to scramble, but he couldn't move his left leg. His pelvis was broken. He screamed again as the night air rushed in on him, twisting his head in time to see a shape fall on him. He fought to bring an arm up to his face, but it was yanked away with a powerful tug. He felt blood rush from his arm and into his face.

The bear raised its paw and swung. Karl heard more than he felt a powerful thump to his neck. He was twisted in a heap. He could no longer move. He could no longer feel the blood on his body. A bear swung its head up and down with his arm in its mouth. Karl was not aware when the bear released its grip.

"What's all the noise about?"

"What do you mean, 'noise'?" Marsha yelled angrily. "Where the hell were you?"

"Right here. Where do you think?"

"How should I know? You take off in the middle of nowhere, a storm coming. For all I know, you could have been in the river. Didn't you hear me?"

Kate regarded her friend closely. She was upset. "No, I didn't hear you. The wind must have carried your voice the other way." Marsha trembled visibly. "Look, Marsh, I'm sorry. I was just experiencing the wind, the storm. I guess I got carried away."

Marsha breathed heavily. She was only partly mollified. "You shouldn't have taken off without telling me," she said.

"I know. I'm sorry," Kate repeated. Marsha did not reply. Instead she closed her lips tightly and stared into the woods. "Come on, let's get back to the tent," Kate said. "The rain has held off long enough. It won't much longer."

It didn't. The rains fell in a torrent. The bears shuffled quietly around the shredded canvas. A pool of blood on the tent floor quickly was diluted. The bears retreated from Karl's campsite. They had made their kill. But they were unsatisfied.

11

Axel left the meeting hurriedly. He had never worried about his wife being home alone before, but now everything seemed different. The asphalt road glistened a shiny black. His headlights reflected on the wet pavement in twin columns of wavering light. He was already driving too fast on the slippery road, but it seemed the trip was taking forever.

When he finally pulled into his driveway, his head ached and the chipmunk bite throbbed. Rivulets of dirt and gravel traversed the driveway, evidence of the rain. A mist hovered in the air, camouflaging a certain crispness left by the storm. The house was dark. He would have expected Janis to wait up for him, or at least leave a light on.

Axel leaped out of the GMC Yukon, leaving his attaché case behind and the key in the ignition. He slammed the door and brought a hand up to his face, falling backward against the car. He rubbed his temples with his fingers for a moment. As the pounding in his head eased, he pushed away from the car and walked through the side door into the house.

Stepping into the kitchen, Axel was greeted by a strong draft. He flicked the lights on. Behind the dining table the long flowing curtains blew in the breeze. The sliding glass door was wide open. Axel walked quickly to the open doorway and gazed into the woods. There was no movement, only darkness.

The door slid closed, thumping with a dull thud as it locked into its runners. The curtains hung heavy with water. He squeezed the fabric, and water dripped onto the floor, splashing in a puddle on the linoleum. Axel stepped carefully through the water and down into the family room. The carpet near the door was wet, and water came to the surface like a sponge as Axel walked through it toward the bedroom.

The door was closed. He paused with his hand on the doorknob and called, "Janis?" There was no answer. "Janis," he called again, "are you there?" This can't be happening! His mind reeled. She must be there! Axel twisted the knob and pushed, but the door did not budge. It was locked, jammed, something. He had to get in! He crashed his shoulder against the solid wood, and it swung open with a bang.

Screaming through the darkness, an inhuman roar bellowed from the bed. Axel froze, reason escaping. The deafening growl surrounded him, held him captive, refused to let him think. The eyes! His mind screamed. The eyes are shining!

Axel stumbled backward out of the room, the echo of the beast pursuing. He pulled the door shut behind him. It must be kept in there! "Janis!" Axel screamed. "*Janis*!" He dashed into the den, the other bedroom, the living room. She was not there. The realization brought his eyes back to their bedroom door. "My God, *no*!" A picture of the torn bodies of the dogs raced through his mind. Frantically he lunged toward the garage.

He seized an ax from the wall and stormed back into the house, racing to the bedroom door. The noise had subsided, but he knew *it* was still in there. With Janis! He rammed the door open and barreled inside. With his elbow he hit the light as he charged toward the bed.

Janis screamed. She held her arms in front of her face and recoiled. Axel stood above her, the ax raised over his head. He quickly turned around. There was nothing behind him. He glanced around the room. There was nothing. He charged toward the bathroom and flicked the light on inside. It was empty.

Axel turned to face his wife. She cowered on the bed, her eyes wide, her face white. She was terrified. Axel stared at her, disbelieving. He could not speak. Janis began to shake visibly.

Axel let the ax drop to the floor and stepped toward her. She drew her breath in deeply and tensed her grip on the sheets. Axel's head was reeling. "Jan, Jan!" His eyes roamed the wall. He did not know how to explain it, even to himself.

"Jan, what was that in here?"

She did not answer, staring at him incredulously. She was still shaking.

"What was that animal in here?" he demanded.

Janis looked at him dumbly. She moved her lips, but no sound came out. She tried again. "What, what do you mean?"

"There was something in here a moment ago. What was it?"

"I don't know what you're talking about."

"It was here. I saw its eyes. You must have heard it."

Janis shook her head slowly from side to side. "I was asleep. I didn't hear anything."

"You must have!" Axel almost shouted. "It was right here. It must have been right by the bed."

"That couldn't be, Axel. I'm the only one here."

"But it roared. Surely you heard it."

"No, no, I heard nothing."

"It was so loud. You must have."

"I didn't, I tell you." She started to shake again.

Axel stared at the ceiling and wiped a hand across his brow. "My God, what's happening?" he said.

Janis climbed out of bed, walked with hesitant steps to Axel, and hugged him tightly. Slowly he brought his arms around her. They stood in an embrace, saying nothing, but drawing strength from the contact. After a long moment they eased away from each other. Janis led Axel to the bed, and they sat down.

"What did you see?" she asked.

Axel studied his wife's face. He didn't know where to begin. But he knew she would somehow understand. "When I opened the bedroom door, I saw a glinting of eyes, like animal eyes. You know, how they reflect at night." She nodded. "And then there was a roar, deep, guttural, like a wild animal."

"Did you see anything? Besides the eyes, I mean."

"No, I don't think so," he said, pausing to search his memory. "Just the eyes. It was too dark."

Janis looked down at the floor. "Honey, there was nothing in here. I didn't hear anything like what you said. I didn't hear anything at all."

Axel looked away from her. "I don't see how I could have imagined something like that." He looked at Janis again. He wanted her to say something. He wanted her to agree. She said nothing, and he looked away again. "It was so real," he said. He could not believe this was happening to him. He had never had hallucinations. Only sick people did, he thought. He lowered his head to his hands, and tears rolled slowly down his cheeks. "My head's been pounding all night."

A glow of distant lightning suddenly illuminated the trees outside the window. The flash disappeared in an instant as a muffled thunder-clap reverberated through the woods.

"Did you take many Darvons today?" Janis suggested softly.

Axel looked at her sharply. Her face softened his stare. "Yes, as a matter of fact I think I took four." He fell back on the bed, staring at the ceiling. "I could have killed you," he thought aloud. He sat up straight and grasped Janis by the arms, turning her toward him. "Honey, I'm so sorry. I could have killed you."

Janis closed her eyes and stifled a shudder. A few moments before, her husband had stood over her with an ax. Was that real? Could *she* be imagining things? It seemed at least as unbelievable as what her husband had described.

"The curtains!" Axel cried. "Did I imagine that too?" He was up off the bed in an instant and half-dashed to the back door. The puddle was still on the floor, and the curtains were still wet. Axel touched them as if he was surprised they were wet.

"Oh, no," Janis said. "I forgot all about the door."

"You mean you left it open?" Axel asked.

"I didn't mean to leave it open. It was so stuffy in here when I got back that I opened it for a little fresh air. I didn't think I was going to fall asleep." Janis took the fabric in her hand and squeezed. Water dripped to the floor. "Oh, Axel. These things are ruined."

"Oh, don't worry about it." Axel touched her on the chin and brought her face up to his. They lingered in a soft embrace until they walked quietly back to the bedroom. They did not speak until after they had made love.

"Let's go to the dunes tomorrow," Axel said.

"Sleeping Bear?"

"Yeah. I think we could both use a day off."

"All right," Janis said, her face brightening. "Let's get up early and pack a lunch."

"Fine. Get me up when you're done."

Janis propped her head up on one elbow and scowled at him. He laughed and rolled over. Janis smiled, a long while, staring at his back. Her arm tired eventually, and she lay down beside him, her hair draping over his shoulder. Nearly asleep, Axel was unaware that her hair was wet.

The drive from Wabanakisi to Sleeping Bear Dunes took about two hours. The two-lane highway snaked south through Petoskey and flowed like a black river along the Lake Michigan shoreline. Black cherry orchards dominated the rolling hillsides along the coast of Grand Traverse Bay. Beyond the bay lay the Leelanau Peninsula, the little finger of Michigan's mitt.

Anytime they came through Empire in the Leelanau, Axel and Janis stopped at the White Pine Inn. It was a simple restaurant with not enough tables to accommodate the summer Sunday breakfasters. Its rough-hewn log walls nestled among a stand of white pine were charming, but it was not the charm that attracted the Michelsons. It was the food. And at breakfast, Axel always made the same order. Broad pancakes with a wall of whipped cream circling the edges and filled with fresh blueberries an inch and a half thick. Other things on the menu were probably just as good, but Axel came here so infrequently that he never found the reason to try anything else.

The coastal dunes in Sleeping Bear stretched for about thirty miles. The park entrance fronted on a modest inland dune. Its surface was pure sand; any of the fragile vegetation had long since been uprooted by the hordes of summer visitors that clambered up its steep incline.

Beyond the crest of the first dune was a desertlike expanse of rolling sand hills cluttered with small stones and scattered wispy blades of grass. An occasional tree clung to the loose soil, its whitened roots tenaciously grabbing the sand like gnarled fingers groping for support. While the wind stole its support grain by grain, it buried a tree farther back by the same measure. Carcasses of trunks stuck eerily out of the sand, their leaves and color and life long gone, suffocated by the shifting dune.

It was a long hot hike from the top of the first dune to Lake Michigan. Axel and Janis rested at the top for a few moments before going on. As they walked, the thick sand sucked at their feet, forcing them to lean forward even while on the flat. It was a difficult traverse to the lake. But Axel and Janis had no complaints. It was a quiet place, with only the wind and the swish of the dune grass carrying sound to their ears. They came on days when it was necessary to be alone, when built-up tension needed a release.

They passed a dune-buggy trail near the crest of the lakeshore dune, where the sand had been eroded down to the hard-packed dirt-and-gravel moraine. The sand on the dunes was actually a thin veneer covering mounds of glacial deposits. Prior to the Pleistocene Ice Age, the Lake Michigan basin was a prehistoric river valley cut through soft limestone and shale. Snow fell in the valley, and as the climate cooled, all the snow that fell in the winter did not melt in the summer. As it deepened, it became more compacted, increasing in density. The ground layer melted and refroze countless times. With each melting, the water would seep into the cracks of the rocks, breaking them up when it refroze. The broken rocks became suspended in the ice and moved when the ice moved. As the snow on the top grew heavier, the ice grew thicker in the valley, and the creeping rock-studded glacier scraped and gouged the land.

Eventually the ice floe was halted by the changing climate. As the glacier retreated, it deposited the unsorted mixture of rock and soil debris in heaps along the edge of the ice. The huge, newly gouged basin filled with water, and its wave action ground its shoreline into sand. The sand along the Leelanau Peninsula was carried by the wind and deposited on the coastal moraines.

Axel and Janis sat atop the sand-covered Sleeping Bear moraine and looked out over Lake Michigan. Dune grass whipped the ground nearby, leaving arcing tracks in the sand.

"Let's go down," Axel said.

Janis lifted her head from her knee and turned to Axel. "Will this be a straight run or a zigzag course?"

"I don't care. Do what you want. I'll opt for speed myself." Axel stood and readied himself for the sprint down the five-hundred-foot sand slope. He crouched at the top of the ridge, slinging his arms back and forth.

"Don't kill yourself," Janis shouted as he began his dash with a leap from the sandy crest. She followed, angling her way down the steep incline, then jumped feet first, landing softly in the deep sand. Axel was halfway down the hill when she got up and angled back across the face of the slope and jumped again.

When she reached the bottom, Axel's pants and shirt were on the beach and he was in his underwear, standing thigh-deep in the water.

"Come on," he yelled. His left hand, still bandaged, was held well out of the water.

Janis stood for a moment, her hands on her hips, considering the invitation. There was no one within sight. She slipped her shoes off and undid the buckle on her jeans. She pulled her T-shirt over her head, her hair bouncing back across her naked shoulders. She unzipped her pants and slid each leg out smoothly. She paused and stared at Axel. He eyed her expectantly. Her eyes followed the hair on his chest down to his waist.

She took off her bra and panties and let them drop on the small pile of clothes. She moved slowly into the water. As she approached, she placed her arms on his shoulders and drew his face to hers. Axel pulled her close. Janis' skin quivered at the touch of his water-chilled body. They embraced, and moving into slightly deeper water, she floated her legs around behind his thighs. Janis slowly rose and sank on the gentle surf, and she no longer sensed the chill of the water.

The waves lapped at their backs as they walked out of the lake. Fine pebbles swished back and forth with the waves, while just beyond the wash, driftwood collected.

Janis and Axel walked to the foot of the dune and lay down in the deep sand. Axel felt perfectly content. He was surrounded by the quiet beauty of the dunes. It was not a spectacular beauty, breathtaking like a mountain valley. But soft. Filled with peace. Rounded hills of sand muted the emotions.

"Every time we come here, everything seems to go just right," Axel said, staring at the sky.

Janis' head was nestled on his shoulder. She hugged him tightly for a moment. "I know. Too bad we don't own the whole park. We could close it all off and have a little house right up there," Janis said, nodding toward the top of the dune.

Axel shifted to his side, facing Janis. He balanced his head on his fist, his elbow jabbed into the sand. "It's nice to see you smiling," he said. "After last night, you should be scared to death of me."

Janis' smile soured, and she let herself drop on her back. "Oh, let's not talk about that, honey. Not now, anyway."

Axel noticed an involuntary twitch in her face. He wished he hadn't brought it up. But it had been just as terrifying for him, he thought. He wanted to talk about it. Opening their bedroom door and seeing those eyes still seemed so real.

Axel looked into Janis' face. Her eyes were closed. He decided to drop it. "It's been a rather eventful last few days. It's nice to stop and just relax for a while."

Janis opened her eyes and sat up, "Hey, how's your hand?"

"Fine. Doesn't hurt a bit. I think they might take the stitches out tomorrow."

Janis reached out and squeezed the bandage. Water dripped out. "You shouldn't have gotten it wet," she said with disapproval.

"I couldn't help it." Axel grinned. "I was out of my mind."

"Oh, you," she said, turning to face the water.

"You can't fool—"

"Axel," Janis interrupted, "you've gone someplace and felt you've been there before, haven't you?"

"Well, yes. I suppose I have. It's probably happened to most people at one time or other."

"Have you ever imagined something and later thought about it as if it really happened?"

"I guess I must have, last night. Didn't I?'

"Oh, I wasn't thinking about that," Janis said. "I mean, have you ever had a rather involved dream, and after you woke up, it seemed so real you began to think it wasn't a dream?"

"No, I don't think so." Axel was perplexed. "Have you?"

Janis looked at him quickly. "Yes." Just as quickly, she turned away, troubled. "I mean, I'm not sure. It seems like I may have, but I don't know."

"Well, when?" Axel asked. "What was the dream?"

"I don't know," she said with almost a gasp. "I don't know why I even thought of it." She shifted uncomfortably, then stood up. "I'm going to wash this sand off, and then I think we should get dressed and go."

"All right," Axel drawled, with reservation in his voice.

"We'll go." He watched as his wife walked to the lake and splashed water over her nude figure.

When Marsha Gutkowski woke Sunday morning, Kate was already coming back from a bath in the river.

Marsha walked to the edge of the embankment and looked down at Kate drying herself with a towel. "Isn't that quite a jolt first thing in the morning?" Marsha asked.

Kate looked up and smiled good morning. "You're not kidding. It's so cold it almost hurts."

"Then why torture yourself?"

"Because when I get out I feel great. Take a dip, and you'll see. You get numb fast, and then it's not bad at all."

"No, thank you. I think I'll wait till later, after I've built up a sweat. Hey, have you looked at the map yet?"

"Yeah. The way I figure it, we should reach Little Two Hearted in a couple hours. With the water from both rivers, the main stream will probably get a little wider."

"Good. Why don't we wait until at least then before stopping for anything."

"That's just what I was thinking," Kate said. "I figured we would be ready for lunch a half-hour or so past the Little Two Hearted."

12

The large black beast twitched its nostrils vigorously. One scent told it there was danger; the other, food. It lumbered slowly upwind, moving its head from side to side. It was wary of the danger, for the bear is a cautious animal. But the smell of the food was strong. It did not matter that the bear was not hungry. It ate all summer long. And it ate almost anything. It ate to add to the layer of fat that would insulate it when the temperature dropped. The bear was not thinking about the cold now. It was thinking about food. And its instincts told it to move closer.

On the edge of the clearing, the bear stopped, alert for any movement. It eyed the strange cocoon-shaped object with interest. There was no movement, and no noise other than the splash of rushing water. The bear walked closer, its gaze fixed straight ahead. The scent of danger was still there, but the bear's other senses told it the danger was remote. And the odor of food was almost overpowering.

The bear stepped up to the cocoon and peered inside. A dead animal lay on the ground, partially covered by the cocoon. After nosing the material to the side, the bear determined the animal had been the unfinished meal of another. Nudging it with its paw, a cloud of flies was disturbed and buzzed into the air. With a quick grunt the bear sank its teeth into the shoulder of the animal and yanked it partway from its cocoon.

The food freed, the bear looked up quickly and surveyed the sur-rounding woods. Sensing no danger, it turned back to its meal and dug its jaws into the carrion.

The water seemed to glide along its course like a huge convey-or belt winding its way through the woods. Kate and Marsha rested their paddles on the edges of the canoe. They were on a broad, relatively straight stretch of the river where they did not have to concern themselves with maneuvering through tight bends or around jutting obstacles. The Little Two Hearted River had joined with the Big Two Hearted a short way back, and the combined waters bulged the main-stream. The women took the opportunity to relax and flow with the current.

Gradually the river narrowed again and the banks grew high-er. As the current quickened, Kate and Marsha sat up straight and grasped their paddles. The women steered to the outer bank, following the deeper water. The canoe turned stiffly left around the bend. The gleaming smoothness of the river was gone, rumpled by the submerged debris of rocks and logs. Kate angled her paddle behind the canoe, steering it by a rounded boulder scraped silver on top from less-accomplished canoeists. Marsha stroked hard in front, her paddle clinking on the side of the canoe as she brought it back and forth. The metallic clang echoed ahead of them through the narrow canyon of birch and cedar trees.

The bear stopped feeding and stood suddenly on its hind legs. Its attention was pricked by a peculiar noise. It sniffed the air for a clue, turning its head toward the water. A rhythmic vibra-tion bounced off the trees, growing stronger with each passing moment. The bear's concern for danger resurfaced. It dropped to all fours and trotted into the woods, leaving its meal behind, and its appetite unsatisfied.

The rough river surface calmed. "Kate," Marsha said from the front of the canoe, "what do you say we pull over up there?" She pointed with her paddle to a sandy embankment on a gen-tle bend seventy-five yards upstream.

"That's a good idea," Kate said. "It looks like a good spot. Maybe even a good place to camp."

"Hey, now you're talking." Marsha twisted to face Kate. "We could have lunch and spend the rest of the day hiking around in the woods."

"Or lying in the sun," Kate said. Her back was sore from a day and a half of paddling. She steered the canoe toward shore.

"Oh-oh," Marsha said. "It looks like we won't be camping here tonight."

The front of the canoe slid onto the sand. Kate saw the waders too, hanging on a branch drying in the sun. "Wouldn't you know it," she said. "I don't suppose whoever's up there would mind us stopping for a while, do you?"

"No, probably not." Marsha stepped onto the ground and pulled the front of the canoe onto more stable footing. "I wonder how they got back here."

"I don't know. There's no road that I know of."

"Maybe they've just floated downstream a ways."

"Maybe, but I would sure hate to paddle back against this current," Kate observed.

The women secured the canoe higher on the shore and started walking up the embankment. Marsha took the last high step and turned to give Kate a hand.

"What the hell . . . ?" Kate said breathlessly.

They stood with their backs to the river, staring at the tent. It was a military-type two-man tent. The front post was askew but still standing. The back post was down. The green canvas drooped sharply from the front, but the women could see where it was shredded in the middle.

Kate started to move slowly forward. Marsha grabbed her arm. Fear pounded in her chest. The peaceful solitude of the forest now seemed menacing.

Kate twisted her arm free from Marsha's grasp. "Stay here," she whispered.

"No, I'm coming too."

"I said, stay here." Kate spoke softly but with authority. She started to walk to the tent. It was about twenty-five feet from the embankment, toward the back of the small clearing. A box dangled at the end of a rope from a tree branch. Kate did not notice it. Her gaze was fixed on the gaping hole in the tent.

She walked slowly, taking great care with every step. The torn canvas was bunched in a small pile on the ground. Kate stopped. A human arm protruded from the crumpled canvas.

"What is it?" Marsha's tone was tense, urgent.

"Stay there," Kate repeated, barely in control. She inched

closer. "Oh, my God!" she gasped. Her hand came up to her face, shielding her eyes.

The body was halfway outside the tent, draped partially in the canvas. It was a man about fifty years old. His head bent grotesquely to the right. His arm was twisted laterally like a tangled piece of twine. Dried blood speckled his face, and matted shreds of clothing clung to the skin. Insects were crawling over him. Burned on Kate's closed eyelids were the torn flesh and empty hole where the stomach should have been.

"Kate, what is it?" Marsha said urgently.

Kate's head spun. It took all her energy to remain conscious and standing.

Marsha took a hesitant step forward. Then she ran up to the tent. A second later, grabbing her stomach, she was violently ill.

The bear paced nervously. The noises ricocheting through the woods were unfamiliar. But the scent was very familiar. The bear's experiences told it to stay away, but the taste of carrion was still in its mouth. And after several minutes, the scent seemed to carry less danger.

"It must have been bears," Marsha said.

"Or maybe wolves," Kate added.

"I don't think there are wolves anymore in the lower peninsula. It must have been black bears." Marsha spoke in hushed tones, as if afraid of being overheard. Her stomach still ached, but she was considerably better than she had been a few minutes earlier. She sat next to Kate on the edge of the overhang, looking down the embankment to the river. Kate sat the other way, staring at the tent.

Finally Kate shifted and started to rise. Marsha turned and snatched her hand. "Where are you going?" Marsha asked, trembling.

"I'm going to cover him up."

"No. We've got to get out of here!"

"I'm going to cover him up," Kate repeated. "And then we'll get out of here."

They stared at each other for a long moment. Marsha loosened her grip on Kate's hand and let it go. "I'm a fool. I'm sorry, Kate."

Kate wanted to touch her friend, to console her, to tell her that was not so. But she was emotionally drained. And there was no time to waste.

Kate walked around the tent to the opposite side of the body. She pushed the front pole down, away from her. The stakes came up easily from the soft soil. After freeing the tent from the ground, Kate pulled the loose canvas over the body. Then she found a small rock, and using it as a hammer, pounded the stakes through the canvas to keep it in place.

Walking back to the river, she felt lightheaded. She was thinking of something to say to Marsha when her eyes caught the cardboard box hanging from the tree.

"Marsha!" Kate said. "He hoisted his food up to keep it out of reach of animals."

Marsha pondered this for a moment, waiting for Kate to note its significance. "Should we take it?" she said finally. "I mean, do we need it?"

"No, don't you see? It's heavy. And for that matter, so is that old tent and his gear inside. He couldn't have been backpacking with all that stuff. And there's no boat. He must have driven out here."

"So there must be a road back there," Marsha said, looking into the woods.

"Right. And hopefully, his car." Kate glanced at Marsha. "I've got to go back there."

"But what if the bears are still around?"

"They're probably not. They come out at night, not in the middle of the day. Anyway, if we find his car, we can get out of here in a hurry. No telling how long it will take on the river."

"All right. But I'll go with you."

"No. You stay by the water. You never know, another canoe might come by."

Marsha watched as Kate walked into the woods. The crunching of twigs and dead leaves telegraphing her approach to the animals of the forest.

The bear was increasingly restless. Although it had stopped pacing, the ground around where it stood remained patted down. The air almost whistled between its teeth. Suddenly it froze; the scent that had driven it away was getting stronger.

Kate saw the vehicle as she passed three large red pines. The glass of the Blazer mirrored the woods around it. She walked excitedly up to it and tried the driver's door. It was locked. She cupped her hands to the glass and peered inside. The button on the other door was also down. There was no key in the ignition. She moved around to the rear of the car and tried to open the tailgate. It was also locked.

The bear listened to the hurried movements. They were unnatural sounds, signifying to the bear helplessness, distress. The feeling of danger was all but gone. Quietly the bear took a tentative step toward the scent.

The Blazer was several feet off the road, and Kate could not even tell from which direction it had come. It seemed like the trail to the west was more recently traveled, but she couldn't be sure. The rains had covered that kind of evidence.

Reluctantly Kate began to walk back toward the river. On the way to the car, the woods had seemed strangely quiet. Now the twigs and fallen leaves seemed to be crackling as if the forest were alive. The wind, she thought.

Marsha turned at the sound of the footsteps. She was still sitting at the top of the bank. "Did you find anything?"

"Yes," Kate replied. "But I don't think it's going to help us. I want to check our map first."

Kate walked down to the canoe and unzipped one of the vinyl bags. After studying the U.S. Geological Survey Map for a few minutes, she slapped it disgustedly on her legs. "The trail roads aren't on the map," she said.

"What?" Marsha's face was expressionless.

"There's a road back there. Probably an old logging trail. But it's not on the map. His car is back there, too."

Marsha's face became more animated. "Let's take it, then," she said.

"Where? Take it where? I don't know where that trail leads. There's probably hundreds of them all through Crooked Tree." Kate dropped her eyes. Now she was sounding foolish. "I'm sorry, Marsh. I didn't mean to snap like that."

She considered their situation at the moment. There did not seem to be any immediate danger. From what she knew of Michigan black bears, it was unusual for them to attack people. And even more un-likely for it to happen twice. They were in the same position they were in before they stopped. They had plenty of food and they knew where they were, at least in relation to the river.

"Let's go, Marsha. We can move fast on the river if we press it."

"But what about the car? Don't you think we should even give it a try?"

"If we go off in the woods, we could get lost and really be in trouble. At least in the canoe we know where we'll end up. It might take a while, but we'll find somebody. We can't do anything for him, anyway." Kate thought for a moment. "And besides, his car is locked, and I didn't see the keys in it. They're probably in the tent."

As far as Marsha was concerned, they could be in the bear's stomach. She was not going near that tent.

The river was immersed in shadow. The sun was still a few hours from setting, but trees effectively blocked its light from the ground below. The water grew blacker, and underwater objects became less defined.

The canoe floated by a stand of jack pine. They grew close together, and only the uppermost branches bore needles. The gnarled branches below the higher, sun-absorbing layer twisted and hooked together in an unending web. Marsha eyed the jagged little twigs with uneasiness. She could never run through there if she had to. The stiff branches would cut her skin like thousands of tiny daggers. She felt trapped.

"Hey, slow down. You're going to kill yourself." Kate was surprised that Marsha had so much energy left toward the end of such a long day.

Marsha stopped in mid-stroke and lifted her paddle out of the water. She was suddenly very tired. "I don't think I can continue much longer, Kate."

"Neither can I. It looks like we'll have to set up camp someplace."

Marsha shivered. Somehow she felt safe on the water, as if cradled in a protective moat. The thought of spending the night ashore made her cringe. "Maybe I can go on farther. We're bound to come to something."

"I wish we would, but we're in the middle of a wilderness. We've been canoeing for hours, hoping, expecting to find somebody. But we won't. Not until we get to one of the landings. And we're both dead tired. We have to stop."

Marsha knew Kate was right, but the thought of lying in that little tent, expecting any moment to see the side slashed open, terrified her.

"I guess we can't keep this up all night," she said finally.

"And without eating," Kate observed.

"Oh, my gosh," Marsha exclaimed. "I had forgotten all about food."

"Well, what would you like for dinner?"

"Let's see, now. We've got beef Stroganoff, chicken cacciatore, or shrimp in cream sauce," Marsha said, mentally checking off their freeze-dried pouches.

"We're just hungry enough that the stuff might taste like it's supposed to. What would you prefer?"

"Whatever bears like least," said Marsha.

Kate's laugh was barely audible, but the tension was broken for the first time since early afternoon. They paddled easily, looking for a high spot to camp.

Marsha tried to analyze her changing attitudes of the last few days. Crooked Tree had taken on such a different atmosphere since they discovered the body. The darkness deep in the woods seemed filled with foreboding. The ferns lost their lacy innocence and were mysterious instead. The arching branches overhead seemed to be closing in.

But it was the same wilderness, the same forest where she had spent the last two nights. It was peaceful to her then. Why should it be any different now? Marsha thought. It was the same place, with the same animals. They had been out looking for forest creatures the day before, and it was practically impossible to find any. The animals were scared. And bears were perhaps the most timid of them all. The constant flow and swish of the water seemed reassuring. Marsha felt protected. Suddenly she remembered hearing that bears were scavengers. They would feed on carcasses anytime they found them. It was just as likely, Marsha thought, even probable that the man was dead when the bears found him.

"Kate, how old do you think that guy was?" Marsha inquired.

"Oh, forties probably. Maybe fifty."

"Do you suppose he could have died of a heart attack or something in his sleep, and then the bears found him?" Marsha turned around to Kate.

"Hey, pay attention. This is a tight turn." Kate's muscles strained as she cut the water sharply with the paddle. The canoe sideslipped around the bend. She looked across the surface of the water in the stretch of river newly opened to them. She was looking for white water or felled trees, so at first she did not notice them.

But they were too large not to notice for long. Kate stopped paddling. She blinked her eyes. She could not believe what she saw. "Marsha," she almost whispered.

Marsha swiveled quickly around. "Oh please, God, no, not us."

The river current was fast. They had traveled thirty feet before making a move. "Get to shore!" Kate screamed. "Hurry!"

The bears stood in the middle of the stream, watching as the canoe approached. Marsha fought the current furiously with her paddle. They were out of control.

"To shore, dammit," Kate screamed. Her words took no effect.

The canoe slipped sideways.

"Help us, please, somebody help us!" Marsha was hysterical. The paddle slipped from her hands, clanged on the canoe, and plunged into the water.

The river drew them closer. Kate felt helpless. She felt giddy, almost drunk. It was like a dream, and she was falling, tumbling through the air forever. It seemed an eternity. It seemed unreal. Almost numb, Kate raised the paddle above her head.

The canoe floated broadside into the black bears. Kate swung the paddle, and one of the bears caught it squarely with its paw. The hard ash snapped like a twig. Marsha scrambled over the side of the boat, half-jumping, half-falling into the water. The canoe listed wildly. Kate tried to steady herself. A bear charged. The canoe flipped out of the water as if made of tinfoil.

Kate plunged into the river, her back crashing on the bottom. Two bears—one for each of us! her mind screamed. Two bears-one for each of us! She wanted to keep from surfacing, to stay covered by the icy blanket. But she couldn't. She was gagging. She had to come up.

Her face broke the surface, gasping for air. It was strangely quiet and dark, as if still enveloped by the water. Her ears suddenly popped, and she heard the screams. But she couldn't see! Where was Marsha? Kate's eyes cleared. She was under the capsized canoe!

Kate was on her knees on the bottom of the river. Her head and shoulders were in an air pocket under the canoe. She grabbed one of the crossbars and held tightly. Her fist clenched even tighter with the screams.

"No, no . . . help me, please," Marsha implored. "Please, Jesus, please."

The water thrashed violently. Snarls and roars punctuated Marsha's screams. Kate's knuckles whitened more. She wanted to cover her ears, but couldn't let go of the canoe.

"Oh, oh, oh nooo." The screams echoed inside the canoe, ricocheting off the aluminum hull. She wanted to go to her friend, and loosened her grip on the crossbar.

The guttural growl was deafening. Kate heard a sickening crunch.

"Please plea . . ." Marsha's voice disappeared into gurgles. The water churned into a frenzied froth. Marsha's voice erupted again. "Let me die, Lord, let me die."

Kate could stand it no longer. She started to go under the side of the canoe, when something nudged her leg. She reached down. The bears' snarls resounded off the trees. They continued to thrash the water. Marsha's voice was silent. It was a hand, Marsha's hand.

"Marsha," Kate said excitedly. She tried to pull her friend up to the air pocket. The hand came up easily. Too easily. The arm was shredded just below the elbow.

Kate stared in horror at what she held. She screamed and flung it down. It floated for an instant before sinking to the bottom.

"No, no, no," Kate shouted, each syllable increasing in volume. She held her head in her hands, shaking it back and forth. The side of the canoe bumped against her shoulder. Unencumbered, it swung around.

There was a splash and a growl next to the canoe. Kate pulled her hands away from her ears. "Me, they're after me," she whispered.

The canoe suddenly rang with a powerful thud. It rocked violently. The side of the canoe lifted out of the water. Kate blinked in the light. The black fur was inches from Kate's face .

She grabbed the crossbar and pulled the canoe back down. The bear bellowed and crashed its paw down again. The aluminum hull crumpled inward where it struck.

Deeper water, she thought. She had to get to deeper water. Kate shifted to a crouch and felt ahead with her foot. She took a hesitant step forward, sliding the canoe with her.

The canoe resounded with another blow from the bear. A dent bulged the top in, just behind Kate's head. It was getting shallower! The bear would have better footing!

Kate stopped and angled to the right. Blind to the world outside, she could feel the current pointing her downstream. She stumbled on a log, falling to her knees. She gripped the crossbar tightly, but the canoe started to float away. Her legs dragged on the bottom, struggling to halt the boat. The side of the canoe buckled. The bear's steellike claws protruded through the thin aluminum. It jerked the canoe violently. Kate braced her legs on the bottom and strained against the force of the bear.

The claws disappeared and the canoe shot away, catapulted by Kate's legs. It drifted quickly for several feet. Kate heard the bear crashing through the water. Suddenly the riverbed dropped from under Kate's feet. She dropped with it, her head plunging underwater. Dangling from the crossbar, she pulled herself up. The canoe glided freely through the deep water. It started to twist sideways, when Kate felt the bottom again with her toes. She planted her feet and stopped the glide. She could hear the bear grunting and splashing the water a short distance upstream. She held tight, hoping, praying she could maintain her balance.

The bear left the water and climbed onto the bank. Kate listened as its vast weight thudded noisily along the shore. After a moment she could hear the bear breathing heavily and growling from the riverbank only a few feet away.

She stood there for what seemed like hours. But still the bear stomped on the shore. Kate struggled with the current, holding the canoe from floating downstream, trying to keep it parallel with the river. She felt several times she could not hold on any longer. But she knew she must.

Exhausted, she almost did not hear the bear leaving. It was

upstream entering the river. Kate listened as the splashing water grew farther away. The snarl of one bear was met by the snarl of the other. A quick series of splashes was followed by a deafening whirlpool of thrashing water. Her two attackers were fighting over something, Kate realized.

She knew she did not have much time. She took a few tentative steps. She could not believe how good it felt just to move, just to bend her legs. She walked slowly along the bottom of the river, guiding the canoe overhead. As it grew shallower, Kate was forced to crouch more and more. Finally she went to her knees. The rocks and debris jabbed into her skin. But she could not stop now. The growls of the bears grew fainter, but their echo still thundered through the trees.

Kate snagged the front of the canoe on the shore. She pulled it back and veered to the left, following the curve of the river. She wanted to come out from under the canoe. But she felt safe where she was. She did not want to see the danger. Just a little longer, she figured, and it would be safe to come out.

In the semidarkness Kate felt strangely calm. The diminishing twilight reflected off the bottom of the river into the hull of the canoe. Shadows rippled across the aluminum in haphazard patterns. Kate felt inwardly at peace. Her body had long ago grown numb to the cold of the river.

There was a crash in the woods. Kate shook her head. She did not know how long she had been walking under the canoe. She did not know if there had been other noises in the woods following her. She did not know if something had been stalking her.

Fear welled in her throat. She stood still in the freezing water. Her body could no longer shiver, and her aching fingers loosened on the crossbar almost in resignation. A whimper pulsing in her chest grew to a sob. It would be over so fast if she slipped under the water. The bear would be cheated.

The canoe rotated untethered cross-stream. With a sudden shift, Kate was knocked off balance. Her body plunged into the water. The cold slapped at her face. She reached for the canoe, but it eluded her grasp. She surfaced, panting. The canoe careened off the opposite bank and cartwheeled into midstream.

Kate's heart raced wildly. She charged after the canoe.

Something was in the water behind her. She was sure of it. Marsha's bloodied arm flashed through her mind. Grabbing the end of the canoe, she glanced quickly around. As she dived under the still overturned craft and surfaced in the air pocket, she realized nothing was there. Nothing was there!

That couldn't be! She'd seen it! No, she'd heard it. She must have heard it. Oh, Christ, she despaired, what's happening to me?

Away. Out of here, she thought. Gripping the crossbar with new resolve, she forged ahead. The river quickly began to get shallower. Kate crouched low, but the water grew shallower still. Wispy green strands of weeds alternated with a gravel bottom. She lay flat and floated until the bow of the canoe ground noisily to a halt. She remained under her cover for a few minutes, listening. There were no heavy footsteps. There were no inhuman growls. She tried to push the canoe with her feet. But it was hopelessly grounded.

Kate finally pulled herself to her knees. With her back on the floor of the canoe, she cautiously rolled it over. The water gurgled by innocently, splashing white droplets in the air. A few stars could just be seen. The trees stood motionless. The forest was calm.

Kate slowly struggled to her feet. She guided the canoe to the shore and pulled it safely out of the current. Then she collapsed on the soft pine needles and closed her eyes. She was asleep in moments. On an uncharted dirt trail a few hundred yards from the river, an automobile engine whispered through the forest.

13

It had become more and more obvious to Sergeant Rademacher that James Davis must be in that woods. Every cabin, every gas station anywhere near 621 between Mackinaw City and Wabanakisi had been checked, and no one had seen him. Every inch of the shoulder had been inspected, and there was no trace of him found. And there had been no ransom demand. By Monday morning Rademacher realized there could be only one explanation. Davis never made it to the road. He was still in Crooked Tree.

Rademacher stood at the top of a tree-covered hill just south of where Davis' car was found. Murph was at his side. Murph had been at his side for more searches than any other dog. But despite his confidence in Murph's ability, he knew there were serious problems. The track was laid five days ago, and it had rained Saturday night. Murph would almost have to stumble on the body to find it. But Rademacher was a patient man and was prepared to cover every square inch of the area if it was necessary. In a way, he felt responsible for the unsuccessful track last Friday. He knew he should not have let inexperienced handlers try to read the dogs. But the pressure had been for immediate results, and he had relented.

Deputy Shank's attitude had bothered him all weekend, and he wondered how seriously his treatment of the dog had affected it. He decided to retrace Shank's steps first.

Murph pranced a short distance ahead at the end of a long leash. The dog's tugging made it difficult for him to descend the slope, but he did not want to restrict the dog any more than was necessary. It needed free rein on a track, and Rademacher did his best to allow it.

It was midmorning, but a line of darkness stretched out before him. Rademacher surveyed the cedar swamp for a few moments. Murph stopped and looked up expectantly. Puddles of black water were scattered between the twisting roots of the cedars. Rademacher spotted what appeared to be a fairly dry path slightly to his right. He led Murph to it and entered the swamp. Neither the stagnant water nor the muck seemed to bother the dog. It kept moving from side to side, sniffing at the ground, as Rademacher struggled to keep pace. His eyes shifted from the dog to the ground in front of him and back to the dog as he stepped from matted roots to soft soil to fallen trunks.

The dog yelped and tugged harder on the leash. Suddenly Rademacher's foot plunged into black slime and the leash slipped from his grasp. The dog ran free as the mud oozed over the top of Rademacher's shoe. He yanked with his foot. The shoe stayed in the muck, held by the suction. Murph was getting farther ahead. Excited, in the middle of a track, he might run off, Rademacher thought. He pulled his foot out of his shoe and charged after the dog, who was barking excitedly just ahead. "Come here!" Rademacher shouted. Suddenly pain shot through his shoeless foot. He stumbled forward and fell face-first into a shallow puddle. He freed one hand and grasped a log. Rademacher tried to struggle to his feet, but he seemed trapped in the powerful suction of the ooze. Shaking his head, he frantically tried to shed the muck from his face. When his eyes cleared, he saw that his hand had not grasped a log. It was a leg. He had found Davis.

Axel Michelson sat uneasily in the doctor's stiff vinyl-covered chair, absently fingering the pages of a three-week-old *Time* magazine. He was behind at the office, and the delay was making him edgy.

"Mr. Michelson?" The nurse placed the telephone receiver back in its cradle.

"Yes," replied Axel quickly, closing the magazine.

"I just talked to Dr. Lewis, and he said he would be delayed a bit. There was an emergency at the hospital."

"Serious?"

"I doubt it. Something about a camper on the Big Two Hearted."

"That's great," Axel said. "Weekend tourist, no doubt. Do you know how long he will be?"

"He said to wait. He won't be much longer."

Axel glanced at his watch. It was almost noon. "Okay," he agreed, settling back into the chair. If he came back in the afternoon, the office would be packed with other patients, and it could be a wait of hours just to remove the stitches in his hand.

Axel did not go back to his magazine. Rather, he thought about being alone with Janis on the narrow beach with their backs against the dune. The sand hill had formed a barrier against the rest of the world, and the swish of the waves on the sand seemed to have washed them of their anxieties. Axel was relaxed. He was content just thinking about it.

The phone rang again on the nurse's desk. Axel listened, sure it was Dr. Lewis saying he could not make it at all. He was surprised when she placed it on the counter and said it was his office calling.

"Hello," Axel said into the receiver. Mrs. Whitesun politely busied herself with something else on her desk.

"Hi, Axel." It was Grace's cheerful voice. "Are you going to survive?"

"I don't know. They might have to amputate."

"Well, that's good. At least you'll be getting your money's worth for spending so much time over there."

"Pretty funny. Actually, I haven't seen the doctor yet."

"Are you going to be there for a while?"

"I'm afraid it looks that way."

"How about if I send some letters over for you to sign? You know, the ones you wanted out as soon as possible."

"That's a good idea. Send Larry over with them."

"If I can pull him out of those books. He's been driving me crazy on this injunction thing."

"Tell him I'll buy him lunch."

"That'll get him, I'm sure."

"Thanks for calling, Grace. See you this afternoon." Axel handed the receiver back for Mrs. Whitesun to hang up.

As he took his seat in the lobby, Axel thought about Emma

Whitesun's name. He knew it was an old tribal name, but he wondered how it originated. Some of her people kept the Ottawa spelling. Others, like Mrs. Whitesun, translated their names into English. Many split their names or adopted new ones. The names were always so melodious, Axel thought, almost like poetry. They usually took an aspect of nature in an attempt to ascribe certain qualities to the infant. More often than not, a person would grow to match the personality of the name.

Ten minutes later, Larry Wolf and Dr. Lewis walked in the front door together. Dr. Lewis had delivered Larry, and as with most of his patients, took more than a professional interest in him. As Larry was growing up, the doctor had been impressed with his energy, enthusiasm, and intelligence. He had encouraged Larry to go to medical school because he knew how a small town like Wabanakisi needed doctors. Receiving the doctor's special attention was not necessarily a singular honor for Larry, and he knew it. Dr. Lewis encouraged every bright youngster to go to medical school. It was his way of ensuring the continuance of the profession.

Seeing Dr. Lewis' arm around Larry and noticing the twinkle in his eye, Axel was almost certain what to expect him to say. While Axel had nothing to do with Larry's decision to eschew medical school in favor of law, Dr. Lewis blamed him for it and rarely missed an opportunity to good-naturedly needle Axel. But Axel was wrong this time.

"I'm sorry I'm late, Axel," Dr. Lewis began, "but I was just listening to the most incredible story."

"What do you mean?" Axel asked. He knew Dr. Lewis was not given to exaggeration.

"Old Butch MacNaughton brought in a . . . you know Butch, don't you, Axel?" Dr. Lewis interrupted himself.

"Yeah, sure, what happened?"

"Old Butch was out fishing by Weynidge Bridge this morning," Dr. Lewis began, "and he says a young girl came floating downstream in a battered canoe, poling herself along with a branch. No paddle, just a branch," Dr. Lewis repeated for emphasis.

"She seemed awfully excited to see Butch, he said, and I imagine, after seeing what she had on, Spike was awfully excited when he saw her." He grinned slyly.

"Anyway, she had him drive her into town, and the way she looked and was talking, Butch brought her to the hospital."

"What was wrong with her? Was she hurt?" Axel inquired.

"Not hurt, really. But she had scrapes and insect bites all over her body, and one hell of a cold."

Larry interrupted. "What from? She spend the night in the woods without any protection?"

"Yes. At least that's what she says. But that's not the worst of it. She claims she and a girlfriend were canoeing yesterday when two bears attacked them. They were waiting for them right in the middle of the river, just standing there."

"Two bears?"

"Yes.

"Where's her friend?" Axel asked.

"The bears got her, so she says. Oh. I forgot. She also claims earlier in the day she and her girlfriend came across a camper who had been mauled in his tent."

"Mauled in his tent?" Mrs. Whitesun repeated incredulously.

"Yes, Emma. Tent was torn to shreds, and they found a man inside, half-eaten." Mrs. Whitesun gasped audibly. "Oh, my word."

Dr. Lewis' manner made Axel think the doctor did not believe her. "Think her story is true, Doctor?" he inquired.

"I don't know, Axel. I do know that hallucinations are funny things. A person can describe them as vividly as if they were real, and in fact probably believes them to be true."

"So you think she imagined all this?" Axel asked.

"I'm not saying that for certain. But I will say I have seen it happen before. The girl did have an awfully rough time last night, for whatever reason. She was suffering from exposure. Everything that happened to her could have prompted delusions. And from what I know of black bears, if there are any out there—because I've never seen any—they are the most timid creatures in the forest."

"As timid as a chipmunk?" Axel asked.

The doctor smiled at Axel. "In any event, we should find out before long if her story is true or not. The sheriff is out searching the woods now."

"Maybe we'll find out right now," Larry said. "A state police

133

car just stopped in front."

They watched a man in a muddied blue uniform climb out of the passenger side of the car with great effort. The driver walked around and grabbed his arm, giving support. As the officer limped up to the clinic, a German shepherd watched from the rear seat of the police car.

"I know I must look terrible," Sergeant Rademacher began, "but I'm not as bad as I look."

"Here. Right here. Sit down for a spell." Dr. Lewis indicated a chair by the door.

"I'm sorry to disturb you at lunch hour," Rademacher apologized.

"Don't be silly," Dr. Lewis said. "What's the problem?"

"I jammed a sharp stick or something up my foot. I don't know if it's still in there or not."

"Were you by the Big Two Hearted River?" Axel asked.

"No, but I was in Crooked Tree, near 621." Dr. Lewis was on one knee, inspecting the sergeant's foot. Rademacher looked up at Axel. "Hey, aren't you Michelson? The lawyer who had a case with Davis last week?"

"Yes, a case scheduled with him."

"I just found him out in the woods. Right near where his car was. Torn to shreds by wild animals."

Dr. Lewis almost dropped Rademacher's foot. He looked at Axel. Axel didn't return the stare.

"Bears?" Axel said at last.

"Could have been."

Dr. Lewis knew what Axel was thinking. "Impossible," he declared. "The last Michigan bear attack must have been thirty years ago, and even that was in the upper peninsula." The doctor's gaze moved slowly from face to face. "It's impossible, I say. Black bears simply don't stalk and kill people, and certainly not three in one week. It has never happened."

Larry Wolf felt an involuntary chill. It was as if icy claws had suddenly gripped his spine. Something forgotten, something heard as a child, erupted in his head. He knew Emma Whitesun was staring at his back. He could feel it. But he avoided her stare. He knew what those eyes would say, and refused to hear it. It *has* happened! they would scream. And it will get worse.

II
Ogochin Atisken

14

The deer's glassy eyes reflected the dim lights. Smoke curled through its antlers. Below it, a bartender dunked glasses in a sink full of sudsy water. He was working fast, washing more glasses than he normally did on a Monday night.

"I still don't believe it," Harry Forstyk declared.

"Don't believe what? Don't believe they were killed?" a man in a blue-and-white flannel shirt asked.

"No, I don't believe the bears did it. I don't see how it could have happened."

"The girl told how it happened to her and her friend."

"That's what I heard. But did you talk to her?"

"Dr. Lewis did," Axel Michelson interrupted. "And Larry and I were there when he got back from the hospital. He told us everything she said to him. Finding the camper's body and the girl in the river seems to verify her story."

"That's right. The godamn bears did it," the man in the flannel shirt said. Axel knew his first name was Dirk, but had rarely talked to him. He had come in the bar with Mike Sizemore and Nels Carlson. Axel, Ted Hiller, Larry Wolf, and Harry Forstyk were sitting at a large round table when they walked in, and the empty chairs at their table were the only unfilled chairs in the bar.

"But it's out of character for them," Harry protested. "Completely out of character. It's rare that a black bear has gone out of its way to attack somebody in Michigan. And now we're supposed to believe it happened three times within a couple days!"

Dirk leaned his broad shoulders forward. "Let me tell you something about the *character* of bears." He sneered, pointing a finger at Harry. "They're mean sons of bitches that will do anything they goddamn well can get away with. The only reason they ain't been killing people right and left is that there's been so goddamn few of them around. Until now, that is."

Harry knew the man was right about the increase in black bear population. If he was honest with himself, he would probably agree the bears had attacked those three people, but Dirk represented everything Harry hated about the new breed of hunter.

"If it wasn't for the conservationists," Dirk continued, "there would be no problem now. In the old days, the bears were controlled."

"Controlled! You mean almost wiped out."

"And it was a damn good thing. No bears meant no bears killing people."

"They didn't seem to bother the Indians much," Harry said.

"Aw, shit. Fuck the Indians. They were half-animal anyways."

Larry grabbed his glass of beer as if he were going to fling it at him, but Axel grabbed his arm, holding it down.

"Whoa, steady there, fella," the big man in the blue-and-white flannel shirt said. He leaned back in his chair, taking his first good look at Larry. He had not known he was an Ottawa. "Hey, I meant no offense. I was talking about a hundred years ago." Dirk managed a strained laugh. "Hell, everybody knows the Indians are just regular folk now. Look at Ted here. No better plumber in northern Michigan."

Larry seethed, but his only appropriate response might land him in jail.

Dirk shrugged and looked to his friends for support. "All I meant to say is, it was a good system in the old days. Bears were always open season."

"Harry," Axel said, trying to steer the conversation away from the building lunacy, "what do you think about the girl in the canoe? She said there were two bears. Do you think it could have been a mother and her cub?"

"And because they plowed right into them, the mother attacked to protect the cub? Is that what you mean?" Harry asked.

"Oh, come on, Fireplug. Why do you need an explanation for an animal acting like an animal?" a man seated on a stool at the bar said.

"Want to know how an Ottawa would explain it?" Larry said, almost in defiance.

"I'll tell you," Hiller quickly interrupted. "They would agree with what Fireplug has been warning us of for years. The bears are ganging up to get back at the hunters."

The group of people that had gathered around the table broke into a laugh. Hiller smiled nervously, but when his eyes caught Larry's they narrowed.

Disgustedly Larry shoved his chair back from the table. "I've gotta piss," he said as he got up and walked toward the bathroom.

Ted quickly drained his beer and followed Larry to the bathroom. When he walked through the double door, Larry was standing at the urinal trough. Hiller stood up next to him, unzipping his pants.

"You know you're not going to help if you start spreading that crazy Indian legend."

"What the hell are you afraid of?" Larry said angrily.

"I know these people. Put an idea like that into the head of a guy like Dirk out there, and pretty soon people will be stirred up and somehow blaming it all on the Indian."

Larry started to reply. Hiller cut him off. "It doesn't matter that it won't make sense. They'll still blame us."

"Us?" Larry drawled sarcastically.

Ted had not urinated, but he was finished. He stepped back and zipped his pants up. "They can make it real hard on an Ottawa in business around here."

When Larry came back to the table, a large crowd had gathered, and Dirk was on center stage.

"Enough bullshit on why the poor bears are not to be blamed," Dirk said. "Before we know it, there'll be a group of assholes out in the woods feeding them, claiming they're deprived."

"Something like this has never happened before," a weathered old man said. "What do you think we should do?"

"What should we do!" Dirk bellowed. "We kill the fuckin' bears."

"What do you mean, 'We kill the fuckin' bears'?" The words dripped from his mouth. Axel could contain himself no longer. "How are you going to find the killers? Which bears are you going to kill? How many bears are you going to kill?"

"We kill every motherfuckin' bear we find."

"That's just great. You going to burn all of Crooked Tree down to get them?"

"If we have to. But we won't. We'll form a posse." Dirk's eyes swept grandly over the attentive faces. "That's right, a bear posse."

"With yourself leading the pack, I suppose."

"Maybe. I'll tell you one thing. At least I have the balls."

"It doesn't take balls. It takes an empty head. Can you imagine what would happen if there was an army of armed men stomping around in the woods on a holy crusade to kill the bears? They would be shooting anything that moved. More people would be killed by bullets than by bear's teeth."

"It wouldn't be so bad," one of the hunters said. "Hell, during deer season there's more men with guns in the Michigan woods than the United States had soldiers in Europe during the Second World War."

"And every year a dozen hunters are shot to death," Axel said.

Dirk broke in, his voice soothing. "Hunting bear is easy. First time I hunted in the U.P., I got seven bear in one day."

"Seven?" someone said with a tone of disbelief.

"Sure. Seven. It's not like deer, who run all over the place. You just have to sneak up on them in their dens. I remember there was an early snow that year, and all we had to do was just follow their tracks to their sleeping holes and blast away."

"What in the world did you do with them?"

"We skinned the first five but were too tired to skin the last two. Hell, that was enough for blankets for my relatives." Dirk's laugh was joined by most of the others in the bar.

"This is sick," Axel said to Harry. "I'm getting out of here."

Dirk was quick to notice the mood as well. He stood on his chair and raised his arms. "Quiet down, men. I say we start organizing right now."

A chorus of assent bounced off Axel's back as he swung through the exit. "Christ almighty!" he exclaimed aloud.

"They've got to be stopped." But he was tired. And he had had too much to drink. So had they, he thought. It seemed unlikely that they would or could do anything tonight.

Axel studied his watch. It was 10:30 already. He suddenly wished he had never come into town. He should have stayed home and relaxed, like Janis. But like everybody else at Smidgeon's, he had wanted to find out what the hell was happening. What he found out was disconcerting. He felt a need to talk to his wife.

The leaves danced their delicate dance to the music of the wind. Janis' long black hair was swept back breezily from her face. She looked skyward as the stars twinkled in and out of view above the gently swaying branches. Ice tinkled nervously in her glass.

It helped her mood to come into the woods. It was peaceful there. Quieting. She bad been inexplicably edgy all evening. Perhaps it was the dreams, she thought. Something gnawed at her, but she did not know what. It was the feeling of leaving on a trip and trying to remember the one item forgotten. There was something to do, but she was not sure what it was.

She had not heard Axel drive up. "Honey?" His voice came from the rear of the house. "Anything the matter?"

Janis turned quickly. "No," she said, walking slowly toward the house.

"That's not what I'd call your best outdoor outfit," Axel observed, smiling.

"I know," Janis said as she gazed down at her silky robe. "I was sitting on the couch looking out the window, trying to relax with a drink, and all of a sudden I had an urge to go outside. I must have just needed some air."

"I know what you mean. It's a beautiful evening."

As she stepped through the sliding glass door, Janis planted a quick kiss on her husband's cheek. "Whew, how much have you been drinking?"

"Oh, a few beers, maybe," Axel said noncommittally.

"Uh-huh," she drawled. "And what did you hear at Smidgeon's?"

"Oh, boy, you wouldn't believe it."

"Why? What's going on?" Janis' tenseness resurfaced.

"Here, sit down," Axel said as he settled into the couch.

"No. Just tell me what happened."

Axel propped his feet up on the coffee table. "They're crazy. They're acting like nuts."

"Who is?"

"Do you know that big guy named Dirk?"

"I've seen him around. I think he's brought his dog, or maybe it was a cat, into the vet's."

"Well, he got the whole place stirred up. When I left, they were forming a 'bear posse.' "

"A what?"

"A 'bear posse.' That's what he called it, anyway."

"You mean right out in these woods?"

"Somewhere in Crooked Tree. But hopefully not right out there," Axel said, gesturing toward the window. "The killings were pretty far away, and no bears have been sighted near here."

Janis' eyes shifted to the floor. "What's the sheriff doing about the posse?"

"He doesn't know yet. But I'm hoping they will calm down and be more reasonable about the whole thing tomorrow. I agree, something should be done. There's probably a sick bear out there, but letting an army loose with guns shooting at anything and everything won't help. The best thing would be to catch it and move it far from people. But do it in an orderly way, with rational people. And let the sheriff or the state police handle it."

"Let's hope so, Axel."

"Yeah, otherwise they'll find more than three bodies in the woods."

"*Three* bodies?" Janis exclaimed. Her eyes widened.

"Yeah, three. I guess I didn't mention they found the girl who was attacked in the canoe."

"Where is she?" she said, trembling.

"She was at the bottom of one of the deep pools in the river."

"No. I mean where is she now?" Her voice was urgent.

Axel was perplexed. He regarded his wife closely. The strain, he thought. "She's dead, honey. Her body's at the funeral home. Her parents were reached, and they asked that she not be left at the morgue. They should be here tomorrow morning."

Janis' face softened. Her eyes blinked shut for a long moment as she exhaled heavily.

"It's late," Axel noted. "Let's go to bed."

"You go to bed, honey," Janis said. The edge was gone from her voice. "I'll be there in a little while. I'll try not to wake you."

"I don't think you'll have to worry about waking me. The alcohol will take care of that."

Janis only nodded. Her contented smile followed Axel out of the room. The uncertainty she felt earlier was gone.

15

Jennifer looked across the crumpled pillow at her husband. As a light breeze billowed the sheer curtains at the window, she clutched the knotted sheet snugly to her neck. Its linear pattern, colorless in the dark, draped loosely over Scott's chest. She reached her hand to the wavy black hair that splashed across his face, curling the long strands around her fingers. A loving tenderness began to kindle within her womb. Suddenly, uncontrollably, her fist clenched.

Scott's eyes opened quickly. "Hey, that hurts," he blurted.

Jenny loosened her grip. "Did you hear that?"

"Oh, shit. Not again."

"But there really was something this time. I heard it."

"That's what you said before."

"I know, Scott, but I can't help it." Jenny was not used to her new name yet, much less living on the second floor of a funeral home. Her voice firm, she added, "I *did* hear something."

Sighing, Scott sank his head deeper into the pillow. "It's my fault for taking this job."

"Don't say that, honey. Where else could two nineteen-year-olds live for free? And besides . . ." Jenny stopped suddenly and jerked up in bed. Her entire body contracted in a rigid brace against the unknown. Motionless, listening intently, she brought her eyes to bear on Scott.

"All right, all right," he said, seeing the fear in her face. "I'll go ask the ghosts to be a little more quiet."

It worked. She almost smiled. "Be careful, Scott," she said as he flung the sheet back.

"The worst thing that could happen is I might stub my toe in the dark. Where's that flashlight?"

"Over here," Jenny said as she reached toward the small table by her. Lifting his Levi's from the floor, he slipped them on. "If I'm not back in a few minutes, don't worry. I'll just be partying with the stiffs."

Jenny sank back into the mattress. She was more at ease. But Scott was not. He had heard a noise as well, a distant clang, as if something metallic had fallen on concrete. The carpeted first floor would not have produced that sound. It could only have come from the basement embalming room.

The funeral home had two parlors, each in a separate wing. It was small by big-city standards, but it fulfilled the needs of Wabanakisi. On the first floor, Scott stepped gingerly through a yawning archway. The flashlight flickered over the furniture, casting spidery shadows on the wall. Scanning the room, he observed that the rows of folding chairs were still in place. A display of flowers was undisturbed. Pulling the draperies back along one side of the room, he made sure all the windows were locked and unbroken. It was unnecessary to check behind the symmetrically placed draperies along the opposite wall. There were no windows behind them.

The basement door was next to the office in the center of the building. Scott paused by it and focused the flashlight's beam on the door-knob. He could picture the narrow staircase, the tables, the instruments. Especially the instruments.

The doorknob was left in darkness as the light flashed down the hall. Scott followed the beam into the second parlor, which appeared to be an empty shell of the first. Where the flowers had been in the other wing there was an empty alcove. Behind it, parted curtains revealed the dull metal jaws of a broad elevator.

Scott walked back to the basement door. The sound, he knew, had come from there, and he had to investigate, not just to satisfy his bride, but because it was his job. With the grisly image of a bear-torn corpse in his mind, Scott reluctantly twisted the brass knob.

As the narrow steps squeaked under his weight, Scott thought about the first time he had followed them down. A withered body had been strapped to a tilted metal table, indented rivulets patterned across its surface. It had reminded him of a meat-carving platter. From yellow rubber tubes inserted in the skin a watery reddish liquid dripped and flowed across the uplifted table to a drain at the end. Scott remembered having to clench his teeth to maintain his composure.

The sharp odor of formaldehyde pierced his unpleasant memory. From the lowest step Scott surveyed the tables. Chemicals and countless persons' life fluids had oxidized the surfaces a brownish gray. He did not linger on their sight. He stepped toward the center of the room, his bare feet cold on the concrete floor.

Hanging implements and coiled tubes lined the wall; jars of chemicals were undisturbed. As Scott inched around the tables, an icy wind seemed to slam his naked chest. At first he thought it was fear.

The door! The refrigerator-room door was open! But it couldn't be. The massive latch could never unhinge itself. Scott stood in stony bewilderment. A pulsing whoosh grew in his ears. The wind. No, there can't be any wind. But still, a rhythmic rush of air. Like the panting of an animal. Could it be imagined? It must be!

Scott moved forward on shaking legs. His fingers pressed against the door and swung its massive weight open. Encompassed by the cold, Scott shivered as the light sliced a rigid line through the icy darkness. Eerie silhouettes projected starkly on the wall. Scott placed his foot carefully in front of him, his moist skin almost sticking to the floor. His eyes quickly darted to the corners of the room. Nothing. He felt relieved.

He started to step back, but his body was propelled forward. His head snapped crazily. A powerful blow struck at the back of his neck. He crashed to the floor in a heap. Dazed, he struggled to rise, but a throbbing ache blanketed his consciousness. With the slam of the heavy door resounding in his ears, Scott sagged to the chilled concrete.

The flashlight wobbled untended back and forth, casting a haphazard beam across the floor. In a moment it came to rest.

Thoughts drifted without direction through his mind. Scenes seemed to swirl in front of his eyes, rotating in a three-dimensional whirlpool. Slowly they were pulled into the vortex. The suction grew stronger. Gradually he became aware of being shaken. His eyes opened groggily.

"Hmmm," was all Larry could manage to say.

"Wake up."

"Mishoo? Is that you?" Larry asked, propping himself up with his elbows.

"Yes. Are you awake now?" Charley Wolf stopped his gentle prodding.

"No. I'm sound asleep. What in the world are you doing?"

"I'm trying to wake you up." Larry's grandfather prodded again.

"What for? What time is it? I'm not getting out of bed."

"It's four-thirty. And I'm taking you to see the sunrise."

"Holy smokes! Are you crazy?" Larry flopped back to the mattress. His grandfather straightened up and stared silently at him. Larry could not distinguish the expression on his face, but he knew what it must be. No use fighting it, he thought. He flipped the sheets to the side and swung his feet to the floor. "All right, I'll come," he agreed, sitting on the edge of his bed. It did not take long for Larry's reluctance to fade. After shaking himself alert and splashing cold water in his face, he was not sorry he was missing his sleep. By the time they were walking up the hill, with Crooked Tree silhouetted against the lightening sky, Larry was glad his grandfather had awakened him. He looked forward to watching the sun rise over the forest.

Their breath almost sparkled in the crisp air. The gently rising hill provided a deceptive test of fitness, as the two men breathed heavily. Larry felt wetness at his ankles. He glanced down. His shoes glistened with dew. Long thick blades of grass, dabbled with droplets of water, whipped his legs with each step.

At the crest of the hill Larry stopped and turned around, panting. His grandfather was just a few steps behind. Ottawa Village was mapped out before him. Beyond the cluster of homes and buildings, rows of poplars divided acres of farmland. A dark line of trees edged the cornfields. Larry sat on the grass to wait for the sun to color the horizon.

"We're not there yet," Charley Wolf said.

"This is fine," Larry protested. "We'll be able to see perfectly."

"We're not to the Tree. We have to get to the Tree." Charley

Wolf did not wait for a response. He kept walking, each step drumming a steady resolve. Larry was left with no choice. He followed.

The barren hill accentuated the massiveness of the single white pine. It rose straight as a Grecian pillar for about 140 feet before succumbing to the force of Mudjekeewis, the west wind. Of the manitous who controlled the winds, Mudjekeewis was the strongest, more powerful even than the dangerous Kabibonokka, who brought cold and ice from the north. The seducer of Hiawatha's mother, Mudjekeewis later faced his bastard son in a battle of revenge.

The taproot from Crooked Tree probably extended downward as far as the tree was high, its centuries-old grasp reaching below the surface of the village. Saved from the lumber mills, nonetheless its timber would have been a mighty prize. It contained enough wood to build seven three-bedroom houses.

The delicate needles, grouped in fives, whistled silently high overhead. Charley Wolf stroked the thick bark, his fingers following the indentations of the deep grooves.

"Touch it, Larry," Charley Wolf said to his grandson, his unblinking eyes staring at the tree. "Feel its coarse skin. Feel the Ottawa blood flowing through it. Feel the pulse of your ancestors." Both hands were spread wide, his flattened hands never leaving its surface, his eyes following the twisting black pattern upward.

Charley Wolf's voice trembled. "Touch the soul of your people. Feel the skill of the proud hunters. The wisdom of the chiefs. The tenderness of your mothers. Let it flow through you as the sap flows through this wood."

The old man's words enwrapped his mind like creeping vines. Larry's fingers gripped the bark, his knuckles whitening with the strain. Something deep within him stirred, spreading like the slowly unfolding wings of an awakening osprey. He felt pride. As it expanded, as the pride grew stronger, his body seemed to weaken.

Charley Wolf slowly pulled his hands away from the tree. His creased face turned toward his grandson. "Feel the strength of your cousins," his voice resonated.

The impact of his grandfather's words slowly registered. Larry eased his grip on the rough bark. His fingers pulsed red. He knew what his grandfather was saying. He knew what his grandfather wanted him to say. But he couldn't. His Ottawa blood was as undiluted as any. But his pride in his people, his pride in his heritage, did not mean he had to accept superstitions.

"Mishoo, I am proud of my people. I do feel their character in my veins. I'm proud of our history. I appreciate the wisdom that led to our beliefs, our legends, because those beliefs, those legends helped us survive in this world. But the world of the Ottawa is different now. The world for everybody is different now."

"No, Gusan, the world is not different. The *people* are." Charley Wolf's voice was strong, distinct. "They don't respect the land. The manitous of the animals are ignored. And what's happening? We gag on our water, we choke on the air. Animals refuse to be born. They refuse to feed us. No, Gusan, the world is the same. And what is happening in the world is exactly what our beliefs told us would happen if the manitous were forgotten."

Larry was frustrated. He could not defend disrespect for the land. And he felt the Ottawa beliefs instilled the proper respect. But they were a device of learning, not a truth of science. He knew his grandfather would never agree. And he knew just as surely he would never accept his grandfather's blind faith.

"Mishoo, I know now why you brought me up here. I know you feel it's for my own good. But I don't accept the legends as true."

"You must, Larry," Charley Wolf shouted, grabbing his grandson by the shoulders. "It's starting again."

"I don't believe in the bearwalk." Larry's voice was certain.

"But it's happening. Just like before."

"I don't believe a man's spirit can leave his body," Larry insisted, "I don't believe it can take over the body of a bear."

"You must believe!" Charley pleaded. "All of us must believe, or we will die as the Mush Qua Tah did. The Ottawas survived then, and they can now. Let Shawonabe practice his evil on the white man. *We* will *live*!"

Charley Wolf's face was frozen in excitement. The creases in his skin seemed chiseled deeper. Larry was chilled. He was not sure what moved him. Was it concern for his grandfather? Or did he fear his words?

As he stood facing the aged man, Larry felt the warmth of dawn on his back.

Jenny jerked herself alert in the bed, her fingers gripping the soft mattress. A deep thud vibrated through the floor from below. "Scott?" she called. There was no answer. She tried again, louder. "Scott?" She sat motionless in bed for long minutes. Still it was quiet.

Her stomach churned. She couldn't stay there any longer. She flung the sheet back and raced to the window. The glow from the streetlights was unbroken by scurrying shadows. She listened in vain, hoping to hear her husband walking up the stairs.

Finally she went into the hallway, calling, "Scott? Scott, are you down there?" There was no response.

Jenny flicked the light switch at the top of the stairs. She knew the manager did not like the first floor illuminated late at night, because he thought it might give passersby an unfavorable impression. But Jenny didn't care. Something bad had happened.

She stepped gently down the stairs, her stocking feet muffling her descent. In the middle of the building by the office Jenny stared in terror: the embalming-room door was open.

As she crept to the top of the basement steps, her mind conjured up images of dead bodies and rotting flesh. Staring into the dark hole, she hesitated.

"Scott? Are you down there?" Silence. She knew she had to go down.

Gingerly she stepped to the bottom of the stairs, where she paused while her eyes grew accustomed to the dark. High on the far wall, shallow windows, frosted to keep out prying eyes, were a source of dim light.

Jenny slowly surveyed the scene. No bodies. Tables, but no bodies. She was thankful. But that smell. An evil, acrid, overpowering smell. The muscle in her jaw strained as her tightly clenched teeth tried to shield her from the odor.

It was damp and cold. It was unpleasant. Jenny moved fast. She walked quickly around the room. She saw no one. "Oh, come on, where is he?" she whimpered. "Please, please let him . . ." Her words trailed suddenly into a gasp. Something was behind her! She whirled. There was nothing. But she had felt it.

A stare. It must have been someone's eyes she felt. But she saw no one. Come on, come on! Shake it! Shake the fear, she thought. She breathed deeply. Again. She swallowed. Her vision seemed to clear. She was calmer.

Another door. A thick door with a heavy latch, like at a butcher's shop. That's where they keep the bodies, she deduced. The heavy thud! The realization electrified her: it must have been that door! He must have locked himself inside. Jenny sprang the metal latch, and it snapped open with a clang. Leaning her body against the weighty door, she swung it halfway open.

A dim flashlight illuminated the cold floor. In the weak glow Jenny distinguished the dark outline of a young woman on a metal cart. She grimaced involuntarily. Squeezing through the partial opening, her foot caught on a hidden object.

"Scott!" she screamed. "Scott!" He lay facedown, his head tilted to one side. Jenny fell to her knees and grabbed him by the shoulders. His cold skin did not react to her touch. Recoiling in dread, Jenny looked at her hands as if to say: It can't be true!

"Ooh," Scott moaned, the noise rippling through his body.

"I knew it," she breathed. "I knew you wouldn't leave me."

His eyes opened as he felt himself rolling to his back. He tried to speak, but his jaws could barely move. They felt cold, distant, as if belonging to another. His wife's tears fell on his face. He tried to smile, but his face seemed frozen. The thought of danger resurfaced. He remembered what had happened. They'll get us both! Aching neck muscles burned as he struggled to raise his head. The door. It was moving! It was going to shut again! His lips parted in a futile attempt to warn Jenny. But he couldn't speak.

She stood and tugged at his arm, her words garbled in Scott's pounding ears. Pushing with all his strength, he stood with her help. The door was still open, he saw, but it was still moving. Everything was moving! He rocked backward on stiff legs, the very walls seeming to wobble with him.

As Jenny's body pressed against his, Scott was able to steady himself. Her warmth gushed into his chest, bringing pulsing life to his sluggish heart. As they locked in tight embrace, the morbidness of the embalming room seemed remote. Concerned only with each other, only with each other's safety, Jenny and Scott could no longer feel the cold. They were oblivious of the mauled body on the cart beside them. They did not notice the fluid dripping from the corner of Marsha Gutkowski's mouth.

16

The breeze brought welcome fresh air through the window. Slender shoots of grass wavered in the wind, their outline distinguishable through the translucent pane of glass. It was partially open, and one of the sliding runners was out of its track. A blue-uniformed state police evidence technician examined the metal runner closely. Sheriff Luke Snyder eyed him expectantly from below.

"What do you think? Will you get any prints off that?" Snyder inquired.

"I don't know yet, Sheriff."

"I sure hope so. It might be our only chance to solve this thing," Snyder said.

The evidence tech was balanced on a metal cart that had been rolled under the basement window. He looked down at Snyder and the others. "The way the window is out of its track, he must have handled it a lot. It would have taken considerable maneuvering."

"And a lot of strength," Scott said. "Look how the metal hinge is bent."

"Yes, it sure is. That wouldn't have been easy," the tech said, turning back to the window. "Anyway, with all that touching, unless he wore gloves, there should be good prints."

The sheriff turned away, shaking his head. "Why would anyone want to break into a funeral home?" he asked, his voice a mixture of disbelief and disgust.

A short wiry man nervously pinched his lower lip. "Kids,

maybe," he said. It was more a question than an answer.

"Kids on a lark would not try to kill somebody," Jenny said with anger, her arm around Scott.

"They might not have realized what they were doing," Sheriff Snyder said softly. "They could have reacted out of fear, like a cornered animal trying to get away." Turning to the undertaker, he said, "Yes, it's possible kids did it. But I doubt it. Are you sure nothing was disturbed down here? Nothing taken?"

"Yes, I'm sure," the wiry man replied, his eyes glancing quickly around the room. "There's nothing down here to take."

"Whoever broke in probably was more interested in what he could find upstairs in your office," Snyder decided. "And he was scared off by Scott here."

"Oh, my, this is terrible, simply terrible." The undertaker could contain himself no longer. "What will people think? What will they say? I'll be out of business. They won't be able to trust me anymore."

"Don't worry. They can't stop dying."

"This looks like a good one," the tech interrupted. A little white cloud materialized as he blew the powder off the glass.

"Is there enough to make a comparison?" Snyder asked.

"Should be, assuming we have a full print to compare with."

"Good," Snyder said, eyeing the window. "He must have been small to be able to squeeze through that little opening."

"He couldn't have been too small," Scott said. "Whoever hit me really packed a wallop."

Snyder regarded the youth out of the corner of his eye. Turning to him, he said, "You say that door was open when you came down here?"

"Yes, just a bit. Enough, though, to let me feel the cold coming from it," Scott said.

Snyder motioned toward the refrigerated room. "The bodies are in there, I suppose?" he asked, his eyes narrowing.

"Yes, we have two deceased in repose," the undertaker said.

"I was hit from *behind*," Scott emphasized. "He couldn't have been hiding in there."

"I know son. But somebody opened it for God-knows-why. Can we look inside?" he inquired of the undertaker.

"Why, certainly, Sheriff," he replied, gesturing broadly. "But I must warn you, it's not a pretty sight."

Snyder stopped. "Why? One of the bear victims in there?"

"Yes, the young lady."

Snyder pursed his lips, exhaling through his nose. He did not like the idea of seeing that girl again. Her dismembered and mauled body was an unpleasant enough sight the first time he saw it. "Why don't you two young folks step back. You don't want to see this," he said.

Scott moved away obediently, taking Jenny with him. Snyder unhinged the heavy latch, his eyes carefully avoiding the body of the young woman on the cart. He had seen many bodies and had scraped many an unlucky driver off the expressway pavement, but none moved him as this one had. He bent down to the floor to look for anything that could have been left behind by the intruder. The cold from the concrete chilled his knee.

The undertaker walked straight to the corpse of the girl. He had cleaned her the best he could the night before. Her condition did not bother him emotionally. The prospect of making her look presentable excited his professional interest. He was concerned primarily with the face. Fortunately, clothes would cover the rest of the body, he thought.

The corners of his lips turned downward as he stood above her, his critical gaze studying her face. There appeared to be something on her cheek, a crusty line extending from the corner of her mouth across her cheek to just below her ear. The undertaker was perplexed. He was sure he had cleaned her face.

He touched her cheek. Where his fingers touched the crusty stain, it crinkled to dust. It was as if she had dripped fluids from her mouth, but that would be impossible, he reasoned. Her body fluids would have settled by gravity. She had nothing to pump them up.

Despite the cold, a bead of perspiration appeared on his forehead. He wanted to open her mouth, but something seemed to hold him back. Was it fear? He had not felt that since he studied mortuary science. He could not be afraid.

Resolutely he placed the forefinger and thumb of each hand at the corners of her mouth. Her lips opened with only slight pressure.

"What?" he exclaimed. Squinting, he looked closer. "That can't be! That can't be!" he shouted, pulling his fingers away in horror.

Sheriff Snyder jumped to his feet. "What's wrong?" he yelled.

The undertaker stumbled away from the cart, his mouth agape. "Her tongue!" he wheezed at last. "Her tongue is gone!"

"What?" Snyder blurted. He had heard, but he did not understand.

The undertaker swallowed again and gasped for air. He turned from Snyder's grasp and looked away. Luke turned to the corpse. The eyes were closed. She looked peaceful. He grabbed her jaw tightly in his hands and pried her mouth open. As her teeth parted, his clenched.

The overhead lighting was not good. But Snyder could see well enough. He understood what the small wiry man had meant. There was no tongue. It was sliced cleanly out of her mouth.

The gleaming yellow ceramic wall tile reflected a hundred miniature white-jacketed figures. The two overhead lamps were bright points of light in each individual tile. In a way, the lights lying over the long tables made it look like an operating room, but less formal. And there were no oxygen tanks, heart monitors, or oscilloscopes. In another way, it resembled a research laboratory, with long benches and bottles of chemicals aligned on glassed-in shelves.

Two stainless-steel tables stood solidly a few feet apart in the center of the room. They were about eight feet long, with sides extending upward all around. At one end, a steady stream of water splashed from a spigot. The tables were tilted imperceptibly, causing the water to flow evenly over the surface of the stainless steel. At the opposite end, the water spilled into deep-cut sinks. A garbage disposal was fitted to the drain in each sink. It was on these tables that the pathologist performed his autopsies.

Dr. Joseph Owanish was less than anxious to begin work. His assistant, Borje Sorensen, could understand his reluctance. The two bodies had been mutilated by wild animals, and one was well on its way to decomposition. The odor of a human body deteriorating was an evil smell, something Dr. Owanish still was not used to after five years as Wabanakisi County medical examiner.

But it was not the smell that bothered him. While his nostrils could never ignore it, he never let it interfere with his job. And the badly ravaged torsos did not make him hesitate. He had seen worse. He knew what caused his palms to sweat. He knew why his heart beat faster and his stomach churned. But he could not say it even within the privacy of his own mind, and least of all to his friend Mitchell Caulley.

He had gone to medical school with Dr. Caulley, and both had worked together for a time at the Wayne County medical examiner's office in Detroit. Mitch was still there, now one of the state's leading forensic pathologists. Joe had left shortly after getting his degree and came back home. Wabanakisi had grown, and the county needed its own pathologist. But Joe had not come home because his people needed him. He came home because he needed his people. He was a proud Ottawa.

"Is anything wrong?" Caulley asked.

"No, not really," Joe replied.

"You don't know these people, do you, Joe?"

"The lawyer by name only. He's been around for a while. We were never acquainted or anything."

"Just the same, I'll take him, and you take the camper. Okay?"

"All right," Joe agreed. Actually, it did not matter to him whom he had. But if that was what Mitch thought was bothering him, he would let him go on thinking that. He had been embarrassed to ask him to help in the first place. After all, Mitch was on vacation and was supposed to be his guest. But he had been only too happy to oblige. There were not many opportunities in Detroit to examine a bear killing.

Borje selected a scalpel from a rack on the wall. He examined the blade by eye, as if he could distinguish imperfections in the razor edge. It was his job to open the corpses and prepare them for the pathologist's examination. Dr. Caulley signaled him silently to begin on the Davis remains.

Borje made his normal thoraco-frontal incision and peeled back what was left of the skin. Under the bright yellow fatty layer, the rib cage was exposed. He picked up the shears and prepared to open the chest cavity. They resembled normal backyard pruning shears, with long wooden handles for good leverage, and short curved blades. He started with the lower rib on the right, snapping it cleanly with one squeeze. He progressed rapidly up the right side, the ribs breaking easily. But the collarbone proved more difficult. Borje climbed on the table, taking care to keep his pants out of the water, and braced one knee against the corpse's chest. He leaned hard on the shears, his face straining with the effort. With a loud crunch, the collarbone gave way. He sighed heavily and relaxed for a moment before beginning on the left side. When he was done, he removed the rib plate, opening Davis' chest like a tin can.

Joe Owanish watched as his assistant moved to the next table. Dr. Caulley stepped up to Davis and began work. He could not help but notice how his friend lingered by the wall, his face ashen.

"Joe, do you want to go home? Leave them both to me?" Caulley asked.

Owanish snapped alert, as if woken from a trance. "Hmmm? What?"

"Do you want me to do both autopsies?" Caulley repeated, frowning with concern.

"Oh, no, I'll be all right," he answered, feeling not in the least all right.

"I don't mind, you know. Are you sure?"

"Of course I'm sure," Owanish snapped testily. Borje stopped what he was doing and looked up. "Hey, Mitch, I'm sorry. I'm just not myself today for some reason. I don't know what's gotten into me. I'll be all right."

Dr. Owanish had lied. He knew what had gotten into him. But he feared admitting it as much as he feared the thought. Oh, God, he wished he could relax. He was a man of science, of reason. So why couldn't he reason with himself? Why couldn't he stop sweating?

Borje walked away from the second table. His work for the moment was done. Owanish stared at the opened body. The easy noise of water tinkling around the corpse was all he could hear. He wished he could just go home and let Mitch do the autopsy. But he knew he couldn't. It was his job. Slowly his feet moved across the tile floor. Stepping up to the table, Dr. Owanish reached for a knife. He stared at the chest of the camper, his eyes unable to look higher. As he began cutting through tissue in order to free the internal organs, all he could think about was the mouth.

He had heard what some of the Ottawa said when they learned of the bear attacks. At first he dismissed what he heard as the predictable babblings of the old. But still, something kept him awake and tossing in his bed all night. In the morning his sheets were soggy with sweat.

He had come to the morgue knowing his people waited to hear from him. Some knew what he would find. Most hoped their uncomfortable twinges would be proved wrong. It was as if the dread of his people crystallized in him, capturing his emotions.

Dr. Owanish laid down his knife and grabbed the remains of Karl Waldemeir's insides and wrenched them free. The heart, liver, lungs, intestines, and the rest of the organs came out together, and the pathologist dropped the bundle across the corpse's legs. He took a 30ml syringe and plunged the needle into the kidneys. As he slowly retracted the glass end, the syringe filled with urine. Dr. Owanish emptied it into a vial for later analysis. He next collected a sample of blood that had pooled in his chest cavity. Owanish emptied that into another vial. Done with the syringe, Owanish selected a scalpel. He had to collect biopsies from the liver, heart, and other organs. When the glass bottles were filled and capped, there was one thing left to be done. Dr. Owanish had to examine the mouth.

Joe glanced covertly at Mitch. He was working steadily, slowly, just as he had in school. Borje was at a bench on the far side of the room preparing chemical solutions for later use in analyzing the specimens. Joe licked the perspiration from his upper lip. His eyes focused on the face of the corpse for the first time. He glanced again quickly at Mitch and Borje, fearing they would hear the thumping of his heart. They continued working. His attention returned to the face, its calmness belying the horror it must have experienced. The lips were closed tight, without a hint of expression, a result of the slackening of facial muscles. Owanish's stare froze on those lips. He pictured himself opening the mouth and peering inside. He watched his own expression for a clue. There was none. The picture dissolved. The lips came back into view.

His hands trembled as he raised them to the face of the corpse. He could not sense the texture of the skin through the rubber gloves. But he could feel its coldness, a coldness that spread up his arms and through his chest. Open it, dammit! Get it over with! In a macabre way he hoped to see what he feared. Then at least the anxiety, the paralyzing feeling, would be gone.

"Hey, this is strange," Mitch said, interrupting Joe's thoughts. "His tongue is gone."

Air exploded from Joe's chest. His hands recoiled from Waldemeir's face.

"Peculiar," Mitch observed, his attention on Davis. "You have a penlight, Borje? Here, let me have a better look."

Borje brought a small flashlight to Caulley. He took it with a wet hand and aimed it in the open mouth. "This has got to be the strangest thing I have ever seen," he exclaimed, with Borje peering over his shoulder. "Joe, come here, you've got to see this. The tongue is shorn completely out of the mouth."

Caulley's head bobbed for better angles, the tiny beam dancing in his hand. "Hey, Joe, come here," he insisted impatiently.

Owanish did not move. He stood tight-lipped by the other table, his eyes fixed on the wall beyond Caulley.

Mitch looked up, annoyed. "I want you to see this, Joe," he said. "I wonder if the bear could have done it."

"No, it could not have been a bear," Owanish said without emotion. "The tissue is cut too cleanly."

Caulley looked up in astonishment. "You're right. It is."

"It could only have been sliced out with a blade," Joe continued. "A blade held by human hands."

Caulley slowly straightened his back. The vacant stare on his friend's face chilled him more than his words. "How would you know?" he said at last.

Joe did not reply. His expression did not change. Inside, he felt strangely calm. The anxiety was gone. The weight of his people's fears unburdened him. He was alone with his own.

"What about your guy?" Caulley asked.

"He'll be the same," Owanish answered, looking at Caulley for the first time. "His tongue is cut out too."

Caulley breathed easier. "There was no hemorrhaging. It was cut out after he died." Joe said nothing. "You'd better call the sheriff," Caulley suggested.

"Yes, I will," Joe said, snapping off his rubber gloves. He turned and walked by the phone on the wall and through the swinging door. Shawonabe has returned, he thought. The bear-walk is with us.

17

Michelson chewed the end of a ball-point pen while studying a case from the Michigan Court of Appeals *Reports*. A yellow pad of paper, half-covered with nearly illegible scribblings, lay on a square leather mat in front of him. His eyes were moving across the page, but he was not absorbing the content. Rocking forward, he dropped the book disgustedly on his desk. He turned back a page and started the case again.

His eyes strayed from the book to a clock on the wall. The morning was half over, he realized, and he had accomplished very little. The oral arguments on the preliminary injunction at Crooked Tree State Forest were scheduled for tomorrow in Bay City, but all he seemed to be able to think about was that "bear posse" running wild in his backyard. He knew he would not be able to concentrate until he talked to the sheriff.

Making up his mind, Axel stood quickly and piled several open case reports on top of each other. Grace looked up from her typewriter as he hurried in with the stack of books.

"Is Larry back there still?" Michelson asked, indicating the room at the end of the hall.

"Yes, he should be. If you sneak up on him, you can catch him before he sees all those books."

"I'll do that." Axel smiled as he walked past her desk.

Larry would rather be working on the injunction anyway, Axel rationalized.

Larry's feet were on the table and his mouth stretched in a wide-open yawn when Axel walked in.

"You must have stayed at the bar late last night," Axel said.

"Are you kidding? If I had, I'd be in jail this morning."

"A-and-B?"

"No, murder."

"I know what you mean. They were pretty crazy." Axel laughed. "Listen, would you mind reading these cases for me and briefing them?"

"No, I don't mind. What about the lease, though?" Larry asked, nodding toward the desk.

"That'll just have to wait. Tomorrow, I mean Thursday."

"Okay. Oh, by the way, would you mind if my grandfather drove down with us tomorrow?" Larry asked.

"Not at all. Do you have relatives in Bay City?"

"No, but Grandfather has an old friend down there, used to work with him at the railroad. I think you know his nephew, Moozganse."

"Sure I do. And if his uncle is anything like him, I wouldn't mind meeting him myself."

"He's even better."

"Good. It should be an interesting trip."

"I hope it's not too interesting," Larry said.

Axel smiled. "I'll be in my office for a while, and then I'm going to call on the sheriff."

Axel left Larry with the books and retreated down the hall. As he passed his secretary's desk, he said, "Grace, see if you can reach Sheriff Snyder for me, please."

Grace nodded and swiveled her chair to her phone. After a minute she said, "He's not in now, Axel. They said he was investigating a breaking-and-entering last night."

"A breaking-and-entering?" Axel repeated.

"That's what they said."

"Okay. Thanks, Grace." Axel replaced the receiver slowly. A breaking-and-entering. He turned the words over in his mind. That did not happen very often in Wabanakisi. Occasionally summer cottages were broken into, but Snyder would never bother to check those out himself. Axel knew well how the sheriff ran his office. People with summer cottages don't vote.

His phone buzzed again. "Dr. Routier is on the line," Grace said. "Can you talk to him now?"

"Sure. Put him on," Axel said.

Grace switched off, and Dr. Routier clicked on. "Hello," the veterinarian said.

"Hi, Doctor. How are you today?"

"I'm fine, Axel. But I was a little worried about Janis."

"Janis? Why?" Axel tensed.

"She hasn't been herself, it seems, the last two days. She's never seemed to have problems with the kennel before, but now she . . ." Routier stopped, not really sure how to phrase it.

"She what?" Axel prodded anxiously.

"She, I'm not sure what. It's hard to describe. It's either she doesn't care about the dogs or . . . I know this sounds odd, but it's like she's afraid to go in the back. Like she's scared of the dogs."

Axel did not know what to say. What Dr. Routier said seemed incredible. The kennel was always more than a business to Janis. She loved the dogs. "Can I talk to her?" Axel said at last. "Is she next door?"

"No, she's not here. That's why I called. When she came in this morning, she just sat in the front for the longest time. Leslie had to practically order her into the back to help give them their medicine."

"Order her? Why wouldn't she want to?"

"I don't know, Axel. And then the strangest thing happened. When she finally did go in the back, the dogs at first became quiet and cowered in their pens. Then a few started to bark, a snapping, vicious growl. In a few seconds all the dogs were scratching at their cages, snarling and barking. I came running over right away, and as I was coming through the door, Janis almost knocked me down. She went tearing out of the building. I yelled, but she wouldn't answer. She looked terrified."

"Where'd she go?"

"I don't know. She jumped in her car and took off. I was hoping you might have heard from her by now."

"No, I haven't. How long ago was this?" Axel asked.

"No more than twenty-five minutes ago. I would have called sooner, but Leslie was kind of shaken up. But the strangest thing was the dogs. As soon as Janis left, they quieted down. I have never seen anything like that before."

Axel was silent for a moment. He did not know what to think.

"Leslie's okay now," Dr. Routier continued. "It's a lot of work for her, but she'll be able to handle things around here for a while." Dr. Routier paused, waiting for Axel to reply.

"I appreciate that, Doctor. I'll try to get hold of Janis right away and find out what's going on."

"Good. You know, Leslie doesn't mind, and it's okay by me. I was just concerned about Janis."

"Sure, I understand." Axel did understand. Dr. Routier thought it was unfair for the young girl to have to run Janis' business, and Axel agreed. "Janis will be okay. She's just been a little upset lately."

"I don't blame her, what with the bears and all," Dr. Routier said.

"Yeah. The killings have everybody upset," Axel said.

"Not that. The fur, I mean."

"Fur?" Axel said questioningly.

"Yeah. The bear fur."

Axel could almost see Routier's puzzled expression. "I don't understand."

"Didn't she tell you yesterday?"

"No. I mean, I don't think so. Tell me what?"

"The long hair found on the collie and the Doberman was from a black bear."

"What?" Axel shouted.

His voice low and distinct, Routier said, "The dogs killed in your backyard were killed by a black bear."

"That's impossible," Axel said. "They were in the garage. Somebody had to open the door to get at them."

"I don't know how it happened, Axel. All I know is that bear fur was on those dogs, and they were killed by that bear."

Axel felt dizzy. The words "bear" and "backyard" seemed to swim in a circle in his head. It shook him more than the news of the bear attacks on people. This was a direct danger to himself and his wife. It was not a remote tragedy to others. He thanked Dr. Routier for calling and hung up the phone.

He sat motionless, almost dumbfounded, for many minutes. He was used to dealing with tough problems all the time. But they were problems of reason. A logical approach would always result in a rational answer. But bear attacks, bears roaming in his backyard killing dogs—it seemed the absence of reason. But there *must* be a reasonable explanation.

Axel sat straight in his chair with his right hand flat to his face, his forefinger across his upper lip and his thumb extending to his eye. He glanced at the clock on the wall. She might be home by now, he thought. He picked up the receiver, the plastic handle still warm, and dialed his home number. There was no answer.

He stood and paced to the window, watching as cars lazily rolled along the storefronts. A black-and-white Chevy with a six-pointed star on the door cruised by. He recognized Luke Snyder's familiar profile in the driver's seat.

Axel watched as the sheriff continued toward the City-County Building. Now more than ever he wanted to talk to Snyder. He had to stop Dirk. When he heard bears were near the Michelsons' house, it would be one of the first areas his posse would hunt. Axel turned and hurried out of his office.

For a Tuesday the sidewalk seemed crowded with pedestrians. Axel wondered if they were as upset at the bear attacks as he was. He looked from face to face as he walked toward the City-County Building. He looked for a darting eye, a twitching lip, an anxious expression. But there was none. He did not detect any tenseness. People smiled and laughed and looked like they always did. Axel did not know if that was good or bad. It might not hurt to show a little fear.

The air conditioner immediately chilled Axel when he walked through the front door. Snyder's office was a large open room with several gray steel desks aligned equidistant from each other. Axel stepped into a reception area, cordoned off from the rest of the room by a chest-high counter. The sheriff was seated on the edge of a desk talking to someone Axel did not recognize. Deputy Shank listened.

Luke Snyder looked up as the air-compression stop wheezed the door shut. "Hello, Counselor," he said. Despite being cross-examined in the witness chair many times by Axel, he still felt warmly toward him. Michelson always treated witnesses with respect.

"Hi Sheriff. I hear business is picking up."

"You mean the B-and-E? I'll say! But that's not the half of it."

"Is that right? Is it privileged information?"

"No, not at all. I'm sure the whole county and probably the state will hear about it real fast. Come on through," Snyder said, nodding toward the upraised counter section.

Axel was intrigued. As he stepped through the partition in the counter, he said, "What's so important about a B-and-E in Wabanakisi that could interest the whole state?"

"It was the funeral home, for starters," Luke said.

"Somebody broke into the funeral home?" Axel said incredulously. "What on earth for?"

"A tongue."

"What?"

"The girl who was killed on the Big Two Hearted had her tongue removed. It was cut cleanly out of her mouth."

"Holy shit!"

"And when I got back here, I got a call from a pathologist friend of Owanish's who was helping out with autopsies at the morgue. He said both Davis and the camper had their tongues sliced out, too."

"Could the bears have done that?" Axel asked.

"Nope. The flesh was severed cleanly. If you saw it, you'd know what I mean."

Something from last night flashed through Axel's head. He shook the thought from his mind as he would a centipede scampering across his arm. "I don't know if it's connected, but I have something else to report."

"What's that?" the sheriff said.

Axel nodded to the unfamiliar face. "Am I interrupting anything?"

"That's okay," the man said. "If it's something to do with the bears, I'd be interested too."

"Axel, this is John Orson," Snyder introduced. "He's a professor from Michigan State University. An expert on bears, I understand."

"Excellent," Axel said, shaking the professor's hand. "I hope you bring some sanity to this whole business."

"I'll try," Orson said. "My first job is to catch the bear or bears that did the killing."

"You don't know how glad I am to hear that," Axel said. "That's why I stopped by. Several men were at the bar last night talking about forming a 'bear posse,' egged on by that big guy, Dirk."

"Yeah, I heard about that," Snyder said. "I don't think there will be any problem, and I don't think there will by any 'bear posse.' Those guys all slept it off by this morning, I'm sure."

"Just the same," Axel persisted, "I'd appreciate it if you would talk to Dirk and tell him to cool down."

"Dirk Vanderlee is more a big mouth than anything. As long as there's no one to follow him, he's harmless. But I'll have a chat with him, Axel."

"Good. I was afraid they would be hunting out by my place."

"I don't blame you," Snyder said. "But I don't think you have anything to worry about. The attacks weren't too close to you."

"The attacks on the people, maybe. But I just found out the dogs that were torn up out back were killed by bears."

"Really!" Snyder exclaimed.

"Yes. They found black bear fur all over them."

"That's incredible," Orson said. "Where do you live?"

"My wife and I live by ourselves, out in the woods, by the edge of the state-forest land," Axel said.

"And bears came onto your land after some dogs?"

"I don't know how they got them. They were left in the garage, and when we got home I found them in the woods just behind our house, dead."

Orson's brow furrowed in thought as he stroked his graying goatee.

"Do you mind if I come out to your place and have a look around?" he asked.

"Of course not. When do you want to go? Right now?"

"No, I'm going to check out the other sites first. How about this evening?"

"Fine. We'll be home," Axel said, "if you think there's no danger of us staying out there."

"It should be all right," Orson said. "Just be careful about going outside, because if you encounter one away from shelter and it decides to go after you, there's not much you could do. No way could you outrun it."

"What if I got up a tree?"

"A black bear can climb a tree faster than a man can run the same distance on the ground."

"That's hard to believe," Snyder said.

"It is, unless you've studied their anatomy. Black bears have a muscle attached to their shoulders that exerts a force directly opposite to the thrust of normal forward movement. It was quite a scientific curiosity until studies showed the muscle was perfect for the thrust needed in climbing a tree."

Orson slowly became more animated, gesturing with his arms. As Axel listened to him talk about his plans for trapping the bears, he was impressed, relieved at the prospect of this man catching the animals rather than the posse on a hunt. Axel was confident that this man of science, this man of logic, held the answers to the mysteries enveloping Wabanakisi.

18

A narrow stream of water splashed on the romaine lettuce in the silver colander. Axel clicked the bread in the toaster down a second time. He wanted it nice and hard for the croutons. Next to the toaster a small oblong package wrapped in white paper sat on the counter. Axel picked it up and slipped his finger under the edge of the butcher's tape, opening the package like an envelope. He had splurged on the strip steaks, which would be easy for him to cook, figuring Janis would not be in the mood to help with dinner.

As he placed the meat on the broiler, his mind considered how his wife seemed to treat the incident with the dogs earlier in the day. It was odd, he thought. At first when he brought it up she acted like she did not know what he was talking about. But Axel knew her well enough to realize then she did know what he meant. Perhaps she was just trying to block an unpleasant event from her mind. If so, that would explain why she finally dismissed the whole thing by saying it was "no big deal" and walking into the bedroom. Axel hoped that was the end of it, but inwardly he had to admit it was a big deal.

He separated a clove of garlic from a fresh bud, peeled the thin skin, and dropped the clove in a large wooden bowl and reached to a knife rack above the counter. He always used the same knife when preparing the salad, a short paring knife with a hardened blade. He liked how it held an edge. There was an empty slot in the wooden rack. The paring knife was missing. Axel checked the dishwasher. A few breakfast dishes sat in the trays, but no knife.

"Janis?" he said. There was no answer. Axel rinsed his hands under the cold water and walked through the family room toward the bedroom.

Janis stood by her dresser, the top drawer open. She turned as Axel walked in, facing him in a navy-blue skirt. Her nipples dimpled through the smooth fabric of her bra.

"I can't find the paring knife," Axel said from the doorway. "Do you know where it is?"

Janis stared with her eyebrows uplifted for a long second. Turning back to the dresser, she said, "I don't know."

"Are you sure?" Axel persisted. "It's usually in the knife rack, and now it's gone."

Janis slid the dresser drawer closed. It was not quite a slam, but the gesture carried a certain finality with it. "I said I don't know," she repeated crisply, disappearing into her walk-in closet. An identical closet, housing Axel's wardrobe, was on the other side of the bathroom door.

Axel decided to drop the subject. He did not want to press it, because he wanted to press something more important. "Janis, when I talked to Dr. Routier this morning he told me about the bear fur on the dogs." The hangers stopped clinking in the closet. "Why didn't you tell me?"

"I must have forgotten," she said as the hangers started rustling again.

"Quit being so goddamned evasive and talk to me," Axel shouted, stalking into her closet.

Janis jumped back and crossed her arms protectively across her chest.

"Don't look so hurt," Axel said angrily. He felt like shaking her by the shoulders, but he moved no closer. "You should have told me."

"I ... I would have," Janis stammered, "but I just forgot."

"It was important. You shouldn't have." Axel glared at his wife. "A bear expert is coming out tonight. He wants to have a look around."

It was Janis' turn to show anger. "What?" she screamed.

"A professor from Michigan State," Axel said defiantly. "He came up to trap the bears that did the killing."

"Why didn't you ask me before inviting him out here?"

"What for? If anything, it will make it safer for us."

"Safer? You call a bunch of strangers stomping around safer?"

"Not a bunch, just one." Axel was becoming defensive.

"You think he'll be the end of it? Last night you were worried about a bunch of men hunting for bears out back. Today you turn around and show them the way."

"This is different. He's a scientist, not a vigilante. Something has to be done about the bears."

Janis turned her back to Axel and stared at the closet wall. Neither moved for at least a minute. Axel's attention was gradually diverted. "Christ, what's that smell?"

Janis turned quickly and glanced at a deerskin handbag hanging from a peg on the wall.

"What's in that thing?" He grimaced.

"Nothing!" Janis said loudly as she yanked the bag off the peg. Brushing past Axel, the purse swinging by its straps in her hand, she rushed into the bathroom. The door slammed, and Axel heard the bolt thud.

He stood staring at the bathroom door for several minutes, unable to think and even less able to speak. It was just as quiet on the other side of the door. Eventually he turned and went back to the kitchen. He selected another knife and resumed fixing the salad.

It had been a silent dinner. Axel had barely tasted the food. The dishes remained unrinsed, stacked in the kitchen sink. The nasal whine of the TV weatherman distracted Axel from the *Detroit News*. He closed the sports section and peered around the edge of the paper. Janis sat at the far end of the couch, her legs curled up beside her, staring unblinking at the bluish glow of the television set.

Axel tilted an ear toward the front of the house, listening as an automobile came to a halt in the driveway. When Janis gave no sign that the sounds registered with her, Axel folded the paper, pushed himself up from the soft couch, and walked to the front door. The sheriff's car was on the pavement in front of the garage, with a trailer hitched to the rear.

Axel stepped outside as Luke Snyder and John Orson slammed shut the front doors of the police car.

"I hope we're not disturbing your dinner hour," said Orson.

"Not at all. We've already eaten," Axel said as he walked toward the trailer. A section of corrugated steel pipe was affixed sideways at the front third of the trailer. "Have you guys been planting sewers or hunting bear?"

"A little of both," Snyder said, massaging his palm across the back of his neck.

"This is one of our traps," Orson said as he slapped the large tube. A deep metallic boom reverberated off the trees.

"I never expected anything like that," Axel said. "I thought 'traps' were those little round things with spikes that snapped shut when stepped on."

"Those are different kinds of traps. I've seen what they can do to an animal's leg, so I stay away from them."

Axel moved closer to inspect the steel culvert. "It must be eight feet. Why so long?"

"To make sure the bear has to go all the way inside to get the bait. If it's too short, it might just be able to reach in and grab the food and run. Or worse, the drop door could hit him in the back and crack his spine."

Axel examined the thick weighted steel of the drop door. "It must be awfully heavy," he observed.

"It has to be," Orson said. "Pound for pound, the black bear is the strongest animal alive."

"Is that right?"

"Yep. Once in the fifties a black bear and an African lion were being trained together in Florida for an act in the circus. The lion attacked the bear, and with one swipe of its paw the black bear knocked it clear across the cage, breaking its neck."

"And you should have seen that canoe," Snyder added. "It was battered like an aluminum cake pan."

Axel shuddered. He pictured a trapped bear trying to work its claws under the drop door. As he thought, something began to crystallize in his head. The garage!

He turned from the two men and raced to the house. "What is it?" Snyder yelled as he and Orson ran up behind him.

"I just assumed somebody pried the door up and the dogs got out." Axel's voice trailed off, his thought unfinished.

Orson crouched next to Axel. He examined the dent in the metal door, rubbing his fingers along the vertical scratches.

Grim-faced, he turned to Axel. "It could have happened. These marks could easily have been left by a bear's claws. But damn," he exclaimed, "I can't imagine a bear breaking into a building like that. Especially with dogs there. You'd expect their barking would scare it off," he said, almost as a question. Orson stood slowly. "Do you keep garbage in there?"

"No, it's out back." Axel twisted the handle in the middle of the garage door and raised it. "Come on in, look around."

Orson glanced around the garage. Tools, garden implements, some seeds. A chain saw, jumper cables, a garden hose hanging on the wall. Nothing that would attract a bear. "If a bear did come in here after those dogs, I can't explain it."

Axel nodded. He had hoped for an explanation, something to ease his mind. "Come on, I'll show you where I found the dogs."

They stepped through the side door leading into the kitchen. The television was still on, but the couch was vacant. Axel turned the television off before leading the men to the backyard through the sliding glass door.

"Did you learn anything at the other places you checked today?" Axel asked as the heavy glass glided shut easily along aluminum runners.

"Learned enough to see that both areas, where the camper was found in his tent and the lawyer in the woods, were heavily visited by a bear or bears. We left a trap at each site."

"And you saved one for my place?"

"Yes. Lucky thing I had one more. I made them for a field study several years ago."

"I'll sleep better knowing there's a trap out here, but I doubt you'll catch anything. The bear the other day must have been a freak thing. I haven't seen one here since we moved in."

At the far edge of Janis' garden Orson stopped suddenly and peered at the ground. In the soft soil a foot had left its impression. The print was wider than it was long, but nonetheless it resembled a human print. Clearly distinguishable were five toes and the ball of the foot. The heel had not touched the ground.

"Bear?" Axel asked.

"Yes. His front left paw."

"Can you tell how big it was?"

"Pretty big. Four hundred pounds, maybe. I've seen larger

prints, but not in Michigan." Orson straightened and looked into the woods. There appeared to be no well-beaten paths. "Let's continue," he said.

Axel nodded and led the way. "So what do you think, John? What has gotten into the bears around here?"

"Normally, I would say that a black bear that attacked a human was either sick, starved, or felt threatened. But there's no shortage of food this summer, and there's no way that camper enclosed in his tent could have posed a threat to his attacker. So that would mean the bears were probably sick. And that's a problem for me. With the sites so far apart, almost certainly three different bears were involved, and it's one hell of a coincidence that three bears became mentally un-tracked at the same time."

"If you're after only a few bears out of perhaps many that live in Crooked Tree, how will you be sure the one in the trap is one of the killers?"

"I won't. But I'll have a pretty good idea as long as the trap is in the killer's territory. Bears for the most part are loners, sticking to their own territory. They mark it with urine or by scratching trees or some-how leaving their scent. There's probably some overlap, but they pretty much obey scent markings, especially when food's plentiful. During its entire life a black bear probably doesn't stray more than fifteen miles from where it was born.

"And bears are creatures of habit. They visit the same spots looking for their favorite food all the time. So the chances are good that the killer bear at some point will visit the same area of the attack. We won't be certain the one we catch is a killer, but it's almost certain that any bear caught in a trap has been at that same spot many times before."

Underfoot, last autumn's leaves crinkled noisily. The midsummer heat was rapidly radiating into the air, the trees effectively blocking the sinking sun, now low on the horizon. The men tramped purpose-fully through the underbrush, Axel searching for where he found the dogs and Orson eyeing the ground for traces of bear activity.

Ahead, Axel saw a tangle of wilted ferns still hanging from the branch where he had lodged them. "Right over here is where I found one of the dogs," Axel said, pointing toward the tree. He approached the site cautiously, as if expecting another gruesome discovery.

"It'll be a bitch wheeling that trap all the way out here," Snyder said, looking back over the path they had just walked.

"Maybe we won't have to. Let me look around for awhile." Orson circled the tree. A small patch of yellow fur marked the spot where the collie had been.

Axel noticed the sheriff looking anxiously into the woods. He was feeling the same apprehension, Axel thought. Turning away from Snyder, Axel looked where Orson looked, trying to see what clues the expert saw. Apparently there were none.

"Shouldn't we be heading back now?" Snyder said. "It's getting dark fast, and didn't you say bears like to feed about dusk?"

"Actually, they'll eat anytime. But you're right, they are night creatures." Orson glanced at his watch and then the sky. "We've still got a good hour of daylight. There's no rush."

"It might be better in the morning, though," Snyder persisted.

"Yeah, but we want to catch the bear tonight."

Axel agreed with that. If the bear was coming back around his house, he would prefer the trap set as soon as possible. He glanced back through the trees toward his house. Momentarily he felt reassured. Then he thought of Janis and a different worry surfaced. He wondered if he should suggest she see a doctor. There was a line between feeling the effects of short-term pressures and an actual mental problem requiring a psychiatrist's help. She was close to that line, he thought.

Axel noticed Orson crouched in a small depression in the ground studying a patch of moist black soil. "What is it?" he asked.

"More bear tracks," Orson said without looking up. "And human footprints as well, just like there were in the swamp where the lawyer's body was found."

Axel hurried to where Orson crouched. He peered over his shoulder, his heart quickening. On the ground he saw the distinct outline of a bare human foot.

"I just don't understand," Orson said, his words almost trembling with uncertainty.

"Maybe the guy who cut out the tongues?" Snyder offered.

"When a bear retraces a path, it will follow its own footprints. I don't know why they do, but they do. And that's what I don't understand."

"What's that?" Snyder asked.

Axel saw what Orson saw, and he understood it even less.

"The human prints follow the identical path of the bear's, just like at the swamp. Each one is in the middle of the paw print." Orson stood slowly and looked from one man to the other. "It's almost as if the person who ran along here had the instincts of a black bear."

Suddenly Axel felt very alone, as if there was nowhere to turn. He could not shake the feeling, even as they worked against the darkness to set the third trap.

19

The village was quiet. No automobile engines disturbed the still air. In the distance the big lake pounded ceaselessly on the beach. The rhythmic slap of the waves on the sand suggested the beating of the drums, their echo resounding now only in dreams. All that remained from the night before was a wispy plume of smoke rising slowly from the hill.

"Are you ready, Grandfather? He should be here anytime."

"Hurry, hurry, hurry. Don't you know you shouldn't hurry an old man?"

"Old, maybe. But slow, never. You must be ready by now."

"Just about. Another five minutes."

Larry looked out the front window. Axel's car was not yet in sight. "Isn't Leon Moozganse the man you used to tell me about as a child? The one whose father was a shaman, a Midewiwin?"

The splashing of the water stopped as Charley Wolf pulled his hands from the sink. He stepped deliberately into the living room. Eyeing his grandson with a narrowed gaze, he said, "Yes, he is. How did you happen to remember?"

"It seems to fit. Now I know why you wanted to make the trip with us."

"You're a smart boy. I was hoping you would understand."

"I understand *you*," Larry said, turning to face his grandfather. "I don't understand the Midewiwin."

"You're not alone, Gusan. You saw the lack of knowledge last night up on the hill. We need Moozganse. I only hope he has not forgotten, like so many others."

A car door slammed out front. Wordlessly, Charley Wolf returned to the bathroom and hurried to get ready. Axel stretched after he got out of the Yukon. As he moved stiffly up the walkway, he noticed a thin cloud of smoke intermingling with the branches of Crooked Tree. His eyes followed the trail of smoke to the ground below the tree. That's odd, he thought. Usually Ottawa festivals were open to all and publicized well in advance.

Larry saw his employer studying the dead fire through the window. He was certainly not ashamed of his people's legends, but just the same, he did not feel like explaining last night's gathering to Axel now.

"Were you able to decipher my notes on those cases?" Larry said through the open door.

Axel looked down from the hill, momentarily startled. "Oh, why, yes. Yes, I did. If I can read my own handwriting, I can read anybody's."

Larry laughed. "I'd offer you some breakfast, but I think we should be going."

"I agree. Besides, I had some orange juice and toast at home."

"I've got a thermos of coffee. We can bring that along."

Larry's grandfather appeared behind him. "I'm set. Let's go."

"Sorry we couldn't drive down to your place," Larry apologized again. He had called Axel the night before and told him he had to leave his car at the service station.

"That's all right," Axel said.

Larry waited until they reached County Road 621 before pouring the coffee. The county-financed highway was much smoother than the weathered asphalt leading into Ottawa Village. He filled the Styrofoam cups only about halfway and passed one to his grandfather in the backseat and handed another to Axel. A third balanced precariously between his legs while he closed the thermos.

"How is Janis today?" Charley Wolf asked.

"She was still in bed when I left, but she seemed okay. Did Larry tell you what happened yesterday at the kennel?"

"Yes, it must have been frightening," the old man said. "I wonder what got into the dogs."

"I don't know. But animals are smart. They can sense when

someone is not acting normally. I must have been awake half the night thinking about it, and the most reasonable explanation I can come up with is that the dogs at the kennel sensed something in Janis. And the crazy thing is, she has been acting different lately."

"What do you mean?" Larry asked with concern.

Axel took a long sip of coffee. Although he had known Charley Wolf for some time, they had never developed a close personal relationship. Axel wondered briefly about the wisdom of broaching such an intimate topic in his company, but he could not help it. He desperately needed to talk to someone about Janis.

"I don't know if anything's wrong with her. Come to think of it, I really can't blame her for acting strange, with all the crazy things going on. Last night, for example, they found naked human footprints right behind our house that matched prints found around Davis' corpse. They think it's the guy who managed to find the bear victims and cut their tongues out."

"Footprints?" Charley Wolf said. "What did they look like?"

"They were small, and the strange thing was, they followed the tracks of a bear almost step for step."

Charley Wolf leaned forward, resting his forearms on the front seat. He nudged Larry softly. His grandson refused to turn around. "The bear tracks were behind your house?" Charley Wolf asked.

"Yes. And another thing. You know the dogs that were killed out there the other day?"

"Bears did it?"

"Yes. They found black hair on the dogs and had it analyzed in Lansing. Janis found out Monday it was from a bear, and never told me. If I hadn't heard from Dr. Routier and brought it up with her last night, she probably never would have mentioned it." Axel glanced sideways at Larry. He wanted Larry to say there was nothing unusual in that, she probably did not think it was important, but he said nothing.

"Last night I asked her a simple question about a kitchen knife that was missing, and she almost exploded." Axel continued, "It's not like her to act that way, is it, Larry?"

"No, it's not," Larry replied quietly.

Axel's moist palms rubbed the steering wheel nervously.

Outside, trees flashed by in a green blur. "And then, the strangest thing of all. A peculiar smell was coming from her purse hanging in the closet, and when I mentioned it, Janis grabbed the purse and locked herself in the bathroom."

"What kind of purse?" Charley Wolf asked, his voice tingling with apprehension.

"A handbag, actually. Made from deerskin by one of the Kishigato boys. I bought it for her a few years ago."

"And the smell came from inside the handbag?"

"Sort of. It was a leather moisturizer she had treated it with, she told me later. That explains the smell, of course, but it was how she acted that bothered me."

"I can understand your concern," Larry said, breaking his silence. More to his grandfather than to Axel, he continued, "You're probably right. She's just uptight about the bear killings. Is she taking some time off from the kennel?"

"Yeah. Today at least. I was thinking she might need to see a doctor."

"I doubt it," Larry said reassuringly. "She probably just needs a rest."

"I hope so. Hell, maybe I'm the one that needs a doctor. Saturday night when I got home after the meeting, I imagined there was a wild animal in the bedroom with Janis."

Larry felt the cushion of the back of his seat depress as his grandfather squeezed it tightly.

"Why do you say 'imagined'?" Charley Wolf said.

"I must have," Axel said matter-of-factly. "There couldn't have been anything else in there. She was all alone."

Charley Wolf sank slowly back in his seat, his gaze riveted on the back of Axel's head. Larry sat unmoving, afraid to look around, afraid to think, wishing he had not heard. He could almost hear his grandfather's thoughts. It all did seem to fit, he admitted inwardly with a chill. For the rest of the three-hour drive, Axel was silent.

The federal courthouse in Bay City was constructed in the 1930's governmental classic Greek style with a massive façade of yellowish stone blocks. The federal bench was the cream of the judgeships, in terms of both security and prestige in the legal profession. Judge Moss, the district judge in Bay City, held the honor of his position highly. He worked hard at his job, providing all litigants a fair treatment in court. That's why Axel felt confident. He knew Judge Moss would more likely be swayed by human interests than by big business or a need to compromise.

Leon Moozganse's house was only a short distance from downtown, and Charley Wolf insisted on walking from the courthouse. It was just as well, Axel had thought, because the hearing was scheduled for ten a.m. and they had only minutes to spare.

He handed his briefcase to Larry and asked him to take it into the courtroom while he stopped by the judge's office.

"Mr. Michelson." Axel turned to face a conservatively dressed man with hair barely long enough to comb. "Good morning, Mr. Mallory. How are you today?" Axel said pleasantly to the attorney for Sunrise Land and Home Company.

"I was fine until I met my client about an hour ago."

"Oh? Why is that?"

Mallory glanced nervously at a woman with a notepad on her lap sitting on a bench staring in their direction. "Perhaps we should step in here," he said, indicating the courtroom. He held the door for Axel and followed him to a long table where Larry sat.

After being introduced to Axel's law clerk, Mallory said, "I wish I had known earlier. I might have been able to save you the trip down."

"What do you mean?" Axel demanded, expecting Mallory to ask for an adjournment.

"My client wants to stipulate to the preliminary injunction," Mallory said sheepishly.

"What on earth for?"

"They say they are afraid of the expense involved in going through some of the same things twice. They feel since Moss granted the TRO he's likely to grant the preliminary injunction, and they would just as soon wait until the full trial on the permanent injunction. Contrary to what you may think, they don't have endless supplies of money."

"You know one of the criteria for granting a preliminary injunction is that the plaintiff is likely to ultimately succeed."

"I know. I explained that to them, but still they want to do it this way. I'm sure you wouldn't be opposed to the stipulation, and I was hoping we could work something out."

"Like what?"

"Perhaps I could stipulate only to the gravity of the issue and the fact that if we are ultimately ruled against there would be irreversible damage to your interests. I could say something like out of fairness to those concerns we would stipulate to a preliminary injunction, but on the understanding that we are in no way admitting who the eventual winner will be. The judge can take it from there."

"Well, conceivably then he could still deny the preliminary injunction, saying he doesn't feel we have shown that we will probably win. I would still have to present extensive arguments on that issue, and we'd be right back where we started. A full-blown hearing."

"I can't imagine the judge denying the injunction on his own after I stipulate ninety percent of the issue away. Besides," Mallory said with a grin, "I already talked to him about it and he said, 'fine.' It makes his job easier, you know."

Axel laughed. "I'm sure it does. Well, in that case, I'm sure we can conclude the hearing in a matter of minutes."

"Good. I'll tell the clerk, and, listen, I'm sorry I didn't find out earlier. I would have let you know."

"Don't mention it. I still would have had to come down to put it on the record," Axel said. He would not have had to work so hard on his arguments, though.

As Mallory left the table to find Judge Moss' court clerk, Axel noticed the woman who had been in the hallway earlier. She had short brown hair, was dressed casually, and still had the notepad on her lap. Axel wondered why Mallory had avoided her.

"Hey, that's great," Larry exclaimed excitedly, barely able to control his courtroom whisper. "We won."

"Yes, we did," Axel said as he considered the woman. "I think."

"That real-estate company must be run by a bunch of jerks. They're not going to save any money on this."

"You didn't buy that bullshit," Axel said.

"Well, yeah," Larry drawled. "Why else would they agree to the preliminary injunction?"

"Maybe because of the lady sitting right over there," Axel said, nodding discreetly toward the woman.

"I don't understand."

"She's a reporter, I bet, and they don't want their proposed development making a lot of noise in the press at the same time the papers are filled with stories about the bear killings. Can you imagine what that would do to their sales? Who would want to buy a house with a bunch of killer bears as neighbors?"

Larry nodded his head slowly with understanding. "And if the arguments for and against developing the wilderness area are not debated in the paper for several months, maybe the bear stories will have blown over and people won't make the connection."

"Exactly. It's a drastic move, but actually very clever. Realistically they have no choice."

The clerk entered through a heavy oak door at the front of the courtroom. He announced the convening of court as Mallory came in the side entrance. Everyone rose as Judge Moss stepped quickly be-hind the bench, his robe billowing behind him. The stipulation was noted for the record, and as Mallory had said, the judge granted the injunction. As quickly as he had entered, Judge Moss hurried back to his chambers. Axel shook his opponent's hand and closed his brief-case, ready to leave. He noticed Mallory hurry from the courtroom, avoiding the reporter by as much distance as he could. Unfortunately, he noted she ignored Mallory as well. Instead, she walked deliberately toward Axel and Larry.

"Now, here's where we publicize our case," Axel whispered to Larry.

"Hello, I'm Sharon Heff from the *Bay City Times*," she said, extending her hand. "Do you have time for a few words?"

"Sure. With the stipulation, I've got all day."

"That's nice. You live in Wabanakisi, don't you?"

"Yes. Actually, just north of it."

"Near Crooked Tree?"

"Yes."

"Great. What about all these bear attacks? How have they affected you?"

Axel looked at her in surprise. "The bear attacks! Aren't you here to cover the injunction?"

"Why, no. I wanted to get some personal reflections on the killings. You know, like what's everyone in the town saying about it?" Axel's expression could not conceal his disappointment. "They're concerned, of course, but most people are confident only a few sick bears are involved," he said, resisting the temptation to scare potential buyers. "A professor from Michigan State—"

"Yes, I know," she interrupted. "What about you? Do you live in the woods?"

"Yes," he admitted reluctantly.

"Has it affected you?"

Axel was uncomfortable. It had, but it was not the type of thing he could talk to a reporter about. "Well, sure," he said. "I'm not going hiking for the time being."

She laughed, feeling somewhat silly. They talked generally for several more minutes and then she thanked them politely for their time and left.

"Did you want to go get my grandfather? He wasn't going to come back until this afternoon."

"No hurry. It's almost eleven now," Axel said, glancing at the large clock set into the marble wall. "Why don't we kill some time and then have lunch."

The two men left the courtroom. Larry was relieved that the Ottawas' rights were upheld and the wilderness preserved, at least for a while, but he savored the victory for only a moment. Then his thoughts wandered to his grandfather and Leon Moozganse of the Midewiwin. Despite the heat, Larry felt his skin trembling. He knew what they were talking about.

The keys pecked a furious refrain as the cursor slid quickly across the screen. Grace typed "Axel Michelson," then, under it, "Counsel for Defendant." Finished, she thought, sighing in relief. She had been working hard lately; too hard. She did not feel sorry for herself. She felt sorry for her daughters. At least they went to school most of the year now and did not have to spend their days at a babysitter's.

Still, Grace thought, she did not have much energy left for them when she got home. They were not getting the attention and affection they deserved and needed. Being without her father, seemed especially harsh on Marcy, the younger daughter. She was shy and withdrawn at times, very much a loner. Lord, Grace wished she could quit her job.

She felt that familiar sting in her nose as her eyes threatened to water. "Oh," she moaned disgustedly. "You're wonderful, Gracie. Feeling sorry for yourself again. That'll really help."

She straightened her back and looked at the monitor. We will go to the lake tomorrow, she thought. It had been perfect weather lately. The kids and I will spend the morning together on the beach. The idea buoyed her. The printer hummed as the last page of the brief fed into the tray. Grace reached for the phone. She hoped Janis was home as she dialed the Michelson number.

Janis answered, "Hello."

"Hello, Janis, this is Grace at the office."

"Yes?"

"I'm glad I caught you at home. I just called to leave a message for Axel. I finished the brief on the Rasmussen case the circuit judge in Mackinaw requested."

"Okay. I'll tell him," Janis said simply.

"And tell him I'll leave it in the top drawer of my desk. I can't come in tomorrow morning, and I just wanted him to know."

"Why not bring it out here?"

"What?"

"Axel told me he wanted it right away. He might not be in tomorrow either," Janis said quickly, the words tumbling from her mouth. "He has to sign it and take it with him up to Mackinaw. It would save him a trip back into town tomorrow."

"But he wasn't going to Mackinaw until next week," Grace said, mystified.

"No. He changed his mind. He's going tomorrow."

"You sure?"

"Positive." But Janis was not positive. Her memory was blurry. He had told her that, hadn't he?

"I suppose I could bring it," Grace said with lingering disbelief. "But he never told me anything about it."

"He would really appreciate it."

"All right." It was a vocal shrug. "I'll leave work early and bring it out this afternoon. You'll be there?"

"Yes, all afternoon. Do you remember how to find us?"

"Yes, I think so."

"I'd better remind you, just to be sure," Janis said, her voice smooth.

"Okay," Grace said, picking up a pencil. "Go ahead."

Janis started to give Grace the directions, the directions from Wabanakisi to their place on the edge of Crooked Tree State Forest, the directions she had given to many people countless times before. She felt dreamy, not really aware of what she was saying. She forgot to whom she was speaking. It was just a voice on the other end of the phone. When she heard the click in her ears, she hung up the receiver. God, she was tired, she thought. But she had to hurry. There was so much to be done.

A short, stout shadow raced along beside the Yukon, the sun only two hours past its zenith. The expressway cut through the flat farmland around Bay City like a fallen birch on the moss-covered forest floor. Long, straight rows of bulbous sugar beets filled the fields. The four men were comfortable in the large vehicle.

"I'm glad you didn't mind giving Leon a ride back with us, Axel," Charley Wolf said.

"No problem at all," Axel replied cordially.

"Seeing me just got him a little homesick, I guess."

"There was more to it than that," Leon Moozganse said.

"My cooking?"

"Hell no! If that was the attraction, I would be heading the other way."

"So maybe I had to coax an old friend a little. It wasn't that hard talking you into paying me a visit."

"You're right. It will be nice to be back, if only for a while."

"How long have you lived in Bay City?" Axel inquired.

"Thirty years. I was transferred by the railroad and after I retired I was too old to move."

"Too old to move," Charley Wolf snorted. "That's a lot of hogwash. I see you're finally living up to your name."

Moozganse and Larry laughed, both glancing at Charley Wolf.

After a moment, Axel said, "Well, what does 'Moozganse' mean?"

"Go on tell him," Charley Wolf goaded. Moozganse only chuckled. "Since you won't, I will. It means 'moose's asshole.'"

Axel glanced over his shoulder in surprise. A grin slowly appeared on his face. "I thought . . ."

"Go on, tell him the rest," Moozganse ordered.

Charley Wolf guffawed. "All right, all right . . ."

"You must be pulling my leg," Axel said. "I always heard names were given to provide an ideal for the child to ascribe to."

"That's right," Charley Wolf said. "And if you ever saw a moose in the wild you'd understand why being called a moose's asshole was really something to live up to. You see, the moose has a habit of rubbing its tail across its rectum and that causes the skin around its asshole to be especially tough. Because of that it was one of the most sought after pieces of the moose's hide."

"All the best moccasins were made from the moose's asshole," Moozganse added.

Axel glanced in the rearview mirror for a closer look at Leon Moozganse. He was an old man. His face was creased and his thick hair bleached white, but from what Larry had told him earlier, he knew Moozganse was actually younger than Charley Wolf.

"Are you coming up for the festivals?" Axel asked.

Moozganse glared quickly at Charley Wolf, his frown adding more wrinkles to his face. Charley Wolf shook his head as if to say: I don't know. Larry did not speak. He wondered how they would handle it.

After a long pause, Charley Wolf assembled his thoughts. "There aren't any scheduled that I know of," he said.

"Wasn't there one last night, up on the hill? I saw the smoke from the bonfire this morning."

"Oh, that was nothing formal. Spur-of-the-moment thing, I guess. It was such a nice evening."

Larry glanced at Axel out of the corner of his eye, aware that Axel understood the religious significance of Crooked Tree. Axel knew that the Ottawas would never disrespect their grandfathers by having a lighthearted campfire under its arching branches. Larry wanted to explain, but he could not find the words. He felt if he spoke it would be showing disrespect for his grandfather. But Axel could see through his grandfather's words. And besides, his wife was descended from the chiefs. He had a right to know what they believed. Even though it was only a legend, he still had a right to know.

"There was a . . . meeting of the village up there last night." Larry announced at last. "Like Grandfather said, it was impromptu. It was brought on by the bear attacks."

"Why would the bear attacks prompt a meeting?" Axel asked.

Charley Wolf and Leon Moozganse remained quiet. Larry looked over the backseat from face to face. Their impassiveness told him to be silent. Turning back to Axel, he said, "Because some of the Ottawas believe they know why the bears are attacking."

"And why is that?"

"The bearwalk. A man's soul leaves his body and takes over the body of an animal. Inhabiting the body of the beast, he can use it for what he wants. As an owl he could fly, a fish he could swim."

"And as a bear he could kill," Axel said.

"Right. It's called the bearwalk because the bear was the most respected of all the animals. It looks so much like man, especially when it walks upright, that the Ottawas consider it their cousin. To inhabit the body of a bear is like the highest sacrament of the art."

"So some Ottawas think that's what's happening now? Somebody is inhabiting the bodies of bears and killing people?"

"Legend says it happened long ago. An Indian by the name of Shawonabe, painted later in legend as the personification of evil, inhabited bears and wiped out an entire tribe, the Mush Qua Tah."

"I've heard of them."

"They were a small tribe that lived in the area of Wabanakisi before the Ottawas came. Their name means 'underground people,' so called because they lived in holes covered by dirt. Every man, woman, and child was killed shortly after we arrived."

"Yes, because the Ottawas conquered them in battle."

"That's speculation. Actually, history cannot explain for certain why or how the Mush Qua Tah were wiped off the face of the earth. To blame it on the Ottawas ignores the friendly history of both tribes and the fact they did live side by side for a while. It seems strange they would all of a sudden fight. And there's no record of serious losses or hardships to the Ottawas at that time. Something as noteworthy as a total victory would certainly be commemorated in song or legend. But there is no such record. Instead, legend says Shawonabe wiped them out. He was a powerful shaman who was accomplished in the art of the bearwalk."

"That's interesting," Axel noted, genuinely intrigued. "But bears have killed before. It doesn't happen often, but bears do kill people. What makes them think this time it's Shawonabe?"

"Because of the tongues," Larry answered.

"What do you mean?"

Charley Wolf interrupted, no longer reluctant to talk. "If someone kills in the body of a bear, he must return and cut the tongue out and save it for protection. Otherwise, the spirit of the person killed will torment his soul. It is said that when Shawonabe died, they found many, many tongues of his victims in his medicine pouch."

"You know, if it weren't so preposterous, I might believe it. It certainly would explain things. But I'm curious—does anyone believe in the bearwalk?"

The silence was chilling. Axel looked at Larry, his eyes questioning.

"Many do," Larry said. "My grandfather and Leon Moozganse do."

Axel looked over his shoulder at the old men in the backseat. Their blank expressions said nothing. Axel's shouted his incredulity.

"That's why Mishoo talked Leon Moozganse into coming up," Larry continued. "His father was a Midewiwin. You would call that a shaman or medicine man, a combination religious leader, teacher, and physician for the tribe."

"There's not much I can do," Moozganse said almost apologetically. "There's so much I don't know and so much I can't remember."

Axel stared intently at the road, trying to mask his feelings. He did not think it was possible for modern people to believe in such things. But he had to be careful. He should not offend Mr. Wolf or Moozganse. They were fine men, perhaps the last of their kind.

"Where is Shawonabe?" Axel asked. "What happened to him?"

"He died two hundred years ago," Charley Wolf replied. "A prison was built for his soul, and he was buried far from the village, far from the lake, far into the wilderness."

"So how could you expect him to be responsible? How could he be the one who retrieves the tongues?"

"He couldn't," Leon Moozganse said.

"Then who?"

"A servant," Moozganse said. "He would need a servant to do it for him."

"But who?" Axel persisted.

Moozganse looked at Charley Wolf. He had just met this man, his eyes said. Charley Wolf leaned forward. "Someone who was available, nearby," he said. "Someone whose small feet would fit the footprints found in the mud, who walked in the feet of the bear."

Moozganse leaned forward, resting his arms on the front seat next to Charley Wolf's. He spoke, his voice a haunting whisper. "Someone who was of his blood, whose eyes glowed with fire at night."

"Someone who was unaware of what was happening," Charley Wolf continued, almost chanting. "Someone who has not been acting like herself. Someone who had a pouch, a *deerskin* pouch to save the tongues."

The barrage of voices ceased. Axel clung to the steering wheel, refusing to hear, refusing to admit comprehension.

"They mean Janis," Larry said quietly. He was glad it was finally out in the open.

Axel looked hotly at Larry. "You think that?" he spat.

"No. I don't believe in the bearwalk." Larry's voice remained calm, barely audible.

Glancing over his shoulder at Charley Wolf and Leon Moozganse, Axel said, "You're crazy! I should never have said those things about Janis on the way down. You've twisted them to fit your own demented little beliefs." Axel had rarely been so angry. Legends are one thing, he thought, but accusing his wife of such gruesome acts was too morbid for words. He was infuriated.

"Janis is upset, emotionally upset. It happens to a lot of people. But spreading shit like that won't help. It'll just make it worse for her. All you have convinced me of is one thing. A psycho Indian is cutting the tongues out of those poor people."

Axel's words rang in everyone's ears. The inside of the car was deathly still. The air rushed through the cracks in the windows, the unnoticed noise now almost deafening. Perhaps Grandfather was right, Larry considered. Perhaps the white man should not have been told. That's absurd, his reason cried loudly. The legends were nothing but stories. They should not hurt people. He understood how Axel felt. But somehow, he felt hurt himself.

Axel glanced at his watch. It was still early, and they were at West Branch already. He wished he were home, with his wife. But he would be, sooner than she expected. Because of the stipulation, he thought, she would be pleasantly surprised when he arrived home so early.

20

The small mammal crept along the broad branch, its steely eyes focused on its prey. The subtropical sun baked the still, humid air under the Siberian forest. The miacid was oblivious of the wilting heat. Its attention was on the paramyid.

Its claws felt the rough bark with uncanny adeptness, gripping it as steadily as if it were the flat ground. Its small bones were guided by thick muscles built for the strength necessary in climbing and killing. Despite being well adapted to its environment, the miacid would become extinct during the Oligocene Period. It would vanish, not because it was unsuccessful in the fight to survive, but because it survived too well. Its adaptive characteristics would evolve as the beast grew larger and more varied.

The paramyid stopped chewing on the leaf. It looked anxiously around, still gripping its meal in its tiny paws. The miacid moved swiftly now, carrying its fifty pounds easily. Its jaws were lax. The paramyid twitched its head nervously, sensing danger. From below it saw its stalker. The paramyid released its food and scampered up the tree, the pounding and scratching just below crashing in its ears. It was fast, but it was not speed that failed the paramyid. Intent on gorging itself, it had allowed the miacid to approach too close.

Mercifully, it was over in a few seconds. The miacid pounced on the paramyid and closed its jaws around the back of its neck. Then it pranced down the branch with the cocky strut of a successful hunter, the paramyid dangling from its jaws. It settled itself comfortably in a crook in the tree, and holding the paramyid in its paws, sank its teeth into the soft flesh. The teeth were sharp and pointed, well adapted for tearing and cutting meat.

Through the eons, the teeth would change as the animal did. They evolved into the tools of the true omnivore, with incisors for tearing and molars for grinding. The same incisors that could tear into flesh could delicately pick blueberries off a bush, leaving the twigs undisturbed.

Across the Bering Strait the miacid's descendants migrated to a barren land, newly freed from a blanket of ice. The family *Ursidae*, genus *Ursus*, populated almost every corner of North America. *Ursus americanus* was the most numerous species, covering the widest range of climate of any mammal except man.

Thirty million years after its ancestors hunted in trees, the *Ursus americanus*, the black bear, clung to the trunk of the hemlock, its forearms stretched out and its bulky body sagging casually. Its nonretracting claws dug deeply into the soft wood. If the bear had to, the strength in its limbs could hold its four hundred pounds suspended for several hours. But it would not have to this time.

The odor of decaying venison had made it stray from the territory. The new area had seemed familiar, though, as if it had strayed there before. Because of the almost overpowering lure of the meat, at first the second scent had gone unnoticed. But it was not unnoticed for long. The bear had stopped suddenly, something nagging at its senses. Its nostrils worked vigorously. Danger! It had smelled danger, and it was close, closer than the bear would have dared to come. Instinctively, it had clambered up the pine.

The danger never materialized, but the scent of the venison was still there. The bear loosened its grip on the hemlock and started its descent. Its claws scratched the bark, guiding it down in a kind of controlled fall. Tilting its head into the wind, reading the air currents, the bear plodded purposefully toward the decaying deer flesh.

Grace turned off the computer. When the baby-sitter had told Marcy and Mary Grace their mother would be by early to pick them up, Grace could hear their squeals of delight through the receiver. More than anything, that had made her day. She constantly worried that spending so much time with another adult would confuse their loyalties and weaken their attachment to her. As a result, she tried to give them her best whenever she could, which gave rise to another worry: that she was spoiling them.

The kids came running down the front sidewalk as soon as Grace braked to a halt. It was a treat for them to be going off with their mother at 3:30 in the afternoon rather than the usual 5:15. Mary Grace jumped into the front seat by her mother, and Marcy had climbed into the back, kneeling on the seat. She always crouched like that when she first got into the car, wanting to be sure she did not miss anything.

"Where are we going, Mommy?" Mary Grace asked, not really caring.

"To my boss's place. Here, be careful of this folder," Grace said as she picked up the manila folder containing the freshly typed brief. She handed it to Mary Grace. "We have to drop that off with his wife."

"Why?"

"Because he wants it."

"What for?"

"Because I said so."

"How come?"

"No more silly questions, Mary Grace. We're going to stop at the laundry first, and then we'll drive out to Mr. Michelson's."

"Mommy," Marcy said from the back seat, "is it true that the Indians are on a warpath and killing people?"

"Of course not," Grace said loudly. "Where did you hear such a thing?"

"Mrs. Smith said they are."

"I don't think she did, Marcy. You probably did not understand what she meant."

"Yes I did," Marcy insisted. "Didn't I, Mary?"

"That's what Mrs. Smith said," Mary Grace interjected. "She said that out West, Indians used to scalp people, but around here they used to cut their tongues out."

"Oh, that's terrible," Grace exclaimed. "They never did any such thing."

"But Mrs. Smith has lived here *forever*," Marcy argued. "She ought to know."

"Well, she does not know," Grace said firmly. She could not believe Mrs. Smith would tell her children such a story. She fought to control her temper. "Mrs. Smith may remember hearing a lot of things from when she was your age, but because she heard them and remembers them does not mean that they are true. When she was a little girl, people did not like the Indians and said all kinds of nasty things about them. A child like yourself would hear these lies and maybe believe them. So listen to your mother: The Indians are not killing people. The bears in the woods killed those people."

Marcy sat back in her seat, her head disappearing from view. Grace hoped she had made a strong impression.

The laundry was in a converted house on Main Street, beyond the drawbridge. Etta Neilson had started washing clothes for neighbors twenty years ago when her husband contracted muscular dystrophy and could no longer work. Etta stayed at home, washing clothes and caring for her husband on the second floor. After he died, she continued washing clothes to support herself. It grew into a comfortable business, and eventually Etta had three people working full time for her.

Mrs. Neilson was a talkative woman, but Grace did not have time to spare. She paid her bill and hurriedly walked to the car with her arms full of the pressed sheets and neatly folded towels. She placed them on the backseat and climbed behind the steering wheel.

As the road narrowed to two lanes and the buildings were left behind, Grace glanced at her watch. Four o'clock. They would be there in fifteen minutes. Plenty of time to come back, eat out, and catch the six-o'clock movie. "Hey, kids, want to go to the show tonight?"

"Yeah!" they screamed in unison.

"Good, so do I." Grace rolled up her window as the car sped faster. The multishades of green in the forest bordered the shoulder of the highway. It was so beautiful, so calm, so peaceful. How could anything horrible be happening in those woods? she thought. The bear attacks did not scare her. She and her children were safe in her automobile.

Gripping the top of the steering wheel, Larry arched his back inward. He had only been driving for a little more than an hour, but the silence in the car made it seem longer. Axel slept beside him, his head balanced between the window and the seat. He had tired rapidly on the expressway, and switched with Larry at a rest stop just south of Grayling on I-75. As they approached Wabanakisi, Larry was reluctant to awaken him.

Larry did not have to. Axel jerked alert with a start and looked around, his eyes wide. Reality rushed to greet his senses. The dream faded, thankfully. It could not be, Axel thought with a mental sigh. It could not happen. But nonetheless the grisly scene from his dream reappeared, and he saw his wife hovering over a mutilated corpse, with a knife in her hand, a knife with a short, sharp blade. The paring knife! His body shuddered as he turned toward the side window, shielding his face from the others. His eyelids closed tightly as he tried to erase the thought, but the picture pulsed in his brain; larger, brighter. Its focus was on the paring knife. It slashed into the mouth. Axel watched as Janis lifted the limp pink flesh from the corpse. Her hands moved swiftly to a bag, her deerskin handbag! "No!" he screamed.

The car swerved into the oncoming lane. Larry quickly steered it back and stared at Axel. The two men in the back leaned forward, their hands tightly gripping the seat. Axel breathed heavily. He was afraid to turn around, but his eyes darted anxiously from side to side. He felt foolish, yelling uncontrollably like an adolescent.

Larry stared at the highway, his face filled with concern. He wanted to talk, but he did not know what to say. He knew what Axel must have been thinking. Nothing else could have caused such a reaction. He felt angry at his grandfather. But it was he himself who brought up the subject, he quickly realized. It was the right thing to do, he reflected. Axel had a right to know. He would hear about the suspicions sooner or later.

"I . . . I . . ." Axel tried to speak. He swallowed with effort. "I don't know why . . . I'm sorry Larry. I . . ."

"That's okay, boss. Don't worry about it. It happens."

"I was dreaming . . ."

"I know, and I can imagine about what," Larry said. "I don't blame you for . . . for being upset."

For screaming like an idiot, you mean, Axel thought. He felt a gentle touch on his shoulder. Axel turned to Charley Wolf's face. The old man did not say anything. He knew some things were best said by silence. He patted him on the shoulder, and Axel understood. It was a pat of patience, not of sympathy. You're beginning to see, the hand said; you will understand.

Axel turned toward the windshield, his shoulders hunching away from Charley Wolf's hand. His movement told the touch he would never see it that way. It said: Your legends are stories, and stories only. It said: My wife is not being controlled by the spirit of a long-dead Indian.

A small green sign—"Wabanakisi 3"—flashed by the side of the car. Axel was glad they were almost home. He wanted to talk to Janis. But what could he say?—"Charley Wolf believes you're inhabited by an evil spirit. Are you?" Axel almost laughed at the thought. But there were still answers to be found, and together they could find them. Axel was glad Janis had stayed home from work and was there now, waiting for him.

Eighteen miles to the north of the speeding Yukon, the Michelson house was quiet. Janis was not at home. She was in the woods.

The heavily padded feet thumped over the springy forest floor. The bear moved steadily but cautiously, drawn by the smell of the meat. The smell of danger was great, but its effect on the bear was not as strong as the prospect of an easy meal.

The bear stopped suddenly, staring at the shiny round object. It was perplexed, perplexed and nervous. It wanted to turn and run, but the smell of the decaying meat was coming from that direction.

The bear circled completely around the rippled object. The scent of danger was all around. It was not a fresh scent, however, like the scent of the deer, and the bear decided to explore more closely. It stretched its neck forward, its nose sniffing the hard exterior. Then it raised a broad paw and ran its claws gently across the cold surface, scratching it slightly. More boldly it banged its paw against the object. A boom resonated from either end, the noise causing the bear to jump back.

From several feet away the bear tensed as the echo slowly subsided. It approached again, moving lengthwise along the large hollow tube. At the end, the odor of food was strong. The bear could see the venison, just a few inches away. But it could not reach the meat. A barrier with holes covered the end of the tube. The bear reached its claws through the grating and pulled. It was solid. It did not move.

The bear continued around the other side of the circular object. There was no barrier. The bear could see the venison clearly at the end of the tube, and salivated over the prospect of eating the meat. But it had never encountered a cave such as this one before.

It put one paw inside and paused while its foot became accustomed to the feel of the cold floor. It was about to take a second tentative step toward the meat when it stopped suddenly. The venison flashed out of its mind. Something else beckoned, something stronger than its instincts. It hesitantly turned away from the meat.

A moment later it loped determinedly into the woods. It was hesitant no longer. It did not move back along the trail it had come. Instead, the bear headed south.

"Is Mr. Michelson an Indian?" Mary Grace asked.

"No, he's not. He's Danish," Grace answered.

"Is Mrs. Michelson Danish too?"

"No, she's an Ottawa. Her great-grandfathers were important Indian chiefs."

"Does she live in a wigwam?"

"No," Grace laughed. "And Axel does not live in a thatched hut."

"Do you think Mrs. Michelson would know if they used to cut tongues out?"

"Of course she would, and she would tell you just what I did. And don't you ask her that question," Grace said sternly. "It will insult her."

"I won't, Mommy," Mary Grace said as she looked out the side window. She put her fingers in her mouth, feeling the smoothness of her tongue.

Grace frowned at what she saw her daughter doing. They were not scared now, just curious. But late at night, alone in the dark, the thought of Indians removing tongues would certainly frighten them. She was angry that Mrs. Smith would tell little children stories like that. She should have known it would scare them. Yet by leaving the kids all day with another person, Grace knew she had to expect such things, especially with an old woman like Mrs. Smith.

They were getting close to the turn. "Mary Grace, open the folder and hand me the little piece of paper on top."

Her daughter did as she was asked. Grace looked at the penciled directions. "No Mailbox" was underlined at the bottom of the sheet. She had thought it was odd when Janis told her there was no mailbox at 621 marking their driveway. But then she realized the Michelsons had a box at the post office. Still, even though it had been a while since she had driven out here, she had thought for sure there was at least a little sign on a tree. It was strange, but Janis said there were no markings at all for their driveway. The way she described it, it was as if they lived down an old logging trail.

As the car drove slowly through downtown Wabanakisi, Axel's embarrassment faded, replaced by a bitter resistance to Charley Wolf's ideas. He was sorry he had lost his temper at the old man, but under the circumstances, it was a normal reaction. When the bears were caught and it all died down, Charley Wolf would realize that his faith in his legends was misguided, that while they were fine reminders of tradition, they were not fact.

"I'll stop by the garage and see if my car is ready," Larry announced.

"Okay," Axel said. "But I think you expect too much from those mechanics. They're only human, you know."

"If they can only pump a little more life into it, I'll be all set. It has to last just one more year."

"That's what you said last year." Charley Wolf guffawed in the backseat.

"That's because I thought I'd be making more money this summer," Larry said with a sly smile as he looked over at Axel.

"I've got bad news for you," Axel said. "If you think your salary is bad now, just wait till you get out of law school."

Larry laughed, steering the Yukon up the driveway into the service station. His old Ford was parked to the side of the garage between two cars that had been demolished on the expressway. After talking to the mechanic, he turned to Axel and gave him the okay sign. As Charley Wolf and Leon Moozganse climbed out of the backseat, Larry disappeared into the office.

Crossing the drawbridge, Axel pressed his foot hard on the accelerator. He was in a hurry to get home.

The bear trotted through the woods, the smell of venison far removed from its mind. Its lumbering movement lacked grace, yet its four hundred pounds moved easily. The bear crashed through the new territory. It had never been there before, yet it was not proceeding cautiously. It did not stop and sniff the ground, nor read the air for wind-carried scents. A few hundred yards through the woods to the bear's right, narrow pavement snaked its way through the trees.

The engine quieted down as Grace eased her foot off the accelerator. She saw the three birches growing from a single trunk on the left, as described by Janis. "Be alert, kids." she said. "Their driveway is near here. It should be just past that yellow sign."

"There's the road," Mary Grace yelled, pointing toward the sign with the curving black arrow.

"Ssh. I can hear you. You don't have to yell so loud."

Mary Grace covered her mouth with her small hand and looked at her mother with smiling eyes.

"Pretty silly, you are," Grace said. She pulled the car off the highway and onto the narrow dirt track. It did not look as she had remembered it. She had thought the Michelson driveway was wider, and covered with gravel.

Axel's car sped along County Road 621. His foot eased on the gas pedal. The scent of pine rushed in the open window. His thoughts wandered to the steel-pipe trap behind his house.

The bear stopped suddenly, its instincts alerting it. There was another shape moving through the trees. It sniffed the air. Another bear! It tensed, ready to bolt, but it did not. Instead, it continued walking slowly forward. From a distance, it was apparent the other bear was paying little attention to it, as well.

The car bounced along the dirt road, long strands of grass tickling its underside. "Mother, does anyone live down here?"

"Yes, I think so," Grace said, but she was beginning to doubt it. This must be the wrong road, Grace thought. But the directions were followed exactly. Could Janis have been mistaken? No, Grace reasoned, the directions could be wrong only if she had done it deliberately. And that's crazy. But the whole thing was crazy. Axel never asked for this brief. What is Janis up to? Nothing, Grace told herself firmly. She felt silly. They liked the seclusion, she thought. Their house was probably around the bend.

Axel could see the car off the road from half a mile away. As he approached, he noticed the front-right corner of the car was jacked up and a man in a checked sport jacket was working on the tire.

Axel eased his car onto the gravel shoulder and parked in front of the crippled auto. "Need any help?" he offered as he walked back to where the man crouched by his wheel.

"No, I'm almost done," he said, wiping his hand across a sweaty brow. "I appreciate you taking the time to stop, though."

"We have to look out for each other up here," Axel said. He started to return to his car.

"Say, listen. How far is Pike Village?"

"There's no direct road. Probably take you forty-five minutes from here.

"No direct road? I thought there was."

"Nope. Not unless you consider driving to Mackinaw and then coming back direct."

"Is there a better way?"

"Yes, if you'll hang on a second I'll get my map." Axel hurried back toward his car.

The bear moved its four hundred pounds closer to the other bear. To its left, its eyes caught movement through the trees. A third bear, it realized. No, two more bears. It stared in their direction.

"I'm scared, Mommy," Mary Grace whimpered. "I don't like it here. Let's go home."

"There's nothing to be afraid of, honey." Grace tried to speak soothingly. Instead, her voice was jagged with tension. "We're almost there. You'll have nothing to worry about in a few minutes."

The unlikely alliance shuffled back and forth. They were spaced evenly about seventy-five feet apart. The bears froze, first one, then the other three. They all heard the whir of the engine.

Grace hoped everything would be all right. So what if it was the wrong road? she asked herself. They would simply turn around and go back. But still, the back of her neck tingled electrically. Why would Janis send us down the wrong road? she thought angrily. Grace glanced in the mirror. She could no longer see 621. If their house was not around the next bend, she would turn, she thought.

Axel's contented expression left his face as shadows from the clouds spread across the highway. The uncomfortable feeling in his stomach was returning. He had repressed his anxiety over Charley Wolf and the bearwalk and Janis for a while. But now it was coming back, perhaps because he was not looking forward to the conversation with Janis. But he had to talk to her about it. He had to help her with her problems. And she with his.

The speedometer needle climbed slowly, one notch at a time. Axel could not explain the feeling, but he knew he had to hurry.

The aimless shuffling of the bears ceased. They moved stealthily forward, aiming to converge on a single area. Nothing would deter them, not even the noxious fumes blowing in from the noise.

Grace eased the car around the bend. It moved sluggishly through deep sand. Getting stuck flashed through her mind. She floored the gas pedal, and the car lurched forward out of the grasping sand. Sweat beaded on her forehead as the engine whirred down. She looked for a place to turn around.

The bears followed the car with their eyes. The sudden roar of the engine did not startle them. They were without fear. Their instincts did not burden them.

The trail was rimmed with earthen mounds, rising about a foot. Ferns grew close to the edge of the road. The car would not be able to turn around, Grace thought, and she would hate to have to back up through the thick sand. Her eyes scanned the other side of the road. A low, dark shape appeared in front of the car. Her foot slammed the brake pedal. Marcy slipped off the backseat and onto the floor. "Oh, no," Grace moaned. A felled tree was blocking the road. "We'll have to back out of here."

The bear reacted instantly. Its prey was immobilized. Its four hundred pounds dashed through the brush.

Mary Grace screamed. "Get down!" Grace yelled. Mary Grace buried her sobbing face in her hands. Marcy pulled the pile of sheets over her as the clean laundry tumbled onto the floor of the rear seat.

The huge black shape came crashing through the woods. The win-dow, it's open! Grace let go of the steering wheel and with both hands frantically spun the window knob. It slipped from her grasp. The crashing noise was louder. The window started to rise again, jerkily, slowly. "Come on, come on," she cried.

Grace saw a second black shape dashing toward the car from the front. Mary Grace screamed. "Over there, help." Grace looked to the passenger side. A third black shape. A third bear! "Drive! Drive!" Mary Grace screamed.

Away, get away! Grace's mind commanded. She slammed the gear shift into reverse. The bear was to the car. Her side window shattered. She screamed and brought her arms to her face. The glass had turned to a spider's web, but it held. She grasped the steering wheel again. The window exploded! Bits of glass sprayed the front seat. A black paw swung into the car. Grace leaped to the other side of the car, hugging her sobbing daughter.

The bear's roar drowned out their screams. The second bear leaped onto the hood of the car and stormed toward the wind-shield. Grace covered her daughter's eyes with her hand, clutching her head to her breast. Mary Grace fought to free herself. The windshield shattered, the safety glass turning into a shield of white crystal. Grace was blinded to all but the three black claws piercing through the crinkled glass.

Grace closed her eyes and bent low, covering Mary Grace as best she could. The bear lunged through the hole, widening it with its body. It seized the cowering animal in its jaws.

Marcy peered frantically through the crack between the front seats. She heard her mother scream. She heard the passenger window burst open. She heard the gasps of her sister. She heard the guttural grunts of the bears. But she could not see!

The trio of animals stretched their heads through the win-dows, snapping and slashing with their teeth. A fourth pranced anxiously in front of the vehicle. There was no more room for it to squeeze into the car. The snarls of the bears grew less urgent, their movements less frantic as their prey ceased struggling. Sensing death, the first bear pulled its chest and head back through the driver's window, dropped to all fours, and quickly disappeared into the woods. It was followed in rapid succession by the other bears, all seemingly instilled with a rediscovered fear.

As the beasts crashed into the bush, Grace's body slowly slumped sideways. Her head came to rest in the center of the front seat, a few inches from the eyes of her younger daughter. Marcy stared through the crack in the seats as though hypnotized. The sound was gone; the fury of a few seconds before had ended. Though her ears rang with the snarls and growls of the bears and her chest pounded the rhythm of terror, she did not move. Her mother was still, so she must be too. Her mother was hiding so the bears would not come back, so she must do the same. She kept her eyes on her mother's face, staring at her mouth, waiting for the word from her lips.

21

The aluminum mast rocked forward, then backward as the sailboat bobbed in the ricocheting waves of the narrow channel. Guy wires eerily stretched from the bare mast like ligaments attached to a skeleton. The boat motored under its own power, its two-cycle outboard whining noisily as the autos waited.

Larry watched as the metal grating of the uplifted bridge slowly returned to the horizontal. The sailboat was safely ensconced in Lake Muhquh Sebing. The line of cars slowly came to life, creeping along the pavement. The battered old Ford jerked into gear as Larry guided it toward home.

It was all so simple for his grandfather, Larry thought. The bearwalk. Shawonabe's spirit leaving his grave and invading the body of a bear. Killing whoever was in his range. Controlling Janis Michelson, using her to collect the tongues, to protect against the victims' vengeful spirits. It explained everything so easily. Larry envied his grandfather's simple resolve, his inner peace. He envied his certainty. He wished it could be explained so easily to him. He wished the gnawing turmoil within him would subside.

Larry considered the seemingly indiscriminate killings during the past week. He considered the Mush Qua Tah and how each member of the tribe was indiscriminately killed two hundred years ago. The deaths were just as senseless, just as undeserving then as they were now. The Shawonabe legend would explain that. It said that Shawonabe was evil, and that his evil grew and festered until it manifested itself in his every action, his every word. The legend told how he killed the Mush Qua Tah, how he was adopted unwittingly by the Ottawas as the lone survivor of their unfortunate brothers. The legend told of Shawonabe's experiments, of his expanding his evil art, of his lust for power. It told of how he threatened the Ottawa tribe, of how a fate worse than the Mush Qua Tah's awaited them. The legend told how the Ottawas stopped his evil, how he was buried far from their ground, how his spirit was left alone with no way to practice his evil. If the legend were true, Larry thought, his questions would be answered. If the legend were true.

But it was not true. Larry knew that. So why were the bears killing, why did they suddenly lose their timidity, their gentleness?

Even more perplexing were the tongues. It was his grandfather's crowning argument, but Larry was not convinced. Axel was probably right. Someone familiar with the legend was playing a macabre joke. He found the bodies and sliced their tongues out. But how would he know where the bodies would be? How would he know where the bears would strike? Somehow, these questions did not provide the test of logic presented by the questions raised by his grandfather. Axel's explanation was just as unlikely, but somehow Larry found it much easier to accept.

Larry glanced at his grandfather sitting next to him in the car, his grandfather who had raised him. It was the first time he could not turn to Charley Wolf for guidance. But he *had* listened to his grandfather's words, he *had* felt his people's chants. They were wrong, of course. But in a perverse kind of way, he was tempted to believe.

The speedometer needle hovered around the forty-five figure. Axel felt anxious, sweaty, but the winding 621 prevented him from driving faster. Still, the pebbles alongside the highway dissolved into a gray-blue as the Yukon passed them. A solid yellow stripe appeared on Axel's side of the broken white line in the center of the road. Farther to the left, three white birches grew from a single trunk. He was a half-mile from home.

Suddenly a human figure dashed through the trees to his right. He glanced down the dirt road. It was a woman. He braked swiftly to a halt. A woman had been running along the old logging trail, clutching something in her hand.

The car engine revved noisily in reverse as Axel raced back to the dirt road. The tires skidded a few feet before stopping on the loose gravel. Axel jumped out of the car, his eyes searching the road. He saw no one.

"Hey!" he yelled. "Who's there?" There was no response. "Hello!" he yelled again. There was no movement. Axel looked up and down 621. It was still. He thought for a moment of getting in his car and driving home. It was not so unusual to see someone in the woods. But there was no car, and the only building within miles was his house. The woman might need help, he thought. He started to walk into the woods.

Axel stepped slowly along the grassy hump in the middle, listening for movement on the twig-and-leaf-littered ground. Everything seemed quiet, but Axel sensed an urgent expectancy, like live coals smoldering under gray ash. He moved cautiously, surveying the brush as he walked.

The forest floor exploded. Tumbling ferns swished the air. One hundred and fifty feet ahead, the woman bolted away from her hiding place by the road. "Hey! I want to help," Axel shouted as he dashed after her. But she kept running, Axel barely keeping her in view through the trees and the shadows. It was not a woman he was chasing. He could see better as he came closer. It was a little girl! "Stop!" he shouted again. Just a few feet more.

He grabbed her by the shoulder and forced her to a halt. She spun around and collapsed on the ground. Her hands covered her face as her breath whistled hysterically between her teeth.

"It's all right. I'm not going to hurt you," Axel said quickly. "I'm not going to hurt you. Calm down and listen, please. You're all right."

Her quivering body stilled, but her arms remained rigid and her face covered. One fist clutched a terry-cloth towel. Axel grimaced as he realized the brown towel was partially soaked with blood. "Here, let go of this," he said softly as he tugged on the towel. "I want to help you."

Her hands slowly unclenched. Axel slipped the towel from her grasp and dropped it on the ground. He gently touched her slender wrists and pulled her hands away from her face. "Marcy!" he said with surprise. She opened her eyes wide, startled.

"Marcy. I'm Mr. Michelson. Do you remember me?" She made no effort to speak. Her face seemed frozen with terror. "Where's your mother?" Her eyes remained wide, her lips unmoving. "Marcy, where is your mother?" She still did not speak. It was as if she did not hear. Axel examined her head carefully. There were no wounds. She did not seem to be bleeding anywhere. Yet the blood on the towel was fresh.

"Come on. Get up and come with me. We'll find your mother." Marcy did not move. "Come on, Marcy," Axel repeated as he took her arm and pulled her from the ground. He held her hand and start-ed to lead her back to the dirt road. Marcy followed, her feet shuffling through the crunching leaves.

Stepping onto the dirt track, Axel surveyed the area. "Grace!" he called. His voice bounced through the trees. Turning to Marcy, he asked, "Is your mother down there?" Marcy did not even look at Axel. He bent down and with one hand turned her face directly to-ward his. "Did your mother drive down this road?" She blinked, but her expression did not change. Axel pressed his lips tightly together in frustration as he studied her face.

Something terrible had happened. Axel knew that, but he was afraid to think what it could have been. He was afraid to think what the blood was from, what caused Marcy's trancelike state. He stared into her face for a clue. There was none. All he saw in her face was her need for medical attention. But he had to look for Grace.

He stared down the dirt trail. He had explored it before and knew it became more and more overgrown until it finally disap-peared. What was this little girl doing coming from there?

Axel took her hand and started down the road. After a few steps Marcy suddenly jerked her hand from Axel's and began shaking all over. "Okay, Marcy, it's okay," he said, trying to comfort her. A tremulous whimper came from deep in her throat. Axel picked her up and hugged her tightly to his chest, swaying from side to side. "Marcy, Marcy, you're all right. You're safe now. Nothing will hap-pen, you'll be all right. You don't have to go into the woods. Come, let's leave here."

Still clutching her tightly to his body, Axel started walking toward 621. The whimpering had ceased by the time they reached the high-way. Axel placed Marcy in the front seat and turned the ignition off. Placing the keys in his pocket, he said, "I'll be right back. I'm going to look for your mother. Stay here. Do you hear me? Stay here." Axel tried to discern if she understood, but her expression remained blank. He turned and walked back to the trail road.

He felt an involuntary chill as he remembered Orson's words the night before. If a bear was once in an area, it was likely to return. Axel surveyed the surrounding woods. He was no longer looking for Grace. He looked for the bear that had torn the dogs apart. He realized grimly that if one attacked, he did not have a chance.

Where the road had cut through the thin topsoil, an irreversible scar of thick sand remained. Axel's feet sank deeper with each step. He noticed a deep gouge in the road, with sand splattered behind it. A spinning wheel, a car! "Grace!" he shouted as he ran toward it.

The rear wheel was pinned against a mound bordering the road. There was something wrong with the car. It wasn't quite right. He was almost upon it before he realized the windows were smashed. He stopped suddenly. He knew without thinking what had happened. The windows, the blood. "Oh, Christ," he said, closing his eyes. He had to force himself to step up to the car and look inside.

"Ahhh," Axel screamed unintelligibly.

It was worse than he had imagined. Grace lay sideways on the front seat, one foot on the floor, the other propped against the dash. Her head was twisted crazily, her neck broken. A young girl was crumpled on the floor. Small cubes of glass were sprinkled throughout the car, their gemlike glitter reflecting the pools of blood like rubies. They were dead. He had no doubt. As he turned to leave, the picture of Grace's face emblazoned on his mind. He saw her blue eyes staring blankly under nonblinking lids. He saw the blood dripping down her neck from her mouth, pried grotesquely open.

Axel started to hurry, glancing nervously around. He knew what her open mouth meant. He knew someone had been there before him. His legs pumped furiously as he dashed toward his car. The bears must still be near. They could leap from the woods at any moment. They could be pursuing right now.

He felt threatened. The danger was real. It wasn't the apprehension he felt when he learned of Davis. It wasn't the uncomfortable twinge that touched him when he heard of the campers' deaths. It was not remote. It was personal. It was close. It was deadly fear, piercing into his chest like a cold blade. He could imagine the bears attacking. He could almost feel their teeth. It was not someone else, but him. His thigh muscles ached with the strain. His car was just ahead. Just a little more.

The dirt road ended. Axel broke out of the woods and circled to the driver's side of the car. He managed a glance down the old trail. There was nothing there. The woods were quiet. Relief pulsed through his head. He collapsed on the hood of his car, his heaving chest expanding and contracting. Gradually he brought himself under control. He could hear the forest once again over his fear. It was still.

He climbed in behind the steering wheel, wondering how to face Marcy. After slamming his door, he looked across at her in the front seat. She sat motionless, staring straight ahead. Axel would bother her no more. He understood why she retreated into her own world. He knew what she must have seen. He knew it would take long and patient care to bring her back to reality. He knew nothing he could say would help.

Axel swung the car around in a U-turn and headed back toward town. Why would they attack an automobile? It seemed so unbelievable, so out of character. The other killings could conceivably be understood, but smashing through windows to get at people in an automobile? Axel knew there must be a rational explanation. He could not think of one, however.

The battered old Ford approached rapidly in the oncoming lane. Axel's initial reaction when he saw Larry's car was to pull off the side of the road and flag him down. He wanted to tell Larry to stop by his house to call the sheriff and check on Janis, but he did not pull over. He knew who was in the car with Larry, and he knew what they would say. He did not acknowledge Larry's wave. He could not look at his car. Though he did not fear the legends, he could not explain the chill that shook him as Larry, his grandfather, and Leon Moozganse passed.

The hospital waiting room was little more than a bulge in the hallway at the entrance. A few hard-cushioned vinyl-covered couches were spaced throughout. Matching chairs, their color rubbed white at the edge of the seats, lined the wall. Axel shifted his weight from one foot to the other as he stood with his elbows on the small Formica shelf under the telephone.

"Hello?" Janis answered unemotionally.

"Hi, honey. I'm in town."

"Oh, Axel, I'm glad you're back." Her voice trembled.

"Is anything wrong?"

"No," she said, then faltered. "Oh, yes. Axel, yes."

"Janis! Janis, what's wrong?"

Janis could not speak, breaking into a sob. "I don't know," she said at last. "I don't know what's wrong."

"Are you hurt, sick?"

"No. When will you be home?"

"Soon, honey, but I can't leave right away."

"Why not?" she said, crying.

Axel wondered if he should tell his wife over the phone or wait until he got back. His mind was too tired and his emotions too drawn to think of anything else to tell her. "I'm at the hospital."

"What?"

"I'm all right, Janis. Calm down. But Grace is dead. She and her older daughter were killed by bears this afternoon."

Janis' forced breathing remained constant. "I'm glad you're all right. But when will you be home?"

"Did you hear me, Janis? I said Grace was dead."

"I heard you," she said between sobs. "If she's dead, why do you have to stay at the hospital?"

"Because her younger daughter is alive. She was not harmed by the bears."

"Was she in the car?" she said urgently.

"Yes, she was." Axel paused. "Who told you they were in a car?"

"You did. You just did, didn't you?" Janis said quickly, the tears gone from her voice.

"Maybe I did. I didn't realize..." Axel did not finish the sentence. He must have mentioned they were killed by bears in their car this afternoon, he thought. Everything was so confusing. "She hid under a pile of laundry in the back. They didn't find her."

"What has she said?" Janis asked excitedly.

"Nothing. She's in shock."

"Did she see what happened?" Janis demanded.

" I don't know. I just said she's in shock. That's why I'm staying at the hospital."

"She must have said something." Janis shouted, her voice no longer trembling. The sobbing had ceased. "She must have seen what happened."

"She probably did. She probably saw everything. Whether she'll ever be able to tell us what she saw is something else."

The receiver in Axel's ear was silent for a moment. "Maybe she'll never be able to say," Janis said evenly.

"Maybe not. But I'd like to stick around for a while to see if she gets any better. Is that okay?"

"Yes, I'll be fine."

"Good. You had me worried for a while there."

"I'm sorry, Axel. I don't know what got into me."

"We'll talk about it when I get home. I'll see you later."

"All right. Good-bye."

"By the way. We got the preliminary injunction."

"Good," Janis said simply.

Axel's hand gripped the receiver for some time after he hooked it in the cradle. He wished Charley Wolf had not made the trip to Bay City. He had given him crazy ideas, Axel thought to himself. Shaking his head, he turned to walk back to where Larry was sitting in one of the vinyl chairs. He was glad Larry had sensed something wrong when he passed him on 621 and had decided to drive back to town after dropping his grandfather and Leon Moozganse.

"Is Janis all right?" Larry asked, putting down the wrinkled magazine.

"Yes, she's okay."

"Did you tell her about Grace?"

"Yeah, she was upset, of course." Axel said, not really knowing for sure if she had been upset over that or not.

"I can imagine. I was too when I saw all those flashing lights and the ambulance on the way back into town."

"Did Snyder tell you anything?"

"You already asked me that, Axel," Larry said. "Just that their tongues were cut out like the others and that you had taken Marcy to the hospital."

"Yeah, I did ask you. Sorry."

"Maybe we should go home. They'll call if anything develops."

"Maybe we should. Right after Dr. Lewis comes out."

"That might not be for a while," Larry noted.

"Someone has to be concerned for her, for Christ's sake. There's no one else."

Larry nodded and reopened his magazine. His eyes moved across the page, but he did not know what he was reading. He was thinking about the bearwalk.

The hospital waiting room was quiet for a long period of time. Occasionally muffled voices or the squeak of a wheeled cart seeped through the swinging doors. The phone had not rung in an hour, and the nurse lazily idled away her time behind the window, waiting for her work day to end at ten p.m.

Luke Snyder stepped through the heavy glass doors, his feet scuffing tiredly on the tile floor. "Axel, I'm glad you're still here," he said.

"Hi, Sheriff. Your work done out there?"

"Just beginning. How's the girl?"

"No change. I think she's asleep now."

Snyder walked slowly to the swinging doors and peered through the small window down the hospital corridor. "It's the damnedest thing I've ever come across in my entire life." The sheriff turned away from the door, reaching his fingers into his shirt pocket. "Maybe you two can help. Whose handwriting is this?"

Axel took the notepaper from Snyder. "Grace's, wouldn't you say, Larry?"

"Without a doubt. What is it?"

"It's directions to that exact spot where you found her in the middle of nowhere," the sheriff said.

"That can't be," Axel said. "She must have followed them incorrectly."

The sheriff simply nodded toward the paper. Axel read it quickly. The three birches . . . before the curve. Yes, Axel realized, it was directions to the road where he'd found Grace. He looked up at Snyder quizzically.

"What do you make of the 'No mailbox' at the bottom?" Snyder asked.

Axel studied it for a moment. "It's as if she expected to find a house down there."

"Yeah, I thought that too," Snyder drawled. "Did you ask Grace to deliver anything to your place?"

"No, I don't think I ever have asked her to drive out there."

"I ask because we found one of your briefs in a folder on the front seat. It was dated today and was unsigned."

"The Rasmussen case?"

"Yeah, I think that was it."

Axel glanced at Larry uncertainly. "That's going to Mackinaw, but not until next week," he said. "She knew that."

"Do you think Janis would have asked her to bring it out?"

"Of course not. She doesn't even know the Rasmussen case exists."

"That's what I figured," the sheriff said, rubbing his hand across the back of his neck. "But I just can't figure why someone would want to set up Grace."

"*Set* her up?" Larry exclaimed. "It was bears, wasn't it?"

"Yeah, bears killed her and the girl, all right. But there was a tree freshly sawed blocking the road. And those directions led her directly to it. The bears must have been waiting right there and pounced on the car so fast she didn't have time to get away. And then someone steps in and cuts their tongues out. It must have been set up, wouldn't you say?"

"I'm not sure what I'd say," Axel said.

"I'd say it's murder," Snyder said, regarding Axel with narrowed eyes. "How or why, we'll probably never understand. I just hope we can find out who. And that little girl in there holds the key."

The swinging doors whooshed open. "You'd better go home, men," Dr. Lewis said. "She'll be asleep all night."

"Will she be able to talk tomorrow?" Snyder asked.

"I doubt it. And if she could, I don't think it would be a good idea just yet to ask her about what happened."

"Will she ever be able to talk about it?" Snyder pressed.

"That I can't answer. The best thing for her now though is time. We'll just have to wait and see."

"Will anyone be with her tonight if she needs help? I'd hate for her to wake up alone in a strange place," Axel said.

"She won't wake up until tomorrow morning. I gave her some pretty strong medication. The hospital can't spare a full-time nurse for her, so tomorrow I'll send Mrs. Whitesun over to sit with her."

"Good. Will I be able to see her?" Axel asked.

"Yes. As a matter of fact, it might help for her to see some friendly faces."

"I'll stop by too," Larry offered.

"Fine. See you in the morning," Dr. Lewis said.

Larry's car sputtered hesitantly before bursting into a loud roar. A week ago, he had barely been able to control the anticipation simmering within him as his mind swirled near the vortex of the Crooked Tree controversy. But now it all seemed so remote. The bearwalk had totally gripped his thoughts.

If the killings were the result of the bearwalk, Larry thought, there was only one Indian who could have accomplished it. There was only one Indian, legend said, who was able to inhabit more than one bear at a time. Shawonabe had worked on the art, honing his skills, becoming more powerful with each success, until he was able to control every bear in the forest, until he was able to destroy an entire tribe. With each kill, with each new tongue in his medicine pouch, his magic grew stronger. With the tongues of the Mush Qua Tah, his power surged to an unheard-of extent, while his magic marched into the unknown.

Though the events of the past week had tightened around his resistance to the supernatural world of his people's past, Larry knew the shrinking circle would never close completely. The bearwalk existed only in the minds of the superstitious. Shawonabe could not be responsible for the recent deaths. He died two hundred years ago. Larry was grim, but determined. He felt confident in his rationality. But as he drove through the darkness, he felt an uneasiness creeping up his spine. Like the cone of his headlights, he felt sure when his thoughts were directed straight ahead, but when he glanced from side to side, there was only darkness.

It was impossible for a dead Indian to practice the bearwalk. But slowly, inexorably, the creeping uneasiness entered his head. He remembered how and why legend said Shawonabe died. And he remembered what happened—or more importantly, what did not happen—after he died.

***

Axel had fallen behind the red taillights of Larry Wolf's car. He felt responsible for the little girl he had just left behind. Her mother had worked for him for a long time and had been a good friend. And it was he who had found her in the woods. He wondered if her father, whom she had not seen in years, would seek custody. He thought about what would be involved if he and Janis adopted her when she got well.

Besides his worry for Marcy, Axel was troubled over who had given those directions to Grace and who had sawed the tree blocking her path. He knew it was impossible that Janis was involved, but he was nonetheless concerned what others would think. If Charley Wolf spread his insanity about the bearwalk, it could only make matters worse.

When Axel pulled up in front of his garage he was still thinking about the bearwalk. Under other circumstances he would be fascinated. Instead, he felt nervous, inexplicably apprehensive. The apprehension suddenly pulsed wildly. The same garage door the bears had lifted to get at the dogs was partially raised. Just high enough to allow a black bear to walk inside, Axel thought. And the house was dark. Not a single lamp glowed through the windows.

Axel got out of the car and approached the garage door unhaltingly. As he raised the door, the headlights from the Yukon pierced the darkness. His shadow projected on the far wall of the garage amidst hanging tools. There was no movement in the garage, no sudden lunge. Axel felt a twinge of embarrassment that he was hesitant to enter his own house.

Janis must be asleep, he thought as he stepped into the kitchen. She probably fell asleep before it got dark and had not left a light on for him. As he stepped by the kitchen table he felt a gust of wind blow into the house. The sliding glass door was wide open, just like before. "Janis?" he called.

He stepped quickly through the family room. The bedroom door was closed, and he thought of last Saturday when he stood at the same spot, opening the same closed door. He remembered the growl, the inhuman roar, the eyes glinting in the darkness.

But it was not the same. His brain was not fogged with Darvon. His eyes were not glassy with the drug. Prepared to defy the hallucination, he flung the door open. It was quiet in the bedroom.

He stepped inside, the blood pounding through his temples. He saw the outline of a figure on the bed. Axel turned the fluorescent light on in the bathroom. Janis' eyes were gently shut. She was sound asleep. Resisting the urge to wake her, he walked into the bathroom and readied himself for bed.

When he came back into the bedroom, his wife still lay on her side, facing the dim light coming from the window. Axel pulled back the sheet and slipped in beside her. He hesitated before waking her. He wanted to experience her gentle beauty, her skin softened by the darkness. His eyes followed the graceful curve of his wife's buttocks as her figure dipped almost unnaturally low to her waist. He reached his hand to her and gently gripped her shoulder. As soon as he touched her, he realized he had made a mistake. Her body tensed. He shouldn't have wakened her. The tender darkness was charged with tension. He wanted to say something, to restore the mood. But his mind could not think fast enough.

He heard the phlegmy gurgle deep within Janis' throat. It was a raspy groaning noise, almost a snarl. Axel raised himself on one elbow and stared in horror at the back of her head. The snarl grew louder. "Hon," he said. "Honey, wake up. It's . . ." He touched her. She spun in the bed, her voice exploding. Her eyes shone at him like luminous disks. Axel pushed himself away. Her eyes glowed in the darkness, reflecting his astonishment, his fear. They forced him off the bed. Axel scrambled backward across the floor until he hit the wall, where he sat propped against the baseboard, his own gaze fixed on her eyes. My God, please don't let it be true! But it was not his imagination. It was real. It was like the last time, but this time it was real.

22

A hotbug's shriek echoed through the woods announcing Thursday's sun. Facing the awakening forest, the dark wood siding of the house blended almost unnoticed. Inside, lacy shadows danced on the wall in time with the fluttering leaves. Axel's eyes absently followed the scratching path of a squirrel scampering across the roof.

He had been awake since before dawn illuminated the sky. And his periods of sleep had been worse than the hours of insomnia. Nightmares rocked his unconscious, until he sprang alert, salty sweat stinging his eyes.

Janis lay quietly beside him. He had not looked at her since she had cried herself to sleep. Axel thought of his shock the night before, staring at those eyes, his mind numbed. He had sat for long minutes on the floor until Janis' eyes slowly cleared, losing their glow. Or perhaps it was his own eyes that finally cleared. He questioned and requestioned himself all night on what he saw. And each answer was the same. It had all been so real. But the more he realized the impossibility of it, the more he was not sure. She said she was having a nightmare at the moment he awakened her. But her scream seemed unearthly, inhuman.

Axel thought of the bearwalk, as he had many times during the night. Charley Wolf was positive Janis was under the same influence as those bears, and there were indications that it was true. The dogs in the kennel, the deerskin handbag, the small footprints, the bearlike manifestations in the bedroom, first

Saturday and again last night. But all the indications, Axel thought, were merely circumstantial at best.

Axel knew that the more outlandish a story an attorney had to persuade a jury to accept, the better the evidence had to be. There was always a point when circumstantial evidence was not enough. Axel imagined attacking his own testimony before a jury on last night's evidence of the bearwalk. Reflect for one moment, ladies and gentlemen, he would argue, on what the witness said. Judge his credibility as you would anyone else's in your daily encounters. Doing that, ask yourself: Could you accept what he said as fact? Ask yourself: Could anyone accept what he said as fact? Could any reasonable person possibly accept something as preposterous as the "bearwalk"? Is it believable, ladies and gentlemen? Is it believable that a dead Indian's spirit inhabits bears and this man's wife cuts the tongues from the victims so their spirits won't haunt his? And you are asked to believe that simply because a tired, confused man with the suggestion planted in his head before he even opened the door tells you his wife's eyes glowed in the dark! If he sat on the jury himself, Axel thought, he would not accept his own testimony. He would require direct evidence.

Janis was disturbed, Axel thought, and she needed a doctor. But the cause of her problems was not the bearwalk. That was superstition. And the more he let it bother him, the more it would cloud his perception of what should be done.

He rolled over on his side and reached to wake her, but his arm stopped, his hand poised in the air. She lay on her side facing the window, just like last night. She seemed equally at ease. Axel climbed out of bed and called to her from the bathroom doorway, "Janis. Janis, wake up." She stirred slightly. "Janis, are you awake?"

Her eyes opened partway. "Yes," she answered.

"How are you feeling this morning?" he asked.

"Tired. And scared," she said. "Axel, what's happening to me?"

Axel saw the fear in her face. "I don't know, honey. But it won't last forever. Right now there are so many things we can't explain. But given time, we'll understand. And when we do, it'll be just as before with both of us."

"I'm afraid that I don't want to understand, Axel," Janis said as her eyes turned away. "I'm afraid of what it might be."

Axel felt his pulse quickening. He walked toward Janis and sat on the edge of the bed. "You're afraid only because you don't understand. That's only natural. Believe me, though, honey, everything will be all right soon."

Janis managed a smile. She leaned over and kissed him on the cheek.

"I'm going in to see Marcy this morning. I want to check to see if there's been any change," said Axel.

"Weren't they going to call if there was?"

"Yes, but she may not have woken up yet."

"I hope she'll be all right. I feel so sorry for her."

"Why don't you come with me?" Axel suggested.

"Oh, no."

"Come on. It might help her."

Janis felt her stomach tensing. An impulse told her to go. But she did not want to. "It won't be any good, visiting her. She's in a trance, isn't she? She won't even recognize us."

"Probably not, but at least we'll be together. It's better than staying here by yourself."

Janis pictured the little girl asleep in the hospital. She tried to picture the room, where it was, what it looked like. But she could not. All she could see was the little girl, unmoving, unseeing. The impulse was irresistible. She would go.

Sitting at the table eating breakfast, Axel studied his wife. She had seemed herself just a half-hour before when she awoke, sensitive and concerned, but now she was barely communicative. Axel wondered if Janis was right, that it might be best not to understand.

The curtain rod squeaked as Mrs. Whitesun pulled the thin cord. She opened the curtains slowly, trying to lessen the grating noise. She had been in the small room by herself for about an hour and was content to sit in the dim light. Only when Dr. Lewis and Larry Wolf entered did she decide to let the sun in the room.

Marcy lay quietly on her back, her blank eyes reflecting the starkly functional furniture of the hospital room. A bedside table was next to her, and next to that were two vinyl chairs, similar to the chairs in the waiting room. A small dresser flanked a wide door to the lavatory. There were no other beds in the room.

"What do you think, Dr. Lewis?" Larry asked.

"It does not look good. I was hoping she would come out of it after a night's rest."

"Maybe she's still feeling the effects of the medication you gave her last night."

"No, that had worn off when I checked her earlier this morning. If it hadn't, she wouldn't be awake with her eyes open like that." Dr. Lewis' head shook ever so slightly as he stared down at Marcy. "You know, shock is a complicated thing. Every human being is susceptible to it. The strength of the stimulus and the strength of the individual determine at what point and how deeply a person will lapse into shock. Here we have a five-year-old girl who witnessed something more horrible than either you or I can even imagine. It's entirely possible, Larry, she may never regain consciousness as you perceive it."

Emma Whitesun looked from Dr. Lewis to the child in the bed. She had been a nurse for many years, and half of those years she had worked in a hospital. She had been exposed to many pitiful scenes, but none moved her as much as the little girl lying motionless in bed, driven into another world by watching the death and mutilation of her mother and sister. She cursed the legend, she cursed Shawonabe to herself.

"There must be something that can be done to help her, to bring her back to reality," Larry said.

"Maybe she doesn't want to," Emma Whitesun said, her eyes still on Marcy. "Maybe it would be worse for her if she did."

"Maybe so," said Dr. Lewis, "but that's not for me to speculate upon." Turning to Larry, he said, "Medicine doesn't hold a cure for everything. If there are psychiatric procedures to help her, they are beyond my knowledge. We're going to have to send Marcy to a specialist. As soon as she's physically able, that is."

Axel and Janis left the Yukon in the parking lot and mounted the steps to the hospital. As Axel spoke briefly with the nurse at the window, Janis noted it was about four feet from the floor. There was no entrance directly into the receptionist's office from the waiting room.

Room 170, she heard the nurse say. She was glad it was on the

226

first floor. Hopefully it would be on the east side of the building, facing the woods. She followed her husband through the swinging doors and down the tiled hallway. A white-jacketed intern passed them hurriedly. She watched as he disappeared through a door marked "Intensive Care." There would always be someone stationed in there, she thought.

Axel turned to his left and rapped lightly on the door. Room 170. The east side of the building. It was all too good to be true, Janis thought. Now she had to check the window. But she felt reluctant to step inside the room. Then she heard Dr. Lewis' voice, then Larry's, and she followed Axel inside. She returned their greetings and listened as Axel asked how Marcy was. The same. Her reluctance faded. She absently withdrew her thoughts from the conversation. She strolled away from the three men over to the window. The nurse was sitting in the chair in the corner.

"What are you doing here?" Janis demanded crisply.

Emma Whitesun was clearly taken aback. The discussion behind Janis ceased. "I . . . I'm sitting with Marcy," Mrs. Whitesun stuttered. "The hospital doesn't have enough nurses to put one on fulltime call, and—"

"I asked her to stay with Marcy," Dr. Lewis interrupted.

"Take it easy, Janis. Mrs. Whitesun is an RN and has been for years," Axel said.

"I'm sorry, Mrs. Whitesun. I don't know what got into me. I was startled to see you there, and, well, I guess I'm just upset by this whole business."

"That's quite all right, dear. I understand." Emma Whitesun was a kind and forgiving woman. She understood how Janis felt. Nonetheless, her narrowed gaze followed Janis to the window.

Deep within Marcy's brain, something stirred. She felt as if she was at the end of a long dark tunnel and people were talking at the other end. She became aware of the light. She was moving down the tunnel. Something touched her through the darkness and nudged her mind.

Janis stared out the window into the woods. The trees came almost to the edge of the building. The underbrush was wild, uncleared. It was a relaxing scene for the recuperating patients, and that's exactly what Dr. Lewis had intended fifteen years ago when he chaired the committee to build the hospital.

Janis smiled. She knew the woods east of Wabanakisi stretched out for miles, broken only by an occasional lonely road, until it became the designated wilderness area of Crooked Tree. She glanced around her. Mrs. Whitesun's head jerked to the bed. With her eyes on the others in the room, Janis reached to the latch on the window, her fingers feeling their way along the aluminum pane. The latch unlocked noiselessly. She turned and walked to the foot of the bed.

The even sheet of light began to separate like melting ice uncovering mounds of dark earth. Shapeless shadows splotched Marcy's vision. She tried to focus her eyes, but they did not respond.

Janis stared down at the little body on the bed, covered by the sheets, and her mind flashed crazily. Another sheet. A pile of sheets. But there was no girl. Where was it? She couldn't see. But she felt it. She felt her breathing become labored, the wetness on her skin, the dizziness in her head. Her hand slipped into her red fabric purse and her fingers touched the narrow metal file. She could no longer hear the voices of the others. She did not see them. She was alone! The file's edge was sharp, one end pointed, like a knife. Now! her mind screamed, but she did not understand what was happening.

Marcy stared at the dark blur in front of her. She no longer tried to move. Her attention centered on the blur in front of her eyes. The pupils narrowed. The fuzzy outline shrank. Janis' shape came into focus. The image was relayed to the brain.

Janis was immobilized. She stared at the girl on the bed, her hand frozen in her purse, studying the unmoving features. They seemed dead. But they weren't! The girl's eyes had darted noticeably. They stared in her face. Janis tried to look away, but she was trapped by those eyes! Janis' purse crashed to the floor.

The tremble started first in Marcy's neck, then spread throughout her body. It brought back a memory of eighteen hours before, a sensation that had gripped her earlier. She had felt like screaming then, but she was unable to. Her control had left her. But it was returning. Slowly it crept into her arms. They began to rise from the sheet. Her elbows bent as her hands progressed toward her face. The control crept into her mouth. Her cheeks twitched as her lips slowly parted. Her mouth grew round in a silent scream. Her face was chiseled with terror.

Then her scream exploded and the terror was released.

The shriek reverberated throughout the barren room. Axel and Larry spun their heads around. The doctor sprang to the dresser. He retrieved a prepared syringe on the tray and doused a wad of cotton with alcohol. Marcy was sitting up in bed staring straight ahead. Staring straight at Janis, Axel realized. The scream was unending.

Janis stumbled backward, her face contorted in agony. Her hands gripped her ears. She shook her head wildly. As Dr. Lewis thrust the needle into the child's tense flesh, Janis spun from Axel and dashed into the ball. The scream from the little girl quickly diminished to wailing gasps.

Janis careened off the tile wall as she lunged down the corridor. Axel caught her after three long strides. He grasped her shoulders, trying to turn her toward him as she struggled to get free. A man in white hospital garb ran to Axel's aid, catching Janis' other wrist. Dr. Lewis burst into the hallway with a fresh needle. He hurried to where Janis writhed between the two men.

In the bedroom the sedative pulsed rapidly through Marcy's veins. She sat hunched forward in the bed, Emma Whitesun's arm around her back. Her unblinking eyes stared at the door where Janis had vanished a few moments before.

Larry stood to the side of the bed, his arms dangling helplessly by his side. The girl who had survived a bear attack and who had presumably watched as her mother's tongue was sliced from her mouth had just gone berserk after seeing Janis Michelson. Janis, the woman his grandfather said was the servant of Shawonabe, the woman whose husband said no longer seemed herself. The thoughts tried to fall into order, but Larry would not let them. He realized Emma Whitesun was staring at him. She sensed what reeled in his head. It had in hers a moment before. But she had calmed herself, calmed herself with the very knowledge Larry was trying so desperately to disavow.

"It's Shawonabe, Larry," she said. He turned away from her, not wanting to hear. "It was Shawonabe," she repeated.

"It's not, it's not," he screamed.

"It was. I saw it in her eyes. You know it was. You saw it too."

"No!"

"Just like the other day in the clinic when the sergeant told us of Davis. We knew what the others did not."

Larry spun to face the nurse. "That's not true!" he shouted.

"It is! I saw the belief in your face then, as I do now. You're an Ottawa, Larry. Don't deny yourself."

Larry did not answer Mrs. Whitesun. He turned and ran into the hall, his feet pounding on the floor as he careened down the corridor. The walls seemed to throb, swelling larger with each pulse. He dashed past Axel, barely noticing Janis seated in the wheelchair. A few more steps and he was outside. The shrinking walls burst into the wide-open sky. Air! He stumbled away from the front door of the building and half-collapsed on the ground. He stared at the grass, afraid to look around, afraid to look at the hospital. He wanted to roll on his back and close his eyes, to blank out what had happened. But his eyes would not close. He feared what they would see.

23

"That might be the best thing."

"What, leave? Run away?"

"No, I didn't say run away. I said take some time off and go on a vacation. On a boat, as far from the woods and Michigan as you can."

"Janis and I can't leave now, Larry. You know that. This is the busiest time of the year for both our businesses."

"How are you going to run them at all with Janis a basket case and you not that much better because of worry over her?"

"This isn't a soap opera. A cruise isn't the cure-all for everything. Maybe we should take it easy for a while, and maybe Janis could see a doctor. But we can do that right here. We don't have to float around some deserted islands baking our heads in the sun, all the time worrying what happens when we get back."

"Sometimes people need a change, if only a change of scenery. And I think Janis does. She might be able to rest at home, but there are some things she can't get away from here."

"Like what?" Axel demanded.

"I don't know."

"Like Shawonabe? Is that what you mean?"

"No." Larry was not sure himself what he meant. He had come home with Axel to help him with Janis, who was still heavily sedated, but there was something else that brought him to the house on the edge of Crooked Tree State Forest. He had come because something pushed him, something he felt but did not understand, something that had been growing inside him since he walked up the hill overlooking Ottawa Village two mornings ago.

"Larry, say what's on your mind," Axel said.

"I think Janis has something to do with the . . . bear attacks."

"What?"

"And more importantly, so does Sheriff Snyder. I could tell what he was thinking, and I'm sure you could too, when he met us at the hospital after the attack on Grace."

"He just had a few questions, a few harmless questions."

"Face it, Axel. Grace was coming out to your house. This place is the only one for miles around. Those directions could have been meant for nowhere else. And the only one to get her to come out here, to deliver your brief, if not you, would be Janis."

"That's absurd."

"Somebody's cutting tongues out of corpses, and everything so far points to Janis. It's only a matter of time before Snyder puts it all together. Don't forget, he's got a fingerprint from the funeral home, and those small footprints in the woods. Sooner or later he'll hear what happened today at the hospital, and for that matter, sooner of later Marcy will probably come out of it."

"If you think Janis is doing all this, why tell me to run? Why not go to the police? You're almost an officer of the court. It's your duty." Axel's tone was sarcastic.

"I would, Axel, but I don't think she's responsible."

"So we're back to the ghosts."

Larry avoided his eyes, his face flushed. "I don't know what we're back to. But a lot of people whom I have trusted all my life think the bearwalk is responsible. Crooked Tree was surrounded the other night by many people from our village, chanting and swaying to music heard only during our cultural festivals."

"You were chanting too?"

"Oh, come on, now. Just because I was there doesn't mean I accept the legends as true. You know there's more to a religion than the supernatural aspect. I felt the other night on the hill was a symbol of our past. If it took a legend to get us there, so be it. Our legends, our religion, is all we have left from our past. It's all I have left that tells me I'm an Ottawa." Larry was reluctant to defend the legends, because it implied he believed in them, when he did not. But there was something about the force of death, the deaths of five people, that made him say what he did.

"My wife is an Ottawa, Larry," said Axel. "I'm practically one myself. In some tribes I would be by virtue of my marriage. I know most of the Ottawas in Wabanakisi County almost as well as you. But until yesterday I'd never heard of the bearwalk, and I bet most others hadn't either. Now, all of a sudden you tell me everyone believes in it. It doesn't make sense!"

"You can't see? You can't understand?"

"No, I can't. I can't see how normal, intelligent people could be bowled over by a superstition in the blink of an eye."

"You're a Christian, aren't you? When did you last go to church, Christmas?"

"What the hell does that have to do with anything?"

"You went then because it's a ritual, a ritual which you keep alive for the sake of your cultural history. The Ottawas do the same with their festivals. But what would you do if Christ came down from heaven and marched down the street? Your belief would be rekindled. You would start going to church. And that's what's happening with us." Larry felt stronger. His own uncertainty was fading.

"Do you really think what's been happening with the bears and the tongues is like Christ walking down the street? Think of what you're saying, Larry. You're saying all the deaths, all the bear attacks, are the result of a dead Indian who decided to come back to Wabanakisi."

"He never left."

"What?"

"His spirit never left his body. It's still in his grave." With each word, Larry became more confident.

"That's impossible, even in your legends. I've listened to your grandfather often enough to know the Ottawas believed their souls left their bodies and migrated to villages in the stars."

"That's true. But only after the proper ceremonies. Only after Ogochin Atisken, the Feast of the Dead, did their souls leave their graves for the celestial villages."

"So why wouldn't Shawonabe's soul leave after this . . . this Feast of the Dead?"

"Because he was never included in the rites. The Feast of the

Dead was never performed for him." Larry's voice was steady, his eyes unblinking.

"You sound like you believe all that."

"I do," Larry said without hesitation. The words came easily. The admission, painless. He did believe. He believed in the bearwalk. He believed Shawonabe's evil controlled the bears from his grave. He believed Janis was his captive. Larry felt calm. The turmoil was gone. He was no longer uncertain. It was as if he never doubted the legends, as if he never had second thoughts about the beliefs of his ancestors. But up until that instant, until the moment he admitted his beliefs to Axel, he would have denied his thoughts. He would have denied his heritage. He felt relieved. And he felt thankful to Axel. It was only through Axel's arguments, through being forced to defend the legends, that he was pushed to this self-realization. He had achieved what he came there for.

Axel studied Larry's face. It was not an anxious face, but the face of a man who was sure in his convictions. It radiated his belief. The expression made Larry's announcement almost natural. But Axel was a reasonable man. *He* at least still possessed his rationality. "I don't understand why they would not have performed the burial rites for him. They would have been done with him for good."

"No they wouldn't have. You have to understand, the Ottawas' concept of the afterlife was not like the Christian one, where there's either a good or bad place. The villages the souls migrated to were very much like the ones in this world. They were faced with the same problems, the same hazards of nature, the same personality conflicts. If Shawonabe's soul had been allowed to migrate with the others during the Feast of the Dead, they feared he would take his evil with him. They feared his medicine would then haunt them for eternity."

"Weren't they afraid he'd bother them in this life if his soul remained here?"

"They were. That's why they built what they hoped would be a prison for his soul. That's why he was buried far into the wilderness. Far from their civilization."

"It gets more preposterous all the time. I can't believe we're sitting here discussing this ... this bearwalk as if we're talking about the latest Supreme Court decision."

Larry was silent.

"Christ," said Axel, "don't you see the flaw in all this? Don't you see where this whole idea of the bearwalk fails, fails in explaining what's going on now?" Standing, he glared defiantly. "Even if true, there's no way the legend can be connected to Janis. The legend says a medicine man, a shaman accomplished in the art, could inhabit animals. *Animals*! Not people. And there's a difference. Animals cannot rise above their instincts, but people have a will, a tool to fight with. They could resist. And a human being has been cutting the tongues out. Even if his spirit is alive, Shawonabe's body is imprisoned in his grave."

"But that's why he died," Larry shouted. "That's why Shawonabe was executed."

"A human being has been cutting the tongues out. Shawonabe's body has rotted away. To collect the tongues, he would have to inhabit a person, not an animal, but a living human being. And people are not included in the bearwalk!"

"Axel, you're not listening. He was put to death."

"I heard, but why? You said it was like a high sacrament, the bearwalk. Others did it. Why would he be executed?"

"Because he was experimenting. He was going beyond the bearwalk."

"But that's still—"

"Don't you understand? He had taught himself to inhabit people. Other human beings."

Axel's breath left him. He slumped back to a chair, barely aware of Larry's voice.

"Why do you think the legend survived for over two hundred years?" Larry roared. "He was the strongest, the worst, the most evil. More than anyone else, he used the black bears to kill. And with each death, each tongue, his power grew. It gave him the power to first enter, then dominate, then control other human beings. But he was executed before he could control all the people in the tribe as he could control all the bears. But he's doing it again. Now. And he's got Janis!"

Axel turned away as Larry got up and walked toward the door where he paused, saying quietly, "I can understand your resistance. I can understand your refusal to accept my words. But you can prove it, Axel. You're in a more enviable position than I was—you don't have to rely on somebody's word. You can prove it to yourself."

The chill in the air seeped through the walls of the house. Dusk darkened the quiet room. Axel lay on the floor, staring into the cold shadows of the fireplace where smoke-blackened brick surrounded a mound of gray ash. Gloom as deep as the charred stone shrouded his thoughts. In the next room, behind a closed door, Janis lay in artificial sleep.

Larry was right on one point, at least. Someone was removing the tongues from the bear victims. But it could not be Janis, Axel thought. No amount of circumstantial evidence would convince him. Why would she do it? She would have no reason to. But why would *anyone* do it? Axel realized no one could have a rational reason to cut tongues from corpses. There was no reason to it unless the bearwalk survived. Survived not in reality, Axel thought, but in a demented mind. A mind familiar with the legend. A mind warped by psychosis.

Even that would not explain everything that had happened. Whoever was responsible knew where the bodies would be. He knew when and where the bears would strike. A psychotic mind, no mind, would be capable of that unless it saw through the bear's eyes. And bears would not kill unless something happened to change their character, unless their very natures were taken over, unless they were controlled. Axel grimaced. He was thinking the bearwalk.

Axel jumped up from the floor, disgusted with himself. For a moment it had no longer seemed absurd. Axel stopped his pacing and rubbed his eyes in a futile attempt to massage his thoughts. His mind did not calm. It remained agitated. The flat palm of his hand moved slowly upward across his forehead, stretching his skin taut. His stomach churned uncomfortably. Christ, he thought, he was thinking himself sick.

He had to end it. He had to prove his sanity, restore his reason. He knew what Larry's final words had meant. He could prove it. He could prove Larry wrong. He could prove to himself the bearwalk was only a legend, a curious footnote in Ottawa anthropology. He could prove that Janis was not guided by a dead spirit, that she did not collect tongues at Shawonabe's bidding. There would be no direct evidence of it. The bear victims' tongues were not in a modern medicine pouch as a talisman against vengeful spirits and a storehouse of power. He could prove it. It would be so easy. He had realized that as soon as Larry walked out the door five hours ago. But he had done nothing. He had felt fear. A deep, suffocating pall. It was like nothing he had felt before. It was more pervasive than the fear of a relative's death, more dreadful than the threat of serious injury. He had to dispel the fear. He had to prove Larry wrong.

The door swung easily open. In the dim light Axel could see the outline of his wife under the sheet. He walked to the bed. She moaned and rolled onto her side at his touch. She was still drugged, and her face was as peaceful as a child's. He was glad she was asleep. *Her* troubled mind, at least, was at rest. Soon his would be too, he thought.

Axel stepped into her closet. The odor he smelled before was not there. He pulled the metal-tipped string hanging from the ceiling. In the light from the bare bulb he saw that the hook the deerskin handbag had hung from was empty. Axel examined the floor. Her shoes were aligned neatly under the hanging clothes. The purse was not on the floor. Axel felt the sweat in his armpits. It must be here, he thought. She would have no reason to hide it.

Axel slipped his fingers between hanging dresses at one end of the closet. He slid the first hanger toward the wall, then the second, their metal hooks rubbing across the wood pole. He searched the spaces between the clothes and the wall behind them. His sense of smell was as alert as his eyes. The leather pouch had a distinctive and piercing odor. The clink of the hangers grew louder. What if he could not find the purse? he thought anxiously. What would that show? Would it prove anything? No. Circumstantial. He needed direct evidence. The wire hangers shrieked across the wood pole. The clothes slammed noiselessly into each other as his arms moved furiously through the rack.

He fell back from the clothes against the wall, his chest heaving. The clothes were compacted to one end of the pole. A dress lay crumpled on the floor. They had not been concealing the deerskin bag.

Axel studied the shelf above the rack. Janis had her sweaters folded neatly in piles for half its length. Shoe boxes and her sewing kit covered the remainder. He reached carefully up to the wooden sewing box, slid it off the shelf, and placed it by his feet. Then he maneuvered the cardboard boxes around. He did not see the light tan of the handbag. His thoughts raced through his head. Scenes of bears and flashing knives crashed before his eyes. Axel hurried. He tried to stay ahead of his thoughts. They pushed him on, faster. He grabbed a stack of sweaters and yanked them from the shelf. The others quickly followed, tumbling to the floor.

Axel burst from the closet, kicking a sweater tangled around his ankle. He charged to the bed, glaring at Janis, breathing heavily. He teetered on the edge of control. He wanted to grab his wife and scream, "Where is it?" He wanted to shake her by the shoulders from her drugged sleep. Instead, he just stared. Stared at her sleeping face, infuriated by her calmness, jealous of her quiet peace.

Suddenly she did not seem so incapable of collecting the tongues. She appeared innocent no longer. Her blank face seemed to mock his nervousness, seemed to challenge his loyalty. Fool, it said. Blinded by your juvenile emotions, you refuse to see. Axel shut his eyes and turned away. What's happening to me? Janis was fine, he told himself. It was he who was mad. But why did she run into the bathroom with the purse? If it were just leather polish, she had nothing to hide. And why was she so interested in where the canoeist's body was, the only body the mutilater had not found first. She had not come to bed with him. She could have broken in the funeral home and been back before he awoke. What made her voice sound so unreal, her eyes glow when he startled her in the bedroom? Why did Marcy break from her trance and scream when she saw Janis? The questions pounded in his brain.

He dropped to his knees and flung the bottom drawer of her dresser open. The smell slammed his nose like a heavyweight's punch. He rocked back. He fought to swallow, to keep the contents of his stomach down. It was the same odor he had smelled two nights before in the closet, but now it was worse.

He stared into the open drawer. Lacy fabrics were visible in the shadows. Light from the closet became starker as the twilight dimmed. Axel's bent knees ached with his weight resting on his calves. His teeth were clenched tight against the odor.

Axel reached slowly into the drawer, his fingers ruffling the silky underclothes. He pushed them aside. The perspiration on his back grew cold as the heat drained from his skin. He felt it! As his fingers touched the smoothly textured purse, they froze, as if touching dry ice.

Axel's hand slowly came to life. Grasping the straps, he lifted the purse from the drawer as if it would explode into dust with sudden movement. The smell was almost overpowering. It was not leather polish. Axel knew it could not be. No polish could smell that foul.

He gently placed the bag on the floor in front of him and withdrew his hands. It was the same hand-crafted deerskin purse he gave to Janis for her birthday three years before. It was a free-form sack with ropelike straps forming a drawstring near the top. It would have been a fine medicine pouch, Axel thought. A tribal shaman would have been proud of its craftsmanship.

Axel felt lightheaded as the blood pulsed quickly through his temples. He was no longer aware of the smell. He was aware of nothing but what he saw in front of him. He pulled the deerskin pouch open and eased his hand inside. Something sharp! He jerked his hand out. A thin line of blood stretched across his little finger. He knew what caused it. The paring knife!

Axel reached in and pulled out a wadded white handkerchief. It was crusty, and in the dim light he could see it was stained brown. Eyes closed, he said, "Please God, let me wake up. Let this nightmare end."

Slowly he opened his eyes and stared at the crumpled fabric in his hands. There was something wrapped inside. Something pliable. He delicately pulled the corner of the handkerchief. His eyes reluctantly peered into the unwrapping cloth. He felt he was intruding, intruding in someone's privacy, prying into a personal tragedy. The stained handkerchief crinkled crisply as it opened.

"My God, my God," he gasped between clenched teeth. The cloth fell from his hands. They were there!

His eyelids wrinkled tightly shut, but etched on his mind was the realization of what he had seen, what it meant. He had seen them! The direct evidence. It could be denied no longer!

A scream pierced Axel's tortured thoughts. It was more than a scream, something less than human. His hands gripped his ears, but they could not block the beastly growl resounding through the room. He twisted sideways and looked up with horror. The growl was ceaseless. Janis' voice—it couldn't be her voice!—was deafening. It shook the sanity from his mind. Terror crackled through his nerves. She hovered above him, standing on the bed. Her nude body rippled with the shrieks. Her face was twisted wildly, almost beyond recognition. Her eyes glowed! They were not human, but the eyes of an animal. They shone like white-hot glass in the darkened room. She raised her head toward the ceiling and thrashed it from side to side. Her mouth was open in a chilling snarl.

The tongues! The five tongues he held a moment before, the decaying organs he had pulled from Janis' purse—Shawonabe's medicine pouch—would not leave his mind. Davis' tongue. The camper's. The canoeist's. No! God, Grace's and her daughter's. He felt sick. Panic. Fear! She could do it to me. She's mad. No, Shawonabe's mad. He could kill me. Janis' neck was puffed out as the growl resonated from her throat. She leaped from the bed, crashing into him.

Axel grabbed her by the shoulders and tried to spin her around. Her naked skin felt leather-tough. She flexed her arms open, flinging his easily from her body. She slashed his throat with her nails, her fingers hooked like claws. As Axel grabbed his neck, searing with pain, Janis hulked over him, slime dripping from the corner of her mouth. He could not overpower her. He was hers!

Suddenly Janis clambered off him. Her hands turned nimble as she gathered up the tongues in the handkerchief and stuffed them back in the purse. The knife! Axel thought. He pushed himself away from her, but her hand retracted from the pouch empty. She jumped to her feet and lurched toward the door. Axel heard her bound through the house.

He must stop her! She would kill again. No, Shawonabe would. "Janis!" Axel screamed. He heard the sliding glass door whine in its runners. Axel leaped up and dashed to the back of the house. She was through the garden, nearing the line of trees. Her thighs flexed with power as her undraped body moved fluidly toward the woods. The pouch swung freely in her hand.

Axel ran through the door. "Janis!" he yelled. "Janis, stop."

She was disappearing through the trees. He ran after her. The soft soil of the garden seemed to grab at his feet. Faster! She was getting away. He crashed through the underbrush. Spindly fern stems wrapped around his ankles. The forest grabbed at Axel. It tried to tell him not to go into the woods. It tried to keep him from the darkened world of night animals.

But he had to press on. He caught a glimpse of her skin ahead. She turned and glared at him. The eyes! They beamed like beacons. He couldn't stop now. He had to save his wife. Naked, alone, she would perish in the woods. He saw the glint of her back in the moonlight. He concentrated on that spot as she disappeared again behind the trees. Intent on catching his wife, he did not see the black shape in the dark. He did not see the black bear.

The eyes! He saw the glow of her eyes. They seemed much closer than she had just been. He could catch her, he realized. Just a little more strength. Almost there.

The growl burst off the trees, echoing in the darkness. The bear reared up on its hind legs, its paws to the sky. Axel collapsed. The beast's jaws gaped wide as its roar bellowed through the night. Axel saw the teeth glistening with dripping saliva. The neck was puffed in fighting posture. Axel's exhausted muscles had no energy left. Unable to move, he slumped to the ground, his face burying in dead leaves.

His thoughts drifted away from him as if they were floating into a starless sky. He tried to keep them in view. But he was fixed to the earth. His thoughts shrank to mere points of light. He was barely conscious. Then they disappeared.

The bear dropped to all fours. It moved slowly toward the crumpled body. A shrill, almost animal shriek crashed in its ears. The bear turned. In the distance, through the tangled vegetation, it saw the glinting eyes.

III

Sweatlodge

24

The moon was at the apex of its arcing path through the south quadrant of the sky. Only part of the Mare Tranquillitatis was still in shadow. The rectangular body of Hercules was bathed in the glow of the moon, while in the north sky Pegasus and Ursa Major, the Great Bear, shone brightly.

Along the dirt road that slashed through the forest, the third pair of headlights flashed off. "It's a good night for us," Dirk Vanderlee observed, staring through the broken cover overhead at the stars. "Nice and clear. Full moon. We'll have good light."

"So will they."

"They don't need it. They use their noses." Dirk turned away from Mike Sizemore and gestured impatiently at the third car. "Let's go. We don't have all night."

"Maybe this wasn't such a good idea," Sizemore persisted, moving closer to Dirk.

"Dammit, shut up," Dirk spat. "I let you talk me out of it the other night, and look what happened."

"But there's something strange going on, Dirk. The bears ain't been acting like they normally would."

"You're goddamn right they ain't. If you all had listened to me Monday night," Dirk shouted, glaring at the faces of the other seven men, "maybe the lady and her kid wouldn't have been killed yesterday. I bet that lawyer she worked for feels differently about it now."

"What will the sheriff do if he finds out about us?"

"Fuck the sheriff. Do you think he'll do a thing that would

lose himself one vote? When people hear what we've been doing, the county wouldn't let him touch us. People are afraid to leave the city limits. They ain't even safe in their cars. All we have to do is bring one bear hide back and we'll be heroes. By next week you'll be leading the whole town into the woods, and before we're through every fuckin' bear in Crooked Tree will be dead."

"Yeah, that's what we came for, so let's get started," Nels Carlson yelled. "And if you want to chicken out, Sizemore, you go right ahead. But quit holding us up."

"Hey, I'm here, ain't I? So don't go calling me no chicken. I'm just being careful."

"Good. We all have to be careful," Dirk allowed. "Now, don't go shootin' unless you're absolutely sure it's a bear. Wait till you can see the black fur. There's eight of us, so we'll pair up. Each pair will lead off in a different direction. Mike, you and me will head north along the road. That's where the bears got the first guy. Whoever goes south, when you get to 621, just go over it and keep going. We'll meet back here before sunup. Okay?"

"Yeah, all set."

"One more thing. If there's any trouble, shoot three times in the air. All right, let's see who gets the most bear."

"Wait a minute. Maybe we should bring something back to prove we got one," Nels said.

"Good idea. How about an ear?" one of the men said.

"You assholes can bring whatever you want," Dirk guffawed. "I know what my trophy will be."

"What?"

"Their motherfuckin' tongues."

The men burst into a raucous laugh. They did not fear the bears. There was no question the enemy would yield to their superior firepower. The only problem would be to find them, they thought. They did not realize that it was themselves that had been found.

The three-way bulb was on at the lowest wattage level, shining dimly through the yellowed silk lampshade. Larry stared blankly at the swirling pattern of the rug. His legs were curled on the old couch, draped with a single sheet. Leon Moozganse was sleeping in his bed.

Larry glanced at the dusty clock face embedded in the pine block hanging on the wall. It was late, but tired as he was, his mind would not rest. When he had walked in earlier that afternoon, his grandfather and Leon Moozganse had known immediately he was changed, but though they listened impassively to what had happened at the hospital, they had not seemed interested in his reaction. They asked only about Janis and Axel. He had wanted to yell at them, ask them what about him—weren't they interested in how it affected him? He had wanted to scream that he believed, that the bearwalk existed. Gradually, though, he had realized his grandfather sensed his conversion and was not requiring him to announce it. He had been thankful for that. Still, he had hoped for a little more.

Now, sitting alone in the living room, Larry had realized they did not know what to do. His grandfather, who knew perhaps more than anyone else in Ottawa Village about the old ways, did not know how to combat Shawonabe. Leon Moozganse, who had grown up surrounded by the old religion, was not himself a Midewiwin. Indeed, Larry had thought, even if he was, how could his magic be expected to stand up to Shawonabe's?

There had been another dance to the Gitche Muhquh Manitou on the hill below the Crooked Tree earlier that evening. They had chanted to appease the great bear spirit, chanted for him to intervene. But Larry had sensed the resignation in his grandfather and Leon Moozganse. He knew what had bothered them, as did most people on the hill. It was not the black bears that were responsible. The Gitche Muhquh Manitou had lost control of the bears when Shawonabe took over.

Larry stared at the telephone on the table at the end of the couch. He had been waiting for it to ring since he had left Axel that afternoon. Michelson must have searched the house by now. He must have found Janis' deerskin purse. And Larry knew what he would have found inside. But when Axel found the tongues and could no longer deny Janis acted for Shawonabe, he would have needed to talk to somebody. He would have called! Maybe he's hurt. Maybe Janis discovered him.

Larry flung the sheet back and stood up suddenly. He would drive over there, he thought. No. It was too late. He would call.

He turned to the phone and lifted the receiver, then silently replaced it. Perhaps he just wanted to be alone with the realization.

The bear stayed a safe distance away. Normally it would have run deep into the woods at the scent and sounds of danger. But it had acted contrary to its instincts several times lately and was almost to the point where it no longer was bothered by the danger.

The scent was very strong at first. The bear was too far away to see them, but it knew there must be many. Then the southwesterly wind brought a varied pattern to its nostrils, and it was momentarily confused before realizing the animals had divided. Were they circling to attack? The bear jerked its head around. It read the air currents for another moment.

Satisfied it had not been sensed, the bear circled to stalk the animals, walking directly into the wind. Its padded feet trod softly over the cushioned forest ground. The bear knew the area well, but the animals were heading out of its territory. Perhaps it could catch them before that.

The noise from the animals was loud and distinct. Something was wrong, the bear realized. They were not camouflaging their steps. They walked brazenly through the trees, as if daring other creatures to show themselves. The bear became more cautious, but it pressed on, something guiding its lumbering movement. Like the last time, it would be easy.

It could see them. There were two upright creatures walking alongside the narrow open hump that cut the forest in half. The bear lowered its head, its jaws slack. It appeared ungainly moving slowly through the woods, but each step was a calculated maneuver. The bear studied the terrain as it moved. A sharp clicking halted the bear. With each step the animals' feet clicked a peculiar sound, something the bear had never heard before. The unfamiliar cadence ceased as suddenly as it started. As its prey receded farther into the woods, the bear moved cautiously forward. The trees ended abruptly, and the bear stared at the long open patch. It was not soft like the ground, but hard, smooth, flat rock.

The bear contemplated the barrier. It had lived its entire life deep in the woods, in its own territory. This was new. It reeked of danger. But so did its prey. The bear dashed across the highway and bolted into the woods, where it stopped, raising itself on its hind legs. It looked around for other bears. They had been there the last time. It expected them again.

The first gunshot exploded in the distance only about fifteen minutes after Dirk and Mike Sizemore began to patrol north along the dirt road. Its quick short snap sounded like a firecracker. They stopped and looked at each other, Dirk expectantly, Sizemore with anxiety in his face. "Maybe they got one," Dirk said, smiling.

"Maybe," Mike replied, avoiding Vanderlee's stare.

They began walking again along the deserted trail as a second shot crackled in the night air. Then a third, seemingly from a different direction. Mike gripped his rifle tightly.

"Hey, take it easy, pal," Dirk soothed. "There's no reason to be edgy with that cannon in your arms. It'll stop anything."

A string of firecrackers seemingly popped in the distance. "What the hell are they doing?" Mike shouted.

"Aw, they're just having a little fun. They probably ain't had a chance to shoot their guns for several months. Either that or they found a whole herd of the goddamn bears."

"I thought we were going to play this safe. Take it seriously."

"We are."

"They're acting like a bunch of kids."

"So what! Let them have their fun."

"Fun! We're supposed to be hunting bear. If there were any around, those guys have scared them halfway to Wabanakisi."

"I suppose that's where you'd like to be too," Dirk taunted.

Sizemore turned and resumed walking north. He never had liked Vanderlee. Now he hated him. The gun felt easy in his hands.

"You know," Dirk said, "you might be right about scaring the bears with all this noise. Perhaps we should split up and go off into the woods." Mike's anger evaporated. The thought of being alone in the woods with the killer bears froze him in his tracks. "No! Are you crazy?" His voice was excited. "We've got to stay together."

Dirk burst into a bellowing laugh which slapped Mike in the face. It was clear to him. Dirk had not intended to split up. He simply baited Sizemore's fear. The rifle shook in his tightly clenched hands. "Shut up!" Sizemore screamed. Dirk bellowed louder.

Sizemore was enraged, blinded to all but the jiggling body in front of him. He was blind to the movement in the woods. His hands squeezed tighter on the gun. The safety clicked loudly. Dirk was silenced, staring in horror at Sizemore.

A pair of eyes glinted in the moonlight behind Dirk. Their flash caught Mike's attention. He jerked the rifle to his shoulder and squeezed the trigger. Dirk dived to the ground as the gunpowder exploded in a deafening flash. The eyes reeled back and dropped. "I got one!" Mike yelled. "I got one!" he repeated excitedly.

"You stupid shit!" Dirk screamed from the ground.

Sizemore dashed past him into the woods, approaching the animal without caution. His mouth dropped when he saw what he had thought was a bear. The gun slipped from his fingers.

"You fuckin' idiot!" screamed Vanderlee. "You almost hit me for a goddamn deer."

The black-bear cub delicately pranced around the stagnant pools of water. Its body bobbed as it bounced easily through the cedar swamp. At ninety pounds, the yearling looked agile. That would change as it grew. It would maintain its agility, but not the appearance of it.

The cub felt bold. Until a week before it had been with its mother, but the biannual mating instinct and the intimidation from the mother's new mate caused the cub to leave. Now it was enjoying its freedom.

The crackling pops in the distance did not concern it. It had survived one hunting season without learning the effects of the gunfire, and right now it had something else on its mind. It was on its nightly forage for food.

It had not been hunting by itself for very long, so sometimes it neglected its sense of smell in favor of its eyesight. It was almost upon the meat before it noticed the strong odor. It was venison, and the cub had not had any meat since before it left its mother. Its forepaws lowered to the ground, and it started to follow the scent. As it neared, the cub noticed a second, equally powerful scent. It was one its mother had run from many times, but the cub did not alter its approach. The odor of venison was too strong.

The cub stopped several yards from the large round object.

The competing scents of food and danger vied for dominance as it peered inside the rippled cave. The venison was at the other end, and the aroma was overpowering. The cub lurched forward, paying no attention to the unnatural feel of the tunnel, its concentration on the hunk of meat at the end.

As it jerked the meat with its mouth, the cave rocked with a deafening slam. The cub dropped its food and sprang about. The entrance was open no more. The cub scrambled to the opposite end, its claws scratching excitedly on the metal floor. The barrier held firm. Its high-pitched howl reverberated in the hollow tube, but its mother was not there to help. The cub dashed to the other end and crashed its paw into the cold latticework metal strips. They did not give. The trap only vibrated. The cub settled back next to the venison, panting heavily. Unable to eat, it only whimpered.

Dirk knew they were in the area where the first bear victim was mauled. It was not the prospect of finding bear that made him choose his course, it was the fact that he would be on an unencumbered path, while the others had to fight the woods in the darkness.

Next to him, Sizemore shifted the heavy rifle to his other arm. Dirk glanced at him as Mike suddenly stopped.

"What's—"

"Ssh!" Mike said quickly.

Dirk looked ahead, where Mike's eyes were focused. He saw nothing in the darkness, but then he heard it too, heavy feet padding through the soft soil. A metallic sound. Scratching. They looked at each other in bewilderment. "What the hell?" Dirk said.

The words were barely spoken when a crash resounded through the woods, a thunderous clang, like a heavy metal door dropping shut. Dirk knew what it was. One of the bear traps! He started to run toward the sound, shouting, "Come on! We got one."

Sizemore looked around. To his left the cedar swamp seemed an impenetrable layer of darkness. He did not want to be left alone. As he started after Dirk, a shrieking howl pierced his ears.

"Ay, hah!" Dirk shouted. "We got one on a silver platter." He was standing at the end of the steel pipe, peering through the grating at the trapped bear.

"It's just a cub," Mike gasped, coming up behind him.

"Cub, hell. He's a big son of a bitch."

"He's not. He can't be more than a hundred pounds."

"Well, it's a hundred pounds we ain't gonna have to worry about anymore," Dirk said as he clicked the safety of his rifle.

"You're not going to shoot him?" said Mike.

"That's what we're out here for, ain't it?"

"We're not out here to shoot caged animals. And a baby at that."

"What the hell you think that jerk from Lansing will do with this bear when he finds it in his trap? Move it a few miles and let it loose. Well, that may be his idea of controlling the bears, but it ain't mine." Dirk cocked his rifle and pushed the barrel through the grating.

Inside, the cub cowered against the far end, its claws scratching loudly on the metal floor. It watched as a smooth stick protruded into the cave.

The stick exploded in a blinding flash, and the cub's left leg collapsed. The roar of the gun was in its ears, and it was not aware its shoulder had been torn open. A second blast erupted, and searing pain ripped into its back. The cub tried to move, but it was immobilized. The stick exploded a third time. The cub did not live to hear the echo.

Dirk squeezed the trigger again, and another bullet thudded into the lifeless body. The roar of the rifle bounced crazily inside the steel pipe. Mike's ears throbbed with the noise. A fifth bullet slammed into the chamber.

"Stop!" Mike shouted as the gun retorted the fifth time.

"Shoot him, dammit!" Dirk yelled. Sizemore did not budge. "Shoot him. That's what we came for."

A few miles to the south, across County Road 621, two men with rifles paused, listening to the booming gunshots resounding to the north. One hundred yards upwind, a black shape in the shadows listened as well. It had heard the noises before. But not since last November. With each blast, the memory grew clearer. The bear abandoned its stalk and ran from its prey, seeking refuge in its own territory.

25

The reptile moved quickly over the leaves and other ground debris, searching for a hole to conceal itself from the day's impending heat. The sun was rising above the trees, and it would soon begin to bake the forest. The snake needed only a small hole. It was fifteen inches long and no wider than the circumference of a nickel.

Axel felt something next to his skin. His leg jerked involuntarily, and he opened his eyes. Trees were above him. He was lying on the ground. Something was up his leg. A snake! It moved suddenly higher, slithering against his thigh. Axel jumped up from the dirt, dancing on one leg, shaking the other. He felt the snake squirming, trying to get away. One more kick and it dropped to the ground. A harmless little garter snake.

Axel glanced around at where he had spent the night. The memory of the bear flashed in his head. He must have imagined it, he thought. It had killed the others. It would have killed him. He walked to where he remembered seeing the beast, and his lips parted as he looked at the ground. The broad impressions in the soft dirt were unmistakable.

Axel wanted to get back to the house, but he had to look for Janis. She might be lying on the ground, a few hundred yards away, just as he had been. His feet shuffled through the dead leaves as he made his way deeper into the woods. It was hard to judge exactly where he had last seen her, but he knew it was approximately where he now stood. To the right he noticed a trail of trampled ferns leading through a muddy dip. Axel walked toward it. Standing above the black ooze, he stared at the tracks of a black bear. In the center of the tracks was the distinct print of his wife's foot following it stride for stride. Axel realized that even if he found Janis he would not be able to help her.

Trudging slowly back toward the house, he found the sliding glass door still open. One side of the curtain hung loosely out the door. Axel straightened it as he went into the house, and retrieved his keys from the countertop in the kitchen. He walked quickly back to the bedroom and looked inside. It was just as he had left it the night before. Axel turned and hurried toward the garage.

A tractor puttered in the cornfield as Axel drove toward Ottawa Village. Ahead, a barely visible plume of smoke rose from the hill above the village. By the time the whitish vapor reached the bend in the Crooked Tree, it was totally dissipated by the breeze.

Charley Wolf and Leon Moozganse were sitting together on the wide front porch. Axel had hoped he would see Larry first, and as he climbed out of the Yukon he stared at the sidewalk, avoiding their eyes.

"Good morning," said Charley Wolf.

"Hi. I stopped by to see Larry," Axel said. "Is he around?"

The screen door swung open. "Axel. What happened to you?" asked Larry. "Your clothes. Your face. You're covered with dirt."

He glanced down at himself. Dirt and mud smeared his clothes. Straggles of decomposed leaves hung from his shirt by their stringlike veins. He rubbed his face and looked at his hand. It was covered with dirt. "Janis . . ." he began hesitantly. "She's gone."

"Here, sit down," Charley Wolf said, standing to give up his seat. Axel accepted the offer, the old wicker chair squeaking as he sat.

"Janis ran away. Into the woods," Axel said, his eyes beseeching Larry for help, but his friend only nodded. "I . . . I found what you said I would find."

Larry looked at his grandfather. "You found the tongues?"

"Yes." Axel looked up at the two old men. "I'm sorry. You

were right."

"That's unimportant," Charley Wolf said. "What is important is, now you believe."

Axel's voice became stronger. "She saw me with the tongues and turned practically inhuman. She growled like an animal, grabbed her pouch, and ran out of the house. Her eyes . . ."

"Yes ?"

"They glowed."

"*Skoda kawin*," muttered Moozganse. "Going in fire."

"I chased her into the woods. I would have caught her, but . . . but there was a black bear standing on its hind legs. I'm not sure what happened then. I must have passed out. When I woke up, it was morning."

"You are very lucky, Axel," Charley Wolf said. "Janis must have saved you."

"And I can save her."

"Shawonabe guides her now. You must remember that. To save her, you must free her from his grasp."

"That's why you must take her away from here," Larry pleaded. "Find her and take her away."

"No, Larry, I can't. I told you I can't."

"But that was before. Surely now you must agree that you have to get away."

"No, that hasn't changed. If I take Janis away, how will I know Shawonabe is not coming with us? And what happens when we come back?"

"But it's your only chance!"

"It's not! It can't be. There must be a way to defeat Shawonabe."

"There is. Get away."

"No, you shouldn't run," Charley Wolf said. Larry looked at his grandfather with surprise. "Shawonabe's power is strong now. Either he would stay with Janis or find somebody else. I agree with you, Axel. You must stay here and find a way to best his magic."

"How?" Axel asked.

Charley Wolf looked out toward the street, shaking his head. "I don't know. I'm sorry, but I just don't know."

"But there must be a way." The old men were silent. Axel continued, "The tongues were collected by Shawonabe to increase

255

his power. Isn't that what you told me before?"

Charley Wolf gazed thoughtfully over Axel's shoulder. "That's true. If you were to seize them from Shawonabe, perhaps his power would be curtailed."

"Curtailed for the time being maybe, but certainly not ended," Moozganse said. "Shawonabe would still be with us. Remember, he didn't need the new strength his modern pouch brings him to control Janis in the first place."

"But if Axel captured the deerskin pouch," Larry offered, "wouldn't that mean the victims would be free to seek their revenge on him?"

Moozganse appeared grim. "They would, but regardless of what happens to the medicine pouch, I fear that while he is in his grave, what revenge they sought now would have little effect on his control of Janis. His torment would be great only if his body was still alive."

"Or if he was in the soul village," Charley Wolf added quietly.

Moozganse glanced quickly from Charley Wolf to Axel, then to the floor.

"What is it?" Axel prompted. "Tell me, what is it?"

"I'm sorry, Axel. There really is nothing you can do," Moozganse said.

"There is, and I can see it in you. Please, you must tell me."

Looking up from the wood plank floor, Moozganse drawled, "Maybe . . . maybe it might . . ." He stopped.

"What?" Axel said fervidly.

"It's impossible. I shouldn't have said anything."

"Tell me!" Axel demanded.

"I'm sorry, I shouldn't have spoken. It would just raise false hopes."

"Stop talking in riddles and say what you mean."

Leon Moozganse cleared his throat and glanced sideways at Charley Wolf. "The only way would be to perform the rites of Ogochin Atisken, the Feast of the Dead, on Shawonabe's body. Only then would he be unable to work his evil magic on Janis, on us."

Axel savored the feeling of hope for a long moment before asking, "Why do you say that would be impossible?"

The two old men looked at each other, and Charley Wolf put his hand on his friend's knee. To Axel he said, "I'm afraid the rituals are lost forever. The Feast of the Dead hasn't been performed in decades. No one alive has even heard the sacred liturgy, much less remembers it."

"And we would never be able to find his body," Larry added. "He was buried somewhere in the forest. It would be impossible to find out where. It's been over two hundred years."

"We could try," Axel said. "There must be some clues as to where he was buried. What did you say yesterday, a prison? You used the same words as your grandfather, 'a prison for his soul.' Why?"

"Because that's what the legend says," Larry answered.

"It must have a reason for saying that. All we have to do is discover it." Axel sat forward in his chair. "And you must know something of the Feast of the Dead," he said to Charley Wolf and Leon Moozganse. "Tell me about it."

"Axel, we tried to tell you," Charley Wolf said soothingly. "We don't know the rituals. You're going to be even more disappointed unless you listen when we say it is impossible to recreate Ogochin Atisken today."

"It's not impossible," he objected, "if you'll only say what you know."

"Anything we can tell you about the Feast of the Dead would be superficial. It's no use without the ceremonial chants."

"Maybe we can piece it together."

Charley Wolf just shook his head. His silence spoke for him.

Axel knew he had to get them talking. "How often was it performed? I gather from what Larry told me it was held for many at one time." No one answered. "Come on," he shouted. "It's my only chance!"

Leon Moozganse wished he had not brought it up. He saw that Axel would not cease until he exhausted all hope. "You're right, it was a communal feast," he began. "Held every ten years or so for all the people that had died since the last celebration."

"And how would they decide when to have it?" Axel prompted.

"The older men, the village elders, would decide."

"Where were the bodies kept in the meantime?"

"They were buried in interim graves. When an Ogochin Atisken was declared, it was the responsibility of relatives to dig up the re-mains. Great emphasis was placed on respect for your elders, your ancestors. If there wasn't, no one could be relied on to prepare your body for the Feast of the Dead."

"But for so critical a religious act how could it be safe just to leave the bodies somewhere for ten years?"

"Buried with them was a funerary mask that became part of the person, imbued with mystical powers, protecting the body until the feast was performed."

"Surely the bodies must have decayed."

"Oh yes. Yes, they did. All that may be left of those that had died several years before could be their bones. The more recently deceased would be in various stages of decomposition. It was the relative's duty to cleanse the body, to remove all of whatever flesh remained. They stripped the corpse to the bare skeleton."

"Was that necessary?"

"Yes. If not, the bones would not acquire a new body in the village of souls. It would be burdened with its rotted flesh."

"What happened to the bones?" Axel asked.

"A huge pit, maybe ten to fifteen feet deep, was dug and lined with the best furs and beaver skins. A scaffold was constructed around the pit, higher than a man's upraised fingertips. The bones were hung from or bound to poles on the scaffolding. Anything the dead might need during their journey to the village of souls was placed in the pit. Hatchets, kettles, beads, clothes. All the very best the relatives possessed, even if they themselves went cold the next winter.

"The feast and praying went on for hours, sometimes days. The names of the dead were shouted out over and over, until finally, at a signal from the Midewiwin, the bones were thrown into the pit. It happened all at once, while the Midewiwin pronounced the ritualistic words that awakened the spirits and sent them on their way.

"When the bodies were in the pit, another layer of skins was arranged over them. Then bark. Finally, dirt filled in the pit and the Feast of the Dead was over. The spirits of the people were released from their bodies and began their journey to their village of souls."

"Larry told me the feast was not performed for Shawonabe. Was that unusual?" Axel asked, trying to assemble all the information in his head.

"Oh, I'm sure others may have been neglected, but that was

because they did not instill in their descendants the proper respect, or because of the immorality of the relatives. But no one, as far as I know, was deliberately kept from enjoying the feast and the opportunity to journey to a village of souls. No one except for Shawonabe."

"And now he haunts us."

"Don't blame the Ottawas, Axel," Charley Wolf said. "They had no way of knowing he would succeed in coming back. They could not foresee the expansion of people inland."

Axel's eyes looked sharply at him. "You mean you think he is buried in Crooked Tree? Near our house?"

"I don't know for sure, but I wouldn't be surprised. Legend does say he was buried far into the wilderness. And if it wasn't for the agreement between the government and the Ottawas eighty-five years ago, Janis would never have come to own your ten acres of the wilderness."

"And until we built a house and moved there," Axel said, "there was no one near Shawonabe. No one for two hundred years that his spirit could inhabit."

"Perhaps. It would explain why he chose Janis, and why he waited so long."

"Then I must search for him near my house."

"Axel," Larry said, "even if you could narrow it down to your ten acres alone, or even our own backyard, you still would not be able to find him. He's buried deep in the earth, and even if there was a marking, it's long gone by now. You would have to uncover to a depth of several feet every square inch of your land."

"Maybe not," Axel said. "Maybe I can learn exactly where his 'prison' is. And I agree. I won't find it digging in the woods. I'll find it written down somewhere. In an old book, hidden in someone's library."

"This isn't a legal issue you're researching," Larry shouted in exasperation. "There's no library on old Indian death rites. Be reasonable. You can't expect to find anything."

"I've heard you say that before. But you always managed to find some law to support our position, no matter how crazy it was."

"Sure, with the help of thousands of pages filled with case summaries from all over the country. There's no such encyclopedia of tribal rituals."

"You don't understand, Larry," Axel said softly. "I have no choice but to look."

26

As the Yukon disappeared around the corner, Larry stood facing the road, his hand on a wooden column. "He doesn't have a chance."

Charley Wolf shifted on the wood slats of the bench. He was not as pessimistic as his grandson. There was something in Axel's tone, in his determination, that made the old man think. "There is a chance, Larry," he said. "A small one, but he still has a chance. If only he could find that grave."

"He'll never find it. And if he did, that's only half of his impossible task."

"Maybe you're right," Charley Wolf had to admit. But he could not disguise the cautious uplift in his voice.

"What are you thinking, you old coot?" Leon Moozganse asked.

Charley Wolf laughed. "I was just thinking that some good may come out of this after all. People are remembering the old ways, and that's not bad."

"It's hardly worth the price," Larry said.

"No, it's not. But as long as it's being paid, it's good to get some benefit."

"Too bad it's a dark page they are remembering," Leon Moozganse noted. "How long do you think it'll be before the people in town hear about the legend?"

Charley Wolf frowned. "I don't know. There's some folk in Wabanakisi as old as us, don't forget. They might know."

"So what if they do?" Larry said. "They surely can't blame us."

Charley Wolf cast a pained glance at his old friend. "You're young, Gusan. You don't know. You haven't felt hate before."

"You're wrong, Mishoo. I've felt discrimination. It's not over."

"You haven't felt hate as we did. Leon can tell you."

The lines in Moozganse's face seemed to sag. "There was a time when a trip to the food store meant you had to endure mocking jeers. I had a son about your age. He tried to stand up to them. Both his kneecaps were broken. The law?" He snorted. "They knew who it was. But nothing was done." The old eyes glistened with the memory.

Larry swallowed with difficulty.

"The effects of the hate, of the physical attacks, of the material success of the whites, was worse than broken kneecaps," Charley Wolf said solemnly. "Our culture was destroyed. Our people lived, but not as Ottawas. They were told by everything around them that their way of life was wrong. Imagine that! A society built on honoring their ancestors, reminded day after day how their ancestors failed."

"Our culture has survived, Mishoo," Larry protested. He had always felt pride in his heritage.

"It survived," Moozganse said, "because of men like your grandfather, and it grows stronger again because of young men like you."

Worn brakes squeaked in the street in front of their house. A green pickup truck with "Tabasash Farms" lettered across the door came to a stop. The driver climbed from behind the wheel and approached the porch.

"Hi, Paul," Larry called. He had grown up with Paul Tabasash, but now saw him only rarely.

"Hi. Glad to see you're not busy."

"Why's that?"

"Hello, Mr. Wolf," Paul Tabasash said as he walked up the broad wooden steps. "We need some help. We thought you might be interested."

"Glad to help if I can," Larry obliged.

"We're building a sweatlodge in Crooked Tree. It was my father's idea. He said it may help stop the bears."

Charley Wolf smiled broadly, his mind racing back to his youth, to a narrow hut ribbed with young saplings and covered with birch bark. He thought of walking in, of seeing the older faces, of being afraid at their stony stares. He remembered the heat that quickly glistened his body with sweat. He had become a man that night. He had dreamed of the whitetail deer and had become a full member of the deer totem. And with the other members of the deer totem had purified himself every summer in later sweatlodges, each time receiving strength and guidance from his patron animal. "Go ahead, Larry," he said.

"I will. I'd be honored."

"When's the meeting?" Charley Wolf asked.

"I don't know," Paul said. "A few days, I suppose. Whenever we finish it. My father said you might join us too."

Charley Wolf laughed. "I'm afraid I'm too old. I can't even keep my own place in good repair." His hand gestured at the peeling paint. "You go build your sweatlodge. Who knows, maybe the Muhquh Manitou will be appeased. Meanwhile, I'll try to coax my friend's magic."

Paul looked at Leon Moozganse. "I hope you succeed."

As Paul and Larry walked toward the pickup truck, Charley Wolf called after them, "If you have problems, maybe I can provide some help after all. You know, advice on construction."

Larry smiled. He knew his grandfather was pleased. Maybe he was right. Maybe some good would come from the bearwalk.

Speeding by his driveway, Axel did not notice the black-and-white car with the sheriffs insignia on the door disappearing up the gravel entrance to his house. His mind elsewhere, he thought of a ritual that took place two hundred years ago. He thought of a lonely grave, far in the wilderness, undisturbed. He tried to picture the grave, the trees around it, landmarks. Unconsciously hoping for some kind of insight, he stared through his thoughts, trying to see. But the trees were fuzzy, the ground indistinct. He could not see. He would have to put his hope in his research.

When he reached Wabanakisi, Axel parked in front of the two-story red-brick library and hurried inside. Smiling at the woman behind the desk, he walked into the room that housed the library's Michigan collection. Whether historic, scientific, or fiction, if it was set in or was about Michigan, or was written by a Michigan author, it was placed in that room. From

Ernest Hemingway to NASA's *Space Atlas of the Great Lakes*, they all had a slip in the two-drawer card catalog on the table.

Axel slid the top drawer out of its wooden box, placed it on the table, and made himself comfortable in one of the chairs. His fingers nimbly flipped to the first card in the section "Indians." He chose what appeared to be the most general, noted the call number, and found it quickly on the shelves.

It was a thick book, well over five hundred pages. Axel leafed to the contents page. "Death Customs, 281." The pages turned crisply. The book had not been opened for a long time.

> ... A burial site was invariably sacred ground, with most tribes taking special precautions to signify them as such. To disturb the sacred ground, even unintentionally, was a sacrilege to the dead. The Apaches sought isolated crevices in the rocks where they would place their deceased relatives. Marking the site they covered the bodies with stones.[48] The woodlands tribes of northern Illinois and Indiana constructed elaborate effigy mounds, usually in the shape of an animal that had special significance to the deceased. The body was buried at the vital point, the heart, and the mound was a lasting reminder of the sacredness of the ground.[49] Many Huron and Algonquin tribes, notably the Ottawas, buried their dead in a communal grave. ...

Axel walked to the table and sat down. He continued reading.

> ... Large wooden posts were pounded into the soil around the filled-in pit. A log-and-bark covering was constructed over the grave which could last for many years, marking the site as sacred ground.[50] In the Northeast, the Senecas and Penobscot tribes ...

Axel scanned quickly ahead, but the Ottawas were not mentioned again. He turned back to page 281. Footnote 50: "Jacques Revard, *Jesuit Relations and Allied Documents, The Travels and Explorations of the Jesuit Missionaries in New France, 1610–1791*, 28: 331–340." Axel took a small slip of paper from an open-ended box on the card catalog and jotted down the citation.

After referring to the card catalog, he selected a second book. Its focus was narrower; Axel could see it gave a more detailed treatment of the different tribes. Each had a separate chapter. He turned to Chapter 7, "The Ottawas." Axel read quickly. He came to a subtitle, "Feast of the Dead":

> ... Located near the natural fur-trade routes of the French, the Ottawas were visited by numerous missionaries. In 1636, Brébeuf wrote the following account after witnessing the Feast of the Dead: ... The graves are not permanent; ... the bodies remain in the cemeteries until the Feast of the Dead, which usually takes place every twelve years. . . .
>
> ... the bodies are to be transported to the village where is the common grave, each family sees to its dead, but with a care and affection that cannot be described; if they have dead relatives in any part of the country, they spare no trouble to go for them; they take them from the cemeteries, bear them on their shoulders, and cover them with the finest robes they have. . . . The flesh of some is quite gone, and there is only parchment on their bones; in other cases, the bodies look as if they had been dried and smoked, and show scarcely any signs of putrefaction; and in still other cases they are still swarming with worms. . . . After some time they strip them of their flesh, taking off the skin and flesh, which they throw into the fire along with the robes and mats in which the bodies were wrapped. . . .
>
> ... each captain by command gave the signal; and all, at once, loaded with their packages of souls, running as if to the assault of a town, ascended the scaffold by means of ladders hung all around it, and hung them to cross poles, each village having its own department. That done, all the ladders were taken away; . . .
>
> . . . We withdrew for the night to the old village, with the resolve to return the next morning, at daybreak, when they were to throw the bones into the pit; but we could hardly arrive in time, although we made great haste. . . . As we drew near, we saw nothing less than a picture of hell. The large space was quite full of fires and flames, and the air resounded in all directions with the confused voices of these barbarians; the noise ceased, however, for some time, and they began to sing--but in voices so sorrowful and lugubrious that it represented to us the horrible sadness and the abyss of despair into which these unhappy souls are forever plunged.
>
> Nearly all the souls were thrown in when we arrived, for it was done almost in the turning of a hand; each one had made haste, thinking there would not be enough room for all the souls. ...

Axel's gaze raced across the rest of Brébeuf's account. Breathless, he returned to a passage that rang in his head: "... *and they began to sing—but in voices so sorrowful and lugubrious that it represented to us the horrible sadness and the abyss of despair into which these unhappy souls are forever plunged.*" His grip loosened on the book. Brébeuf did not know, Axel thought. The Feast of the Dead was foreign to him. He did not realize what the Ottawas were doing. He did not realize their sorrowful voices were waking the spirits and sending them on their way to their heaven, an afterlife as different from Brébeuf's as their existences on earth.

Axel looked to the end of the passage. Footnote 21: "Brébeuf, *Jesuit Relations and Allied Documents, The Travels and Explorations of the Jesuit Missionaries in New France*, 1636, J.R., 10: 265–305." The same citation as before! Axel quickly scribbled it under the other, cramming it at the bottom of the small slip of paper. Perhaps another missionary had made a more accurate record.

The librarian was engrossed in a book. "Ma'am, excuse me," Axel said.

She peered over her glasses with a trace of annoyance. "Yes?"

"I found mention of a book—*Jesuit Relations and Allied Documents*. Do you have it here?"

Her face warmed immediately. "Oh, I wish we did," she said as she turned her book over and placed it open on the desk in front of her. "But there's not many of that collection around. They're old, you know."

"Yes, I can imagine. What is it, exactly?"

"Oh," she cooed, "it's a marvelous collection of writings by the Jesuit missionaries who worked around here when the French controlled the Great Lakes. It's quite unique, you know, for an area to be so blessed with so rich and detailed accounts of history."

"How detailed?"

"Very. Seventy-three volumes' worth, covering the period from 1610 to 1791."

"Where would I find a set of them?"

"Well, let's see," she pondered. "University of Detroit, I suppose. They're a Jesuit school, you know. And University of Michigan, of course."

Of course. The U. of M. library. It had everything. "Thank you," said Axel, turning to leave. "You've been very helpful."

"Oh . . . oh," she stuttered. "Was there anything in particular you wanted to know?"

"No, not really," Axel lied, moving closer to the door. He stopped. It was worth a try. "Well, actually, I was researching the Feast of the Dead."

"Oh, that's marvelous. Ottawa history is fascinating, you know."

"I know. Do you know anything about the Feast of the Dead?"

"Of course. I know everything about it. It's still celebrated, you know. Every year."

"*What?*" Axel almost shouted.

"Yes. Every year. November first."

"That's impossible. I was told it hadn't been performed for decades, maybe centuries."

"Not like they used to, perhaps. It changed dramatically over time. Originally it was a Huron custom which the Ottawas borrowed when they lived in eastern Canada. But as the Ottawas were driven west-ward by the Iroquois Confederation, the feast gradually changed. With the coming of the white man, it changed even more. But it's still celebrated today. Only, now they call it All Saints' Day."

"You mean the Catholic holy day?"

"Yes, that's it. When the missionaries were converting the Ottawas, their old beliefs gradually became Christianized. The missionaries found the Feast of the Dead distasteful, but it was strongly rooted in the Indians' culture, so the Jesuits eventually convinced them to do away with the actual rites and symbolically remember their ancestors every year on the Catholic All Saints' Day. It seemed to be the perfect solution."

"Yes, I should say," Axel said thoughtfully. "Well, thanks again."

He was across the drawbridge and past Ted Hiller's plumbing shop before he felt the full impact of what she had said. The Feast of the Dead celebrated every year? Symbolically, she had said. The festival the village held every November? Was that the old Feast of the Dead? Could the sacred chants have survived and they didn't even know it?

The wheels of the Yukon spun on the gravel as he hurried down his driveway. He was anxious to call Charley Wolf. At the sight of the black-and-white car, his chest tightened. He had not expected visitors. Least of all Sheriff Snyder. Another killing? he thought. Perhaps worse: *They've caught Janis.*

27

The rhythmic chopping of sharpened steel striking wood grew louder as Larry and Paul Tabasash trudged deeper into the woods. Paul had parked his truck behind two other vehicles on one of the many overgrown trail roads that ribboned the state forest. A mile from 621, the cars would not attract attention.

By the time they reached the clearing, Larry's shirt clung to his sweaty back. Several men were already working. One put down his ax and came over to them. "Hi, Paul."

"Hi, Dad. I brought some reinforcements."

"I can see. With this heat we need all the help we can get."

Larry noticed a pile of newly felled saplings. Their smooth bark was broken only where the branches had been stripped. The leaves and twigs constituted a second pile. They would provide some of the insulation, Mr. Tabasash explained. As Paul's father described the activity, Larry studied him closely. He was about the same age as his father would be—or would have been: Larry did not know which. After the brief survey of the sweatlodge site, Tabasash asked Larry to come with him to find some birch.

"We passed some on the walk from the car," Larry noted.

"I know, but I think there'll be more this way," he said as they moved out of the clearing, heading north. "I noticed how the land was a little lower."

"We don't want to have to drag the logs too far, do we?"

Tabasash looked at him, his eyebrows upraised and an amused twist to his lips. "We won't drag them anywhere. We just want the bark."

"Oh," Larry said simply.

After a few minutes, Larry eyed several white trunks of birch through the trees. "Over here," he directed. He led Tabasash to five medium-sized birches growing from a single root network.

"Good," Tabasash said as they approached. "These look fine." The papery bark was broken only occasionally by black splotches.

Tabasash slipped his black-handled knife from its sheath on his belt. He selected one of the trunks and sliced an even vertical line from as high as he could reach down to the ground. He was careful to cut through only the top layer so they could peel a continuous strip from the tree.

At about two-foot intervals he sliced a horizontal line completely around the trunk. With the tree prepared, he edged the width of the blade under the bark and pried the end loose. He moved slowly around the tree, the bark peeling easily. After two layers were removed, Tabasash cut the bark evenly from the trunk. It dropped to the ground, coiling like an apple peel.

The underbark had the same pattern of blemishes, but it was yellowish, almost metallic in color. "You have to be careful not to go too deep," Tabasash instructed. "Otherwise you'll kill the tree. In another season," he said, rubbing the silky new bark, "this would be ready for harvest."

He handed his knife to Larry, who wedged the length of the blade under the bark. Slowly he separated it from the tree. Halfway around the trunk, the bark cracked and split.

"Equal pressure, all along the strip. Try again."

He did. The rest of the strip came off evenly, and Larry sensed an inner exhilaration. He had heard much of his people's history and legends from his grandfather, but he had rarely participated in what must have been such a common job as stripping white birch.

As he started his second strip, Larry wondered if he would be more like Paul if his father had been around to teach him. Would he have learned the old crafts and never left the village for law school? He forced himself to concentrate on the bark. Almost done. No cracks.

"How's Axel Michelson been doing lately?" Tabasash said suddenly.

The birch bark split. "Okay," Larry breathed, his response a question.

"Just wondering. You're pretty friendly with him, aren't you? I mean, he's not just a boss, is he?"

"No, we're friends." Larry was guarded.

"Has he said . . . talked about Janis at all?"

"Sure, she's his wife." Larry was not going to make it easy for him.

"I know . . . but, I mean, has he said anything odd about her? Since the bear attacks?"

Larry ignored him as he finished peeling the cracked strip. As it dropped to the ground, he turned back to Tabasash. "No. Why should he?"

Tabasash's eyelids drooped. He stared at Larry as if to say: Come on, you trust me, don't you?

There was no use pretending, Larry decided. "He knows about the bearwalk."

"And?"

"He believes."

"What about Janis?"

"He's trying to help her."

"How?"

"He's looking for Shawonabe's grave. He wants to perform the Feast of the Dead and release his spirit."

"He *wants* to *what*?"

Larry looked at him silently. He had heard.

"He can't do that. You told him, didn't you?"

"I told him he wouldn't succeed."

"You've got to do more than that. You've got to stop him!"

"He'll never find the grave. It's impossible."

"But what if he does? You wouldn't let him dishonor our ancestors like that, would you?"

"It wouldn't dishonor anyone. It would only stop the killing."

"Don't you know why the feast was not celebrated for him?" Tabasash's face was intense.

Larry did know. The implications had not occurred to him, though.

Tabasash looped a fatherly arm around him. "Come on, son. Let's finish up and get back to the lodge site. I know we can count on you."

Luke Snyder stood with his back to the Michelson house, his right hand at his waist, just above his holster. He had taken to wearing his gun lately, confident the .357 Magnum would drop a black bear in its tracks.

The sheriff stared into the woods. He had walked out to the trap with John Orson and had been as perplexed by what they found as Orson was. He left him there eventually to come back to the house for a discreet look around. Now he stood pondering the entire improbable set of facts. A car pulled up in front of the house.

Janis or Axel? Either one, he did not look forward to what he had to say. He walked around the side of the house, where Axel met him with an anxious glare.

"Hello, Axel." His face was grim.

"Sheriff," Axel nodded. "Anything the matter?"

"Checking the traps."

"Oh?"

"Orson's out there right now. He's resetting it."

"*Re*setting?"

"Yeah. Crazy thing. The trap was sprung. The bait's gone and the drop door's down, but no bear."

"How could that have happened?"

"Either the grating was raised to let whatever was caught out or it was propped up until the meat was removed." Snyder regarded Axel closely. There was no visible change of emotion. "In either event, it would take more cunning than any bear would have."

"I suppose. What about the other traps? Same thing happen to them?"

"No, only to yours."

Axel shifted uncomfortably. Where's Janis? he wanted to scream, but he had to continue the charade. "I would have thought by now at least one bear would have been caught."

"One was. Last night, in the trap set by where Davis was found."

Axel faced Snyder. "Is that right? Was it one of the killers?"

"Hardly. It was a cub, a yearling." Snyder turned away for a mo-ment, spitting between his teeth. "It was dead. Shot ten to fifteen times while it cowered in that steel pipe."

"Oh, Christ. Who would have...?" Axel stopped. He knew

who would have done such a thing.

"Yeah. I'm going to talk to him later. I was kind of hoping to talk to Janis too, while I was out here. You wouldn't happen to know where she is, would you?"

"Uh, I guess she's probably at work. At the kennel." Axel could feel his voice growing weak.

"Nope. I checked. Hasn't been there in a couple days."

"Maybe she's in town someplace."

"Her car's in the garage. I looked through the window."

"You don't miss much. Why all the interest in Janis?"

"Come on, Axel, I'm your friend. Don't look at me like that. There's a lot of pressure on me to stop whoever has been cutting out those tongues. Especially with the state police looking over my shoulder. If I don't talk to her, they will, as soon as they piece together what I have."

Axel was cautious. "And what have you pieced together?"

Snyder shook his head slowly and looked down at the ground. "I heard how that little kid went crazy when she saw Janis. She's the only witness we have so far."

"Janis just happened to be standing there when she came out of her coma. It could have been anybody."

"Yeah, I suppose. But it sure would explain things. It would explain what Grace was doing down that old trail road. The way I figure it, she must have thought she was going to your house—it's the only one around, and she did have your brief. Now, if that's true, the most likely person to ask her there would be either you or Janis. And you were in Bay City."

"Do you really believe Janis is the one that's cutting out the tongues?"

"It's not a question of what I believe or want to believe. You know that. It's what the facts indicate."

"Come on, Luke, use your common sense. Janis couldn't be involved."

"I hope you're right. But I just don't know what to think. I've already had two anonymous tips that Indian black magic is responsible. They said evil spirits inhabit bears and cut out tongues for trophies or some such nonsense. Lord knows where it will all end."

"I just hope it's soon. How is Marcy, by the way?"

"Who?"

273

"The little girl in the hospital. Grace's daughter."

"Oh. They took her to a clinic outside Detroit to see some specialists. Last I heard, she's still in a trance. They wouldn't let me get near her to try to ask a few questions."

"That's probably for the best," Axel observed. "Sooner or later she'll come out of it."

"They might not even let me talk to her then," Snyder said forlornly.

"Maybe by then your friend Orson will have solved our problems."

Snyder shifted gears. "I know Janis is an Indian, but is she an Ottawa? I mean, is she originally from this area? I never really knew her, you know," Snyder added almost apologetically. "You know how it used to be, we didn't socialize much with the Indians."

"Janis is the daughter of an Ottawa chief and has lived here all her life."

"She would know the local legends, then, I suppose."

"Probably. Like every other Ottawa around here."

"Do you know when she'll be back?"

"No, sorry."

"I've got a good fingerprint from the window of the funeral home. Maybe if I could compare it with Janis', we could settle this once and for all and I wouldn't have to bother you any more."

He took Axel by surprise. "All right. When she's back, we'll come in." He hesitated. "Oh, I forgot. I'll be heading down to Ann Arbor this afternoon. I've got some research to do."

"What's the matter," Luke said, "our library not good enough for you?"

Axel managed a laugh. "U. of M.'s law library."

"I guess it can wait. I don't expect them to match anyway. It'll let me cross something off my list, though."

Axel was weary of being on the defensive. He was glad when Orson appeared from behind the house.

"Hello," Orson greeted. "Did the sheriff tell you about our trap?"

"Yes, he did. The bears somehow got the bait without getting caught."

"The venison is gone, that's for sure. Whether the bears figured out how to do it is another matter. Sheriff," he said, a businesslike tone to his voice, "I poked around some more and found something interesting. Footprints near the trap. Small ones, like the other day."

Axel did not look at Snyder, but he felt his calculated stare.

Orson broke the silence. "Anything the matter?"

"No, no," the sheriff said. "We should be getting back."

"Uh, perhaps you could take a plaster cast of those prints, or whatever you do." Orson's tone was almost apologetic. He was treading in another's expertise. "It might be the tongue cutter."

A look of displeasure crossed Snyder's face. "All right. I'll call the state police evidence tech."

Orson quickly grasped his first lesson in policy-agency rivalry. He told Axel the trap was reset and asked him to call if he heard it slam shut. By the way, hear anything unusual last night? Axel had to lie again.

As they walked to their car, Snyder said, "Don't forget to bring Janis in, when you have a chance."

"I won't. And thanks, Luke." Axel watched as they maneuvered by the Yukon, the sheriffs car rolling down the slight embankment that stretched across the driveway and in front of the house. When they were out of sight, Axel hurried into the house. "Christ!" The refrigerator door was wide open. Food was strewn on the floor. "Janis!" He dashed into the bedroom. The bathroom. Empty. He returned to the kitchen. Thank God Snyder missed this, Axel thought. Or had he?

A milk carton on its side had emptied half its contents on the floor. Axel picked it up and put it back on the metal shelf in the refrigerator. The cellophane around a package of hot dogs was torn open and the meat was partially devoured, gnawed only in the middle. Fruit was smashed and half-eaten. A head of lettuce had rolled under the table. Axel picked it up and examined it. It looked like someone had bitten it like an apple. If was as if an animal had gotten into the refrigerator.

Axel gathered up the food and returned it to the shelves. Anything partially eaten he placed in a mixing bowl, which he slid beside the milk carton.

She was alive. Axel knew that. But what had she become? He was grim as he finished cleaning the kitchen, picturing her alone in the woods with the bears. The thought chilled him. She could not survive forever out there against the elements and Dirk Vanderlee's posse. As he picked up the phone, he told himself she was safe.

"Hello," the voice rasped.

"Mr. Wolf. This is Axel Michelson. I think I may have found something important."

"Yes?"

"All Saints' Day. November first. Is that when the Feast of the Dead is commemorated?"

There was a long pause. It was as if the receiver went dead.

"Mr. Wolf? Are you there?"

"Yes, I'm still here."

"Well?"

"I hadn't thought of that, but yes, you're right. Ogochin Atisken is remembered on All Saints' Day. Sort of."

"So the Feast of the Dead is still celebrated." Axel's voice crackled with excitement in Charley Wolf's ear.

"You could say that."

"How? How is it celebrated?"

"It's celebrated with a Mass, a Catholic Mass, and silent prayers for our deceased during the offertory."

"And?"

"And that's it. Maybe at one time there was more. Back when our religion was strong and Christianity was new. But not now." His voice became sympathetic. "I'm sorry, Axel, but no one alive remembers."

No one alive, his mind repeated. Axel knew he would have to turn to the dead. The *Jesuit Relations* could hold the clue. "I'm going to have to drive to the library in Ann Arbor," he announced. "But before I do, I've got to find Janis. Then—"

"What will you do if you find her?" Charley Wolf interrupted.

"I don't know, but I can't just leave her out there."

"She's Shawonabe's now, and the only way to save her is to break his hold. If you feel going to Ann Arbor will help in discovering the secrets of the Feast of the Dead, you must do it. And if she does come back, Larry and I will be here."

"But how can I be sure she can survive until I get back?"

"Axel, Janis is probably the only safe human in Crooked Tree. She is protected by the bears."

The realization was chilling. After a moment Axel thanked

him and said good-bye. He quickly packed some clothes, grabbed his briefcase, and after dropping a fresh legal pad and a couple pens in it, ran out to the car.

It was a little after four o'clock. He would be in Ann Arbor by nine or ten. He would need a full night's sleep to prepare for the research tomorrow. One more thing to be done. Axel dashed back into the house and made sure the back screen was unlocked and the sliding glass door ajar. The animal might have to feed again.

28

The conversation seemed far removed. It was as if Larry were eating alone instead of with his grandfather and Leon Moozganse in the kitchen. Leon had to repeat himself before Larry looked up. "You should be in good spirits. Learning about the sweatlodge used to be the happiest time in a young Ottawa's life."

Larry nodded.

"Wait till the ceremony. You will learn much more."

"I'm not sure I'll be going."

Moozganse deferred to Charley Wolf. "Why wouldn't you go?"

"I don't know. They might not want me."

"What are you talking about?"

"I'm too close to Axel. They might not want me there, if I don't try to stop him."

"You told someone what Axel is doing?" Charley Wolf guessed.

"Yes. And Tabasash thinks that if Axel is allowed to celebrate the Feast of the Dead, Shawonabe's spirit will go to the soul village and torment our ancestors, the very thing they tried to avoid. And he'll be there when our souls enter."

Charley Wolf looked across the table at his old friend with saddened eyes. The pain of ignorance hurt him deeply. "That is not true."

"But isn't that the purpose of Ogochin Atisken? Send the spirit to the soul village?"

"It is."

"Then how can you not be concerned over what it might mean if Axel succeeds?"

"Neither I nor Leon is concerned, because we know the old religion. The reason the feast is delayed for so long and not celebrated at each individual's death, and the reason for a communal grave, is to ensure the souls are not alone in the next life. Those for whom the feast is celebrated at the same time, whose bones are mingled in a common grave, migrate to a single soul village. No one else will be there, and no one else will ever arrive after them. The heavens are made up of countless soul villages, each one separate and unique. So you see, the danger Shawonabe presented to our ancestors no longer exists. If the feast were celebrated for him now, he would be destined to roam eternity alone."

"But what about Tabasash?"

"Many are unschooled in the old ways. You should know that. They may think they understand, but in reality their knowledge only scratches the surface."

Larry flushed. "I'm sorry, Mishoo."

"Don't worry. What Axel seeks to do will cause no one harm."

Larry looked to Leon Moozganse. The crinkled face nodded its agreement.

"You still look concerned," Charley Wolf said, "Don't you believe your grandfather?"

"Oh, yes . . . yes, I do. And I'm very relieved. But I was wondering what Tabasash might do. He seemed so sure of his belief, so insistent that I stop Axel."

"Don't worry about him. He's a good man. He would not do any-thing foolish."

"You're probably right," Larry agreed. His grandfather knew him better than he did. He should know. Still, Larry felt apprehensive. His grandfather had not been with Tabasash in the woods that afternoon.

The forest seemed unusually quiet. A low-pressure system had drifted across Lake Michigan, bringing with it still, humid air. After the sun had set, a cloud front moved shoreward from the lake and now hung heavy in the night sky.

"Do you think it's smart, coming back to the same spot?" Nels asked.

"I thought we discussed that already," Dirk said, leaning against the side of his car, a rifle cradled in his arms.

"I know, but I was thinking. People weren't too happy when they heard about that cub. Maybe somebody—the sheriff—will come out here looking for us tonight."

"That fuckin' asshole hasn't worked a minute past five o'clock since he's been in office. You think he's going to come all the way out here just on the possibility of catching some bear killers?"

"Well, he suspected you right off, didn't he?"

"Yeah, so what? He didn't do anything, did he? I practically told him I shot the little fucker, and he still didn't do a damn thing."

"But what about the people? Everybody I heard talking about it seemed . . . well, disgusted."

"To hell with them. They don't know what's good for 'em."

"I don't know," Nels drawled. "That's what you said last night."

"Hey. You're starting to sound like Sizemore."

"No I'm not, I'm just—"

"Then shut up."

"I was just trying to say maybe we should move to another spot. I want to shoot these bears as much as you do."

"Look. We got a cub last night. That means its mother must be nearby. All we gotta do is find it. That's a hell of a lot better than any other spot you could pick out."

A shaft of light ricocheted off the trees. Nels spun around to see headlights bouncing jerkily down the dirt road. "Is that Metz?" he asked breathlessly.

"Sure. Who else?" Dirk stepped into the middle of the trail.

"The sheriff?"

"If it is, so what? No law against standing in the woods holding your gun, is there?" He walked up to the car as Bob Metz got out.

"I brought my cousin along to get in on the fun. Jasper," he said, motioning to the hulking figure, "this is Dirk. And Nels."

"Hi," Dirk said evenly. He regarded the big man carefully. Dirk did not meet too many men taller than himself. "I hope you can shoot," he said, his voice a challenge.

"Sure he can," Metz said. "As good as me."

"That's what we're afraid of!" Nels chortled.

"Just listen to me and don't go firing unless I say." Dirk stared at the big man. "That goes for everybody." His gaze shifted to the other two men.

"All right. Don't get excited," Metz said.

"Come on. Let's go."

"Go? What about the others?" Nels questioned.

"There aren't going to be any others."

"I thought you said we'd have even more tonight," Nels demanded excitedly.

"I can't help it if most people around here are assholes." Not waiting for a reply, Dirk turned and walked north along the trail.

As the four men moved silently along the dirt road, the air seemed to grow heavier. Nels sensed something he did not understand, something that filled him with dread.

The huge black shape was almost indistinguishable in the shadows. From a few feet away it could have been an old white-pine stump, but the heavy panting was unmistakable. The bear breathed lustily, its thick coat a handicap in the sultry air.

It was in new territory with the smell of danger reeking in the air, yet it felt strangely at home. It had known where the hill was, the narrow clearing that snaked its way through the woods, and even where to find the circular cave.

Twigs crunched behind the bear. Approaching steps padded across the soft ground. The bear did not lurch away. It had known the intruder would come. It had known others of its kind would be there. And it knew they would be there for the same reason.

The intruder plodded heavily up to the circular cave. Its nostrils flexed rapidly as it examined the unfamiliar object. Ambling around the length of the object, it almost stumbled over the other bear.

They studied each other carefully, sniffing first each other's noses, then their bodies. They looked very much the same: the same shaggy fur, the same weight, and both were males. Under other circumstances a chance meeting would have rocked the forest with a mighty battle. But the bears knew they shared a common purpose.

The intruder turned and loped up the small embankment to the narrow clearing. It stood on its hind legs and read the air. Slowly it lowered itself to all fours, its nose still seeking the scent. The bears' eyes seemed to communicate silently. The intruder turned with a grunt and made its way down a slight incline on the other side of the clearing. After a while the shuffling of vegetation ceased. The bear knew the intruder was in place.

The bear shook its head. A heavy glob of saliva flung to the ground. Almost immediately, more drool formed at the corners of its mouth. Hot and restless, it began to pace alongside the cave. It paused at both ends long enough to sniff the grating. It had enjoyed the easy meal and hoped to find something it might have missed. But the meat was eaten and the cave was now closed. The bear glared impatiently at the road.

The men puffed and panted in the dead air, sweat soaking their shirts. Thick sand tugged at every step. Beads of moisture collected on Nels' forehead. He wanted to turn around and walk back to the cars. But he did not want to go alone, and wondered how to make the suggestion.

"Hey, Metz," Nels wheezed at last. It was almost too hot to talk. "Did you think it would be as warm as this?"

"Nope. Now I know why hunting season is in November."

"Are you going to stay out all night?"

"I don't know," Metz parried. "What about you?"

"We'll stay until we get the job done," Dirk said forcefully.

"But it's so hot. Maybe we should—"

"I'm calling the shots here, and I say we continue walking."

"I don't mean we should give up the hunt for good. Just tonight, maybe, while it's so hot."

"And what are you going to say when the next lady and little kid get torn apart by bears? 'Sorry, but I was too hot'?"

"No," he said meekly.

"Then shut the fuck up and keep that gun ready."

Nels could feel Dirk's eyes boring into him. Even under the cover of darkness he was forced to turn away.

"We'll stop at the trap," said Dirk. "Maybe we can take cover and wait for them there."

The bear's eyes were almost closed as its snout jutted upward in the air. It did not have to rely on sight. Its sense of smell would tell it what it needed to know.

The scent languished in the still air, while the sound carried swiftly. The bear had heard them before its nose was alerted. Now it concentrated on reading the slow-moving clues. It was the smell of danger, and it was getting closer, but the bear did not try to get away. This was what it had waited for.

Sweat streamed down the smooth underside of his arm. Nels gripped his gun tighter, his muscles dulled with the strain.

"You know, perhaps we're going after the wrong thing," Jasper said quietly.

"What do you mean?" Metz asked.

"All these people had their tongues cut out. It had to have been done by a person, and it was probably an Indian. They have a belief, I heard, that says a man can use a bear to kill. But it's effective only as long as he cuts out the tongue of the victim."

"That's just a lot of horseshit."

"Maybe. But maybe some smart Indians are making it look that way. They ain't never been fond of us whites, especially since this injunction shit."

"So what are you thinking?" Metz said.

"I'm thinking maybe we should be hunting some redskins."

"Don't worry about the arrow flingers," Dirk said, his tone conveying more than his words.

"Why? What do you have in mind?" asked Nels, not sure he wanted to know.

"Me? Nothing," Dirk said. "But maybe I heard about somebody else that's going to take care of them. All we gotta do is keep up our side of the bargain."

Nels shuddered. He sensed being involved in more than he wanted.

The bear could now distinguish four similar but very distinct scents. Its chest pulsed with the heavy beat of its heart as it crept into a bramble thicket a few feet from the cave. Its breathing was even; it was no longer panting. It took little notice of the quiet, determined shuffling approaching through the thick sand from the north.

Two more bears stepped almost in unison, the second behind the first, following it track for track. Except for the muffled swish of scattered sand, they moved silently. They could not see the first bear, but they sensed it was there. As they stood in the clearing, another shape approached on their trail. It moved between them, standing upright, and surveyed the surrounding area.

A tangle of bramble ferns rustled a short distance into the swamp. The bear enmeshed in the woody shrub sensed the smell of danger a few feet away at the top of the embankment. Though it was close, it seemed remote, as if the scent was not as strong as it once was.

The two bears turned and strode into the woods opposite the cedar swamp. They were followed closely by the upright creature, its thin hairless body melting into the shadows of Crooked Tree.

The road had dipped low. To the left of the hunters, a thick wall of cedar crowns formed an almost impenetrable barrier. To the other side, oaks towered above them. Ahead, a small knoll further closed them in.

"Boy, if ever there was a place for an ambush, this would be it."

Dirk grabbed Nels by his shirt and spun him around. "I told you to shut up!" His hand squeezed Nels' chest, pieces of cloth and loose flesh caught in his tight grasp. Then slowly, loosening his grip, Dirk said, softly, "If an ambush is what you want, an ambush is what we'll have."

With his free hand, Nels massaged his chest.

"We'll set up right here," Dirk said.

"Hey, what's that?" Metz almost shouted. He pointed with the barrel of his gun down the embankment into the swamp.

The bear's jaws were slack, its breathing measured. It could see one of the men standing on the edge of the clearing. A quick lunge and it would be in reach. The bear readied itself.

Dirk ran to Metz and stared into the darkness. "It's the trap," he said excitedly. "Let's check it out."

Dirk took two steps down the embankment and slipped. He struggled to his feet and half-slid the rest of the way as the others stumbled behind him, hurrying to see.

The bear steeled its muscles. It was as still as death. The prey was almost within its grasp!

"It's closed!"

"It can't be," Dirk said. "That must be the back."

Metz shuffled to the other end. "No, that's the front."

"Well, son of a . . ." Dirk dropped to his knees. He peered through the metal grating. "Nothing. Damn!"

Nels' voice trembled. "How could that happen?"

"How the fuck do I know?" Dirk snapped.

"Maybe it was the guy who cuts the tongues," Jasper said. "I told you we should have gone after those red bastards."

"Who cares what happened to the trap? It don't mean shit to us."

Dirk glared at the others, then waved his arm at the road. "Let's get out of this hole. We're not accomplishing anything down here."

As the others started up the ridge, Nels breathed deeply. His arm ached from carrying the eight-pound rifle. Stepping toward a mass of bramble fern, he leaned his rifle against the stout underbrush.

Dirk stepped into the middle of the trail. "We'll wait for them on the solid ground over here," he said as he led Metz and Jasper into the woods opposite the trap.

Sweat dripped from Nels' handkerchief as he squeezed it with his tired hands. He shook it open and rubbed his arms, the thin cloth quickly saturating again. He looked up to the ridge, but the others were out of view.

The bear stared at its prey. It tensed to spring. But it couldn't move. Something gripped its muscles and held them motionless.

"Hey. Out there! I heard something!" Metz cried.

Nels grabbed the barrel of his rifle and dashed toward the embankment.

"There was something in the woods," Metz whispered. "Big. Heavy."

The bramble rustled behind Nels. He did not hear it, his attention intent on the voices.

"We all heard it," Dirk breathed. "And it probably heard you. If you'd shut up, we could get a fix on it."

On the ridge, Nels saw the three figures in the darkness and hurried beside them. The brush crashed in the darkness.

Something large was moving through the woods. The men tried to see, but it was no use. The oaks blanketed them from what little glow there was from the starless sky. Whatever it was, it moved powerfully.

"Let's fan out," Dirk whispered. "Then we'll walk toward the noise."

They inched through the woods, partly by plan, partly by necessity. At a few feet away, objects lost their design and became darkened shapes. Dirk glanced nervously from side to side. He would not have believed any place could be so dark.

Ahead of them three hulking shapes clung to the ground. Slowly, through the dense air, the bears discerned a trace of familiar scent, an acrid, pungent odor that made them look toward the woods, thinking escape. They smelled it rarely, once a season, when the air was changing from warm to cold. It was a faint reminder of death, but the bears were unable to run away.

Nels looked to his right. Dirk was a shapeless shadow stalking through the trees. Beyond him, invisible in the darkness, Metz kept pace with halting steps. At the far end, Jasper plodded deliberately over the spindly ferns.

The bears strained to see each other in the darkness. Their enlarged retinas were blank; there was no light to reflect in them. The bears moved slowly, silently, as if guided by the same instinct. One slunk to the north and settled a few feet to the side of the approaching path. Fifty feet directly south, two bears crouched among the ferns side by side. In between, the fourth creature, still upright, stood behind the Y of a tree trunk split close to the ground. A free-form sack dangled from one of its forelimbs. Suddenly the sack slipped to the ground.

The men froze. Jasper raised his weapon to his shoulder and pointed toward the noise. Christ! he realized, he couldn't see the sight at the end of the barrel! He would be shooting blind.

"They're out there." Dirk's loud whisper wheezed through the woods. "Take it easy."

"Yeah," Jasper breathed to himself. "Take it easy." He lowered his rifle and resumed his cautious walk. The slow crunching to his left told him the others were continuing as well. Ahead, tree trunks were silhouetted, black on black. His eyes scanned the ground. Two stumps were directly in his path.

The bears were hardly aware of each other, their concentration focused on the approaching animals. They held as steady as they could. But their powerful muscles could remain tensed only so long.

The stumps! Did they move? No. The ferns around them must have shifted in the breeze. Jasper gazed beyond the low black shapes into the woods. Suddenly his mind shouted: There is no breeze!

The bears exploded from the ground. Jasper stumbled back, screaming. A bear was on him. His gun crashed to the ground.

Metz saw the flurry to his right, but was afraid to shoot. He might hit his cousin.

Jasper tried to turn, but a bear's jaws tugged at his side. Blindly he groped for his rifle as the bear's teeth ripped through the soft flesh. Then the second bear pounced, and Jasper shrieked into the darkness.

Metz heard a rushing of dead leaves behind him. "Help him!" Dirk shouted, but he stood frozen with fear.

The bear's lightning paw slashed across Jasper's chest, leaving a gaping wound from neck to stomach. As the others approached, the bears leaped from their prey and plunged into the darkness.

Dirk almost tripped on the body. He bent quickly to Jasper and felt the rushing warmth. Metz stumbled up to him, gasping, "Jay, Jay."

"Get back," Dirk commanded.

Metz did not hear him. "Jay," he repeated, his hand fumbling for his flashlight. The beam lit up the corpse. His cousin's body lay mottled with blood. "I killed him!" he shouted.

"Shut up!" Dirk yelled. He tried to grab him. But he was too late.

Metz broke toward the road, his rifle falling to the ground. "I killed him!"

"Come back!"

The footsteps quickly receded into the darkness. It was quiet for several seconds before Nels spoke. "We gotta get outta here," he gasped.

"You're staying. We can get them."

"No!" he yelled.

"They've killed too many people. We have to get them."

"You're insane!" He stumbled backward.

"Stay here!"

Nels turned and started to run, his rifle firmly in his grasp.

"Come back . . . *deserter!*"

Dirk jerked the gun to his shoulder. His finger squeezed. The fleeing shadow crumpled to the ground as the gunshot cracked through the heavy air. Its echo pounded into the skulls of the bears. The faint, acrid odor they detected earlier seared their nostrils. It was the most dangerous smell of all. The bears' collective instincts shouted to run. Instead, they shuffled nervously among the brush.

Dirk lowered the rifle as the ringing in his ears slowly subsided. His thoughts cleared less swiftly. Nels had been leaving him to die, Dirk told himself. He only acted first.

He glanced quickly about. How many of *them* were there? He could not fight them by himself. It would be suicide. He must retreat. There was no shame in that, but which way was the road? A nervous laugh escaped from the back of his mouth. The road was this way. He was sure of it. His legs stepped hesitantly. They were less sure.

One more. The bears heard him moving slowly in the direction he had come from, and began to creep through the underbrush, converging on the last of their prey. Keeping low, the slight creature approached the dark outline of a man on the ground. Twenty feet ahead, a bear's heavy paw stepped on a fallen branch.

Dirk heard the snap and whirled around. They were following him!

He aimed his gun and blasted into the darkness. "Come on, you fuckin' bears. Come out of there!"

The naked creature dropped flat to the ground. Its ears gradually cleared from the deafening roar, and it stood up. Grasping the sack, it stepped hesitantly forward. The bears had continued moving. It had to keep pace.

Dirk crunched slowly through the brush. He could see the hump of the road. Just a little farther and he would be to the sandy trail. The bears tensed. They must strike together. And quickly. Their heavy feet drummed the ground.

Dirk heard them coming and began running blind. The woods rustled in the darkness to his side. There were too many! He couldn't fire fast enough. He reached the clearing with them only yards behind.

The trap, thought Dirk. They couldn't get him in the trap. He dashed through the sand, his eyes scanning the darkness. A growl resonated from the trees behind him. There it was! He sprang down the embankment as the bears broke into the clearing together. Dirk's foot snagged a bramble fern and he stumbled, the rifle falling to the ground. The bears were in the road. No time to pick it up.

He grabbed the metal grating, and the latch snapped open. The door rose with a jerk. Dirk swung his legs in the pipe. The bears were only feet away. He could feel the ground shake. He pushed himself under the trapdoor and let it go. The metal grating crashed. An instant later, the pipe jerked forward. A bear had smashed into the door.

Dirk clambered to the far end of the trap. Twisting quickly around, his back pressed against the cold grating. He was safe! "Ha, *ha*," he screamed, his voice caroming off the steel walls. "I did it! I won! I outsmarted them all!"

The upright creature dived to the sandy soil. The bellowing screams startled it. It watched as a bear smashed its paw into the grating. Dirk stared at the three-inch claws protruding into the trap. The bear tugged mightily. The pipe slid an inch forward. But the door was unbent.

"Ah, *ha*!" he screamed. "I'm locked up and you can't get in. I'm safe! In your trap!" Dirk rocked with hysterical laughter.

The bear moved back to the others, its throaty snarl like tumbling gravel. They did not want to concede, but they did not like waiting so close to the smell of danger.

Dirk lay on his back with his head and shoulders propped against the end of the enclosed tube. Fatigue encompassed him like a thousand tiny probing fingers. Why are they so quiet? He could hear them shuffling in the swamp, their growls low. It was almost as if they were waiting for something. Dirk felt a quickening of his pulse. Though safe, he realized he was totally helpless.

The smooth-skinned creature stood on the ridge staring at the circular object. It could see the shapes of the bears shuffling nervously to the side. It knew their prey was inside the metal cave. The creature moved silently closer.

Dirk rolled to his stomach and peered between the metal hatchwork. His head throbbed at the temples. Something nagged at his memory. The bait! If the bears had sprung the trap earlier, they could do it again. "Get outa here!" he yelled. "You got your share. Now go, leave me alone. Please . . ."

A high-pitched shriek shattered the dead air. Dirk couldn't breathe, he couldn't move. It had sounded unearthly. Something gently nudged the pipe. Dirk spun around on his knees and scrambled toward the trap door. He crouched, frantically scanning the metal wall. The trap door wiggled imperceptibly. Suddenly there was a thud on top of the culvert.

"That's not going to help!" His voice boomed in the narrow confines of the pipe. The echo was almost gone when his shaking voice yelled again. "Fucker! Climb up there all you want. You still can't get in!"

His breaths erratic gasps, Dirk inched to the door. He didn't notice the bear splashing through the muck until it was almost to the trap. The bear roared and crashed a heavy paw into the grating. Black ooze splattered across his face. Then the rasp of metal on metal grated in his ears, and he watched in terror as the door began to rise.

The bear watched too, snapping its jaws. Dirk could see little but the great white teeth dripping with saliva.

Stop! Please make it stop! Dirk stared at the rising steel strips. "Leave me alone, please," he whimpered. "Please help me. . . ."

The bear lunged into the cave. Its lightning-quick head seized a flailing foot and crushed it with its teeth.

Dirk heard his bones crunch above the resounding roars. Pain exploded up his leg. He could think of nothing but the pain. He screamed in agony.

The bear jerked forward and seized the soft flesh of the neck, trying to crush out the sound. When it released its grip, the head slumped forward. There was no movement.

The bear glanced at the close walls. It felt trapped. Its steel-like claws scratched across the corrugated metal. Freed, it turned and loped into the cedar swamp. As it retreated from the circular cave, it felt strangely calm.

A metal latch clanged on top of the cave. Two feet thudded to the ground by the entrance. The creature stood upright for a moment and surveyed the swamp, then bent low and peered in the open mouth of the trap. The dead body was slumped at the far end. The creature crawled into the cave, dragging the sack beside it. A few moments later it emerged and padded across the clearing into the stand of oaks.

29

Sunlight penetrating translucent leaves colored the small patch of wilderness amber. The bears shuffled nervously in circles over the dry moss. They had covered six miles of new territory since the night before, walking due west. When they met the fifth bear, they ceased their trek and began their wait. It seemed a tenuous alliance, held together by an invisible thread of common purpose.

Seated on a red-pine log, ignored by the bears, the figure of a woman hunched forward, huddled alone in her nakedness. Her un-blemished breasts pressed against her thighs, and a tired head rested on scratched knees. Long black hair brushed across her expressionless face and dangled almost to the ground. By her feet lay a stained deerskin pouch.

The bears realized the creature's weakness, yet they did not desert it in the woods. They sensed its strengths as well. The woman had not the natural tools of the bears, but it followed them and used an agile mind to read their actions. So when the five bears tensed, their necks puffed, staring toward the same hillock, the woman stared where they did.

After several seconds she could see what they had detected. Two black bears sidestepped around the hill, one loping easily behind the other. They halted their approach a few yards from the trampled circle of vegetation. The seven bears stood motionless, their snouts raised in the air. The woman knew there would be no confrontation. As she settled back on the red-pine log, the two newcomers joined the pack and gradually adopted the hypnotic shuffle of the others, their ears tuned to the same rhythmic chopping resonating from an unseen location through the woods.

The young wood sliced cleanly under the force of the hatchets. As Mr. Tabasash and his son gathered the last of the saplings they would need, Larry and the others worked on the lodge. It was slowly taking shape.

Larry grunted as he twisted the hand auger, something their ancestors had to do without, he thought. That and the twine would be the only accoutrements of modern civilization.

Two poles were sunk into narrow holes. Larry stopped long enough to watch as the men bent them toward each other, hand over hand. Where the tips overlapped, they were bound tightly with twine. Larry resumed digging as they made sure the fourth rib was secure.

In a moment he heard the sweeping swish of saplings being dragged to the clearing. The sound of Tabasash's voice drifted over to him seconds later. As he grew nearer, Larry yanked the auger from the ground and moved to a new spot, turning his back on the approaching steps. The steel screw bit the earth greedily.

"That's good muscle, but come here."

Larry sighed. He turned and stepped reluctantly back to the hole he had just walked away from. "What's wrong?" he asked, looking at the dirt.

"It's not deep enough. Should be another ten inches at least. When it's tied down, its liable to snap right out."

"The others haven't," Larry argued feebly.

"They might, when the other weight is added."

The others wouldn't, Larry knew. He had dug them deeper.

"Not as bad as rolling boulders up here, is it?" he said.

"No, I suppose not."

"Good," Tabasash declared. Larry started to move away, but Tabasash grabbed his arm, holding him firmly. "Did you tell him?"

He looked at Tabasash for the first time.

"You stopped him, didn't you?"

"Actually, I haven't seen him," Larry said matter-of-factly.

"He's a white man. You heard how they smashed up Hiller's

shop last night. That's how they reward an Indian who tries to make it in their world."

"Michelson had nothing to do with that."

"Dammit! If you don't stop him, we will."

"What do you mean by that?" Larry snapped.

"Exactly what I said. Axel Michelson is not going to do the Feast of the Dead."

This has gone too far, Larry thought. "I talked to my grandfather about it," he said evenly. "He said there's nothing to worry about because the souls only go to villages with those they are buried with. There's no mingling."

Tabasash appeared thoughtful. "Your grandfather said that, eh?"

"Yes."

"Well, he don't know everything. I heard some of the others say differently."

"They're wrong. You know my grandfather. You know he knows more about the old ways than anyone else."

"Maybe so. Still, isn't any need to take chances, is there?"

Axel paced quickly along the broad sidewalk. It cut diagonally across the core of the University of Michigan campus. Early morning after Labor Day and the Diag would be swarming with people. Now, only a few summer-class students lounged on the grass under the ninety-year-old elms.

Axel entered the Graduate Library and walked directly to the second-floor bank of computer terminals. It was the university Mirlyn online catalogs. He did a search for Ottawa references. Advanced search, History. *Jesuit Relations* was the fifth cite! He hit the Print Screen key and waited impatiently for the page from the printer.

Axel checked the call number against a locator chart on the wall, then made his way into the old wing of the building and down three flights of stairs. Opening a leather-upholstered door, he was greeted by an attic smell. The light was dim. Two bare bulbs lit the narrow corridor along the wall.

In one of the far stacks Axel found a brown-backed set of books that occupied four shelves in the center. Axel squinted at one of the volumes. It was too dark. He looked around for a switch. A segmented chain hung from a fluorescent light fixture. It flickered to life.

Axel stared at the faded gold lettering. *Jesuit Relations and Allied Documents, The Travels and Explorations of the Jesuit Missionaries in New France.* Eyewitness accounts of the meeting of two cultures, the writings of the earliest Western people to encounter the native Great Lakes population. Axel rubbed his hand across the backs of the books. Nervous anticipation tremored up his arms. He wanted to begin, but he was afraid it would not be there.

His hand lingered a few moments longer before he scanned to the end of the set. Volume 73. Index. It did not slide easily from the shelf. Axel opened the old book carefully. Under "Burial Rituals," Brébeuf was the first citation. His fingers gripped the book tightly. There were five more: "Bressani 22: 140. Breve 9: 31–33. Lalament 21: 199. LeMercier 11: 13 1. Ragueneau 29: 285."

Axel pulled a pad from his briefcase, rested the old book on an open shelf, and jotted down the citations. After assembling the five volumes, Axel moved to a wire-mesh carrel at the end of the stack.

Volume 22 was thinner than the others. As he opened it, a small cloud of dust floated in the air. He read Bressani's passage in a hurry. It concentrated on special customs for those who died a violent death. There was no description of the Feast of the Dead. Volume 21. Lalament described the first burial, immediately after death. Again, nothing on the Feast of the Dead. Without enthusiasm Axel read the accounts of the other Jesuit missionaries. None came close to Brébeuf's detail.

Axel looked through his wire cage into the dimly lit stacks. Row after row of books sat quietly, their mute voices taunting his frustration. Alone, on the drive down the night before, Axel had thought about the *Jesuit Relations.* He had not controlled his expectations. Gradually he had become confident they would hold the answers. He had felt it was only a matter of time, of research, and Janis would be back with him. Now he felt dejected. He suddenly considered, for the first time since she had disappeared into the woods, that he might never see her again. He bit his pen top. He rearranged the books. He read the citations again. Anything to chase that thought from his mind.

"Hey, Lare." It was a young man in his teens, his arms full of dead wood. Another approached from the trees just behind him. "Could you give us a hand? I saw a good red-pine log other side of that hill yesterday. Should burn real good."

Larry stared at the young man. He was slow in comprehending what he had said. "I . . . I can't."'

"Okay. Just thought I'd ask." He gave a facial shrug to his friend, and they walked toward the pit.

Larry's eyes followed them over there. Christ! He's staring at me! his mind cried with a start. Tabasash was standing by the pit, an easy grin on his lips, staring unflinchingly at Larry.

Dropping the auger, Larry stalked away from the clearing toward the dirt road. He did nothing to camouflage his departure. His feet crashed heavily on the crisp ground, anger smothering his fear.

First one bear noticed it. Then another; then the rest. One of the animals was moving away by itself. The woman could see something was wrong. As she jumped to her feet, two of the bears darted through the woods. The other bears watched them retreat into the trees. Threatening to follow, they stayed, their anxiety tenuously quelled.

Speckled patches of flickering light jittered nervously across the ground moss and graying twigs. Larry hurried through the woods, his shoulders hunching. He felt alone. The voices of the men he left at the clearing diminished to occasional syllables before dissolving totally into the wind. His hot anger had evaporated, leaving only a chill. It was a good distance to the overgrown trail road. He felt naked, unprotected.

The bears' overrested muscles strained with each pounding step as they crashed through the woods. One had been there since the night before; the other, almost all day. Their impatience had sought a nervous release, their restless energy an outlet.

A gathering rumble swayed the greenery somewhere behind Larry. Like a wall of water cascading down a dry ravine, the breeze rushed across the treetops, rustling the leaves in an approaching wave. The tumult broke above his head, the branches swaying in a tumbling green froth. The sudden gust seemed to waken the forest into a thrashing frenzy. Below the protective canopy, except for his rushing feet, it was dead still.

Their breath gushed in even pants, exploding from their

throats with each thrust of their forelegs. Their heads were low-ered, jaws slack. The tall broad-leafed ferns were back-high. They saw their prey!

Another rush gathered in the forest behind him. Larry heard the second wave of crashing vegetation. More wind. But some-thing was different. He whirled around, his eyes scanning quickly over the fern tops. He saw nothing, yet he turned and started to run.

Their prey was escaping! The bears split apart and began to circle to either side of the animal.

Thoughts raced through his head. He was running out on his people. He had doubted his grandfather. He had turned his back on Axel. He wasn't helping him. Worse. He had tried to dis-courage him. He was useless, of no value to anyone anymore.

Something nagged at the bears' purpose. It slowed their move-ment, even though their prey was within reach.

Larry pushed his way through the tangle to his old car. He heard the wind thrashing the leaves, but did not notice that the trees were still. The door opened with a grinding creak. He leaped inside and closed the windows.

The bears halted, staring at each other through the olive greens. They'd done it before. This prey was still within reach, but they sensed their prey controlled the power of escape. Like the last time, they had to use surprise. One bear suddenly raised its head and looked back in the direction they had come from. Then the other bear felt it too and checked its forward movement.

Larry placed his key in the ignition. The bears wanted to charge, but they could not move. The car lumbered forward, the spinning rear wheel grasping solid dirt. Luckily, Larry thought, he was not boxed in. He squeezed by the other cars in the nar-row road and began to accelerate.

Their fury smothered, the bears turned abruptly around and pounded irritably back toward the others. It was only one, their primitive minds declared. There will be more, many more, later.

Tabasash plunged the hand auger deep into the hole. He worked fast. Six of the ribs were in place. Cross poles were already being lashed to the frame at the other end. They would be finished tomorrow, Tabasash thought. At dusk they would assemble.

Axel raised his tired eyes from the open books as the clicking of heels stopped directly overhead. The low ceilings in the old stacks were translucent, allowing Axel to see the outline of a pair of shoes above him. Four wheels of a librarian's cart tailed behind. He was easily distracted after five hours of scanning the online catalog, jotting citations, searching for books, and reading passages.

After a few moments the soles above him scuffed on, the cart squeaking behind. Axel glanced through three pages of his scribbled citations, most of which were now preceded by an ink check mark in the margin, then returned to the narrow book in front of him. When he had opened it a few minutes before, the binding had cracked. He had noticed the only date stamped on the date-due slip pasted inside the front cover was 1-17-53. Chapter 6 was headed, "Feast of the Dead:"

> Variations of the death custom known as the Feast of the Dead were performed by many of the Great Lakes Indian tribes encountered by the early missionaries. Because the rite conflicted with Christian burial, it became a prime target for elimination. Ironically, contact with the whites at first made the missionaries' task more difficult. New cultural pressures and especially the fur traders induced a kind of pan-Indian culture that spread across tribal boundaries. With the new exchange of information between the tribes, rituals like the Feast of the Dead became wider, and for the moment at least, more entrenched. The Ottawas in the northern lower peninsula of Michigan, the Ojibwas in the upper peninsula, and the Potawatomi along the coast of Lake Michigan down to Indiana became known as the Three Fires. . . .

The chapter's focus proved to be on the cultural impact of the Europeans on the Indian burial rites. It contained little description of the feast itself, and nothing regarding the actual rites.

Axel turned to the bibliography in the back of the book. Under "Feast of the Dead" there were two citations. The first was to Brébeuf. The second was new. He stared at it for a moment. He did not recognize the citation system: "Chigishig, 'Ogochin Atisken.' WPA Historical Records, Keonah, Folder 5, Item no. 37."

After jotting it on his yellow pad, his eyes lingered on the Chigishig citation. He wondered how old it was. What was Chigishig's purpose in writing it? Who was Chigishig? The more he stared at the name, the more questions rolled across his mind. Suddenly Axel jumped from the chair and walked hurriedly to the catalog room. He did a search for Chigishig, but the system responded: *Sorry. There were 0 results for your search.*

The Works Progress Administration screen indicated there were over 60,000 listings. He narrowed the search, but there was nothing for "Historical Records," nor Chigishig. Axel turned and made his way through a side door to the Documents Room. No, congressional documents only are kept here, the man behind the desk said. Try the microfilm index. Another room, this one filled with hulking microfilm viewers. He checked the catalog. "Chigishig. WPA. Ogochin Atisken. Feast of the Dead. Historical Records." Nothing. Where next?

He dashed down the marble staircase, his yellow pad clutched in his hands, and into the administrative offices. Inside the cluttered room, Axel paused, his eyes searching for someone to approach.

"You look lost."

The voice startled him. Axel turned around. "Yes, I am."

She toothed a friendly smile. "Maybe I can help."

"I was hoping someone down here could tell me something about the historical records of Roosevelt's Works Progress Adminstration."

"Did you check—?"

"Yes," he interrupted. "I checked."

A smile flashed across her face again. "What is it you wanted to know?"

"I'm looking for this," Axel said, pointing to his notes, "but I have no idea what this citation system means."

She took the pad from Axel and thought for just a moment. "It's been a while, but, yes, I've come across references like this before. Occasionally we have a request for a WPA file folder."

"You mean you have them here?"

"No, sorry, we don't have any of them here. And I really don't know where this particular one would be. You see, the Historical Records was a major project of the WPA, and its job was to find and list research works from all over the United States and organize them in a systematic fashion. The aim was to preserve unpublished research projects before they were lost or forgotten. This one here, what was it? Chig . . .”

“Chigishig is the author’s name.”

“Indian, isn’t it?”

“Yes. Ottawa, probably.”

“Well, this could have been an independent project of his, or perhaps a master’s thesis that was never published. Whatever it was, there must have been something unique about it. The Historical Records people were very selective.”

“How would I go about finding it?”

“That’s the problem. The WPA had a number of storage spots around the country, and after they were given a file number, they became part of the National Archives. So this paper you’re looking for could be in Washington or any of a dozen other libraries God knows where.”

“There must be a master list telling where to find them,” Axel reasoned.

“If so, I’ve never seen it. And I know we don’t have it.”

“Then the citation itself must give a clue.”

“Maybe. Let me have a look again.” She stared at the yellow paper. “Name, title, WPA, file folder. It must be this Keonah.”

“A town perhaps?”

“Perhaps. Let’s try the reference room.”

At the top of the marble staircase they turned to their left and entered the mammoth reference room, its ceiling arched high overhead like the Roman Pantheon. At a desk in the center of the room she pulled a hefty book from under the counter. “This is a cities atlas,” she announced. The tissuelike pages breezed through her fingers. She paused almost in the middle. “Here’s a Keonak, ending with a k.”

“That might be it. Nothing with an *h*?”

“No. It says it’s an Ottawa village near Superior, Michigan. That’s the U.P., isn’t it?”

“Yes, I think about fifty miles west of Sault Sainte Marie, on Lake Superior. But I’ve never heard of an Ottawa village nearby.”

“Let’s see here,” she said, her face disappearing into the book. “It says it had a population of 830 in 1940. Could be a ghost town now.”

“Can we check to see if it’s a WPA storage site?”

“If it is, the records would be noted in the local library.” Another huge book slid from the shelf and thumped heavily on the open atlas. "American Library Listing" was in bold print on the cover. "Nope, no Keonak, or Keonah. Let's try Superior." Axel watched as the woman's eyes darted alertly through the columns of fine print. "Superior Public Library," she read. "Holdings: 10,000 books; depository for Northern Michigan Historical Society."

Before Axel could speak, she turned and walked briskly toward the far end of the room. He hurried after her. At the far wall she disappeared into a cubbyhole in the corner and emerged with an old yet unweathered broad book. "*Haner's Guide to Archives*," she said lowly. Axel was not sure if she was speaking to him or to herself.

"Michigan, Michigan, ah. Northern Michigan Historical Society." She skimmed quickly over the description of the society, its funding, membership, purpose. Documents, Custodian of Works Progress Administration Historical Records. "Here it is!" she said excitedly.

Axel looked over her shoulder and read where her finger pointed: "Specializing in Ottawa history, legends and religious ceremonies." "Ah, ha!" he shouted, his voice echoing in the huge chamber. She beamed broadly at him. Axel kissed her on the forehead and raced the length of the room. Within minutes he was in his car and leaving town.

The fatigue of a full day in the library caught up with him around Flint, an hour north of Ann Arbor. But gradually Axel settled into the synchronized groove of long-distance travel. Four hours later, on the horizon, a blinking red light seemed to flash in slow motion. Five hundred feet above the Straits of Mackinac and ten miles from his car, the beacon hovered as if in midair, the suspension bridge invisible in the night. The Yukon sped northward along I-75, its twin cones of illumination the only wrinkle for miles in the blanket of darkness.

Once past the Mackinac Bridge and into the upper peninsula, he would stop for the night. It would be no more than seventy miles in the morning to Superior. That distance and another thirty miles southwest from Mackinac, and he would be back in Wabanakisi Sunday afternoon. Then he would find the grave.

As he neared the towering suspension bridge, the link between the two peninsulas, he shifted uncomfortably in his seat. The possibility that Chigishig's paper did not contain the holy chants kept running through his mind. Like the others, the citation could hold nothing new. How could he hope an unheralded research project of one man contained what published histories did not?

But it must, his emotion implored. Chigishig's research was at least seventy years old. There may have been those alive then who remembered, who had heard their grandfathers speak the holy words of Ogochin Atisken. Chigishig's work was not done with the cold eye of a historian, but the passion of a member of a dying culture. If he recorded the Feast of the Dead, he would have included the critical part. As an Indian, he understood the meaning behind the feast, the significance of the chants. He was not a Jesuit describing a heathen oddity, but a proud Ottawa struggling to preserve the secrets of his people's most important religious ceremony. It must be there!

The rubber tires suddenly began their whine over the metal grating of the bridge. Axel began to relax. The five-mile-wide strip of water undulated with rolling surf two hundred feet below him. The strait, connecting Lake Michigan with Huron, was at the hub of twenty percent of the world's fresh water.

Axel turned the volume of the radio higher. The sky was clear and the eleven-o'clock news from Chicago's WLS came in strong.

"In the headlines, three more bodies are discovered in northern Michigan's bear country, the President promises that the economy. . . "

Dread filled his chest. "Janis? No! Don't let it be her. I need more time, just a little more time."

The introduction ended. "Three men were added to the rising death toll in Michigan's Crooked Tree State Forest earlier this evening when sheriff's deputies found their bodies near a mechanical bear trap. A source close to the investigation said the men had formed a hunting party last night to seek the killer bears that have been terrorizing the remote area.

"Two of the men had been mauled to death by bears, while the third victim had died from a bullet wound in the back. The sheriff would offer no explanation, but others speculated that the man was accidentally shot by one of his hunting partners.

"When asked if the peculiar form of mutilation was repeated

on these corpses, the authorities refused comment, pending autopsies.

"Meanwhile, in Lansing, Governor Frederic Andrews warned . . ."

There was no doubt in Axel's mind who the three men must include. A morbid sense of relief settled his nerves. It was one less hazard for Janis to face.

30

Sweaty grime caked his skin. With windows closed to thwart night mosquitoes, the Yukon became an unventilated oven as the sun rose steadily. Late the night before, the car had rolled into the roadside rest area ten miles north of the bridge. It was a few minutes off the Interstate on M-123.

The passenger seat was reclined. Axel turned uncomfortably. His body was sticky. His mouth dry. Groggy and sore, he climbed out of the car. A few minutes later he was back on M-123 heading northwest. The rolling tree-covered landscape of the lower peninsula changed almost immediately above the straits. The Laurentian Shield formed the bedrock of the U.P., a mass of granite that extended from Hudson Bay to the northern Great Lakes. Waterfalls and rocky escarpments highlighted the rugged terrain.

After an hour and forty minutes Axel was in Superior. The town had a permanent population of 1,248, announced a black-and-white sign at the corporate limits. The small community sat on a sandy spit of land which gradually narrowed to a hooked point jutting into the icy waters of Lake Superior. Hence the town's nickname, Ice Pick.

The houses were clustered together at the wide base of the point. Spiking north along a solitary street, the business district extended like a wavy tendril of a bottom-heavy tuber. The stores along Whitefish Avenue were not close together, as in Wabanakisi, but spaced along the narrowing point. To the right, through the gaps between the buildings, Axel saw a small pier harboring the town fishing fleet, Superior's one and only industry. Westward, white sand, fuzzy with sparse dune grass, stretched behind the shops to the rolling whitecaps of the lake.

He drove slowly, studying each building along the road for the library. A quarter-mile ahead, a white-brick lighthouse complete with a circular two-story turret sat almost at the point's end. Axel negotiated the narrow isthmus to a small parking lot in front of it. To one side a state historical marker identified the lighthouse as a ninety-year-old landmark. A flock of white and black birds hovered around the top of the tower. He could see there was no longer a beacon behind the glass. To the other side of the entrance a simple, neatly painted sign declared, "Library." Axel hurried inside. Books lined the dimly lit interior from floor to ceiling. He realized quickly he was alone. He nosed his way through a door into a side room. A narrow cot stretched along one wall. Linoleum covered the half of the room opposite the bed. It apparently was the kitchen.

Axel stepped back into the main chamber. He found no catalog. Searching closer, he noticed the books on the shelves did not bear any coding. He felt as if he had walked into someone's private house. A metallic ping came from above. Axel noticed a circular steel stairway in one corner. Someone was coming down.

"I didn't mean to intrude," Axel said.

"You didn't. I saw you from above. I was feeding my seagulls. Ever watch how they can grab garbage in midair? Anyway, the library's public." The man was in his late twenties. His wind-lashed hair was blond, his beard blonder.

"Well, I'm glad you're open."

"I'm not. Never on the weekend."

"Oh." Axel glanced at the front entrance. "The door was open."

"It always is. I live here."

"Uh . . ." Axel hesitated. "I drove all the way from Ann Arbor last night . . ."

"Don't worry about it. I don't keep regular hours anyway. Actually, I'm open anytime somebody wants one of my books."

"That must be a lot of work."

"Not really. Winters are long up here, and most people have already read everything I have."

His beard was thin. Axel could see his skin through the wispy strands of hair. "Well, I was looking for something in particular. Do you have a catalog?"

"Nope."

"But you must. How would you know where everything is?"

"I have a good memory."

"You the only one?"

"Yep."

"Oh. I thought the Northern Michigan Historical Society was located here."

"I am."

"Aren't there others?"

"Oh, sure," he agreed expansively. "But he died."

"*He* died?"

"My father. Actually, for a short time the society had three members, but my grandfather died when I was four. Then my dad died eight years ago, and membership dipped to one."

"Why do you keep it up?"

"Kind of traditional, I guess. And besides, it gives me a little prestige. A downstate professor comes up just often enough to make the townspeople think they've got something important here."

"And they don't?"

"Oh, they do. Me. And my books. You know, the federal government stores some of its papers with me."

"I know," Axel said. "That's why I came, to see the Works Progress Administration Historical Records."

"Oh. You must be another professor," he said happily.

"No, just a student of history." Axel smiled. "Where would I find 'Ogochin Atisken' by Chigishig? Folder 5, Item—"

"Hold it, hold it. I'm not a tape recorder. Now, what is it?"

"Folder 5, Item 37."

He thought a moment. "Three quarters of the way up and on the lake side."

"Up there?" Axel said, pointing to the circular staircase.

"Yep. No one looks at them much. You can use the room at the top. The light's better."

The metal steps spiraled up the narrow tubelike tower. Axel could see the floor dropping from under him through the grated stairs. The round walls were lined with dusty books and papers neatly arranged. Axel looked up through two stories of circular bookshelves toward bright sunlight above. It was almost dizzying. It was like a nightmare before a final exam, with all the books he had not read spinning before his eyes.

About three-quarters up, on the north side, he saw a series of wide manila folders. Axel's fingers guided his eyes across the lettering. F5 121-37. His breath stopped. Here it was!

The folder opened crisply. Yellowed pages were stapled in bunches. He quickly leafed through them. The last one read: "'Ogochin Atisken,' by Andrew Chigishig." Below that, at the bottom: "An independent research project, requirement for Master of Fine Arts degree, University of Michigan. Submitted June 6, 1885." The date blazed in his eyes. There would have been people alive whose memories went back to the 1700's! And they would have memories of what their fathers and grandfathers taught them. The eighteenth century! Before widespread settlement by the whites in the north! Axel slammed the folder shut and dashed up the steps.

As he pulled himself through the narrow hole in the floor, brilliant daylight blinded him. He was in the glass-enclosed light room at the top of the tower. The beacon was gone, its pedestal now a table. Axel sat in the solitary chair. Outside the windows, a flock of seagulls squawking hungrily rose to greet him.

Axel read hurriedly. It was carefully hand-printed, the strokes of a man with purpose, determination. Written in academic style, the background and purpose of the Feast of the Dead were discussed first. The paper described how deep the pit should be, how far across. The construction and design of the scaffold were minutely described. The removal of each shovelful of dirt, Axel realized, the placing of each wood plank, was a religious act. It had to be done properly. And Chigishig was giving a detailed account.

The paper was laced with Ottawa words. But still his eyes moved swiftly, his mind drinking up every detail, his heart feeling every word. It described the role of the Midewiwin, the torching of the fires, the gathering of the crowd. Chigishig's academic style had slowly eroded. It was not an impersonal study, but a desperate grab for survival. The steady print pulsed with meaning:

Then came the climax of Ogochin Atisken, the very purpose of the elaborate feast. It was time for the release of the spirits from their earthly existence. The pit prepared, the people mournful, the medicine man, adorned with funerary mask, shrieked above the growing rabble. His voice was the signal. The people began to cry, "Ayee-ee Ayee," over and over. Their calls grew louder with each syllable. They shouted to awaken the soul, asleep in death. Their voices turned to shouts, their cries to chants. They told their dead to wake, they pleaded for them to heed their calls, to begin their journey. They screamed individually, wrapped in private fervor, their shouts forcing the souls to depart from their bones:

Jeeb yuk gah ni-bah jik, nish kahk.
Noon dwish-nahng ga kah yak meen wah nish kahk.

Gee nish kah-yak guh zee lahm je mah-jah-yak.
Ka go zeg ze kam je mah-jah-yak guh che nahd-mah goom.

Shkwah nish kah-yak mishoo ook-mis ga guh wahb mahk.
Noong go dush guh mah jahm.

Oo-dan-we che shpim me a tak guh zahm,
Ga neen we dush je wahm dahs yahng mee-bahd bik guh bee dah
zam mahn-pee ni-ka-yah.

Nish kahk guh mah jahm, nish kahk guh mah jahm, nish kahk
guh mah jahm . . .

Axel leaned back, his gaze looking at but not seeing the impatient birds flapping outside the glass. He floated in his thoughts, thoughts not of Chigishig or the Feast of the Dead, but thoughts of Janis.

County Road 621 for part of its length between Mackinaw City and Wabanakisi balanced precariously along the edge of a bluff overlooking Lake Michigan. Axel could see the treetops plunging to the shoreline a half-mile to his right. The late-afternoon sun reflected off the dark lake surface in mercurial blotches, shifting and sloshing on the choppy water. Sunday boaters seemed headed inland, some returning from Beaver Island, twenty miles offshore.

As he had during most of the drive down from Superior, Axel

thought about the location of Shawonabe's grave. "A prison for his soul." The words turned over in Axel's head, but it ended there, with words alone, "a prison for his soul." He needed something more. Inspiration. A spark. An idea. Axel needed something else to unlock the phrase's meaning.

Ottawa Village seemed unusually quiet for a Sunday afternoon. Larry's car was in front of his house, but the place looked deserted. Axel knocked on the front door. After a moment he heard steps approaching.

"Hello, Axel," said Charley Wolf.

"Hi. I was afraid no one was home."

"Just keeping the heat out." He noticed the anxiety in Michelson's face as he held the door for him. "Janis has not returned. Larry checked your house."

The pain flashed only briefly in Axel's eyes. "I've got something to show you." He pulled a folded yellow sheet of paper from his pocket and flattened it on the dining-room table as Leon Moozganse appeared from the kitchen.

Charley Wolf hunched over Axel's handwriting, his head bobbing as he read.

"Do you know what the words mean?"

Charley Wolf inched the paper toward Moozganse. "Leon's better than me at things like that," he said.

Larry entered from his bedroom. "What's that?"

"The sacred chants of the Ogochin Atisken," Charley Wolf said.

Larry's lips parted in a quiet whisper. "That's . . ."

"It tells them they must awake," Moozganse paraphrased. "It says they must begin a journey. A journey to a new place. Their souls must leave earth with the others. It tells them they will go to their own village in the sky and staring down on us their happiness will brighten the night's darkness."

"Ogochin Atisken has been rediscovered," said Charley Wolf. "I never thought it possible."

Axel's satisfaction lingered merely a second on his face. "We have to find the grave."

"Axel, what we said before still holds true. I'm afraid we can't help in finding the grave. We can't because we don't know."

"But maybe you do," Axel insisted. "Maybe something you once heard when it seemed unimportant is still in your memory."

"I'm afraid not. No one liked to talk about Shawonabe, even when I was growing up. Everyone knew, of course, and my father made sure I knew the legend. But as you can understand, it isn't something you wish to dwell on."

"Tell me again about it, Mr. Wolf. Shawonabe was adopted into the Ottawas..."

"...after the massacre of the Mush Qua Tah," he obliged. "They did not realize until later that it was he who was responsible. Eventually, as you know, he was executed and buried deep in the woods, away from the village, and, as you've heard, in a prison for his soul."

"And what else about this prison?"

"There is nothing else."

"What could it have been? Some kind of special coffin?"

"Maybe," Larry said. "But that wouldn't help you. If it was, it would be buried in the ground with him."

"A structure above the grave, then? Made from logs perhaps?"

"It could have been, but it would have long since rotted away."

"Could he have been buried above ground?" Axel asked.

"No. They would have feared an animal dragging the carcass back toward the village," said Moozganse.

"Then they must have worried about what would happen if Shawonabe's body came close to anyone." Axel spoke quickly, his thoughts racing. "He was buried far away because they feared his spirit would leave his grave and inhabit an unwary Ottawa."

"That's true," Charley Wolf observed.

"If they were aware of the possibility of Shawonabe inhabiting someone who walked near his grave, then the prison must have had a second function. It must have served as a warning to any traveler or hunter to stay away."

"Then it would have had to be highly visible," Larry said.

"And permanent. Something that would warn people for all time that Shawonabe lay buried there."

It all seemed so logical, so simple. But where? A charged silence gripped the room as they all searched their memories for something they might have seen in the woods. A rock formation, perhaps, a boulder. Anything that was out of place. Axel mentally scanned the area around his house. There was nothing unusual about it. Deeper into the woods he was less sure. He had never really explored the virgin forest that stretched behind their property for miles. "If only we could see," he said despairingly. "If only there were something to make us see."

"Maybe there is," Charley Wolf said. "There is to be a meeting tonight in the woods, a ritualistic assembly."

"Mishoo!"

"What kind of assembly?" Axel prompted.

"A sweatlodge has been built, and tonight they are going to pray to the manitous for protection and guidance."

"A sweatlodge? Where young men received visions that guided their lives?"

"Yes. Perhaps you would be so enlightened."

"No!" Larry shouted. "That's Tabasash's doing. You can't go."

"Larry!" Charley Wolf commanded, his voice strong. "He has done a good thing."

"But he's twisted everything."

"Learning is painful. Much has been forgotten. At least he is helping show us some of the old ways."

Their voices were urgent, their views strident. As they debated, the prospect simmered within Axel's head. The sweatlodge would provide no divine intervention. He didn't expect a vision. There were no miracles. But maybe, he thought, just maybe it would provide the spark he needed. Something might be said, something could surface that was long forgotten, aroused from somebody's subconscious that provided the answer. "Larry," Axel interrupted, "I want to go."

He stared at him. "You can't," he said in a voice that stilled the room.

"Why?"

Larry averted his eyes. "Because you're not an Ottawa."

Charley Wolf glared in disbelief at his grandson. "*You* can bring him there, Gusan. *You* can be his sponsor."

"I know, but I won't." His grandfather would not understand, Larry thought. Axel *must* not go. He turned and stalked out of the house.

Charley Wolf covered his shame with words. "You know Tabasash. Go to him. He'll take you to the lodge. I'm sure of it."

"What about you?" Axel pleaded.

"The lodge is for younger men. I am as fit as I can be for my age, but I'm sorry to say the ceremony might be too much for my old heart to endure. The heat takes a lot out of me."

"But what would I say to Tabasash?"

"Axel," Charley Wolf said with authority, "he knows about Janis. All the Ottawas know. Go to Tabasash. He will understand."

He would go. Axel knew he had no alternative.

Tabasash had been the last to leave. He had sat on the ground alone and studied the finished lodge. The rounded hump of white birch mottled with black resembled a fungicidal growth gone wild. The bark covered a layer of leaves and grasses used as insulation. A narrow four-foot-high door was the only opening. In a few hours the place would be alive again. As Tabasash walked into the woods, he felt satisfied.

The woman paced slowly around the well-trodden ground. She was hungry, drained. But there was more to do. Suddenly she crouched to the ground.

The nine shaggy black bodies were dead still. They smelled the last one moving away from the clearing. Their anticipation grew. But the bears remained where they were. They sensed it would not be long.

Tabasash relaxed in the lounge chair. Paul was asleep in his room, gathering energy for later. A light tapping at the door brought Tabasash to his feet. It was Axel Michelson.

"Come in," he said, his voice stuttering with surprise.

"I hope I'm not interrupting anything."

"No, I was just sitting."

"Good. I came to talk about the sweatlodge."

"Yes?"

"I want to go. It might help me."

Tabasash turned away. He did not trust his expression. "You've been doing some research lately?"

"Yes." A hint of surprise in his voice.

"On the Feast of the Dead?"

"Yes," he drawled.

"Have you found anything?"

"I've been fortunate. I found what I looked for. Now I just need to put it together. I hoped the sweatlodge might help give me direction."

"I see," Tabasash said evenly. "You would need someone to vouch to the manitous for you. Have you talked to Larry?"

"Yes, but he refused."

"He did? Why?"

"He said because I was not an Ottawa."

"He said what?"

"He won't vouch for me because I'm not a member of the tribe."

Tabasash's gaze narrowed. "Anything else? Did he say anything else?"

"No. What else would there be to say?"

"I don't know. That just seems so odd..."

"I thought so too."

"He said nothing else."

"Nothing."

Tabasash's face smoothed. Finally he said, "Be back here at eight o'clock and you can come with me." As Axel turned to leave, Tabasash added, "And, Axel. Don't tell anyone where you are going."

Alone, Tabasash settled again into the soft lounge chair. The easy drowsiness was gone. He was in a state of anxious relief. Suddenly there were more preparations to be made. He reached for the telephone on a nearby table.

31

A forest at dusk has a certain stillness to it, a certain time-stopping quality that is a tenuous truce between two relentless antagonists. Like waves of armies taking, then losing front trenches, the dusk is a no-man's-land. It is a moment of fragile peace whose milky veneer covers but does not conceal gathering shadows. As it slowly smothers the energized activity of daylight, it quietly sets a match to dormant forces of night. Standing in the woods, Axel sensed the silent foreboding of the encroaching darkness.

Most of the men shuffled impatiently, waiting for the lodge to be ready. When eyes met his, they looked away. Axel tried to mask his discomfort. It was the same for everybody, he told himself. They all suffered the same anxiety.

Two sweaty figures toiled by a roaring fire. Armed with long poles, they maneuvered rocks, some the size of basketballs, around the perimeter of the blaze. The heat near the pit was staggering. Axel watched from a distance. The two men huddled together, gesturing toward the fire, their voices drowned by the crackling wood. Axel observed closely. It would be his turn later.

One of them wedged the end of his pole between two of the rocks and pried it away from the edge of the burning pit. He spat on the stone, the moisture disappearing in the sizzling puff of vapor. He nodded at the other man and rolled it farther from the fire. Discarding the long pole, blackened now at one end, he reached for a shorter but thicker log.

Axel watched as they hoisted the rock between them, cradling it with two stubby poles. Their shoulders rippling with the effort, they stepped haltingly to the low opening to the lodge and disappeared through a hanging cloth doorway. In a moment they reemerged and selected a second stone.

Like the others, the two men had familiar faces, but Axel could not remember their names. Odd, he thought. There were none of Janis' close friends present.

His grandfather was right. Tabasash was a good man. He truly thought Axel was worse than a mortal danger to his people. It was understandable, in fact admirable that he would do anything he could to prevent what he feared. Under the same belief, any honorable person would react similarly. Tabasash's problem was in his conception, not his motives. Larry's mind was clearer as he trudged down the gentle slope. The long walk on the beach had settled his nerves. Now all that remained was to explain himself to Axel.

It was time. The bears' agitation slowly congealed. The smell of danger was as strong as any the seventeen bears had ever sensed. Yet they were unafraid.

The woman stood on a rotted stump, her wild eyes staring up the hill. Saliva collected at the corners of her open mouth as her breasts rose and fell. Like the bears, she sensed the impending attack.

Charley Wolf eyed his grandson stonily as he walked into the house.

"I'm sorry, Mishoo. I had to do it. You haven't seen what has happened to Tabasash. And if I had tried to explain to Axel, he would not have believed me. He would have wanted to go anyway."

Larry's grandfather stared at him with chiseled features. Finally his face softened. "You must have had your reasons, so I'll accept them."

"Thank you. I appreciate your trust in me." Larry walked toward the telephone. "Now I can call Axel and try to explain."

"He won't be home. He went to the lodge with Tabasash."

Larry froze in horror as the consequences slowly registered.

"He couldn't have!"

But the old creased face nodded affirmatively. "He did."

"They'll kill him!"

Axel estimated there were thirty men, most of whom had been at the meeting on the injunction the previous Saturday. That meeting was only one week ago, yet it seemed an eternity. His world had changed since then. And so had the focus of the assembly. Now it was they who would teach him.

The mound of heated rocks had grown smaller, but a number of stones still remained on the periphery of the fire. As the latest pair of workers emerged through the curtain, they placed the wood poles, now scorched in the middle, on the ground. "It's ready," one of them said.

The men began to disrobe. Tabasash nudged Axel. Like the others, he took off his clothes and stacked them in a little pile. One by one the men stopped to crawl through the narrow opening into the lodge. As Axel neared the door, he glanced anxiously about. Larry was nowhere to be seen. Why wasn't he there? Then he felt a gentle push from behind and went in.

A solid wall of heat smacked him in the face, stealing the breath from his lungs. Stumbling forward to a place in the center, he sat heavily next to Tabasash. Directly in front of him was a second pit, smaller than the one outside. The rocks filled it completely, piled in two rows. In the middle, a kindling blaze flickered its dancing light off the arching ceiling. A man could stand straight, Axel observed, only along the structure's axis.

The fire reflected off the others, their bodies already glistening with sweat. Axel's skin quickly moistened as well. By the time the last man crawled through the opening, the lodge was quite full. Squatting on the ground, their legs folded, each naked body touched those all around, forming a single mass of flesh.

In the dim light, his eyes stinging from dripping perspiration, Axel could not distinguish faces beyond the second row opposite the pit. Next to him, Tabasash breathed deeply, holding the air in his lungs seemingly beyond endurance. Axel stared into his face. His eyes were closed, his features unmoving. Come on, breathe! Axel said to himself. Finally Tabasash exhaled noisily.

Axel felt the human mass begin to pulse. He looked around.

One by one the men began breathing heavily. Axel too sucked the hot air deep in his lungs, searing his throat. An eerie panting hovered above them like a suffocating blanket. The composite body convulsed with each breath, rocking back and forth. Faster. Axel breathed faster. Deeper. A rush of dizziness surged into his head. Suddenly the lodge exploded in a single booming beat of a drum.

"Ah-eee!" The scream dropped like lead in the thick air. The hair at the nape of Axel's neck stood on end. A second scream exploded from the other side of the room. The drum beat again and grew quickly into a pulsing rhythm.

Axel looked to his side at Tabasash. The man's eyes were open but vacant. His body began to sway from side to side. Axel's did too. Then the body next to him. A growing wave rippled around the lodge.

Tabasash began to shout, his voice rising, then falling, in time with the drum. The air seemed denser, almost cloudy. Axel's vision was fuzzy. Suddenly a flash of light burst into the room. Two men were crawling out the entrance. Through his dizziness Axel could hear the blaze still crackling outside. Some of the others imitated Tabasash's tremulous chant. A rumble rasped in Axel's throat. It grew to a moan. The curtain swung open, and the two men returned, bearing a smoking rock. Captured in the building fervor, Axel heard his own voice explode in his ears. He shouted at the ceiling. His mind could form no words. He screamed without meaning. The lodge resounded with thirty voices in a deafening cacophony of noise.

The ungodly din resonated through the trees. On the hill, looking down on the roaring fire, the bears congregated in tense silence. They glanced uneasily from one to the other. It was something they had never heard. They glanced nervously at the woman. But she could do little to soothe their vibrating nerves. The raucous screams pounded fear into her as well.

The old Ford screeched sideways to a halt. Larry had missed the turn. He backed up and gunned his car onto the barely visible dirt track, praying that Axel was unharmed.

As the road twisted through the trees, the headlights speared crazily ahead, bounding up and down and rocking from side to side. In the daylight, at a cautious speed, the rutted trail had been a difficult traverse. Now it was madness.

The road dipped quickly to the left, too fast for Larry to react in time. His car bounded over a hump and into the woods, stripping the bark off a hemlock. The sound of splintering wood gave way to grinding gears as the car lurched back to the road.

A tree appeared in the cone of his headlights, the road jogging to the side. Larry twisted the steering wheel, soft ground fighting his muscles. A metallic crunch crashed in his ears. The car grazed off the massive trunk and continued barreling over the road.

He must be almost there. It was only a mile off the highway. Larry glanced into the woods, his engine racing wildly. Darkness camouflaged familiarity. He looked back just in time to spin around a gentle turn. His lights reflected back in his eyes! He slammed the brakes, and the car skidded into a parked truck. Crumpling metal and glass shattered the night. Larry vaulted forward, his head cracking into the windshield.

He slumped back in his seat, the motor sputtering for a moment before stalling. His skull pounded. Out. Get out. Through the woods. It wasn't far.

"Assert your will, Gitche Manitou, assert your will over your earthbound servants," a voice behind Axel cried.

"Deliver us from the evil one from the south," cried another.

"Enlighten our cousins, O powerful Manitou, give them strength. . . ."

Ottawa phrases interspersed the English. Axel tried to listen, but they made little sense. And it was so hot. His body seemed not his own. Listen! he tried to command himself. But he couldn't. The screams, the drum, the heat! "Janis!" he shouted. "Please, God, help her. Janis!"

The woman grabbed her ears. Her face contorted in near-agony. Forward! The direction suddenly crashed in her head. The bears heard it too! They were moving down the slope.

The trees seemed to shimmer like heat above a mirage. Larry stumbled to one knee, his hand gripping his forehead, trying to still the spinning sensation. His stomach churned like a malevolent brew. Suddenly it contracted, and his mouth violently exploded with puke. Bending low to the ground, he retched again and again. Slowly his body calmed. He asserted control. His head stilled. He forced himself to his feet and surveyed the woods. Which way? It all looked the same.

The line of black bears inched stiff-legged down the hill. They moved cautiously, the bellowing noises demanding respect. Behind them an upright figure slunk through the trees, her bronze skin glowing gold from the aura of the blaze. A sack slung from her drooping arm. The noise still boomed loudly in her ears, but now it was only an amorphous sound, the individual voices lost in collective rabble.

The bears halted thirty feet from the clearing. Suddenly the curtain flung open, and one, then another animal appeared, carrying something in their arms. The bears watched as the creatures dropped a heavy boulder in the flames, orange streamers erupting from the glowing ash. Keeping their distance, the bears began to circle the mound.

Larry hurried through the darkened forest. Invisible twigs scratched his face. This must be the right way, he told himself. A yellowish glow glimmered in the sky. The fire! In a moment he heard the voices, shouting and screaming and chanting. It was like nothing he had ever heard. Axel must be alive, he prayed.

The bears were at either end of the mound, their pincer movement beginning to curve around behind it. They were still safely covered by the woods. Hearing something, the first bear stopped unexpectedly and stood up.

Air burning his raw throat, Larry pounded toward the birch-covered hump. His eyes were fixed on it. He did not notice the movement to his right.

The flames shot higher. The two men curled the boulder with the poles and struggled to raise it off the ground. Suddenly a darting shape appeared from the darkness. It was one of the young men of the tribe, they realized.

"Hurry up. You're late."

"I know," Larry gasped. He noticed the clothes scattered about, and disrobed quickly. Blood pulsed in his aching forehead as the sickness returned. His stomach felt as though it had been hit with a steel rod. He leaned against the arcing wall for a moment before he parted the curtain and moved inside. Crouching at the doorway, he could only distinguish dark shapes swaying in the dim light. Slowly his vision adjusted, but the faces remained unrecognizable. Dirty sweat streamed across their cheeks as their mouths were contorted by wild screams.

Above everyone else's, a voice cried, "In our moment of sacrifice, help us do what we must do." It was Tabasash, Larry saw. And next to him was Axel. Can't he hear? Doesn't he understand? Moment of sacrifice!

"Muhquh ogiwena ogasawan midash ogiwenigan . . . "

Larry perceived he had gone unnoticed by the mesmerized gathering. His eyes stinging, he surveyed the lodge. Axel was opposite the door on the other side of the pit, separated from Larry by a solid mass of fleshy bodies. As he crouched indecisively in the doorway, a thought gnawed at his deliberation: There isn't much time.

"Protect us from the southern spirit," a voice called. "Defeat Shawonabe's magic."

Tabasash's eyelids locked shut. From deep in his throat his voice boomed into the low-ceilinged room. "Great Muhquh, the man from the south steals your servants, he abuses your generosity, he works evil on us. Protect us. Seek vengeance on him who insults you, who threatens you. His power will grow until you have no more earthly servants. Our cousins will be our cousins no longer. They will no longer possess keenness of spirit and gentleness of body. They will no longer be yours! Seize their souls! Seize them before it is too late!"

The babble had fallen to a murmur. As Tabasash became silent, it gradually rose again. The voices pulsed with the fervor of rediscovered faith. The narrow perimeter of the pit was Larry's only unobstructed path. He slid a careful foot forward. The nausea was returning. He tasted bile in his throat. His muscles weakened. His unsteady legs began to tremble. Struggling to maintain his precarious balance between the fired rocks and the row of jutting knees, he swayed, then plummeted to the ground.

The rocks! The realization was simultaneous with the pain. Black smoke appeared where his arm touched the searing stone, and he could smell his own flesh.

At first he didn't feel the powerful hand gripping his side. But when he rolled forcibly away from the pit, the saving grasp was unmistakable. "Don't move! You'll get hurt." It was Shigwam, the farmer. Larry's eyes closed without replying. He lay on the big man's lap for a moment, trying to regain control over his muscles. Slowly he managed to pull himself to his knees, and grimacing against the pain, looked toward Axel. He appeared to be in a trance. His head lolled from side to side, his mouth gyrating with incomprehensible sounds. It was apparent he did not know what was going on.

Axel felt more than heard the endless rhythm of the drum. His eyes were mere slits as the sultry air above the stones rose in wavy streams. Across the pit the faces grew increasingly distorted. Axel tried to focus, but the transformation continued. Animals. Grotesque visages.

They must be illusions, he shouted inwardly. It was the heat. He was losing control. Bears! They had the faces of bears.

The heat intensified the surging pain in Larry's head. Leaning behind Shigwam, he peered over a row of laps. Realizing it was the only way, Larry started to crawl on his hands and knees over the jutting legs. The swaying men barely noticed him as he glided over their wet skin and wedged himself next to Michelson, Tabasash on the other side. "Axel," he said urgently, grabbing his arm. "Axel. Listen to me . . ."

Axel tried to see through his thickening thoughts. Images floated by as if in slow motion. "Janis," he managed to gasp. Swallowing, he repeated her name again. He tried to concentrate on her, but dammit! Something interfered. A voice was close. His body jerked. Someone was tugging at him. Someone was calling his name. He turned to the person at his side. He tried to focus.

"Axel. Do you hear me?" Larry whispered.

It was Larry Wolf! But he had not been here. How? his face questioned.

"Can you hear me?"

Axel struggled with the word. Finally: "Yes."

"You have to leave. You've got to get out of here." The words spilled from his mouth. His head pounded.

Leave? "No," said Axel. Janis needed him. If only he could clear his head!

The heat, the pain, hammered Larry's lucidity. He had to make him understand. He had to make Axel leave before he passed out. "Get out of here!"

"No. I'm vouched for by someone else."

"I know, I know, but listen to me. They're going to kill you!"

"What!"

"They're going to kill you!"

Axel stared at the sweat-streaked face. "That's not true."

"Tabasash didn't bring you here to help. He brought you here to stop you from performing the Feast of the Dead. He's going to kill you." Larry's head nodded forward. The dim glow on the ceiling whirled in his eyes. "Believe me," he breathed.

But it seemed beyond belief. "That's impossible," Axel said. "There would be no reason for it."

"Don't you understand? They don't want Shawonabe's spirit to go to the soul village. They think his evil would be a hundred times worse than it is here."

Axel stared with growing horror at the small flames in front of him. It made sense, he slowly considered. Of course. That's why the prison for his soul. Why hadn't he thought of that before? But why hadn't Charley Wolf? "Larry, why wouldn't your grandfather fear the same thing?"

With halting breaths Larry explained. Then, knowing Axel had been warned, he allowed himself to retreat from the pounding in his head and the burning in his arm. His eyes closed, Larry slumped into unconsciousness.

Axel glanced toward the doorway. A solid layer of bodies blocked his path. The heat! It wouldn't allow him to think. More than that. His legs felt as if they were on fire. At first he thought it was just the pressure of Larry's body. But he could feel the searing heat of the rocks growing hotter. He was closer to the pit! He was being pressed toward it. Axel felt the gentle pressure behind him as the human mass inched him relentlessly forward.

He would have to do something fast! His attention was drawn to the two stubby poles. He grabbed one and shoved the other at a man near him. They had been taking turns keeping the stones hot. It was now his turn. Out of the corner of his eye Axel saw Tabasash rise halfway to his feet. The log was heavy in his arms. One swing and Tabasash would be out. But there were too many others.

Axel edged the pole into the pile of rocks and maneuvered one away from the pit, all the while his body keeping sway to the beating drums. Tabasash slowly sank back to the ground. The other man rose reluctantly, joining Axel at the side of the pit. Together they hoisted the rock and stumbled with their load through an expanding steam of bodies. The door was just a few steps away. His partner stooped low and labored through the small exit. Then Axel was outside and the chill air splashed around his body. It surged into his lungs. Hot sweat turned icy.

"I'll build up the fire," the man said. "You pick out another stone."

Rolling the biggest rock he could find from the fire, Axel positioned it between the scorched wooden carriers. With the flames rising, Axel grasped the ends of the poles opposite the lodge. The bronze figure finished tending the bonfire and joined him, hesitating a moment before turning his back to Axel and grabbing the poles.

Cradling the hot stone, they raised it with difficulty. Axel followed step for step toward the lodge. The man disappeared through the curtain. Axel knew if he entered again he would never come out alive. The rock was in the doorway. Now! Axel flung the poles from his body. The rock thudded heavily to the dirt directly in the middle of the entrance as he dashed around the lodge.

The drum stopped and a rush of frantic voices followed him. Hurry! his mind screamed. The rock would not hold them for long.

The bears watched as the creature moved erratically away from the hole in the mound. It seemed as if their patience was about to be rewarded.

Axel didn't hear the growls. His concentration was on the Ottawas who were past the rock and giving chase. The bears tensed to strike, but then hesitated, confused by the multitude of scents.

Axel didn't see the low black shape. But he felt the soft fur on his legs as he somersaulted over the beast and sprawled to the ground. Ignoring him, the bear looked toward the mound and reared on its hind feet. The other bears did the same. Axel saw the black shapes all around. He scrambled to his feet. A surge of frightened energy propelled him into the woods as terrified screams echoed behind him. The noise became deafening as the bears erupted in a destructive frenzy.

Partly from fear, partly from a glancing blow, a charging Tabasash sailed forward, slamming his chest on the darkened earth. From the ground he stared with immobilizing horror at the thrashing beasts surrounding him. He pushed himself forward along the dirt to get away from the carnage.

Behind him, he heard a shout: "Back to the lodge!" But he couldn't. The bears stood in his path. He struggled to his feet and started to run. The noise of the ambush quickly retreated behind him.

Axel ran almost blind. Obstacles concealed by the shadows appeared suddenly in front of him. But he charged forward on a dodging path, his muscles flexing under his taut skin. Branches slashed at his face as woody bushes scratched his naked body. His lungs pounded, pumping night air into his heaving chest. A cooling sensation wakened his heart, then spread to his limbs. Freed from the oppressive atmosphere of the lodge, his mind began to clear. It cleared from the tranquilizing heat, only to jump to the racing madness of danger. He was being pursued! Axel could hear the forest exploding behind him.

The snarling turmoil raged in Tabasash's ears. But it was stationary! He was getting away. Then he realized Axel was getting away too. He had run in the same direction. Toward the cars.

Tabasash could see the hurrying shape. The carnage at the lodge receded from his thoughts. Fear for his own safety was removed. If he had to sacrifice himself, he must. It was for the tribe!

Axel's bare feet pounded across the forest debris. Fear steeled his soles. He could not feel the jutting sharpness of dead twigs and felled branches. Rivulets of blood streamed unnoticed down his legs.

Through the pain, the fear, the crashing vegetation in his ears, something tugged at Axel's thoughts. Now that he was freed from the sultry heat the thought had gradually grown in his mind. What was it? The lodge. Something said at the lodge. The bear was getting closer. He saw the cars ahead. But the beast was only feet behind.

A dull blow slammed into the back of Axel's legs. He sprawled to the ground, spinning quickly to face his attacker. It was Tabasash! There was no bear! Axel tried to rise, but

Tabasash was quicker, lunging over him. Axel kicked upward with all his remaining strength. His bony foot crashed into Tabasash's dangling testicles. The Indian screamed and fell heavily to the ground, his hands between his legs.

Axel pulled himself up and looked around. The cars were directly in front of him. Seeing Larry's Ford, he ran over and jumped inside. It was his only chance. The key *had* to be there. He felt by the steering column. It was! As the motor slowly turned over, Tabasash violently flung the passenger door open. Axel jerked the gearshift into reverse and pressed the accelerator to the floor. The engine roared into life, but the car did not move. It was snagged on the vehicle in front. Tabasash lunged headfirst across the front seat as the car ripped away from the truck's bumper and lurched backward, scraping against an oak. Tabasash's face contorted with pain. The tree crushed his legs, yanking him effortlessly from the car.

The engine revved high in reverse as Axel tried to guide it over the weaving narrow trail. There was no place to turn around, and his neck ached as he strained to see out the back. The road curved sharply at the top of a rise. Axel jerked the steering wheel, and like a tugboat in reverse, the car barreled into the woods, piling green froth to either side. Refusing to slacken his pressure on the accelerator, Axel aimed between the larger trees. The auto charged through the underbush, snapping saplings bumper-high and toppling them onto the roof. For an instant the car was airborne as it sailed over an embankment before thumping heavily back in the road, its underside brushing the earthen hump in the center of the gouged tracks.

In a blur through the trees Axel saw headlights flashing by. The highway was near. The forest ended, and he squealed onto the asphalt, skidding clear across County Road 621 before grinding to a halt on the gravel shoulder opposite the rutted trail. Axel slammed the gearshift and the car lurched forward.

Cold air rushed in the window, chilling his naked body. With head-lights smashed, the car moved as if in a black tunnel. Axel leaned close to the dash, following the splitting seam of the trees above the roadway.

Trailing the auto, silhouetted against the starry sky, the blunt head of a heavy owl soared through the air. Its powerful wings thrust it forward. Its dagger-sharp talons dangled below. Wide eyes stared earthward.

The thought returned, nagging his awareness. What had they said? Something he had not heard before. *The evil one from the south*. It had been repeated again and again. It meant something, but what he wasn't sure. He needed to relax and organize his jumbled thoughts.

As the blind auto limped along the highway toward home, the words "from the south" echoed in Axel's head.

32

The heat seemed even more intense. Blood flowed freely. Agonized moans had replaced the frenetic chanting to the black-bear manitou. The healthy tended the wounded, while Larry remained in an unconscious heap by the pit.

"We're okay in here, we're okay. They won't come in," John Shigwam said.

"They could. The walls are paper thin." Oliver Reedwhistle had not even wanted to come to the sweatlodge to begin with. His brother had talked him into it. And now his brother lay dead outside.

"I said they won't. Not while Gitche Muhquh is with us. Shawonabe's afraid of losing his control."

"But surely he's stronger than the manitous!"

"He's not. They would have attacked earlier, while we were all inside. It would have been easier for them."

Wide eyes stared at Shigwam above sunken cheeks. Reedwhistle said nothing. He was afraid to move.

"Now, let's count how many there are," Shigwam said, turning away from the cowering figure.

"Father? Father? Are you here?" Paul Tabasash propped himself on his elbows. Blood trickled down his cheek and dripped to his chest. "They got my father! He's still out there!" he shouted, struggling to his feet.

Shigwam halted Tabasash's advance, gently forcing him back to the soft dirt. "Your father's gone, Paul," Shigwam said evenly. "He's dead. There's nothing that can be done now for him.

You must save yourself."

"No . . ."he whimpered.

"I count twenty-six," a man said.

Shigwam slowly rose to his feet. "Good. We still have numbers. We'll be all right in here."

As if to disagree, a guttural roar exploded outside the lodge. The men froze, each head turned toward the small open space of the doorway.

The bear stared at the black hole. Its teeth flashed in the firelight as its cavernous mouth spread wide. The thick hair by its snout was matted with blood. It growled with all its fury. The other hulking black shapes began approaching the bark-covered hump in the clearing.

Behind the mound, the woman scurried among the lifeless bodies. She paused briefly at each one, bending low by their heads. As she moved, her breathing seemed to constrict. There was something different. The faces were in her memory. Her heart beat faster. She moved to another. The jaw pried easily open, and her fingers groped for the soft flesh. The blade cut cleanly through, and the tongue pulled free in her hand. She rocked forward, her thoughts wrenched apart. Something shouted in her head to stop. The knife slipped to the ground. She felt weak, as if about to collapse. Slime dripped from between her fingers. The tongue oozed fluids. "Ohh," she moaned.

Then slowly her body stilled. Strength returned to her muscles as her breathing became even, her features neutral. She opened the deerskin pouch and let the tongue slip inside. Then she retrieved the knife from the ground. The wrenching realization had subsided. The glimmer of memory was gone.

Axel sank into the soft cushions of the sofa, sore leg muscles twitching in his thighs. His head pounded, but he knew he had to resist sleep. Something had to be done for Larry, for the men at the lodge. And he sensed that the location of Shawonabe's grave was in his grasp.

Evil one from the south. Why would they call him that? He was a Mush Qua Tah, and they had been geographical contemporaries of the Ottawa. It must have some other significance, but his mind could fathom no logic. Maybe the others had been right. Perhaps it was impossible. At least in the library, researching the sacred chants, he was on familiar ground. But this! He was handicapped to begin with—he was not an Ottawa! How *could* the significance of the phrase be apparent? He needed help, he realized, from someone who had been raised in the Ottawa discipline. And Larry needed his help.

He reached for the telephone and dialed with jerky haste. The tiny speaker rang unhurriedly in Axel's ear. The silence hung long between rings. Axel could not hear the old man moving slowly toward the phone. He could not see him stumble over the stool in the darkened room. He could not see him grope for the clanging box. The eighth ring jangled defeat in his ears. The receiver loosened in his grip.

"Hello?"

"You're home!"

"Axel? What's the problem?" said Charley Wolf.

"Something happened at the lodge," he gasped. "The bears attacked."

While Axel explained, Charley Wolf listened impassively. When he was finished, the old man said simply, "But were you enlightened?"

"I said Larry's still there. We have to get others and go back. Maybe the sheriff—"

"No," he stated forcefully. "It will do no good. You must perform the Feast of the Dead. It's the only way to help those in the woods, the only way to save Larry, if he's . . ."

Axel understood. "Evil one from the south. They kept referring to Shawonabe as that. What does it mean?"

"Why? Is it significant?"

"I think so, though I can't decide why yet."

"Well, I'm sorry, but I don't think it's going to help much. It's just his name."

"His name? I don't understand."

"Shawonabe," his voice hyphenated slowly. "It's Ottawa for 'man from the south.' "

An excited tremor rippled lightly through Axel's mind. "But he was a Mush Qua Tah, wasn't he?"

"He was a Mush Qua Tah like he was later an Ottawa. He had been adopted into their tribe, just as he later was into ours."

"Where had he come from?"

"I don't know for sure, except that he appeared one day at the Mush Qua Tah village. He had been traveling by himself, walking from the south. The Ottawa knew this, and when they adopted him into our tribe as the sole survivor of the massacre, they named him Shawonabe."

With singleness of concentration Axel's mind became clearer. His memory grasped for direction. "What tribe had he come from originally? Does legend say?"

"It may have, but I don't know. I guess it was never important. I would say, though, he was probably a Potawatomi. They're the only tribe that lived south of the Ottawa along Lake Michigan."

The realization exploded, it was something he had read. "Could he have come from farther south? Somewhere below the Potawatomi?"

Charley Wolf considered the suggestion. "I suppose. It would have been a long way to travel by foot, though."

"But it was possible. He could have come a long distance."

"Yes."

"He could have come from the woodlands of northern Indiana and Illinois?"

"He could have. Or even beyond. Who knows how many other tribes he was adopted by."

Thoughts were taking shape. A pattern was emerging. He needed to think, to organize.

"Wait a minute," Charley Wolf was saying. "What does it mean?"

"I don't know yet. Maybe nothing. I'll be in touch later."

As the flames died down, the bears grew nearer. But they dared not enter the mound where a whimpering cry continued unabated. The connecting moans of the injured men still provided a sorrowful threat. "We've got to get rid of these rocks," gasped Reedwhistle. His eyes were half-closed, his body streaked with muddy sweat.

"We can't," a voice disagreed. "The Muhquh Manitou is all that protects us now. If we give in to our comforts, we show the great spirit we are unworthy of saving."

"Look what your great bear spirit has done for us so far. Do you think it cares about us? What about Tabasash and my brother out there on the ground? What protection did it give them?"

Except for the dying cry, the lodge turned silent. Animal snarls outside heightened the tense atmosphere. His challenge unanswered, Reedwhistle crawled toward the pit and grasped one of the scorched wooden poles, lifting it from the ground.

Shigwam shook off his trance and leaped up, jumping on the pole with his bare feet. It slammed to the ground, pinning Reedwhistle's thin fingers underneath.

"I don't pretend to know what our grandfathers knew," Shigwam said, holding Reedwhistle to the ground. "But the bears are staying out there and are not coming in. I say there's no reason to risk things changing."

"But the heat ..." Reedwhistle gasped.

The plea had no effect on Shigwam's steely expression. Slowly the men sank back into their pain. For just a moment the suffocating heat had been forgotten. But now they paid for that brief reprieve. They became aware of heat rushing around their bodies, squeezing their struggling lungs.

Beyond the insulated walls of the crude room, the woman turned suddenly toward the woods. A familiar scene flashed through her mind. It was her territory. A creature moved through the shadows. A command took hold of her muscles. She began to move away from the clearing, heading toward the south.

Four black shapes turned and loped after her. There was other prey in Crooked Tree.

Axel paced back and forth, sifting through his thoughts. He wanted it to be true, but he could not see how it would have been possible. On the one hand, it would make sense. A prison, as permanent as the earth. Designed in his people's custom. Highly visible—a warning to all who unwarily approached.

Yet at the same time, the tribes had been so removed. They lived in different worlds. How could the Ottawas have heard of the concept, much less mastered the techniques necessary? The question unanswered, Axel tried to remember what else was in the passage, but it was no use. He had read much during his research. Had skimmed through innumerable pages.

Innumerable pages. Other books. A thought began to form. Axel became motionless. What was it he had read? Elsewhere. At U. of M. Like the burial customs of the woodland tribes in Indiana and Illinois, it had seemed insignificant. But now it provided the missing logic: The pan-Indianism! The thought burst in his head. The Three Fires! It was a time of exchanging ideas, contact between the different tribes. The fur traders opened cultural avenues among the Indians. They borrowed from each other. The Ottawas could have known, they *must* have known of the major customs of their neighbors. *They must have been exposed to the woodland practice of building effigy mounds for the deceased.*

It was all so logical. Shawonabe, the man from the south, had been buried, as his people were, in a mound the shape of an animal. It was to be his prison, his prison for his soul. And it was a readily visible warning to the others.

Axel's dizzy exhilaration quickly subsided. It was far from over. The grave, the effigy mound, still had to be found.

Reedwhistle lay awkwardly against the arcing wall. He had hoped for coolness by the narrow opening, but the sultry air acted as an impenetrable barrier, and sweat continued to stream across his skin.

Heat penetrated his skull, fragments of thoughts stumbling haphazardly in his mind. The threat of the bears receded from his consciousness, their growls from his hearing. The unrelenting heat became his sole agony. His eyes peered through a filmy veil. Outside, it was cool. And he was so close. The door was open. He could crawl through. It would feel so good. Reacting slowly, Reedwhistle rolled to his stomach and began to inch toward the opening.

The woman stalked hurriedly in the dark. Guided as if by instinct, she avoided the hidden obstacles. Ahead, the four bears were mindful of her limitations, their pace geared to her progress.

As the procession wound single file through the woods, the glow from the clearing diminished. The five creatures moved with singleness of determination. One of the animals had escaped. But it was still within reach.

***

Axel sat at the kitchen table, his fingers tapping the hard surface. Staring at the liturgical words of Ogochin Atisken spread in front of him, Axel considered the last, perhaps unsolvable mystery of Shawonabe's grave.

Earth piled in a horizontal facsimile of an animal should be readily apparent. The effigy mound—*if it exists*—should have been discovered years ago. He should have seen it himself, Axel considered, if it was anywhere near.

Sensing the doubt, Axel stood quickly and paced through the family room. All aspects made sense only if there was a mound. From the south. The woodland tribes. Pan-Indianism. A prison. A warning. It had to be! It seemed the inescapable conclusion. But where? The question bounded urgently through his thoughts. His pacing had carried him to the front room. Settle down. Relax, he told himself.

Axel stood motionless in the middle of the living room, pensively studying the thick carpeting. It may no longer be so apparent, he considered. The years have concealed it. It might have eroded to ground level. Or it could be concealed by its size! If it was so large that it could not be grasped in a single glance its shape would be impossible to discern. An inexplicable chill rippled through his skin. The thought tumbled over itself in his head as if it somersaulted down a staircase. Each spinning revolution crashed growing realization in his mind.

One part of a huge effigy mound would look like a normal ground formation. Its whole would be unrecognizable. Axel tried to picture it. A short rise. An earthen ridge running through the woods. My God! The ridge!

Axel lunged toward the front window. In the darkness, bathed in a glow from the house, he could see its shadow, a black band extending the breadth of his vision. He stared in awe, unable to move. The realization seemed unfathomable. It couldn't be, he thought. But the ridge was there, his driveway rising gently over it before reaching the garage. Three innocent stairs carried the front sidewalk over it. The scene of him digging into the side of the ridge, placing the steps, flashed through his head. It had seemed such a normal chore.

Shaking off his thoughts, he dashed out the door and into the front. Collapsing to his knees at the foot of the gentle rise, Axel touched the ground. With his palms flat against the ridge, he reverently caressed the delicate grass. The effort it must have taken, he considered. The purpose for it. Whether from the cool of the night or the discovery, Axel began to shake. He knew what he had to do. He was close to the last step, the performing of the ritual. It would release Janis from the world she had entered, it would bring her back to him. But somehow he was afraid. He was afraid what he would find when he began to dig. Axel stood and studied the ridge as it trailed into the woods, disappearing in darkness. It must be huge, he thought, covering many square feet. He remembered the passage clearly. Shawonabe's body would be found at the heart, the vital point of the effigy.

He took a step forward, then seemed to freeze as he touched the stair. He looked toward his house, planted squarely on top of the mound. It took on a different, foreboding appearance. It was an imposition on the past, an ignorant slap at a people's ingenuity. Axel had to force himself to ascend the rise he had vaulted up without hesitation many times before. For almost a year they had lived on Shawonabe's grave! It was barely comprehensible.

Inside the house Axel went to his office, to his desk. The left hand drawer. It wasn't there! Damn it! He thought for a moment. The last time they had used it? On Isle Royale, backpacking. Axel raced down to the basement to where their camping gear was stored. He checked the side pockets of his pack and found the GPS. He turned it on and the two inch screen flashed with light.

Axel grabbed a flashlight from the kitchen and went back outside. At the front door, he paused to scroll through the topographical map downloaded into the GPS. He marked the coordinates of the house, then long strides brought him quickly back to the base of the ridge. He checked the coordinates on the GPS and marked it as a waypoint. Glancing at the house, Axel took several measured paces. He took another reading, marked it, then flicked to another screen. A short vertical line appeared, connecting the two waypoints. It was working!

He continued to the edge of their front yard, marked a waypoint on the first screen, then moved on. After a few minutes he was well into the thickness which surrounded his yard, and the line marking his path had grown. Axel turned and shined the powerful beam along the ridge back toward the sidewalk. The light shone evenly along the rise in the earth. It was still straight. He had not missed any imperceptible curves. Turning away from the house, he took another several strides.

Reedwhistle crawled toward the door. He was sure he would die from the heat. He had to make it outside to the reviving coolness. But his strength was almost gone, his muscles expired. His neck could no longer hold his head erect. His face flopped in the dirt. His body convulsed in near-despair.

The suffocating air filled his lungs like hot sludge. His chest labored with each breath. The heat! He was being roasted alive. Shakily he rose a few finger widths from the ground. With dizzying reserve he pushed forward. Outside, he could see the ferns, the trees. They rustled gently in the breeze. The breeze! His only hope. His eyes saw only the relief. The black shapes, the glinting eyes, the glistening teeth, were invisible to him. His head was outside. Just a little more. The air slapped his naked skin. He would make it! His ears could not hear, but strength was returning. The agony was behind him.

"Stop him!" Shigwam's voice bellowed through the lodge. No one moved. Shigwam stumbled toward the door and grabbed Reedwhistle's ankles. There was a moment of weak resistance. Then a growl exploded, and Reedwhistle's feet were wrenched from Shigwam's grip and pulled through the opening. Shigwam pushed himself away from the door, his eyes affixed in horror. He listened to a dull ripping, a sound like wet cloth being torn apart. A sharp cracking brought his hands to his ears. But still he could hear. He could hear the man being mangled by the beasts. He gripped his head, but the noise was ceaseless. He could stand no more. Shigwam collapsed to the ground.

The bears pounded heavily through the woods. The woman gradually lapsed farther and farther behind. But she was approaching her territory. She would not be lost. And the bears sensed an urgency. They could not smell the animal, but they knew it had left its protection. It would die easily.

Axel moved slowly through the thick vegetation several steps at a time. He paused frequently to use the beam like a surveyor's line, ensuring overall definition to the small fragments.

The line curved gradually until Axel was now at right angles to his initial direction. He clicked to the second screen which connected his waypoints. At this scale, the two inch screen could not display the full path. But it was working, it *had to be* working! Axel followed the ridge, curving gently inward until it angled sharply to the south. The matching coordinates were carefully plotted. Axel paused to check his progress on the second screen. Damn it! It was out of alignment. He had made a mistake. It was the tiny buttons, the darkness, his haste!

He erased the last waypoint, then retraced his steps. He entered it again, then checked. The line appeared to be tracking as he expected. He suspected it would turn westward in a short distance. But under the ferns the contour of the ground was hard to distinguish.

After only another fifteen paces, about forty feet, the ridge angled to his right. Axel plotted the change of direction carefully. He continued another thirty feet before the ridge altered its course once again toward the south. Axel studied the two inch screen. As best he could tell, the hind legs were completed.

As he moved, a trail of broken fern stems marked the outline of the emerging mound. Camouflaged under two hundred years of growth and regrowth, it was easy to understand why he had never recognized the shape. Underbrush obscured all but a few feet at a time. But here it was! An effigy mound on a scale as grand as any produced to the south.

As he turned eastward again, following the inside of the forelegs, excitement burned throughout his body, and he fought the urge to move faster. The map had to be as accurate as possible. The heart on this scale could cover many square feet.

He slashed at the ferns in front of him with his foot, then tumbled forward as the ground dropped away. He steadied himself and shined the beam. A muddy slit in the earth extended through the ridge. Footprints, the same he had examined with Snyder and Orson five days before, were still visible. The dip must have resulted from erosion by centuries of rainfall. He hurried ahead.

Something brushed his head. Dried ferns twisted together hung from a branch. Axel's light flashed around him. The trap was closed! The bears must have returned. Shaking off a feeling of growing terror, Axel forced himself to continue. As he neared the mound's chest, an owl's hoot suddenly burst from the canopy above him.

A scream erupted in their massive heads. Nothing was smelled, nothing seen, but the bears felt a sudden danger, a suffocating threat of defeat. It was not outwardly perceived. But it was real, and it pushed them faster. The forest pounded with their desperate charge.

The woman could no longer hear the bears ahead of her. But she felt the same urgency, the same fear. She knew that aside from the bears, only one animal lay ahead of her. It could not prove hazardous, but her inner survival seemed in jeopardy. Her bare feet moved faster. Sharp ground debris went unnoticed. Her body plunged toward the verge of total exhaustion. But something whipped her resistance unmercifully. Unknown danger propelled her after the bears.

The ridge emerged from the woods. It dipped slightly, graded for the driveway. Axel stepped quickly across his front yard, his cautious attention to detail abandoned. He took one last reading—at the sidewalk, by the steps, where it had begun. The waypoints were linked. The path he had traversed should be joined in the shape of the effigy mound. If it had worked.

Axel hurried into his office, then turned on the desktop computer. As the operating system loaded, he plugged a USB cable into the front panel and connected it to his GPS. He called up the pre-loaded software, then downloaded the topo map of Crooked Tree State Forest with the waypoints he had just mapped.

The image appeared in stark contrast on the screen. Axel was transfixed by the design. He had known what it would be for some time, but as he stared at the outline of the effigy mound, he was overcome with awe. Projected on the map was a miniature of the earthen ridge that surrounded his house. Clearly drawn was the unmistakable image of a black bear. Shawonabe's grave. An effigy mound which had locked his evil in his rotten corpse for more than two hundred years. A prison as inescapable as any devised by the ingenuity of man. Inescapable until Janis took up residence within its very confines. Until his wife provided the unwitting vehicle for Shawonabe's escape.

Axel looked outside into the darkness. He had to hurry. The bears could be nearing the house. He moved quickly to a book case and began searching Janis' zoology books. He pulled a tall one from the shelf. *Mammalia Anatomy*. He flipped through the pages to a series of animal diagrams with clear plastic over-leaves. Each plastic sheet added a new layer of internal organs. Coyote. Deer. Moose. Bear! He turned the book sideways and laid it flat on the desk, next to the diagram of the effigy mound. The heart was even with the bear's lower neck and straight up from its forepaws, cradled between its powerful shoulders. Axel carefully moved the mouse to the exact location on his diagram and marked the coordinates of the outline of the heart. He would dig in the center. Shawonabe's bones would be there!

Axel hurried to the garage and pulled a long-handled shovel from a rack on the wall. His ax lay just below it, leaning against the bare wood. With the tools he stalked through the kitchen, snatching the print-out of the map, and with the GPS, slipped it in his pocket.

The rear glass door slid open with a heavy whoosh. Outside, Axel headed toward the bear's heart. His thoughts were on the ritual before him, his attention diverted from the growing tumult in the forest.

The bears could see the glow through the trees. They crashed relentlessly toward it, their powerful strides flattening the under-brush. A scent grew in their nostrils, the scent of the solitary ani-mal, its odor betraying its movement away from the structure.

Excitement deafened Axel's senses. He crossed the forgotten garden. But their approach could no longer go unnoticed. My God! Axel swirled to his left. The crunching vegetation was unmistakable. Dropping the shovel, he broke for the house. It was only a few yards. But the bears were already at the line of ferns by the north edge of his yard. A black shape burst from the cover into the open. Then another. Axel tripped on the step and sailed onto the linoleum, the ax crashing heavily on the floor. The first of the beasts appeared on the concrete. Axel lunged and slammed the door, but it was only glass. Steel claws could shat-ter it effortlessly. Axel struggled to his feet. He froze with hor-ror. Across the flimsy threshold the snarling head of a killer raged.

33

The storm had originated in Canada, picking up moisture as it crossed Lake Superior, then Lake Michigan. Its leading edge touched the coastline, sending gusts billowing inland.

Wind assaults a forest by degrees. Tips of pine trees jutting above the leafy canopy lean away from its approach. Then heavy oak branches slowly come to life and sway in rippling waves. On the ground the wind gradually filters through, causing elegant ferns to jerk inelegantly.

With the initial gust racing unencumbered far ahead, the wind finally touched the woman's naked body. Physical exertion had doused her skin with wet streaks. The breeze chilled her. But she was almost there.

The thick woods ended abruptly. With deliberate steps she moved toward the clearing at the back of the structure. She saw the bears charge toward the house, then stop and rear up on their hind legs, bellowing their fury. The woman approached warily. The animals seemed alien to her for the first time since their association began. And the house. It was familiar. She was in her territory.

Axel clutched the heavy ax tightly as he stared through the trans-parent barrier between himself and the bears. The overturned kitchen table was braced against the glass door. It would be difficult for them to break through. He would have a few moments with the ax.

One of the bears charged forward and pressed against the glass. The clear panel bowed inward. He raised the ax to his shoulder, but the bear backed off with a deafening growl. Captured in its gaze, Axel stared into it cavernous mouth, its teeth like white iron spikes. Light reflected in the wild animal's eyes. They shone like burning embers among dead ash. They burned his sight, forcing him to turn away. But still those eyes! The image of the creature's death stare would not fade.

Something brushed against the glass. The bears became quiet. They were coming in! He raised the ax, his teeth clenched. Janis! Her face was inches from the glass. "Janis!" he screamed. Startled, she stared into the house.

It was his wife. Yet it wasn't. Her gaze was vacant, her expression barely human. Cracked lips were parted in a silent grunt. Roughened by exposure and covered with insect bites, her naked body pleaded for care. A large bruise splotched her right shoulder. Her tangled hair resembled the matted fur of the black bear.

Axel moved toward the door. He could see the bears gathered a few steps behind Janis, standing quietly. He knew she acted in partnership with them, but he never could have imagined seeing her standing amid the killers.

He followed the curve of her arm down to her smooth waist. The deerskin handbag dangled from her hand. Axel gasped. Directly below it was the map print-out with the diagram of the effigy mound. And dripping onto the center from the stained pouch was a darkish liquid.

Grimacing, he returned his eyes to hers. It wasn't Janis who performed the macabre deeds. She was as much a victim as the dead, and she couldn't last much longer without him. A glimmer of recognition livened her eyes. He glanced toward the bears. He needed just seconds to pull her inside.

The ax head clinked softly to the linoleum. With his foot Axel maneuvered the table from the door. The bears panted heavily. Axel reached for the latch as Janis' gaze followed his fingers. In a moment she would be his. The latch clicked.

Suddenly her expression changed. Her eyes took on the fury of the bears as she lurched for the door. It wrenched open a few inches in its runners. Axel could feel her hot breath through the narrow crack as he struggled to slide the heavy glass door back into its slot. He felt it moving. A fraction more. It was in. The latch dropped.

Janis screamed a wild cry, her arms flailing with angry defeat. Then she turned suddenly and stepped aside. The bears! Axel grabbed the wood handle of the ax. A bear charged, its claws bursting through the middle of the glass. The door shattered, sailing sharp fragments through the room. The beast was coming inside!

Axel spun and dashed into the bedroom, slamming the door. He could hear the bear in the kitchen and knew the door itself offered little protection. It would splinter like plywood. Grunting with effort, he maneuvered the heavy dresser in front of the entrance.

As it slid into place, a bear's paw crashed into the door. The wood split, rocking the dresser forward. Axel leaned his back against it, holding it firm. He needed Janis' dresser to use as a brace. The door pounded with the furious onslaught of the bear as Axel dashed across the room and began dragging the second dresser to the door. When it rested firmly against the first, he grabbed the ax and chopped the floor at the base of Janis' dresser. The carpeting cut evenly. Then the wood cracked and the bottom edge of the dresser dropped an inch and jammed against the jagged floor. He was safe, the door was secure. The bear realized it a moment later and howled in protest.

Axel sat on the bed, studying his blockade. Light from the ceiling fixture cast eerily on the disheveled room. He could hear movement through the walls. The house was full of bears! The beasts would try again. The windows were high from the ground, but the bears might be able to reach them. Axel stood quickly. A dark shape moved just outside the electric glow. One of the bears. Standing motionless, Axel listened as it became silent. He whirled around, his eyes searching the corners of the room, grazing off the walls, peering into the darkness outside. They were there, he knew. Come on, get it over with, his mind shouted. His hands strained as they gripped the smooth handle of the ax.

Movement in the family room. A chair tumbled. The pop of a lamp bulb. Then the wall exploded with pounding fury. Axel could hear the wood cracking. His body shook. He imagined the gaping jaws, the tearing claws. Pound for pound, the strongest animal alive! The paneling splintered with an explosive crash, and the inner wall bulged. Each pummeling blast pounded fear in his brain. He raised the ax above his head as the plaster burst in a cloud of powder. A black paw poked through a small hole, and he readied to swing. But the bear, the wall, disappeared. The lights! They were out. The power had been shut off. Unseeing, Axel listened as the beast worked furiously, enlarging the hole. He swung the ax blindly and it crashed into the wall, splitting the plasterboard. His pupils slowly dilated. A shadow. He swung again and the bear howled in pain, disappearing from the hole.

Behind him the windows burst under a powerful blow. Glass flew inward, minute particles scratching his neck. The bear widened the jagged hole as Axel lunged across the room. With all his weight behind the ax he brought it down on the intruding forepaw. The bear shrieked, and as it dropped heavily to the ground outside, a portion of its paw fell to the bedroom floor. As he struggled to yank the ax free from the window ledge, a sound like human wailing wavered in the air. Its high pitch stabbed paralyzing terror in his spine. The ax jerked from the wood, tumbling Axel backward to the bed. He lay still, listening to the pitiful crying of the animals. Gradually the wailing became more distant as they retreated to lick their wounds. But there were others. And Janis.

Axel listened tensely. He listened for breathing, movement, anything. Rapidly flowing blood thumped in his ears. It beat rhythmically, resolutely. It almost deafened him to the sounds coming through the hole. It was a few minutes before he heard it, before he realized what it was.

He moved closer to the hole in the wall and stared toward the sound. It grew louder, broken only by halting sobs. It was Janis.

"Axel." Her voice was sweet. Innocent. "Axel, help me. Please . . ."

Axel glanced through the hole. There was no movement. No hulking shadows. His wife's cries tugged at his heart. They floated hypnotically in his head.

"Axel, please." Her tone was frantic. "They're going to kill me. You must help me!"

"Come and get me, you bastard!" he screamed, his body shaking with rage. "You goddamn bastard!"

Janis' silky voice hardened; she laughed a harsh ugly sound that echoed through the house.

"Give her back to me!" he shouted.

"Go to sleep, my sweet," Janis said. "Go to sleep, and she will come to you."

He sat heavily on the bed, trying to block out her voice, until against his will he lay back, his eyes open, staring at an imageless ceiling.

Lying on the bed, his feet dangling to the floor, he could no longer resist his fatigue. As the taunting laughter subsided, the last of Axel's energy escaped.

Janis stood by the shattered back door, her back bowed under the weight of her tired body, her bare feet torn by the scattered glass. She had been outside too long. Her meager food could not sustain her. She needed sleep, but she knew she could not be discovered here. In the woods, where it was safe, she could rest.

Janis limped through the broken door and away from the house. The two remaining bears sensed her importance and followed her into the woods.

The storm set siege to Crooked Tree State Forest. The rain came in sporadic torrents, each outburst connected by a steady but gentle drizzle. Intermittent gusts of wind lashed the rain horizontally. It blew through the shattered window, spraying water throughout the house.

His mind lazed over peaceful thoughts. His eyes were on Janis' lips, Sleeping Bear in the background. He could not hear her words, but he felt their meaning. The warm sun moved steadily across the deep blue. Water lapped at their feet. Under the protective blanket, discomfort grew. Something pecked at his face. Gnats? He tried to brush them away. But the intruders were persistent. The sweeping dunes became marred with jittery scars. Like white blips on an old movie film, the tranquil scene became obscured. The blips became more insistent. The celluloid flaked away.

Axel's eyes jerked open. Rain pelted his forehead. He sat up straight in the darkened room and felt frantically about himself on the bed. The ax lay next to him. Gripping it, he stumbled in the darkness toward the side table. The clock radio hung by its cord from the table. It had stopped at 12:30. He had been asleep a few hours, he guessed. Peering through the hole to the family room, he heard and saw nothing. If the bears were gone, he would have to act fast. He was the only one who could stop Shawonabe.

After dropping the ax into the next room, Axel squeezed through the narrow hole and eased himself to the floor. Squatting in silence, he detected no movement.

Slowly be crept toward the kitchen, searching about the floor until he found the boxy flashlight. Although the lens was cracked, it still flickered to life immediately. He directed the light out the window. There were no moving shapes within sight, but he knew he had very little time.

He spun the overturned table out of his way and eased through the gaping hole in the sliding glass door. Outside, he moved the light about until he found the map of the burial mound. He still had the GPS. He picked up the longhandled shovel and hurried into the woods.

Under the thickness of the leaves the rain lessened. Axel came to where the mound dipped, and followed the lower level to a tight bend. He was at the neck. He shined the light on the water-faded diagram and estimated the distance to the small outlined heart. He carefully paced eleven steps, then he stabbed the shovel into the ground at his feet.

He checked the coordinates on the GPS. He was close. A few more feet to his left. He stopped and stared at the ground in front of him. The black earth held his gaze for several moments before he drove the ax deep into the dark soil. The center of the beast's heart. Shawonabe's grave.

Axel turned the light off. The bears could not be too distant. Perhaps in the downpour their sense of smell might fail them. As he lifted the shovel and began to dig, he realized he was sweating despite the cooling rain. He was afraid of an evil far more terrifying than the bears alone.

The top layer was a spongy mass of leaves and twigs that had yet to decompose. The dull blade of the shovel cut through with difficulty. Rich black topsoil, heavy with water, sank to a depth of six inches. He did not know how far down he would have to go. Below the thin veneer of black dirt, the soil turned sandy. Eons of glaciation had made it so. It was lighter than the thick mud on top, but more likely to collapse. He would have to make the hole wider still. Axel stopped suddenly, the shovel poised under his foot. The sand meant something else. Good drainage. He shuddered with the realization. Perfect for preservation. Shaking the thought from his mind, he resumed digging.

When his waist was even with ground level, Axel paused to rest. Above him, leafy branches pulsed downward with each gust of wind. Creaking a dozen feet away, a scaly-barked jack pine spit woody fragments into the air. Its needleless branches jerked like thrashing daggers, reaching for Axel's vulnerable skin. The shovel bit deep into the ground.

Three miles into the wilderness, Janis screamed. Her eyes snapped wide and her breasts heaved, while air gushed like hot steam from deep in her throat. The animal was outside! She felt the wrenching, tearing danger, and struggled through the twisting branches, fighting to be free. Outside the narrow confines of the den, she ran toward the house, the bears a moment behind.

The shovel clunked hard on a hidden obstruction. Axel dropped to his knees. He felt a tubelike extension a few inches under the sandy soil. After determining it was only a root, Axel stood. With the surface at neck level, Axel had to reach up for the ax. As he chopped the stubborn wood, vibrations rippled through the dirt. The unsteady walls weakened further.

At the surface the pit was seven feet long and four feet wide. It sloped downward almost imperceptibly to his feet, where the bottom was slightly smaller. As he yanked the root segment from the ground, his hands felt black mud. Like on the surface. He crouched low, the steep sides looming above him. He stood suddenly and heaved the root to the side, trying to ignore the possibility of the hole collapsing. But the thought was too terrifying to repress. The bears at least would kill quickly. But buried alive, death would be slow, his gasps for air yielding only mouthfuls of earth.

The bears crashed through the rainswept forest with unrelenting fury. Their outer fur glistened with water running over natural oils. They were too far away to smell the animal, but the bears knew exactly where it was. And the knowledge alternately brought terror, then killing anger. It had to be stopped. The underbrush crunched with their powerful strides.

With the support to one side gone, the rain-soaked dirt sagged. In the hole, Axel worked desperately. As it deepened, the possibility that he had chosen the wrong spot to dig became greater. It was only a rough diagram. He could miss the burial chamber by just a few feet and never know it. But two hundred years' gradual accumulation of debris would have buried the body deeper. It was to be expected. Axel strained, the dirt flinging higher, wider.

The wall collapsed, sliding downward like a miniature avalanche, tumbling noiselessly around Axel's feet. The pungent odor of wet earth wafted in suffocating vapors in his nostrils. The pit stabilized, but his feet couldn't move! Axel bent low and clawed frantically. One leg pulled free. Then the other. But still his fingers gouged at the soft soil. He fell to his knees, attacking the soil with crazed energy. His mind pictured sinking walls, slowly covering the hole. He had to stay ahead of them. Faster!

Suddenly his nails hit a hard surface. It wasn't flat, his fingers could tell. It was like a face, but twice the size of a normal head. Axel withdrew his hands in horror and turned on the flashlight. A grotesque visage stared at him across the steamy void. Its eye sockets were empty holes. Its mouth protruded from the mask like the snout of an animal. Carved teeth were bared in a chilling snarl. Unblinking in the harsh light, the lifeless funerary mask gazed in defiant silence.

His fingernails thick with dirt, grime caked on slick skin, Axel was immobilized. Deep inside, a blaze of growing terror raged. In his knees, through his body, he felt but did not understand a building tremor in the soil.

An eerie glow emanated from the ground like an iridescent mushroom. The bears beat the cushioned forest floor with heavy blows as they ran toward the light hovering in the dense air. Rain smothered any wind-carried scents, but the bears knew it was there. Alone. Unprotected.

Their aching muscles lost their fatigue. The prospect of a kill excited them. They reached the hole in the ground. The animal cowered at the bottom, its back to them. Their fury unleashed in a bellowing roar.

The sound exploded in his ears. Rocked from the dead stare, Axel spun around. Leaning over the pit stretched two howling bears. Dirt sprayed his face as their forelegs inched closer to the edge. They were ready to spring! Axel grabbed the shovel and jabbed it at the beasts. A mighty paw swung, catching the steel blade in the center with its ironlike claws. The metal shovel snapped with an ear-wrenching clang, the half-blade flinging into the soft wall of the pit. Axel fell backward. His hands grasped the stiff mask in desperation. He dug his fingers under the broad edges, but the earth did not want to give it up. Then it jerked free, and Axel jumped to his feet, brandishing the fragile mask in his outstretched arms. He shoved it toward the bears, who howled in protest.

They were moving back! Axel lunged closer, forcing the bears away from the edge, their fury shattered by fear. He flung the mask toward them, and they lurched to the side, the leathery visage falling in between.

Axel stared at the hulking shapes peering down at him. He could see their tongues curled between parted fangs. Their glowing eyes stared as if transfixed. But not by him! They stared at the ground he stood on. Following their gaze, Axel saw what they saw, what held them back. In the center of the mask's imprint, flecked with sandy soil, was the mummified face of a long-dead corpse. Axel stared at the still form. It lay encased in a shroud of dirt and creeping roots. Dark brown leathery skin fit snugly over the skull. Sunken cheeks outlined the jaw and facial bones. Eyelids drooped into empty sockets. The lips were shriveled, baring black teeth in a sardonic grin. Axel wanted to look away, to climb out of the grave, but he was trapped. The bears waited atop for him. His only chance was to finish what he had come for.

Reluctantly he knelt beside the hideous face. His fingers eased the dirt from around the skull. His thumb inadvertently poked through the papery chin, and he retracted it, gasping as if he had touched venomous coral. Above him, he heard the bears prance close to the edge once again, their weight sending shock waves through the ground. A clump of dirt splattered by the corpse's head. Axel brushed it away.

The neck was no wider than the circumference of the spinal cord. Shrunken to the skeleton, it covered in tight relief segmented bones. Axel dug carefully, the throaty growls vibrating in his ears. A glob of foamy saliva dripped like glue from a bear's mouth. The hot drool slobbered on Axel's neck and slimed down his back.

As he worked, a sense of the unreal took possession of his body. The very evil in the ground seemed to infect his legs, numbing them as it spread upward, killing feeling as it moved. His chest, his heart captured, Axel felt as though be were floating. The evil crept further. A thick dullness settled over his thoughts. His eyes blinked shut. He fought to open them. No! he screamed inwardly. He must not fail. With gritted teeth he scraped the last of the dirt from the corpse's torso.

The rib cage was outlined tightly with the shrunken leather. The skin drooped where the stomach had been, encasing like a taut sheet the pelvis and hip bones. The arms were folded across its chest.

Grasped in its bony fingers was a shriveled slab of tanned deerskin, humped slightly in the center. Staring at the pouch, Axel rose slowly to his feet. There could be no mistake. It was Shawonabe.

Axel stood, and from his shirt pocket pulled a soggy sheet of paper. He brought the beam to focus on the blurred ink.

"Aye'e', Aye'," he cried, his voice ringing through the dripping rain. "Aye'e', Aye'," he shrilled in a growing cascade of primitive forces. Again he screamed, and again, the words designed to wrap around the skeletal corpse and take it in their hold, to grasp it with unyielding force.

The cries seared the bears' skulls. They rose together, guided by the same impulse, and standing on their hind legs, roared with a force that shook the moisture from overhanging leaves. Then they fell forward, their forepaws thudding heavily into the soft, wet earth. The impact loosened the wall. Part of it slid unnoticed to Axel's feet.

"Jeeb yuk gah ni-bah jik, nish kahk.
"Noon dwish-nahng ga kah yak meen wah nish kahk."

The words flowed from his mouth. A mystical tension gripped him. The sacred chants of Ogochin Atisken were being recited in ceremony for the first time in decades, perhaps centuries.

"Gee nish kah-yak guh zee tahm je mah-jak-yak.
"Ka go zeg ze kam je mah-jah-yak guh che nahd-mah goom."

His voice rose, then fell, then rose higher. His chest heaved with the effort. The energy of forgotten years, lost peoples, pulsed through his veins.

"Shkwah nish kah-yak mishoo ook-mis ga guh wahb mahk.
"Noong go dush guh mah jahm."

Axel shouted defiantly to the Midewiwin. His strength had returned. The tendons in his neck stretched with unbridled vigor.

"Oo-dan-we che shpim me a tak guh zahm,
"Ga neen we dush je wahm dahs yahng mee-bahd bik guh bee
dah zarn mahn-pee ni-ka-yah."

"Ee-ah!" The shriek drowned his chants. Axel spun around. It was her! Shawonabe's servant! Her scream tore his swelling confidence. His eyes grew wide with horror.

Janis stood tall at the end of the grave, a boulder in her upraised arms. It hovered above her head while white foam bubbled at the corners of her mouth. Her eyes shone like red flares.

Axel froze with dread. Her arms were moving! He leaped forward. The rock sailed inches over his head and sank heavily into the base of the far wall. Enraged, she dropped to her knees and slashed with hooked fingers at his eyes. Her nails dug into his check. Axel grabbed her arm, his face burning with pain.

Janis fell headlong into the grave, a flurry of loose dirt following her. She twisted on the ground and slammed the bottom of her foot into Axel's kneecap, tearing the cartilage. As his leg bent crazily backward, he screamed, falling on her.

She struggled in Axel's grasp as he squeezed her tightly to his chest, trying to immobilize her. The ceremony was almost complete. But as her face pressed against him, she bit into the thin muscle between his shoulder blade and neck. Axel screamed in agony and rolled to his side, trying to push her away. But her grip did not loosen, and the teeth sank deeper.

His hands gripped her throat and squeezed. Her eyes bulged until she opened her mouth in a suffocating gasp. Axel rose slowly to his feet, dragging her upward by the neck. Her fingers clawing toward his eyes, Axel crashed an open hand across her face. She flew against the end wall, her back flattening against the dirt. It held her upright for a moment before she slid unconscious to the ground.

Her battered nude figure crumpled at the far end of the grave. Blood, *his blood*, dripped from her mouth. He forced himself to look away. But the Feast of the Dead was not over. The gnashing of the black beasts shook him from his trance. His torn knee buckled, collapsing him to the floor of the pit. Staring at the growling jaws, Axel twisted around and struggled to one knee. With the paper in hand he continued the ritual.

"Jeeb yuk gah ni-bah jik, nish kahk.
"Noon dwish-nahng ga kah yak meen wah nish kahk."

His voice was weak, stuttering for strength. It grew stronger.

"Nish kahk guh mah jahm, nish kahk guh mah jahm, nish kahk guh mah jahm . . ."

Axel shouted louder. His throat rasped with the effort. Blood flowed freely from his wound. His knee throbbed with ceaseless pain. His voice yelled in wild frenzy. The bears' roars grew with his. Their growls cracked through the forest, boomed in the pit. But his voice was louder. Theirs ceased. The mad snarls stopped.

The bears pushed frantically back from the open hole. Danger exploded in their minds. They turned and dashed into the trees. Their flight carried them in different directions. The ferns, bushes, saplings, snapped under their rushing weight. Fear propelled their retreat.

Axel heard the receding tumult. They were gone! It was over! Shawonabe was defeated. His pain forgotten, he turned to Janis and leaned against the earth wall. It moved. He glanced quickly upward. The wall was collapsing! He tried to stand, but his torn knee would not respond. Mud dropped heavily on his shoulders. He slumped to the ground, unable to withstand the pressure. The dirt encased his body like wet cement.

He fought to keep his last air. But it was no use. The weight squeezed his lungs. As he gasped for breath, flecks of dirt sucked into his mouth.

Suddenly a sharp edge jabbed into his lips. The pressure increased. It was *his* teeth, his eternal sneer! Shawonabe's withered jaw bit into Axel's face. With unbridled horror Axel realized that in defeat the soulless corpse was grinning in taunting revenge.

Larry stared through the open doorway. The heat had diminished inside, yet his skin was still streaked with sweat. The low moans behind him had long since faded from his hearing. Outside, the blaze had been reduced to embers. Near it lay the torn carcass of Reedwhistle, his skin glowing red from the dying fire.

Larry's gaze moved blankly from the corpse to the pit to the dark woods. An undercurrent of impatient growls ceased suddenly. Larry could see jerky movement in the shadows. He steeled himself for their charge. At the least it would finally be over. His eyes closed. The underbrush thrashed violently, but the noise retreated. They were scattering. The bears were fleeing into the woods!

His chest was almost stilled. His thoughts distant. The increase in pressure was slight. At first it was unnoticed. But gradually it scraped at Axel's receding consciousness. His ears became aware of a rhythmic scratching somewhere above. It grew louder. The dirt became less weighty. Then he felt it.

Frantic hands clawed at the ground on his back. They dug into the soil. He felt them at his head. The sides of his face. They were lifting him out. Air! It rushed over him in a cooling wave.

His lungs wheezed, his throat gagged. Coughing, Axel spit wet sand from his mouth. He struggled for air. It surged into his chest. Smooth hands brushed the mud from his face. Rain pelted his skin with reviving freshness. Gentle fingers brushed his eyes clear. Long strands of hair caressed his cheeks.

His shoulders moved with creaking effort. As his gritty fingers felt the naked skin, soft lips brushed against his. It was a gentle kiss, a kiss that had been alive in his memory. It had seemed such a long time since he had felt it. Now the feeling resurrected.

She stood and helped him to his feet. Then they climbed out of the grave.

Like a ragged whip flailing a rocky breach, the lake-born wind tired, leaving the forest as it had been. The trees calmed to an easy sway in defiant gesture to the dying storm. Vertical rain fell in a quieting blanket. Like flitting fingers dancing over a canvas tent, the rain tapped a pittering refrain on the uppermost branches. From leaf to leaf the water cascaded until dropping softly to the ground.

Epilogue

The colors meshed in irregular swaths like the brush strokes on an impressionist canvas. The deep scarlet and tantalizing gold of the maples gilded the picture with baroque elegance. Heart-shaped aspen leaves splashed as brilliant as a sunburst. While the pines maintained their stable green, the burnished copper of the oak leaves exhibited imposing strength.

Piercing the gentle gyrations of the changing trees, the afternoon sun cast lively shadows of muted hues. The black bear was blind to the multishaded glow. But it had felt the same forces that acted on the trees. Its den was deeper, under heavier brush than the bear had been used to during the past several months. Fresh vegetation matted its floor.

As it ambled awkwardly over the crunching ground, a foreign scent stabbed its consciousness. The bear stopped suddenly. Fear robbed it of its hunger. The scent drifted lazily on the westerly air currents. It was the smell of danger. The bear didn't wait for it to get stronger. It turned and dashed with terror-filled strides deep into the woods. As it retreated farther into the wilderness, its limp was barely noticeable. The bear had not been slowed a step.

Axel glanced quickly at Janis. Her eyes darted a nervous reply. The black-and-white car ground to a halt in the driveway. Luke Snyder was alone. His face showed pained exertion as he pulled himself from behind the wheel. Axel leaned on his rake. Janis slowly rose behind the half-filled plastic bag.

"You could be out here forever with that thing," Snyder said.

"I know. Silly, isn't it?" Axel smiled.

"How are you two?"

"We're fine. When did you get back?"

"Last night. Godawful trip it was. It took longer to get from Detroit to here than from Florida to Detroit. That old plane was like a bus, stopping at every airfield it could find."

"How was Marcy?" Janis asked.

"Oh, she's fine. Real fine. I met her new folks. Good people. They told me she never mentions Michigan anymore. The psychiatrist down there called it repressed anxiety."

"That's just as well," Axel said. "She'll be better off not remembering."

"I suppose you're right," he said. "It's over anyway."

"Yes. For all of us."

Snyder nodded, his lips pressed tightly together. Turning his back to Janis and Axel, he stared out toward the woods. "If you don't mind, I'll make sure the trap's still all right."

"Sure, go ahead, Luke. Nothing's been there to disturb it in over two months."

"Maybe you can join me, Axel."

"You go on. I'll be out in a minute."

As the sheriff's footsteps grew fainter, Janis said quietly, "Don't lie to him, Axel. I don't want to live our lives that way."

Axel was expressionless. "Let's see what he wants."

"We're at peace with ourselves. And that's all that counts."

Axel followed Snyder's path behind the house and into the woods. When he reached the trap, the sheriff stayed crouched, peering into the open culvert at the dried meat. "John Orson will be collecting his traps soon," Snyder said. "Before next month and the first snows, anyway."

"Good. The hinges would be rusted shut by the end of the spring thaw."

"Funny, I suppose he could have taken them away in July."

"He could have. But how was he to know there would be no more bear attacks?" Axel was cautious.

"You're right, Axel. How could he have known? But no matter," Snyder said, pushing himself up. "As long as it's safe now."

Michelson was silent. Snyder stared at him for the first time. "It is safe, isn't it, Axel?"

"Yes, Sheriff. It's safe."

A small smile relaxed Snyder's face. Turning back toward the house, he asked, "How's Janis been?"

"Fine," Axel said. "The kennel's going strong again, and she's been just fine." The two men were silent, the only noise the crunching of dead leaves under their feet. Nearing the house, Axel stopped and gripped Snyder's arm. "Luke, Janis is fine. But she wants—"

"You know," he interrupted, gently pulling his arm from Axel's grasp, "there are some things the law just can't deal with. Now, you're a lawyer and might not accept that. But just ask an old sheriff and he'll tell you it's so. Sometimes, no matter what the case is, if the evidence won't be believed, it's no use going to court. And sometimes it's better that way. Sometimes there's no one to blame."

A door slammed in front of the house. As Axel and the sheriff stepped through the back door into the kitchen, Janis was leading Larry Wolf in through the front. In one hand he carried a gallon jug of cider, in the other a large manila envelope.

"Back for the weekend, and I knew you couldn't wait for this to come through the mail," Larry said.

"From Bay City?"

"Yep. The permanent-injunction order."

"Great. I didn't trust Sunrise Land and Home when they said they were dropping their development plans. But I guess this makes it official."

Snyder grinned. "Can't blame them for not wanting to build houses out here now, after last summer." Reaching into his shirt pocket, Snyder pulled out a stack of tickets. "You going to be up again at election time, Larry?"

"Sure, I'll be here for the All Saints' festival at the village."

"Good. You're a student again, so take a free ticket to my fund-raiser election eve."

"You won't get reelected passing them out like that," Larry said.

"No, but maybe your boss here might be kind enough to contribute."

Axel laughed. "Wouldn't miss it."

"I think you should make it to the festival, Sheriff," Larry said. "Never know, might help."

"I'll be there, Larry. And the way I hear it, a lot of people from town will be there too, if they're welcome."

"Always have been."

"Is that a jug of cider for drinking or building up your muscles?" Janis said as she brought four empty glasses from the cupboard. Larry smiled and placed the jug on the table. Then the four of them sat down.

After walking their visitors back to the cars, Axel and Janis watched as they disappeared through the trees. The engines whirred faintly. Then with a distant roar they were gone.

With his arm around her shoulder, Axel squeezed her tightly to his side. Janis turned her head and looked at her husband. Her face was soft, her smile gentle. A quiet content was wordlessly conveyed.

They walked slowly toward the house. As they stepped up the low embankment that stretched across the front yard, Axel felt a relieved tremor in his chest. The effigy mound was safe.

A few hundred feet away, under a thick blanket of newly fallen leaves, Shawonabe's grave lay concealed as it had been for two hundred years. Next to him, at the heart of the earthen bear, heavy dirt covered a second Ottawa.

The remains of Oliver Reedwhistle, brought to the mound the night of the sweatlodge, lay shoulder to shoulder with the evil Midewiwin's. He was a victim of the bearwalk, a victim to whom the Midewiwin had been unable to return, a victim from whom Shawonabe had been unable to retrieve his protective talisman. And wrapped tightly in Reedwhistle's hands was a stained deerskin handbag, a modern medicine pouch.